It was one of th...a
flawless white-blue sky and temper... o
the high eighties. For almost three hours the players
had been battling it out for a place in Wimbledon
history – to have their names immortalised in gold-
embossed letters on the championship board.

Sitting in the players' enclosure, the sun beating
down on her head, was Lauren Kendall. Having
watched Josh play in countless tournaments across
the world, she was used to her husband turning a
match around. But she'd never had to sit through
anything like this. Nothing so utterly nerve-racking.
She pressed clenched hands against her mouth, willing
him to win.

Also by Emma Davison

Catwalk

The Game

Emma Davison

CORONET BOOKS
Hodder and Stoughton

Copyright © 1996 Emma Davison

First published in 1996 by Hodder and Stoughton

First published in paperback in 1996
by Hodder and Stoughton
A division of Hodder Headline PLC

A Coronet paperback

A CIP catalogue record for this title is
available from the British Library.

ISBN 0 340 65989 0

Typeset by Hewer Text Composition Services, Edinburgh
Printed and bound in Great Britain by
Cox and Wyman Ltd, Reading, Berkshire

Hodder and Stoughton
A division of Hodder Headline PLC
338 Euston Road
London NW1 3BH

For Greg
My best friend

ACKNOWLEDGMENTS

The professional world of tennis is mind-bogglingly complicated so I am deeply grateful to the following people who helped me overcome what felt like a truly daunting task. They include: Roy Fisher, Chris Bailey, Andrea Charlton, Chris Ling, Paul Hutchins, Andrew Castle, Mark Bullock and Cliff Bloxham.

In particular, I would like to thank Ken Whetherly who opened all sorts of doors including those to the All England Club – I shall never forget that first thrilling taste of Wimbledon. Without him I couldn't have got the book started.

I am immeasurably lucky to have found in Peter Robinson an excellent literary agent, as I am to have Carolyn Mays as my editor for a second time.

In addition I'd like to express my thanks to Tim Hulbert for his valuable input and finally to my grandfather, James Bramwell, for his unstinting support and belief in me.

Emma Davison, 1995

SEEDS

For the clear voice suddenly singing,
high up in the convent wall,
The scent of elder bushes, the sporting
prints in the hall,
The croquet matches in summer,
the handshake, the cough, the kiss,

There is always a wicked secret,
a private reason for this.

Auden

1

It was Josh's turn to serve. The first ball hammered down the middle, smacked the net tape, hovered there for a second as if it hadn't quite decided which direction to take, then rolled back onto his side. Cursing angrily at himself, Josh tried to block out the lamenting groans ricocheting around the court. Popular though the one-time Wimbledon champion Max Carter was, everyone wanted a fifth set. Here was a chance. Could Josh do it?

Someone – probably the fat woman three rows from the front with a coffee flask and weighty packed lunch stationed on her pink sunburnt knees – had carelessly dropped an empty packet of crisps. Just as the tall Australian was about to serve, the cheese-and-onion bag was swept up by a gust of hot air and floated nonchalantly onto the court.

'One moment,' petitioned the English umpire, sweating discreetly within the confines of his formal asparagus-green jacket.

A red-faced ball girl rushed to retrieve the offending article. But the bag, with determined independence, floated upwards beyond the poor girl's reach, then veered off to the left.

'*Hurry* please.'

A few spectators giggled, enjoying a moment of light relief. But most of the thirteen thousand spellbound tennis fans squeezed on to the packed Centre Court were crossing their fingers that the unseeded Australian could hold on to the match. What had begun as a foregone conclusion in the American's favour had turned into a truly riveting men's final.

It was one of those rare perfect July afternoons with a flawless white-blue sky and temperatures burning into the high eighties. For almost three hours the players had been battling it out for a place in Wimbledon history – to have their names immortalised in gold-embossed letters on the snooker-green championship board. The Australian, Josh Kendall, had been two sets down and love-four in the third, but had managed to cling onto the match. Now, on a tiebreak in the fourth, he had a set point.

Sitting in the players' enclosure, with the sun beating down on her blonde head, was Lauren Kendall. Having watched Josh play in countless tournaments across the world, she was used to her husband turning a match around. But she'd never had to sit through anything like this – nothing so utterly nerve-racking. She pressed clenched hands against her mouth, willing him to win.

Crisp bag captured, everyone settled back down. A hush descended as Josh prepared once again to serve. Wiping sweat from his freckled brow, knotted with tension, Josh fixed his gaze on the American patrolling the far-end baseline. He pitched the ball high into the air, arched his back like the string of a bow and onto the ball brought the face of his racquet crashing down.

An Indian linesman wearing a red turban threw his arm out to the side, indicating that the ball was long.

'Six-five, Kendall.' The air crackled with nerves.

Josh lost the next point which brought the score to six-all and groans of disappointment from the crowd. Lauren closed her eyes. To those watching her she seemed to be praying. Then Max made a careless backhand pass into the net. A vital point to lose at this stage of the match but his inscrutable expression made it impossible to guess what was going on in his mind.

'Seven-six, Kendall.'

With a desperate strike, Josh took a massive risk and went for his shot, pelting a devastating second serve into the far right corner.

'*He's done it with an ACE!*' shrieked the presenter from the BBC box, banging his hand down on the desk with such force that his co-presenter spilt his cup of Nescafé. 'He's taken the fourth set! *Now* the match comes alive. Oh, yes! And just *look* at the support he's getting from the crowd. Max Carter's shaking his head as if he can't quite believe it – I don't think any of us can. My word, what riveting play we're seeing from this quite exceptionally plucky Australian. An hour ago we all felt that it was over for Kendall. But not any more. We've got so many twists to the plot out there, I doubt even Agatha Christie could have dreamt up better.'

Eyes shining, Lauren Kendall cheered her husband on as he walked back to his chair, determination stamped all over his face. She felt unspeakably proud. All signs of fatigue were now gone. His eyes blazed, focused. A new confidence radiated from him. The press box was suddenly looking very full, smelling an upset as the number three seed tried to work out what had hit him. Having been two games away from match point, Max was now in serious trouble.

With Lauren was Sol Martin, Josh's coach, and Lottie Roach. Aware of the cameras recording her every move, Lauren had been able to keep a rein on her nerves. Ten-year-old Lottie, however, had been on such tenterhooks that she'd bitten off what remained of her fingernails.

'Lottie, how about a chicken sandwich? There are two left in my bag,' Lauren suggested.

'Oh, I couldn't even *think* about food. I'd be sick!'

The little girl fidgeted restlessly in her seat and gnawed on the end of a straw. Lottie's face was extraordinarily mobile, questioning and expressive. Her toffee-coloured eyes remained glued to Josh who, during the changeover, had draped a green towel over his fair head. He was drinking greedily from a plastic Coke cup.

'Do you think he's feeling nervous?' she asked.

'I expect he's beyond that now,' Lauren said, allowing herself to relax for the first time since the match had started. She tossed her thick mane away from her shoulders. 'He had Max running all over the court.'

'Wasn't that last serve *brilliant*?' Lottie's young high-pitched voice sounded breathless. 'I don't think even Ivanisevic ever served that hard.'

Sol glanced up briefly from the scribbled notes he'd been making during the match to bring up with Josh later.

'That's because you're biased, sweetheart,' he said with a grin.

Ironically, it had been Sol who only three years ago had helped coach Max Carter to his first Wimbledon victory, bringing the American's total grand-slam titles to three. No one quite knew the circumstances under which the two men had parted. But seven years was a long time for a player to stay with the same coach. It was rumoured that Max had simply outgrown Sol and for the moment was going it alone.

'How about some more of your lemonade?' Sol suggested.

Lauren observed the empty bottle next to Lottie's feet. 'I'm afraid we've finished it.' Her cornflower eyes twinkled with amusement.

Normally, Lottie would have immediately owned up – she would certainly have been made to apologise if her mother had been around. It was wrong to have drunk so much of Lauren's home-made lemonade, especially as she'd been so nice and everything. Oh, but it was so hot and she'd had to do something to anchor her nerves. To add to her troubles, Lottie was desperate to go to the loo. She'd been hanging on for almost an hour waiting to see the outcome of the fourth set. She'd now have to wait until the end.

'Time.'

As the players were applauded enthusiastically back on to the court, Lauren, just for a second, caught her husband's eye.

'You can *do* this,' she mouthed to him.

Josh winked to show he'd understood. Much to the BBC producer's delight, both actions had been caught on camera.

'Don't get too cocky yet, champ.' Sol murmured nervously. His note-making abandoned, the coach edged forward in his seat, chin in hand, and watched Josh with intense concentration, 'He's just gotta work at that first serve.'

As if by telepathy, Josh promptly polished off an awe-inspiring ace.

'Cor!' a spectator said. A few people nearby laughed.

Lauren let out a little gasp.

Sol heard her. He glanced in her direction. All colour had drained from her face.

She placed an experimental hand on her belly and nudged the stretched, distended flesh as if she were checking the outcome of a newly baked cake. As the wave of pain subsided she smiled into Lottie's wide, worried eyes in reassurance.

'I'm okay. It's just that if I sit still for too long he wakes up. Here,' she took Lottie's hand and placed it on her stomach.

'*Oooh*!' Lottie jumped slightly as something knobbly and hard pressed indignantly against her hand. 'I felt that.' She glanced at Lauren curiously. 'How do you know it's a he?'

'Because he kicks like a boy. Probably a future Gary Lineker.' She made light of it, but the spasm had been one of many during the match. She frowned. The baby wasn't due for another week but the gap between each contraction, she felt sure, was lessening. Shifting position, Lauren moved her legs further apart to accommodate the egg-shaped bulge.

As is so often the case after an angst-ridden tiebreak, the fifth set developed much more rapidly. Max dropped his serve in the second game – no doubt unnerved by the dazzling performance from Josh. It was as if he were playing a different man. Max was further handicapped by a seniority in age of seven years and the prolonged match was beginning to take its toll. But when someone shouted out, 'Come *on*, Max,' in a for-goodness-sake-pull-yourself-together voice, he managed a wry smile and a shrug which seemed to say, 'You come down here and see if you can do any better.' For the twenty-five-year-old Josh, after the arduous uphill slog in levelling the match, it now seemed as if nothing could stop him from realising his life's ambition. Adrenaline shooting through his veins, he looked as fresh and as energetic as he had been while warming up. Having the crowd on his side certainly helped.

'Five-*three*,' squealed Lottie, pushing her fringe impatiently from her eyes, 'and Josh has the break. If he can just win this next game—Oh, *ple-ease*, let him do it.' She chewed fretfully at her lip.

Lauren understood her youthful enthusiasm but she hardly dared to share it. Josh, like many good players, had so often thrown away a match he had already bagged up – often at match point. Sol was thinking the same thing. When it came down to it, a player's nerve simply bottled. Hell, there were hundreds of first-rate hitters on the circuit. What separated the guys at the top, and what kept them there, was the ability to hold their nerve when it counted. Watching his Australian protegé, Sol hoped to Christ Josh could do the same.

'Thirty-fifteen.'

'*Get on with it, Kendall*!' a voice cried from deep within the crowd. 'You can do it, mate.'

'Come on, darling,' Lauren murmured.

Max made mincemeat of Josh's serve, powering his return straight at his body. Rotten tactics, Lauren thought protectively, but 'the jammer' was often effective because it gave the opponent absolutely no room to make a decent return. A retaliating Josh aced Max on the next point.

'Forty-thirty.'

'Oh, my God. Oh, *my God*!' squeaked Lottie, grabbing Lauren's arm.

The spectators were making so much noise now that the umpire had to ask for quiet five times. Still they shouted. Josh, serving for the match, paced restlessly at the back of the court, bouncing the ball against the face of his racquet as he waited for the furore to settle. Lauren held her breath. Her insides curdled. She could hardly bear to watch. All their dreams, the plans they'd made together depended on this next point.

Josh's serve was a surprise. As Max had predicted, it went to his backhand but landed at such an acute angle that it took everything he had to keep it in play. A powerful forehand sent it back. But Max handled it well, getting in nice and low. His drop shot forced Josh to scramble to the net. Whack! A beautiful cross-court return and now it was Max doing the running. The public drew in its breath. Max just reached it in time and was forced to hit it blind. The lob sailed into the air and landed inside the baseline. Josh, convinced the ball was going to go out had slowed up his pace and was forced to make a clumsy return. It dribbled over onto Max's side. As Josh sprang forward he slipped and fell awkwardly. The crowd groaned. But quick as a flash, he was on his feet again, his eyes glued to the ball. Too late, Lauren thought, gripping the sides of her seat. He'd left the court wide open for Max. She swallowed anxiously. Instead of going for an easy smash, however, Max played a vicious backhand to the far left baseline. An impossible return. Or was it? People would talk about the next shot for years to come. With superhuman strength, Josh threw himself across the court, his expression that of utter determination, and leaping into the air hit one of the most sensational backhand returns Centre Court had ever seen. Max could only turn and watch helplessly as it landed nimbly inside the sideline.

'Game, set, match and championship to Josh Kendall. Four-six, three-six, seven-five, seven-six, six-three.'

The crowd erupted.

Lauren blinked incredulously. 'My God! He's done it!'

'YES!' bellowed Sol.

'*Brilliant, brilliant* Josh has WON!' shrieked a thrilled Lottie.

Throwing his racquet into the air, Josh put his hands to his face in a moment of wonder, then punched his clenched left hand victoriously towards the players' enclosure where Lauren, Sol, and Lottie had all jumped ecstatically to their feet whooping with delight, arms high in the air as they applauded his victory.

They all hugged and kissed one another quite overcome with emotion – this would be a moment they would remember for the rest of their lives. Not only was this Josh's first grand-slam title, but what a way to have achieved it.

Lauren winced as another contraction gripped her insides but fortunately with all the fuss going on around her no one noticed. The Carter contingent sitting in front of them obligingly turned and held out congratulatory hands while all around them the noise swelled to an astonishing level; royalty, the committed tennis fans, the Debentures whose financial contributions had helped maintain the club's impeccable example, the young kids with dreams of one day becoming champions themselves, security guards, off-duty linesmen and umpires, veteran players who returned to this, the greatest tennis tournament in the world, to relive old memories, all applauded the sheer guts and beautiful play of the Australian.

The two men, who only moments before had been trying to destroy each other, now approached one another as friends. Max, gracious in defeat and always a favourite with the crowd, climbed over the net and put his arm round Josh, sealing his congratulations with a firm handshake. Those close to the front heard him say,

'You played a hell of a match, pal. Congratulations.'

With its usual efficiency, the award ceremony was quickly in place. The vanished net had been replaced by an orderly row of linesmen. The ball boys and girls, who had been carefully picked from local schools and had been in training for six months, assembled in two lines facing one another, their hands clasped tidily behind their backs. While the players towelled down and slipped back into their sweatshirts, Alan Mills, Wimbledon's veteran referee, explained to each of them the procedure. A great cheer went up as the Duke and Duchess of Kent, the latter wearing an alluring banana-yellow dress, walked onto court. They stopped to chat with some of the ball boys and girls, then took their positions by the trophy table which had been draped with the Union Jack. As was customary, the defeated finalist went up first. There were resounding cheers for the Floridian Max Carter who ambled up to the Duke with the ease of a cat.

The ever gracious Duchess spoke to Max at great length. To the eyes of the greedy press their animated conversation appeared warm and affectionate. Not surprising really, as Max was a previous Wimbledon champion and had twice been a finalist, the two had got to know each other quite well.

Then it was the turn of the champion. Lauren wept with joy as Josh, cheered on by the crowd, accepted the heavy silver cup, a cheque for £345,000 and warm congratulations from the Duke. He had gone beyond all expectation, realised his greatest ambition. As the new Wimbledon champion, the tennis world lay at his feet. He could do anything now. Lauren, more than most, knew what that meant to him.

Watching her idol, Lottie was experiencing somewhat ambiguous emotions: a new seed of unease began to sprout. It was dawning on her that she could no longer expect to have a monopoly of Josh. Shifting in her seat as she contemplated this worrying notion, she wondered at the same time why the chair felt warm and damp. She placed an experimental hand beneath her. Mortified, she found that in the excitement of Josh winning she had wet herself. Her cheeks burned. Oh, the humiliation of it. How was she going to get out of this without anyone noticing?

But as it happened, no one did. The clapping persisted while Josh proudly held the great glinting cup above his head for the press. Some of them urged him to kiss the trophy. He had just placed his lips against it when he suddenly became aware of a separate commotion. Instinctively his head swerved towards the players' enclosure, and saw his wife slump forward, her face crumpled with pain. On either side, Lottie and Sol were trying to support her.

'Oh, Jesus!' Thrusting the trophy into the arms of Max hovering nearby, Josh sprinted across the court towards her. People tried to make way for him as he clambered up through the crowds, intent only on reaching his wife. Not since Pat Cash's win in 1987 when he'd clambered through the fans to reach his family had there been a final like it. The press went berserk.

'Lauren!' Lowering himself over the wall Josh's foot landed on the plastic lemonade bottle which crumpled and split under his weight. 'Lo, darling, talk to me.'

Gripped by another contraction, Lauren could only gasp, 'The contractions—Josh, I think my waters have broken.'

'Bloody hell!'

'Guess the midwife was right after all.' Lauren laughed a little hysterically.

By now, several 'Shorrock' security guards and three committee members were on hand to help. Quickly summing up the situation one of them plucked out his walkie-talkie and holding it to his mouth urgently demanded an ambulance. Three more guards formed a wall against neighbouring spectators wanting a better look.

'What's going on?' one of them asked.

'Someone's having a baby.'

'What here? Blimey. Sue, get my camera out. Quick!'

'Can you *please* give them some room,' barked a Wimbledon official, his huge walrus moustache twitching furiously.

Another committee member offered to give Josh a hand but the champion irritably waved him off. He gathered his wife's slumped body into his arms, murmuring to her as he walked through the gate exit. He was followed out by Sol and a trembling, white-faced Lottie.

There were swarms of people everywhere, some trying to help, most just getting in the way. Somehow Max Carter had managed to shoulder his way over to them but was stopped by a fan proffering a glossy programme.

'Your timing's off, pal,' Max snapped, roughly pushing the man away. As he reached Josh, he said, 'Anything I can do to help?'

'Could you see Lottie gets home, mate? I don't want her coming to the hospital.'

'Oh, but I want to . . .' Lottie's protest was cut short.

'No argument, young lady.'

So when the ambulance arrived, Lottie was forced to stand back in the confusion with everyone else and watch Lauren, leaning heavily against Josh, being bundled into the ambulance and driven off to a cacophony of shrieking sirens.

*   *   *

At first the nurse wouldn't let Josh go in with her. Without him, Lauren's fears increased. Her contractions were now coming every six minutes and in between them anxiety was causing cramp in her stomach. She was convinced she was moments away from delivering.

'Where's my husband?' she croaked, as she lay like a sacrificial offering on the birthing table. She heaved her swollen body into a more comfortable position.

'He'll be here soon enough. You just try to relax now. Try to concentrate on your breathing.'

'I'm having second thoughts.'

'It's a bit late for that, dearie.' The midwife smiled indulgently. She'd heard it all before.

'I feel like a beached whale.'

'Not for much longer you won't. I'll be back in a while to check your blood pressure.'

'In a while' stretched into an hour, then rolled into an agonising second hour. Lauren lay suffering each strengthening contraction. Alone, she was seized by self-doubt, amazed at her stupidity in thinking labour could be an enriching experience. She didn't want a baby. She wasn't prepared. She couldn't survive much more of this pain either. What on earth had possessed her to think she could get through this ordeal without the aid of drugs!

In a brief break from pain she studied the stark dimpled white walls that looked like cottage cheese, the tired linoleum, the grey, unyielding table they'd put her on, her bloated, bursting vein-scored stomach that she no longer recognised or liked. She wanted to die.

With the onslaught of her next contraction, she screamed. A nurse she hadn't seen before popped her head around the door.

'Try not to do that, love,' she said. 'You need to save your energy for the hard part.'

The hard part! Where *was* Josh? He should be here with her.

'Help!' she moaned as the nurse's white shoes swished softly away and the door swung closed behind her.

Sometime later she heard the door suctioning open, then voices. Exhausted, Lauren propped herself up on her elbows. Rather a lot of people entered the room. One of them thankfully, was Josh. He looks tired she thought lovingly.

'I'm so proud,' Lauren murmured, as he bent forward to kiss her.

'You had me so bloody scared out there. When I heard you scream I didn't know *what* to think.' Josh's voice was hoarse and croaky as if he hadn't used it for some time.

Lauren was beaming at him. 'Darling you did it. You *won*.'

'Don't go tiring her now,' warned the midwife.

Josh ignored her. 'Is there anything I can do, anything at all you need?'

Lauren managed a small grateful smile. 'Just don't leave me again.'

He folded her hand between his. 'Don't worry. Not even old bootface over there will budge me now.'

'Shush,' said Lauren giggling, and glanced at the midwife in case she'd heard.

But the midwife was checking her blood pressure again. In the background was the ominous rattle of a hospital trolley. There seemed to be hands on every part of her body: rigging her up to the foetal monitor, ointments being smeared onto her now exposed belly. The pain returned. Professional voices faded in and out like the tide. Anxiously Lauren gripped tightly on to Josh, unaware that she was squeezing the blood from his hand.

'Getting closer, are you, Mrs Kendall?' asked the midwife. 'Let's have you lying back now, there's a good girl.'

The door reopened. In strode the doctor who bore a marked resemblance to John Major. He looked desperately tired. That makes two of us, thought Lauren wearily. She wondered if he was up to the task.

John Major smiled benevolently at her and she responded by putting all she had into the corners of her mouth. With that smile she willed him to like her, to get this over with quickly, to treat her in the same reverent way he would if she were his own daughter. Josh was murmuring to her.

'I love you, Lo.'

She collapsed between two colossal contractions and someone attached a suction apparatus to her stomach. Someone else, she could feel, probably John Major, was prodding between her legs. What a sight she must be, lying here like a massive blancmange in her clinical hospital gown covering every part of her except her vagina, displayed for all the world to inspect. Hovering on the dim periphery of consciousness, she thought: Do you? Do you really love me even like this?

John Major surfaced for air. 'Cervix isn't fully dilated yet. She's got a couple more centimetres to go. Give it a bit longer.'

A bit longer, thought Lauren in a panic. I'll be dead by then.

'Keep breathing, Mrs Kendall, you're doing fine.'

Another devastating wave of pain. Lauren gripped her thighs and panted until she thought she would hyperventilate.

'We—wanted—a home—birth,' she gasped, her face bathed in sweat, 'the birthing pool—we'd said.'

'I know, Lo. I know. There just wasn't enough time. Try not to talk. Save your strength.' Tenderly Josh stroked damp hair back from her forehead.

As the pain intensified the urge to push became unbearable. Lauren was desperate to go to the loo. She tried to concentrate on her breathing, on what they'd taught her to do in the antenatal classes, but things were exploding inside her. She wondered if this was what it felt like to be murdered. Her bowels felt ready to burst.

'Not yet,' the midwife said, reading her thoughts, 'or you'll tear.'

She didn't care. She couldn't stand this any more. She just wanted it to be over!

'Get it OUT!' she screamed. 'Just get it OUT OF ME!'

'Okay, Lo. You're okay.'

The contraction diminished. Lauren fell back against the bed, limp with exhaustion. It was so hot. How could they bear to be in this suffocatingly airless room. Couldn't someone open a window. She wanted to ask but felt too depleted of energy.

'I'm just going to have another look, Mrs Kendall. I need to check your cervix.'

Again! She hated them doing that. There was more than enough pain to contend with. The door opened again with a pneumatic hiss. Somewhere in another room she could hear the muffled anguished moans of some other poor woman, no doubt going through the same nightmare. Then someone fixed a plastic mask over her face and the moans stopped. That was when she realised the moans had been her own.

'Cervix is fully dilated. She's ready.' The contractions had recommenced. Lauren remembered how determined she had been not to take drugs – refusing to harm her baby in any way. Feeling as she did now she'd have cheerfully knocked back gas, Mogadon, air, pethidene. To hell with the consequences.

'Okay, Lauren. Push down now,' said a voice.

Hallelujah! Willingly she obeyed.

'That a girl,' urged Josh, forty minutes later.

'Bear down. Come on, bear down!' The midwife joined in.

'You can do this, Lo.'

'But I can't, I *CAN'T*!' shrieked Lauren, feeling as though she were giving birth to England, Scotland and Wales all rolled into one. Sweat poured from her body, blood and greenish water oozed from between her legs, 'Oh God, I'm so tired. Why won't you let me *sleep*!' she was crying hysterically.

'Can't do that yet, Lauren. Now come on, there's a good girl. Keep going. We're nearly there now. You're doing really well.'

If only the midwife would shut up! Lauren pushed with the last vestiges of strength she had left even as she felt her insides burn and splinter. She pushed for Josh next to her urging her on, she pushed for her parents who had longed for this grandchild, she pushed for the slim body that had got waylaid somewhere and which she yearned to have restored to her, most of all she pushed for the life she had held inside her for nine months. She could feel the lips of her vagina burning as they gave way, the baby's hot, wet head burrowing towards light. Josh had gone down the other end to watch.

'*God*, Lo,' he was feverish with excitement. 'This is so beautiful. It's coming out. STREWTH, I can see its head.'

'Almost there. Now, *come on*, Lauren. Bear down. One more time. *Push*.'

'AAAAAARH!' The strength of her scream penetrated the walls, shot along the hall and could be heard three floors down in reception. *This* was what it felt like to die. With one last desperate push, Lauren gave it everything she had, feeling veins bursting all over her body. Almost anticlimactically, the rest of the baby's body slithered out and into Josh's waiting arms. Triumphantly he held it up just as he had his Wimbledon trophy just a few hours ago, grinning stupidly, tears of joy rolling down his cheeks.

'Oh, Lauren, darling. *Look*! It's a boy,' he said, his voice so choked with emotion it was barely audible. 'It's our beautiful, beautiful boy!'

When Josh finally emerged, looking dishevelled, unshaven but ludicrously happy, he found Max Carter sitting in the maternity ward lounge engrossed in *Cosmo*.

'They get you to write down fifty ways of making out with your partner. I could only come up with ten. Guess I'm losing my touch.' Then, as if he'd suddenly tired of the glossy magazine, Max chucked it disparagingly onto the side table. 'So. Spill. How's the mother?'

'Sleeping. Poor Lo's all in.'

'You look as if you could do with some sleep yourself.'

'I do feel beat,' Josh yawned widely, 'but Lo's the star. Turned down all the drugs they threw at her. Reckon it's down to all those yoga classes she's been so keen on. Ten pounds! Can you believe it? A ten-pound baby boy!'

Max grimaced. 'She must be pretty torn up.'

'Yeah and weak with it. They're stitching her now – couldn't face it, mate. Tell me – did Lottie get home all right?'

'One of the courtesy cars took her. I put her in it myself.'

'Good one, mate. I owe you.'

A Tannoy message was blasting out of the intercom, doctors dashed through the puke-green doors. Josh glanced at the clock on the wall, rubbed his eyes. 'I said I'd call Lauren's parents as soon as there was any news. How long have you been here?'

'Couple of hours.'

'Then you'll have sussed out where I can get myself some coffee. I'd kill for a cup.'

Max indicated doors to his left. 'Machine's through there but I don't recommend it. Tastes like dishwater.'

'Just as long as it keeps me awake.' Josh leaned back

against the wall and slapped his forehead several times in astonishment. 'I still can't fucking believe it, Max. I'm a dad!'

'And a new Wimbledon champion – in case it slipped your mind. Or was your giving me the cup back at the All England Club a sudden change of heart?' Both men grinned. 'Hell, Kendall. I've been in this game for a long time and thought I knew all the publicity stunts, but getting your wife to go into labour on court takes some beating.'

'Isn't she bloody marvellous!'

'You might not think the same of the press. There's an army of them camped outside the main entrance and they ain't about to go away. Lovely as Nurse Hodges here is,' he said, winking at a very pretty nurse wheeling through a patient, 'it's not her they've come to see.'

Josh shrugged his shoulders. 'They can wait. Where'd Sol get to?'

'Downstairs trying to keep the press off your back.'

'In that case I definitely need some coffee.' A doctor sped past them, his white coat flapping like sails. About to follow him, Josh swivelled round.

'Hey, Max,' he said quietly.

'Still here.'

'Today can't have been easy for you. Your coming here like this . . .' he paused, embarrassed. 'After the first two sets I've got to admit I thought I'd lost it – you were playing faultless tennis. I couldn't get an edge. I just want to say thanks. It really means a lot.'

Max waved away the sentiment. 'Go on. Get out of here. Lauren'll be wondering where you've got to.'

The Australian's face relaxed. 'Right.'

And with one of his wide, infectious smiles, Josh, smug and grinning with triumph, turned back towards the high-pitched sounds of his newborn son.

2

Melanie Roach had watched the men's final at home. It had been tempting to use her complimentary Centre Court ticket but in the end she had given it away, preferring to watch in privacy. Armed with a tartan rug and Sunday papers packed with shots of Liz Hurley and Hugh Grant, she lugged the portable bedroom set and extension lead into the back garden and settled herself under the shade of the apple tree. She wondered, as she watched the players stroll confidently onto the court, if she'd regret her decision not to go. It had always been such a treat. Her closest friend Gillian Twist had said she was mad to have passed up such an opportunity, although it hadn't stopped her from going in her place. Perhaps she was mad. A fly landed on her leg. Melanie flicked it away, sighing gently. No, her instincts felt right. She would have just caused friction. Besides, she had things to do. Now that the damp had finally been fixed in the spare bedroom she could get on with repainting it. The upstairs room (used for Lottie until she had outgrown it and moved into the one across the hall) was small with even, unexceptional walls and a solemn rectangular west-facing window that looked out on the road. The muted pine furniture and landscape paintings on the walls that Melanie herself had painted added a harmonious quality to the room. She was glad watercolours were back in fashion. During the first term of her adult education art course she had found it difficult getting to grips with the glutinous power of oils. Watercolours were much more her and now her canvases were filled with wild flowers, domestic animals, dreamy country landscapes. With the residue of the recession still very much around, Melanie felt sure that what people wanted was a revival of delicate, pretty, familiar things.

During a break in the second set she nipped back into the welcome cleanliness of the house to make a cup of tea. Wicklow, a Stygian-black kitten, catapulted in behind her on the rampage for food. Lottie had found it crying piteously in a ditch one day and had carried it home in the pocket of her school blazer.

'Lottie, you *can't* keep that here,' Melanie had said, grimacing as her daughter placed the rain-sodden animal on the just washed, spotlessly clean kitchen floor. 'We agreed, didn't we? No pets.'

Lottie buried her nose in the kitten's wet fur.

'Mum, he's nowhere to go. He'll die if I put him back.'

'That's not our problem.'

But Lottie had cast those big pleading eyes at her and she had caved in, agreeing he could stay for just one night.

'And you've never looked back, have you, Wicklow, you little minx!' The kitten blinked at her with his green marble eyes and purred hopefully.

While the kettle boiled Melanie rummaged through the fridge trying to find the small jug of milk she had put there that morning. Bother. Sure as eggs are eggs Lottie had given it to the cat or chucked it out – another thing to add to the shopping list. Not having the strength to walk up to the Broadway in the hope of finding something open, she left her tea black, then as an afterthought added to the tray a slice of lemon sponge cake. She told herself that she was enjoying having the house to herself. Lord knows, it was a rare enough luxury; no noise, no meals to prepare, no ten-year-old's demands. A whole afternoon of peace and quiet. But Melanie wasn't good at being on her own. Perhaps if she had been given a chance to live by herself after leaving home, explore her independence, she might have grown to like it. But then she'd never been given the chance.

She often wondered over the years whether in fact she would have married Andrew Roach had her parents not been so persuasive. Certainly she had been attracted to his being a doctor – one with excellent prospects. The confident way he carried his tall good-looking frame also impressed her. His parents had money, something her father was happy frequently to point out. *He'll set you up for life, lass,* he would stress eagerly. *You'll find nowt better.* It had all happened with such dizzy speed. Andrew, sensing her reservation when he proposed, had suggested that perhaps he should take a job offered to him in the north and see if, when he returned, she felt differently. The possibility of losing him frightened Melanie. Soon after, they were married.

Three years later, in the small Gladstone Road house – a wedding present from Andrew's parents – Melanie gave birth to Lottie. It should have been a time for celebration. But then followed Andrew's traumatic collapse and the diagnosed brain tumour. Terminal, they had said, with no hope of his seeing the end of the year. Melanie's mouth tightened as she remembered the brief period during which Andrew returned from hospital a diminished figure worn down by drugs and fear. How could the doctors have got their prognosis so catastrophically wrong? Sometimes she found herself wishing he *had* died instead of having the breakdown that followed. At least then she could have forgiven him for walking out and leaving her to cope with a small baby. This way they'd all suffered. When Lottie reached her second birthday Andrew had gone, leaving Melanie Gladstone Road and a small allowance in the divorce settlement. By then he had given up practising completely, sold his half of the Wimbledon surgery and squandered the profits on a small plot of land in Surrey.

His intention was to build his own house. But no sooner had the structural walls been erected than Andrew lost interest, gave up and walked away. Just as he had with her and everything else in his life. In a way, Melanie could understand the pathetic, wretched man he had become. To live each day wondering if it was going to be your last, there didn't seem much point in making long-term commitments. But he had a daughter. *Lottie*. He should have tried. With her, he should have made more of an effort.

Bees droned sleepily in the lavender and heat as she carried her tea back out into the sun. Melanie's eyes drifted to the noise reverberating from the TV. Josh's serve had just been broken and he was now two games to four down in the third set. During the changeover the BBC camera homed in on Josh's face. This was the bit she found painful, watching Josh looking into the stands as he was doing now, looking for his friends, for the support that he needed, knowing that it wasn't Melanie he was looking at but *her*. That hurt. Josh got up from his seat and spoke briefly to the umpire. As he rushed off court (presumably for a loo break) a BBC commentator discussed Josh's serve which, in his opinion, had simply gone to pieces. Then the guest commentator (a retired tennis player who had shown great promise in the eighties but, like so many potential stars, had never quite fulfilled it) said that luck had had some hand in Josh's making it to the final; it had been an easy bottom half draw for him, particularly as the seed he had played in the third round had been forced to pull out after straining a muscle in his back. That wasn't fair, Melanie thought crossly. Over the past two years Josh had more than proved just how good he was. The significance of what she'd just said struck her like a blow; the last two years. Had it really been that long?

'Now then,' John Barrett, the commentator, continued as Josh reappeared on court chaperoned by a steward, 'let's see whether Kendall can pull himself out of this mess. He's got a long way to go, but the important thing for him now is not to worry about that. He needs to focus his mind on one game at a time. That's all he can do, don't you think, Bill?'

There were shouts of encouragement from the crowd and a close-up of Lottie chewing her nails, the pregnant Lauren looking grim but composed. Melanie glared at her clear, milky skin, the unpainted lips (something she had never dared do herself even though she hated wearing make-up), then switched off the set unable to watch any more. She would hear the outcome from Lottie soon enough.

In need of a distraction, Melanie re-entered the house which was cool and dark. She washed up the tea things, noticing irritably how the inside of her mug was beginning to stain. She put it to one side to bleach later on. Upstairs she changed into a clean, but well-used pair of dungarees. She'd had them for almost ten years and they still fitted her. At least she had her figure, she thought grumpily. In front of her dressing table she examined her face. Her nose was small and sharp, her brown eyes insignificant without make-up. She leaned towards the mirror tilting her head from left to right looking for the encroaching signs of ageing. Then she centre-parted her hair, using the sharp nail of her index finger as a comb. She picked up a brush and roughly scraped her thick dark hair back into a ponytail, her brow pulled into a frown.

Lottie arrived home in a fever of excitement. Yelling to her mother she rushed upstairs and burst into the spare bedroom.

'Mum! Mu-um! Lauren started having her baby and Josh had to take her to hospital and . . .'

'Be careful of the . . .' Melanie's voice warned. But it was too late. Lottie had cannoned straight into the 2.5-litre can of gloss paint. She froze and watched it ooze like lava over the floor. 'Oh, Lottie, for God's sake. Don't just stand there. Go and get something to clean it up with. Quickly!'

Buggerbuggerbuggerbugger. Lottie muttered her new word under her breath as she raced back downstairs, Wicklow scampering playfully behind. As always she jumped the last five steps and landed with a terrific thump.

'Lottie. *Hurry*!'

She inspected the spotless kitchen for clues. What did one use on spilt paint? Lottie grabbed what was closest to hand: a kitchen towel roll, a sponge and a dishcloth that had been draped over one chair to dry. As an afterthought she went back for the bottle of bleach parked on the sink shelf.

'Here, give that to me,' Melanie snapped, grabbing the kitchen roll. She had already scooped up quite a bit of the gluey liquid while waiting, using the lid from the can and a paintbrush. Now she tore off several sheets of paper and dabbed irritably at the wooden floor.

'No, Lottie, *not* the bleach.' She scowled, as Lottie got down on her knees to help her mother, the edge of the day's excitement somewhat blunted. 'Honestly, Lottie, you're a walking *disaster*.'

Lottie's cheeks blazed, 'Sorry.'

'And for heaven's sake straighten your shoulders. They're all hunched.'

It took half an hour but they managed to get most of the paint off. Any remaining marks would eventually be hidden by new carpet. Relieved, Lottie gathered together the pile of used paper towels as instructed, and crammed them into a shiny black rubbish bag.

Back downstairs, Melanie was chopping onions and Lottie, fresh from a much-needed bath (the soiled knickers secretly consigned to the laundry basket) relayed the day's news.

'Josh was *fantastic*! Everyone thought he'd definitely lost but you should have heard the noise when he took the third set. Did you see me on the TV?'

'A number of times – chewing your nails. I wish you wouldn't. You have such pretty hands.' Lottie, perched on the kitchen table swinging her thin legs, guiltily sat on her hands. Melanie sniffed.

'Mum, you're supposed to put a digestive in your mouth when you chop onions. It stops you crying.'

'Bit late for that now.' Melanie frowned at her daughter's face which was more flushed than usual. Probably forgot to put on the sun block she'd given her.

'Max Carter was really nice. He talked to the Duchess for ages – she's really pretty and I think he's a bit in love with her. Then later on, he came and sat with me even though he'd lost and everything, right up until the courtesy car came. He said he was going to the hospital after he'd had a shower. Do you think we could go too? I'm dying to see Lauren's baby. Oh, *please*, Mum, say we can.'

'No. We cannot.' Melanie wiped her nose with the back of her hand. 'It's much too late and you should be thinking about doing some homework. You've got school tomorrow, remember?'

School. Yeuch! Her least favourite place in the world. Sulkily, Lottie pushed herself off the table and sat on the floor further away from her mother who was shovelling bits of onion into a hot oily pan. A small basket of tomatoes stood on one side. Melanie picked one up and plucked out the stalk. It fell to the floor and Wicklow, having finished his supper, skipped over and sniffed it with interest. To Lottie it looked like a fat black spider. Wicklow soon got bored with the inanimate object. He parked himself on Lottie's lap and licked his salmon-flavoured lips with satisfaction.

Melanie gave her daughter a sideways look. 'What's happening about the school play? Have you learnt your lines for next week?'

Lottie puffed out her cheeks and played with her fringe. 'Do I have to? It's such a stupid song . . .' Her voice grew duller as she spoke. 'I think it's so unfair that bloody Arabella gets to play my part just because she's pretty.'

'Nothing in life is fair, darling,' said Melanie, with just a trace of irony. 'Get some knives and forks out for me, please.'

Lottie dragged herself up from the floor and opened a drawer. 'If I promise to do all my homework tonight could we at least call Josh and find out if the baby's been born yet?'

Melanie poured on top of the softened onions whisked eggs, which sizzled and bubbled.

'I shouldn't think he'll be back from the hospital. It's only been a few hours.'

'*Oh, go on, Mum!*' Lottie's reedy voice pleaded. 'I'm desperate to know what's happened.'

Melanie glanced over her shoulder at the beseeching face of her daughter. She had hoped to avoid this. That, after all, had been the whole point of not going to the match today. But she couldn't let Lottie down and if she was honest, she also wanted to know. Removing the pan from the heat, she wiped her hands on her apron, picked up the portable phone and dialled the number.

'Josh?' There was a pause. 'Hello, Josh, it's Melanie. Look, I'm sorry to bother you but Lottie's desperate to know what the outcome is. If you get a moment perhaps you could give her a quick call.' She was about to hang up then. 'Oh, and congratulations,' she added lamely. 'I always knew you'd do it one day.'

'Answer machine,' she explained to Lottie as she hung up. 'I expect he'll call in the morning.'

'That's *so* frustrating! I'll never be able to sleep. Can't we try him again later?'

Melanie gave her one of her looks that left no room for argument.

'Supper, homework, then bed,' she said firmly, 'and put Wicklow outside. He almost chewed through the kettle flex last night.'

An hour and a half later, upstairs in the small confines of her room Lottie flopped on to the single bed crushed against the wall. From the pocket of her jeans she withdrew the two chocolate biscuits she'd sneaked out of the kitchen while her mother wasn't looking. She popped one of them into her mouth. On her chair was an orderly pile of clothes put there by Melanie, clean, ironed and ready for the morning. She shifted her eyes, determined to banish school from her thoughts. The Habitat gingham duvet cover was almost obscured by the amount of frilly pillows adorning it. Amongst these, propped up with a certain air of importance, was Dimble, a large powder-blue rabbit whose zipped tummy held her nightie. Josh had brought it back from a trip to the States. Above the bed was a shelf groaning under the weight of tennis books and magazines and a treasured dog-eared copy of *Swallows and Amazons*. Alongside were her schoolbooks and a collection of pencils and rubbers. Each one had her initials clearly marked. Her dressing table boasted a cornucopia of miniature bottles of bubble bath and body cream, all neatly displayed. Lottie admired and sniffed them a great deal but the cosmetics were never used – she was a hoarder by nature and found it hard to part with almost anything. On the back of the door was a giant poster of Josh taken during last year's Australian Open. This was partially obscured by her costume for the end-of-term play.

Glaring with passionate loathing at the stiff pink wings, Lottie sighed heavily and threw an arm over one eye. Well, it wasn't fair. Who wanted to be a stupid fairy in some stupid boring play anyway? Arabella Villiers, the most popular girl in the school, had landed the coveted role of Titania, queen of the fairies. Gossip circulating around the school was that Arabella's mother, once a celebrated actress herself, was bringing the director of a well-known acting school to watch her daughter perform. As most of the girls in Lottie's year dreamed wistfully of a Hollywood future, there had been talk of little else.

Springing up from the bed Lottie knelt in front of her mirror and unplaited her hair, pulling her fingers through it to separate its wormy lines. It wasn't pretty hair like Arabella's. It hung limp and fine like baby hair and filled with electric sparks when she brushed it. Not that she minded, but having inherited so few of her mother's tidy features, she could have at least been given her thick, richly brown hair. Lottie practised raising her eyebrow – all the girls in her class were doing it, but so far she had only managed to work out one side. After a few failed minutes with her right eyebrow she returned to her bed. She felt suddenly very sleepy. So much had happened today. Josh was the new Wimbledon champion. And Lauren was having her baby. She hoped it would be a girl.

Once, at Gillian's house when she was very small, she had watched their cat having kittens. The cat had lain on her side in a box next to the washing machine as though very ill, face jerking, tail lashing angrily to warn off anyone trying to get too close. It seemed like ages before anything happened. She almost gave up waiting. And then she saw the tiny bluish bag slide out. The cat instantly ripped the tiny blind beast free of its bag of skin, then began licking it until it uttered a thin whiny mew. It reminded Lottie of a bald mouse. Then it all started up again and she watched five more births. She went home feeling exhilarated, fascinated by what she had seen but adamant that such a thing would never happen to her.

Now she had something else to get excited about. Before tucking her up in their spare bedroom the night before,

Lauren had mentioned that her parents were celebrating their ruby anniversary. The event promised plenty of entertainment and would bring together family and close friends. How did she feel about going too?

'You might enjoy it, getting out of grimy London for a couple of days,' Lauren had encouraged. 'I know how much my parents would love to see you again. Mum even said something about running a junior tennis tournament.'

'And don't think we've forgotten that it's your birthday on the Sunday,' added Josh. 'Turning eleven is a big one so how about we throw you a wing ding of a party?' He held up his hands as if to defend himself. 'I know what you're thinking, but it won't just be boring grown-ups. There'll be plenty of kids your age.'

It all sounded so wonderful Lottie could hardly wait. She had frequently drooled over pictures of the Millers' large seventeenth-century Sussex house which proudly boasted a tennis court, heated swimming pool and two acres of sloping garden. They even had dogs. And now she was going there. She had something of her own to look forward to. But moments later, her bubble of excitement burst. Rolling onto her side so that she was facing the wall, Lottie clutched Dimble for comfort. There was a problem.

How in the world was she going to persuade her mother?

3

Miss MacKenzie was having a fit. A costume belonging to Bottom had mysteriously disappeared overnight and couldn't be found anywhere. Under her strict instructions two members of staff and three seniors had been dispatched to find it and on no account were they to return empty-handed. During the dress rehearsal Lottie overheard some of the girls whispering – 'Fancy dress—got drenched in the pool—nearly peed myself—if Miss MacKenzie ever finds out—sssh. Promise you won't—' She guessed what it was they had been up to but kept her mouth closed. She only wished they had taken hers.

Miss MacKenzie, a thin insomniac who taught English and drama, had been with the girls' school for nine years. For eight of them she had organised the summer play which had always been met with unstinted enthusiasm by her pupils. Not only had Miss MacKenzie directed but she had also organised the music, the sets and props and provided costume patterns. This year, however, some of the girls' eagerness seemed to have waned. Miss MacKenzie blamed this on television. In her opinion the girls watched far too much of it. Parents ought to be more selective in what they allowed. The BBC still produced really excellent drama. What possible good could come from all the mindless violence, those dreadful soaps, and presenters who couldn't even speak the Queen's English?

'Those of you who have taken part in my other productions' (she made 'productions' sound like an RSC tour), 'will know that I expect full participation from my girls. Any nonsense,' she singled out the troublemakers with her flinty eyes, 'will be dealt with swiftly. Now, regarding your costumes, I've spoken to the head and she has graciously agreed to let you make them during your needlework classes.'

A few of the girls groaned. Sewing was about as popular as maths and domestic science. Lottie couldn't thread a needle to save her life, whereas both Esme, her grandmother, and her mother were excellent seamstresses. They had tried to teach her but Lottie would just look and say, 'Yes, I've got it,' while the instructions slid through her mind like water. She was too proud to admit to this character flaw, but after four botched attempts and a great deal of wasted material, kind Mrs Garrett who taught needlework had taken the pattern home and made it for her. Lottie didn't have the heart to say she hated it when Mrs Garrett brought it back. And all because Miss MacKenzie had robbed her of the role of Hermia.

'Charlotte, dear,' said the drama teacher in the sugary voice she put on when she wanted her own way, 'although I think you make a very nice Hermia, I think that you would be better suited to playing one of the fairies. It's only a small part, I know, but the smaller roles are often the more difficult. You're one of my brightest girls, dear, and I am confident that you can do this.'

Lottie had looked at Miss MacKenzie's earnest smile with suspicion. But she knew better than to argue. She was simply no match for the English and drama teacher.

With only a week to go before the end of term, the school hall was already packed with parents. It had been tastefully decorated with leaves, bracken and tiny fairy lights. Mothers chatted animatedly to one another, discussing their plans for the summer holidays. Fathers, fatigued by a long hot day in the office and too much lunchtime booze, stifled yawns and gazed mindlessly at the thick, plum-coloured velvet curtains. Behind them the cramped space was vibrating with excitement. Girls struggled with hooks and zips, giggling nervously. Mums who had volunteered to do the make-up, were busy transforming fresh faces into mythical forest creatures. More pupils, already dressed, stood to one side going over their lines. Arabella Villiers, Lottie noted grudgingly admiring, was wearing the long sylphlike floaty skirt she had coveted and tiny silk pumps with pale pink ribbons that must have cost a fortune. She was having her picture taken for a local paper.

'That's great. Thanks very much,' said the photographer recapping his lens. 'Maybe we could get one with your mother after the show?'

'I'm sure she won't mind,' Arabella smiled sweetly. 'Don't forget to mention that I came top of my form in English and won first prize in the high jump.'

'Sporty as well as pretty, hey?'

Lottie turned away, sickened by how easily things seemed to fall into place for Arabella. Couldn't they all see her for the fake she really was? She reminded Lottie of the old Hollywood films they showed on Saturday afternoons on the box, where girls swanned around in *Gone with the Wind* gowns all sweet and demure, then sneaked off to the loo to say horrid things about each other.

Determined to show Arabella that she at least was quite unimpressed, Lottie trotted off to the only mirror provided, which was slightly warped, and inspected her appearance. Oh! She was a little taken aback by what she saw. This wasn't at all the effect she had wanted. The angry creature that gazed back at her looked more like a pixie than a fairy in those rotten emerald-green opaque tights she had been forced to wear and the mincy tutu which itched horribly and barely skimmed the top of her thighs. Lottie could have cried at the sight of her short spindly legs, her very *worst* feature. For a moment she imagined herself in Arabella's butter-yellow skirt. Oh, yes. Much better. And it nicely covered up her ankles. Lottie's eyes travelled up to her hair and froze. Someone had put sticky tufts into it so that she looked as if she had been electrocuted, and silver glitter that they used to put on Christmas cards in art had been smeared onto her lips and cheeks. This was not the magical transformation she had dreamt about.

Stealing a glance round the room in the hope of finding someone else who looked like she did, Lottie caught Arabella's watchful gaze. Triumphantly, the star of the show cast a slow scornful smile, then resumed dusting her perfect oval face with pale powder, her golden curls engagingly piled high on her head like a crown.

'Miss MacKenzie! Miss MacKenzie!' panted the Australian PE teacher as she thundered across the room. 'We've found it! We've found the costume. Someone had stuffed it inside one of the study hall desks. It's a bit wet, I'm afraid.'

'Thank goodness.' Miss MacKenzie grabbed the costume and rushed over to Bottom's dresser, the PE teacher struggling to keep up with her. .

'Quickly now,' she snapped. 'Don't just stand there dawdling.' She clapped her hands briskly at the poor fat girl who was playing the part. 'We've no time to lose.'

Five minutes later Lottie was standing in the draughty wings plucking nervously at her hated tutu. Someone had sat on her costume and one sad wing now hung broken and lopsided. It was too late to fix it. She just wouldn't think about it.

'You look really nice,' she said to Tess, who was playing Helena. They sat next to each other in class and once Tess had asked her back to her house for tea. 'Are you feeling nervous? I am.'

'A bit,' Tess admitted. 'Do you like my new hairband? I got it in Peter Jones.'

Peter Jones. Just hearing the name made Lottie shudder. They used to go there to buy her school uniform. Whenever she was naughty, Melanie would threaten to leave her in the badly behaved children's department. Lottie used to imagine rows and rows of cramped, airless cages with little children locked up inside, their pleading arms reaching through the imprisoning bars. Knowing now that no such place existed, it still gave her nightmares.

Tess startled her out of her thoughts by uttering a high-pitched shriek. She had located her parents in the third row.

'I do hope Daddy doesn't fall asleep like he did last year. Where's yours sitting?' she asked, remembering that Lottie's mother was rather pretty.

'Oh,' stalled Lottie, 'Mum hasn't arrived yet. But she's definitely coming.'

She'd promised she would. Someone turned the lights out. Intently Lottie listened to late arrivals scraping their chairs, the preliminary coughs and shushes. Then there was a brief moment of silence followed by a speech given by the head mistress. The spirited applause turned Lottie's stomach to liquid. She had always suffered from the most dreadful stage fright. Even her debut at four (playing a snail) had ended in tears after her knickers had collapsed around her ankles. Josh had been living with them by then for more than a year. If only things were still the way they used to be. If only Josh still loved her mother.

Wrapping her arms protectively round her chest, Lottie was suddenly unable to remember a single thing she was supposed to do. For a moment she panicked, then realised that she didn't appear until Act Two. There would be enough time to go over her lines.

A small collection of girls about to go on, squeezed in front of her. Arabella was one of them. They were all so tall. It wasn't fair. Lottie couldn't see a thing. Just as the curtain rose unsteadily, Arabella imperiously made her way to the front, and glanced slyly over one shoulder at Lottie.

'What's the matter, squirt? No one bother to turn up then?'

Lottie bit down on her lip. Bloody Mummy. That was it. She would never, *ever* speak to her again!

The first scene went off without a hitch. Miss MacKenzie ran around the room checking everyone's costume, making sure they got on stage on time and occasionally shouting. In the back of her mind she was still fuming about Bottom's costume. She was going to have everyone punished if the culprit didn't own up before the end of term. No pupil had ever got the better of her!

In Act Two, Puck, much to the annoyance of Arabella, made a grand entrance and promptly stole the show. Not only was she very funny, she was the only cast member who hadn't fluffed her lines. Lottie peeped out from behind one corner of the curtains. She could see Arabella's glamorous mother sitting in the front row, jiggling one of her feet in its high-heeled glossy shoe. The fact that she was nothing like as pretty as Melanie surprised Lottie but also gave her a certain amount of satisfaction. Sitting on Mrs Villiers right was a grey-haired man with a notepad balanced on his lap.

Flower of this purple dye, Hit with Cupid's archery,
Sink in apple of his eye, When his love he doth espy,
Let her shine as gloriously, As the Venus of the sky,
When thou wak'st, if she be by, Beg of her for remedy.

Oberon's speech, spoken confidently because his lines had been Sellotaped to a tree, was slightly spoiled by a commotion coming from the back of the room.

'Gosh, isn't that thingummy?' whispered Snout, vying for a better look over Lottie's shoulder.

'Who's thingummy?'

'You know, the man who—'

'Charlotte!' Miss MacKenzie hissed in the backstage gloom, 'Come here, you silly girl, or you'll miss your cue.'

Miss MacKenzie's hand clamped down on Lottie's arm and wrenched her out of the way so that Titania could go first. She then unceremoniously shoved Lottie out onto the stage. Dazed by the bright lights, Lottie tried to act as she had been instructed, as much like a fairy as possible. She flitted over to the other fairies and immediately Mrs Garrett plunged the school piano into life. They all began to sing.

> *You spotted snakes, with double tongue,*
> *Thorny hedge-hogs, be not seen;*
> *Newts and blind-worms do no wrong;*
> *Come not near our fairy queen.*

Oh, Lottie thought, tripping over the words. If she could just get through this without messing it up. After they had finished, Arabella (alias Titania) lay down under the papier-mâché tree and leaned against it. The tree promptly fell over and hit Oberon squarely on the head but fairy one wasn't to be deterred. She launched straight into a soliloquy about spiders and beetles and long-legged spinners. Lottie, chewing on her bottom lip, was trying to remember what a spinner was when Oberon growled at her,

'It's your go.'

She gazed out at the politely expectant audience and for a moment her mind blanked. Then, hesitatingly, she opened her mouth and said in a small, quivering voice,

> Hence, away! now all is well.
> One aloof stand sentinel.

Amongst the giggles someone began to clap loudly from the back of the room. Lottie wanted to die. How *embarrassing*! But having already lost her concentration once, she wasn't about to do so again by sneaking a look. Exiting to the sounds of 'Tu-whit, Tu-whoo' (someone with an even smaller part than her), Lottie shrugged her shoulders up and down in a vain hope that her damaged wings would spring to life.

Backstage was a tangle of arms and legs as everyone struggled into their next costumes – some of the more senior pupils were playing as many as three different roles. A crowd had collected around the mirror. Lottie, relieved to have got through her first and most difficult scene unscathed, stood slightly to one side, silently muttering the song the fairies all sang at the end so that she wouldn't forget it.

'Have you seen who's out there?' one of the girls was saying.

'Arabella's mum. So what? I've been round for tea enough times.'

'No, stupid. Not *her*. The tennis player – Josh Kendall.'

Like finely tuned antennae Lottie's ears pricked to attention.

'What? The Australian who won Wimbledon? Good one, Tabby.'

'It's true. Daisy reckons he came in a Porsche.'

'A Porsche!' said a chorus of awe-struck voices.

'Have a look when you go on if you don't believe me. He's standing at the back.'

'Girls, girls! Don't stand around gossiping. You should be waiting in the wings. Come on now. Chop, chop!'

Lottie couldn't believe it. Josh. Her Josh! Here! She chucked her copy of *A Midsummer Night's Dream* to the floor and rushed to the edge of the stage and peered out. Straining her eyes, it took a few seconds to adjust, but sure enough, there he was, standing a foot taller than all the other parents. Goodness, he'd brought Nana. Clutching a handbag, her grandmother was sitting in the last aisle seat with her hat and coat still on and Josh behind her. Tears sprang to Lottie's eyes. She simply couldn't believe it. Josh and Nana, the two people she loved best in the world, here at her school. Arabella came offstage wearing a smug smile.

'That photographer took my picture again.'

'Don't know why,' tossed Lottie. 'You can't act for toffees.'

Arabella's painted mouth fell open in astonishment. 'But,' Lottie added, full of a sudden confident joy, 'you do look good as a codfish.'

At the end everyone was bundled back on stage to rowdy applause. Miss MacKenzie followed and was congratulated on all her efforts. Tess presented her with a massive bouquet of flowers.

Lottie changed as fast as she could. Out of the corner of one eye she saw Arabella's mother arrive with the grey-haired man. Here we go again, she thought, her mood darkening. Then an extraordinary thing happened. After only a few spoken words to Arabella, the man politely bowed farewell then approached Puck (played by Camilla Snodgrass) on the other side of the room. Well, thought Lottie in astonishment as he dished out his card and handed it to the impish blonde, serve Arabella right for being such a know-all. Then Josh appeared and all thoughts of Arabella vanished.

'Come here, star.'

Ignoring the envious neighbouring eyes, Lottie flew into his opened arms, hugging him with a fierceness that surprised them both. 'Hey,' chuckled Josh, 'I didn't know fairies were so strong.'

'I never in a million *years* thought you'd come. Oh, Nana,' said Lottie turning to hug Esme. Her grandmother's emerald-green coat matched her shimmering eyeshadow and her skin felt soft and powdery, like a peach that needed to be eaten quickly.

'Wouldn't have missed it for the world, my little duck,' she squeezed Lottie tightly.

Lottie didn't know which of the hundred questions she had buzzing round her mind to ask first. 'How's Lauren and the baby?'

'Both doing fine. Lo's pretty tired with all his night feeds and she's a bit sore, but looking forward to spending some time in Sussex.'

'Haven't you got a name for him?'

'We're still arguing about it. I rather like the name Polly!'

Lottie pressed both hands against her mouth and giggled. 'Did you really come in a Porsche?'

'Aye, that we did,' Esme flashed her special smile. 'I thought we were going to take off in it. It goes ever so fast.'

A boy of about ten rushed over and stopped in his tracks a foot from Josh.

'Can I have your autograph, please?' he asked nervously. In his hand he held out a pen and a small book.

'Sure, kid.'

'And one for me mam?'

Arabella was leaving. She was so busy glaring daggers at the theatre director still talking to Puck that she almost collided into the wall.

'Didn't think much of her,' sniffed Esme, carrying her handbag over her wrist like the Queen. 'Bit too la-di-da for my liking.'

'Oh, that's Arabella. She's very popular,' admitted Lottie.

'Aye, well, she's not a patch on you.'

Miss MacKenzie, mingling in the hall with the delighted parents, overheard one of her pupils talking about the Wimbledon champion. A terrific tennis fan herself, she deftly extricated herself from an admiring father and rushed backstage. It took her a moment to overcome her surprise when she saw that the pupil he had come to see was Charlotte Roach.

'Well, now,' she said breezily, hoping her just reapplied perfume wasn't too overpowering, 'what did we think of our little Charlotte, then, Mr Kendall? Not quite the performance we might have liked, mmmmh? But then we can't all be megastars, can we?' She smiled meaningfully at Josh.

'You underestimate, Lottie, Mrs eh—?'

'Miss MacKenzie,' she placed heavy emphasis on 'Miss' and proffered a slender, bony hand. 'And may I say how delighted I am that you managed to come to our little extravaganza.' She flourished a hand then modestly placed it on her silk bodice.

'Had I known that you were . . .' her voice trailed off at this point and unable to help herself, raised an incredulous eyebrow in Lottie's direction. 'Yes. Well perhaps you'd like to join me with some of the parents for a glass of wine? I'm sure they'd be *thrilled* to meet you.' The invitation clearly didn't extend to either Esme or Lottie.

'Thanks, but my priorities are with these two beautiful girls. I'm taking them out for a meal.' Josh put his arm around Lottie who gave him a sweet little conspiratorial smile. 'You about ready to go, darling?'

She quickly held up her schoolbag to show that she was, then turned to her teacher.

'Bye then, Miss MacKenzie. Hope I didn't let you down tonight.'

'No, dear,' Miss MacKenzie said, failing to keep the disappointment from her voice as the Wimbledon champion turned and walked out of her life without even saying goodbye, 'you were fine, just fine.'

The rest of the evening seemed to pass in a dream. Squeezed into the back of the red Porsche, Lottie chatted incessantly while they sped along Wimbledon Park Road. They passed the All England Lawn Tennis and Croquet

Club protected by a barbed-wire wall and large steel gates through which she could glimpse the tantalising military green stands. Lottie's heart quickened with excitement. Just a few days ago she'd been there.

As it was such a nice evening Josh had suggested going out for dinner, but Esme was tired from the heat and wanted to get back to her house in Bushy Meade. At the door, she insisted they both come in for a cup of tea.

'I'll put the kettle on. There's some nice cake too,' she called from the adjoining kitchen that smelt of baking and faint traces of gas. 'Dundee cake, ginger biscuits, some jam tarts made this morning,' she tempted, knowing what a sweet tooth her granddaughter had. 'Or what about a slice of bread and jam?'

'That's all you have?' said Josh, winking at Lottie. 'A man could go hungry hanging around you.'

Esme elbowed him gently. 'Oh, he's a devil, this one.'

'Come on you,' he steered the old woman out of the kitchen. 'We'll do all that.'

Esme hovered, reluctant to give up her domain. But the heat was getting to her and her varicose veins were playing up. She could do with putting her feet up. Back in the adjoining living room, she eased off her shoes and wiggled her plump toes gratefully. Patting the chair next to her, she said, 'Josh, you come and sit over here and tell me about that new baby of yours.'

One of the gas rings was still on. Lottie quickly turned it off and opened the kitchen door which led out to the garden and a long line of washing.

'Herman!' she shrieked, as the small black-and-white terrier scurried into the room. Deliriously he circled her feet, pawing at her legs. Lottie bent down and rubbed his tummy, 'Are you hungry too?'

From her chair next door, Esme chuckled. 'Bound to be. Go on, Lottie, give him some cake. But mind you mash it up for him. And watch out for nuts. They make him choke.'

Herman's great shame in life was that he only had four of his teeth left. Melanie blamed Esme for constantly feeding him sweets. He never had proper dog food. He ate whatever Esme was cooking for herself. Nana didn't have many teeth either. Her grandmother was the only person Lottie knew who could take out a section of five bottom teeth.

While Josh used the phone, Lottie filled the kettle and got some cups from the cupboard. The kitchen was full of old-fashioned things; a coronation tea caddy; pictures of the Madonna, Jesus on the cross; a wooden plate rack; a tiny gas fire; a big slab of brown soap that smelt manly and filled both her hands. On the small kitchen table were three crocheted mats like her mother had. They were made of a biscuit-coloured silky thread and shaped intricately like a spider's web. Lottie could never imagine making anything so fragile, so fine. But Nana was clever like that. She found the cake and put it on a flowery plate then added a few chocolate biscuits as an afterthought – Josh loved them. She filled the fat teapot with boiling water and carried the rattling cups and saucers into the living room.

'You're a good girl,' sighed Nana, as she sipped her tea. 'Nothing quite like it.' Never in all Lottie's life had she seen her grandmother drink anything else.

Josh returned from making his call and sat down next to Lottie on the sofa. She picked up a chocolate biscuit and thought about Arabella's floaty skirt.

'I didn't have a very big part today,' she said.

'It's quality not quantity what counts,' sniffed Esme, her diamanté earrings glinting like tears.

Josh put his arm round Lottie and pulled her closer. 'Has Lottie told you she's coming to stay with us for a few days, Esme?'

Lottie beamed. 'Lauren's parents are having a party at the

weekend, Nana. They've invited lots of people and there'll be kids my age and everything. I've seen pictures of the house – it looks amazing; dogs and cats and horses. There's even a pool.'

'A pool. Fancy!' Esme was impressed.

The conversation drifted back to the new baby, with Esme clucking sympathetically as Josh described Lauren's ordeal. The heat and excitement of the day made Lottie's mind withdraw. She picked up Josh's hand and examined a scar that ran along the inside of his palm. Although it had long since faded a bruise-coloured weal remained. She ran a finger along its edge curiously. 'I got it as a boy,' Josh had once told her. Coming home from school he had stumbled on three men trying to steal his mother's jewellery. A fight had developed, Josh decked two of them and the men had fled. More than that he wouldn't say. But Lottie thought it incredibly brave. Just the sort of thing Josh *would* do.

Josh opened the living room door and a warm breeze immediately wafted through from the kitchen. Lottie looked lovingly at the familiar surroundings crammed with possessions; Nana's knitting with the needles pushed through the wool lying on a footstool; the chewed and battered basket in the corner where Herman now lay curled, his old, rheumy eyes watchful; sepia photographs of her grandfather, stiff and proud in his uniform, his long bony face slightly in shadow. He died before she had a chance to know him but her nana spoke of him so much Lottie felt she did; a smiling Melanie holding her as a baby. As always, Lottie studied the picture with curiosity. Melanie hardly looked old enough to be a mother – more a schoolgirl with her long thick hair pulled back in bunches and slim as a reed.

'That's one of your favourites, isn't it pet?' said Esme, watching her. 'Your mother used to bring you round in your pram. We'd pop you in the garden like, all wrapped up and ne'er a squeak of complaint.' She smiled proudly.

'Your granddad used to say you were prettiest baby he'd ever seen.'

Lottie's eyes returned mournfully to her younger, prettier self. Here in the warm crowdedness of her grandmother's house she felt a sudden ache of homesickness. If she could only remain here for ever. She didn't want to go back to school, not for one more day. She hated it. It was obvious she didn't belong there. She wasn't like the others. She didn't know why exactly, but she could sense it. Other girls had fathers, best friends, visited each other's houses to watch television, swapped clothes and magazines. Hanging back in corners, twisting the end of her short plait, Lottie would observe them in the playground, huddled in secret conspiring groups, whispering and giggling together, practising dances, playing netball. She longed to know what it was they talked about. She yearned to be part of their exclusive world. But even more she wished she didn't have to go to school at all but could be alone to think her plan out properly. Because her plan was a big one and would take an awful lot of working out. Sometimes she wondered if she was a bit too ambitious for her own good. But she never allowed herself to think that way for long.

After tea, Lottie was worried Josh would be too full of cake to remember his promise of dinner. But the Porsche roared straight past her house. The phone call he had made from Esme's had been to Lewis Roger who owned the popular wine bar Volleys in Wimbledon Village. From three o'clock food stopped being served but for close friends like Josh, Lewis sometimes made an exception. A little shiver of excitement filled the room as Josh entered. Lottie grinned proudly as heads turned in their direction. She had never been inside Volleys before but had, on many occasions, watched several top players going in and out during Wimbledon. Curiously, she glanced around the dim bar bustling with noise and music. Stuck to the walls was a myriad of tennis memorabilia. She gawped at photographs of a very young (and skinny) Becker shaking hands with Lewis; Agassi's Nike hat signed and mounted; easily identified caricature sketches of Martina and Steffi; old wooden racquets crossed together like the Wimbledon logo.

With a sense of unreality Lottie let Josh order them both hamburgers and milkshakes. This was like the old days when Josh used to take her to the local fair or on day trips to the sea where she could eat all the sweets she liked without being told that her teeth would fall out and run freely along the pier, the wind stinging her cheeks. She could remember the first day she had learnt to swim, and Josh bragging about how she would one day swim the channel; when he brought home stilts for her seventh birthday so that she could totter behind, matching him in height, at least for a few seconds until she collapsed laughing and laughing so hard she almost peed her pants. In those days Josh didn't have a car so they took the underground. Lottie's hand carefully tucked into his, she would watch in awe the trains accelerate into the deep black tunnel, their squealing wheels spitting out a shower of blue sparks like fireworks. Captivated, she believed they were spirits of dead people trying to find a resting place. She was never quite convinced about heaven though. It sounded warm and nice when Melanie talked about it, but like Father Christmas, nice things weren't always real . . . Oh, bugger! Mum!

Her eye spun to Josh, wolfing down his food. Like a child he was jamming matchstick French fries into the thick tomato relish that had little bits in it then popping them into his mouth. Melanie never let her do things like that. Or that, she thought, marvelling at the sight of Josh licking each of his fingers with aplomb.

'Josh?'

'Mmmm?'

'Mum's going to be mad. She was supposed to be picking me up from school.'

'Don't worry about it,' he mumbled, rinsing down his food with some Coke. 'We spoke earlier. She knows you're with me.'

'She does?' That floored her. 'Then how come she didn't . . .?' Lottie glared at the green-and-white-check tablecloth. 'She could have come. She could have made the effort. I've never had a speaking part before.'

'Don't be too hard on your mum, sweetheart. She sounded pretty crook when I called. Flu, I reckon. She'd have come if she'd been up to it, wouldn't she?'

She stirred her milk shake around with the straw and licked froth from it with her tongue, exploring it thoughtfully like a cat. A television screen suspended from a wall was showing a basketball game.

'While we're on the subject of your mum, I mentioned your birthday.'

Lottie nibbled her bottom lip.

'Guess you never mentioned my suggestion to her, eh?' Josh polished off the rest of his double cheeseburger.

'I meant to,' she said defensively, shifting in her chair. 'There just never seemed to be the right time. What did she say?'

'Not much. Think she was too out of it to take in what I was saying. But no worries. We'll get it sorted.' His eyes dropped to her empty plate, 'Oye, I thought you said you weren't hungry?'

Lottie flashed him a mustardy grin.

Going home she was allowed to sit in the front of the Porsche. It *was* like flying. She felt the thrill of scary excitement as Josh revved the engine then let it purr as they stopped at the lights by Ely's department store. Lottie felt sure everyone was looking at them. Being with Josh was like being part of the best of everything: swimming;

Christmas-tree lights; roast chicken; flying on a plane; Nana's home-made jam tarts; the first day of spring. Oh, if only today could last for ever.

When they turned down Gladstone Road, however, Lottie's exhilaration had dimmed. Despite Josh's words of reassurance earlier, her mother's moods were often unpredictable – *especially* when it came to Josh. She clambered out of the car and the front door burst open.

'Darling!' Melanie rushed out to greet her and Lottie wondered why her mother had on the thick bottle-green sweater she normally wore in winter. 'Sorry I couldn't make it – feeling a bit under the weather. Were you very good?'

'Brilliant,' said Josh, wrapping an arm around Lottie, 'Winona Ryder's got some stiff competition. How are you, Mel?'

Their eyes met for a moment, then sought safer places to rest.

'It's just this damn cough,' she said, coughing. Her daughter was still hovering close to Josh, gazing up at him with puppyish awe. Just for a second Melanie frowned as if this annoyed her.

'Lottie?' she coaxed. 'Lottie, love, come here.' But Lottie refused to move staring mutinously at the clusters of pink roses clinging to the front of the house. 'I really am sorry about the play. But I took some medicine the doctor gave me and it knocked me out. Am I forgiven?'

Her mother looked so awful Lottie suddenly felt ashamed.

'It wasn't all that good,' she mumbled by way of an apology, 'and Arabella Villiers knocked a tree over.'

Melanie reached down and plucked at a few weeds pushing through the cracks of stone slabs. 'Well, get yourself inside. It's draughty this evening.' She risked a glance at Josh as she pulled herself up.

'Would you like to come in for a drink?'

'Thanks, Mel, but I'd better be heading home. You know how it is.'

'Yes,' she said with a trace of bitterness, 'I do.'

A look passed between them.

'Nana gave me a present. See, Mum. Here,' Lottie held out a book for Melanie's inspection.

'That's nice, dear,' she said, but Lottie could tell her mother's attention was elsewhere. It always was when Josh was around.

Josh jiggled his car keys. 'Right. Well, I'm off.'

Lottie's face fell. 'Won't you stay even for a little bit?'

'No can do, sweetheart. But you've had me for most of the night. Do you want to tell your mum about the weekend now?'

Melanie looked quizzically at Josh.

'Yes, what was that all about? On the phone you said something about Lottie's birthday?'

'Lauren's parents are having a do at their Sussex pad. There'll be other kids there – we thought it would be fun for Lottie.'

Melanie glanced accusingly at her daughter. 'But that's next weekend. Why didn't you mention this to me before? I've already made plans for your birthday.' That was a lie. She hadn't given it much thought at all. Not yet, anyway. But faced now with the prospect of Lottie going off with Josh and that *woman*, it seemed suddenly vitally important that she didn't go.

Lottie regarded her mother with suspicion. 'What plans?'

'Well . . .' Melanie began thinking quickly, 'I was going to do a picnic lunch and a trip down the Thames. We could get Esme along too. Now, wouldn't that be nice?' Unfair of her to use emotional blackmail but she could already feel the parental reins slipping from her control.

'Oh, Mum. *Please* let me go. It's going to be so much fun. They've got a tennis court and everything.'

Melanie could see she was fighting a losing battle. She switched tactics.

'Why don't we talk about this in the morning? You've had a long day, darling, and there's still four more days of school. Go on, up to bed now. I'll be up in a bit to tuck you in.'

Lottie glared at her mother. She had that strained look, those tiny lines at the corners of her eyes and around her mouth. Lottie sulkily dragged her feet forward. 'That means you're not going to let me go. I *never* get to do anything fun!'

'Thanks very much, Josh,' said Melanie angrily, once Lottie had disappeared up to her room. 'Bloody typical of you to have the effrontery to make plans with Lottie without first consulting me. It puts me in an impossible situation. Honestly. Why should I be the one who has to tell her she can't go?' Hands on hips, she glared at him.

'You could just make it easy on the kid and say yes. It doesn't have to be like this.'

Melanie stepped further forward and pulled the front door closer behind her as if she were afraid that Lottie might hear them.

'Now look, Josh. You disappear for months with that—' she seemed unable to say Lauren's name, 'with only a few snatched calls, the odd postcard and that's supposed to keep Lottie happy? It's not good enough, and neither is it fair. You can't play games with people's lives the way you do on court. Josh, she's just a child. She needs stability not your emotional roller-coaster rides.'

A car drove violently past them and screeched round a corner further down the road. Josh watched it disappear then turned back to face her.

'Mel,' he said, 'you're her mother. No one's trying to take that away from you. But I'm fond of the kid and she likes hanging around me. What's wrong with her getting away for a couple of days? She rarely gets to meet kids outside of school.'

He was right, of course. Lottie had few friends to play with, but it galled Melanie that she was the one who made sure Lottie did her homework, got up in time for school, who reminded her of her responsibilities around the house. It meant that she always looked like the spoilsport, the villain. She looked at Josh with reluctant curiosity. Still maddeningly attractive – blazing blue eyes, long aquiline nose and high flattened cheekbones that gave him a heroic look, golden hair curling at the collar of his denim shirt. She thought; if we'd had a child together, would it have looked like you? Under the glare of the harsh streetlight, Melanie was suddenly acutely aware of how untidy she must look – no make-up, her hair messily tied back with an elastic band. Oh, what did it matter anyway! Josh had long since lost interest in her.

'So,' he tried after a few lapsed moments, 'how's work been going?'

'Bits of temping here and there. I can't really do more because of Lottie, but the money helps with bills. At least I don't have a mortgage.'

She thought back to all the years she had supported Josh while he was trying to make it, about the money he must now be raking in. Not that he offered any of it to her. Their worlds had become quite separate, distanced by his marriage and ever increasing success. Her eyes narrowed with resentment.

'Go on, then,' her tone was bitter, 'take Lottie on your precious weekend. If that's what she wants I'm not going to let you turn her against me by saying no.'

'No one's trying to.'

'Aren't they?' she said harshly.

'Of course not. Lauren and I . . .'

But she had launched into a prolonged fit of coughing.

'That sounds nasty, Mel. You should get it seen to.'

'Bloody cough,' she snapped, angry with herself. 'Look, it's late and I'm tired of arguing. It's all you and I ever seem to do these days. Go home, Josh. Go back to your wife and son.'

For a moment Josh studied her. He slowly shook his head and sighed. 'Whatever you say, Mel.' Then he turned and walked back to his car.

Melanie stood smouldering, watching from the doorway as he drove off until the Porsche was no longer in her sight.

4

'Okay, baby, which way?'

'Left, I guess. No, hang on. Take a right.'

Max Carter shifted down into second gear. 'You sure?'

'Not one hundred per cent.' Tiffany Forbes gave an exasperated sigh. 'Hell, I don't know.'

'It might help if you used the map.'

'And just what do you think this is?' From her lap Tiffany lifted the map, folded into a manageable size, and waved it in the air. 'Half these tiny roads ain't even on this thing.' She scrutinised the map again then looked up decisively. 'Okay, go left. It's definitely left.'

They turned into a narrow Sussex lane groaning with so much hedgerow that there was practically no room for the car. Tiffany, squinting against the glare of the sun bouncing off the red-hot bonnet, could hear things thudding against the expensive paintwork. She sneaked a glance at Max. He'd hate that, she thought. Hate the idea of his precious car getting scratched: never mind the fact that he got given a new one every year. Men and their cars. She could hear her mother's voice saying: 'Men who get a new car every year usually have trouble committing to a relationship.' She consigned the maternal advice swiftly to the back of her mind. Her mother wasn't right about *everything*, after all!

They shot round a vicious S-bend, its verges laced with cow parsley. What would happen, she wondered, if they were to meet an oncoming car.

'Gee, this lane's skinnier than an anorexic.'

Max gave her a quick approving glance. 'Not one of your problems thankfully.'

She reached over and cupped his groin. His penis felt fat and warm through the padding of his trousers.

'How's the hand doing?' his voice softened, all buttery and warm the way she loved best.

'Better.' They both glanced at the angry red mark which dragged from her wrist to the knuckle. Tiffany touched it cautiously. 'D'you think it'll scar?'

Max's hands tightened round the steering wheel. 'You should have let me go after that little punk when I had the chance.'

'Oh, right. And have yourself beaten up – or killed. No way, Max. We did the right thing.'

She turned her head away and gazed out at the fields beyond the hedgerows, then suddenly pointed to a private opening in the road.

'Hey! I'm sure Robert said something about willow trees and a gravel drive. See. Over there?'

'Great,' Max muttered, throwing Tiffany against him as he made the sharp turn, 'we might just about make it in time for lunch.'

The car slipped through a mossy stone gateway supporting two chipped, bulging urns. On the right Tiffany could just make out the faded stone engraving, Willow.

'Bingo,' she said, breathing in the heady scent of honeysuckle on the late July air.

As they drew up outside the Millers' splendid thatched house, two giggling young children raced across the croquet lawn. They almost collided with the car.

Max braked abruptly. 'Watch it, guys!'

Tiffany stepped out of the car. 'Howdy.'

'Hello,' said the boy politely. He couldn't have been more than seven. 'I'm James and this is my new friend Lottie.

She plays really good tennis and we're going to watch the Flintstones.'

'A good choice.' Max opened up the boot. 'How are you, Lottie? Josh here yet?'

She smiled shyly. 'We drove down last night with Lauren and the baby. I'm having the *best* time.' Lottie glanced curiously at Tiffany then back at Max. 'How did you do in Sweden?'

Tiffany raised an eyebrow.

'Made the semis. Then got thrashed by Rafter. I tell you, these young Aussies are getting out of hand.' Max grinned, showing her that what he'd said was meant in jest. 'The French Algerian won.'

'Wolff Bohakari?'

'Yeah. He's a good player when he's not smashing racquets. Where is everyone?'

'We're all down by the pool,' cried a voice, 'making the most of this *fabulous* weather.'

A tall handsome woman wearing a sombrero and carrying a tray of glasses was crossing the lawn towards them. Two panting golden Labradors tagged behind.

'We were beginning to think you'd got lost,' she said. 'I'm thrilled you could make it.'

'Kay,' said Max, kissing her warmly.

Kay Miller rested the tray on the bonnet and took off her sunglasses, then directed her smile at Tiffany. 'Now you,' she said, 'must be the ravishing Texan we've been hearing so much about.' Max sent her a warning glance but Kay ignored it. 'How on earth did you survive the car journey? Max behind a wheel is the devil himself.'

'He is kinda fast,' said Tiffany, darting Max a secret smile. 'It's nice to meet you, Kay. You have a real pretty home.'

'We think so. It's taken lots of work *and* money to get it

looking the way it does now. I've been having a love affair from the day I first set eyes on it, which was just before we were married. But I'm not about to tell you how many years ago that was or I'll sound as old as the house.' She smiled conspiratorially.

One of the dogs was sniffing Tiffany's crotch with frantic excitement.

'Tadpole, *get down*!' ordered Kay. The Labrador flopped immediately into the pose of a Landseer lion. 'I hope you like dogs, Tiffany. Satchmo's a terror,' she indicated the Labrador peeing against a large willow weeping over the lawn, 'but Tadpole, here,' she stroked the second dog's blond tufty chin affectionately, 'couldn't bite through a doughnut, could you, Taddy.'

Tadpole barked obediently.

'Mrs Miller!' James, who had been waiting patiently for the grown-ups to finish, tugged at her cotton skirt. 'Can we go and watch the Flintstones now?'

'Aren't you hungry, dear? We're just about to have lunch.'

'Yes, but can we have it later?'

'Go on then. You can take these glasses in for Mrs Poole to wash on your way. No, not you, James. Lottie.' Gingerly Lottie picked up the tray from the car bonnet. 'Just be careful,' Kay instructed. 'Robert will have a fit if any of his precious mowers get broken.'

But Kay doubted they had heard; the children had already turn-tailed and were making their way up the front steps, the Labradors bounding along behind them.

'Come on then. Let's get you both a drink. You must be gasping. We can leave your luggage until later. You haven't missed much. Robert couldn't get the barbecue to light – the firelighters fell in the pool or something silly – so lunch is very late.'

Kay linked arms with them both and like a dowager

duchess directed them down the sloping lawn towards the noise and laughter coming from a swimming pool and summerhouse walled off by stout yew hedges. An attractive man wearing shorts, who Tiffany guessed to be in his late sixties, was turning blackened sausages and chicken breasts on a hot grill. He wiped his spare hand on his apron to greet them.

'Max,' he said warmly, 'good of you to come.' He was less formal with Tiffany and kissed her on the cheek. 'Hello, there, I'm Robert Miller. Glad you could make it. Traffic bad?'

'Not really. But we had a slight incident on the Talgarth Road,' said Max, with a slight edge to his voice.

'Sounds intriguing.'

Tiffany explained. 'This guy ripped off my Cartier watch while we were stopped at the lights.'

'Good God! How on earth did that happen?'

'He was so fast neither of us had time to react. I had my window rolled down and my arm hanging out of it. He just appeared from nowhere, grabbed my watch and ran. Unreal!' As she spoke, Tiffany could feel herself being scrutinised. A few feet away a young woman with aggressively short marmalade hair was stretched out on a pool chair. She was smoking with deep, resolute drags.

'Were you hurt?' asked Robert, concern in his voice.

'Some,' admitted Tiffany, 'but I guess it could have been a lot worse.' She held out her hand for them all to inspect, rather enjoying the attention she was getting. 'Apparently, it happens all the time.'

'You poor girl. You must let me do something about that,' said Kay worriedly. 'Don't want to get it infected.'

'Oh, that's okay. I had some antiseptic in my bag.'

'Well, I hope you were insured,' said Robert soberly.

'Robert's very keen on insurance policies,' Kay explained

to Tiffany, 'I think even the dogs are covered.' They all laughed.

Max had sloped off on the pretext of getting drinks, but Tiffany could see him weaving his way over to a small group gathered on the other side of the pool. She identified Josh Kendall holding a baby, but she didn't recognise the blonde woman next to him or the skinny red-headed guy lounging in a pair of parrot-green shorts. His sprawled tanned legs, broad shoulders and wavy hair pulled back into a ponytail were all giveaway signs. Tennis player, for sure.

'Sukie,' Kay gestured to the girl with the marmalade hair, 'come over and meet Tiffany Forbes. She's from Texas. This is my younger daughter, Sukie,' she said, as the girl got up from her chair and approached them. 'Darling, you were in Houston last summer, weren't you?'

'Only for three weeks so I can't claim to have seen much.' Sukie ground her cigarette butt into pulp with her foot and pushed her tinted glasses more firmly onto her retrousse nose. 'Are you from there?'

Tiffany shook her head. 'My hometown's a small place near Wichita Falls – close to the Oklahoma border. Dad moved to Florida some years back. I have a house nearby – Dad and I are pretty close.'

Sukie's eyes ran over the Texan's clothes as if she were labelling and pricing each item. 'And what do you do?' she asked bluntly.

'Works on that Bermuda tan of hers most of the time.' Max grinned, back with drinks. 'Sukie, you're too nosy for your own good. Wine okay, hon?'

Tiffany smiled at him as she accepted her drink. 'You don't want to go paying too much attention to Max. My father owns a string of horses and I help out when I'm there. Do y'all ride?'

'Not if I can help it,' Sukie said rudely. 'Horses and I don't see eye to eye. I got kicked very hard when I was about four. Now I keep a safe distance.' She put out a hand to stop the Millers' neighbour who was going round with a bottle of wine filling people's glasses. 'Any chance of some slimline tonic, Jeffrey?'

'Absolutely, old girl. Hang on a sec.' He turned to Max and held out his hand. 'Jeffrey Rutherford. Bloody good final, sir. Fine match. Yes, uhumph. Play quite a bit myself.'

While the men talked, Tiffany turned to Sukie. 'You reducing?'

'Sorry?'

'Slimline tonic. I figured you were reducing.'

'Absolute waste of time if you ask me,' sniffed Jeffrey, whose capacity to follow two conversations at the same time was remarkable. 'My wife's been dieting for years and looks exactly the same.'

Tiffany gave him a sugary smile. 'Where I come from the men like their women with plenty of curves.' To add emphasis to her point she ran a slow lingering hand down the side of her shapely hip. Max hid his smile in his glass.

'Yes, uhumph. Yes, right,' Jeffrey spluttered, his complexion shifting from a subtle shade of pink to brick red. 'Right. Tonic coming right up. I say, anyone else for a top-up?' he yelled, making a hasty exit.

'I just love teasing these Englishmen,' giggled Tiffany. 'They're *so* cute.'

'Aren't they just,' Sukie replied a bit waspishly.

Max kissed the back of Tiffany's smooth neck. 'How about coming over to say hi to Josh?'

'Let's do it.' But Tiffany's smile faded once they were out of Sukie's earshot. 'Damn it, Maxy! What is her *problem*? That's some chip she's walking around with.'

'Sukie's a well-balanced girl with chips on *both* shoulders. Hates competition but she does have her moments.'

'Now's not one of them, that's for sure!'

'She's probably pissed you don't have to work for a living.'

Tiffany raised an indignant eyebrow. 'She's a script editor for Carlton TV. Money always seems to be a sore subject.'

Two young boys were bomb-diving in the pool. Tiffany, anchoring herself to Max, stepped sideways to avoid a tidal wave.

'Tiffany!' Supporting the baby over one shoulder, Josh rose and kissed her warmly. 'I don't know how you always manage to look as though you've just stepped out of the pages of *Vogue*, especially in this heat. I'd like you to meet my wife, Lauren.'

The woman who held out her hand was like a shampoo commercial – radiant, glowing with health and vitality. Her features seemed to leap from her face and pitch themselves towards you – the wide bleached denim-blue eyes set off by neat eyebrows, the strong nose, the large mobile mouth which had opened into a dazzling smile. Even the tiny gap in her two front teeth was beautiful. Never in all her life had Tiffany felt so threatened.

'Hello,' Lauren said warmly, 'you're even lovelier than Max described you.'

Tiffany, who rarely blushed, did so now at the unexpected compliment. 'Is this your little boy?' she asked, as much to hide her confusion as anything else. She put a hand up to stroke one of the baby's tiny fingers. 'He's just adorable. How old is he?'

'Four weeks.' Lauren said it proudly, as if her son had just won a scholarship to Oxford.

'Here, take a pew.' Josh pulled up another chair. 'Move your backside, Luke,' he said to the redhead nearby. 'Tiffany, do you know Luke Falkner?'

Tiffany shook her head. 'I've seen you around with Max.' Luke stopped cramming peanuts into his mouth. 'How're you doing, man?' He turned to Max. 'Caught your match in the quarterfinals. Manliekov got a bit out of hand.'

'Can't stand the guy. I've played him three times now. He aims his shots right at the head and that's dangerous.'

'Yeah, I've heard that. I've also heard you're going to write a bio.'

Tiffany glanced at Max with surprise. 'Is that true, Maxy?'

'It's a maybe. That's all.'

'I'll bet you could tell a few stories,' said Luke with more than a trace of admiration in his voice. 'A legend like you.'

Max laughed. 'A legend, hey? Now I feel ancient!'

'Max, we've got to get you round to see the house,' said Josh.

'How long have you had it now?'

Josh turned to his wife. 'About a year, isn't it, Lo?'

'And to think we so nearly lost it.' She smiled. 'Come for a meal before you fly back – both of you,' she said, including Tiffany.

The baby started to cry. 'Uh-oh. The unmistakable sound of hunger.' Lauren rose stiffly and held out her arms to Josh. 'I'll take him up to the house, darling. He probably needs changing.'

Josh held his son high in the air and grinned at him adoringly. 'You heard what your mother said, champ. Time to go.'

Lauren adjusted the delicate lace hat so that it shielded his tiny head more effectively from the afternoon glare. She lowered him into his Moses basket.

'Sorry,' she said to Tiffany, 'but time's not your own once you've had one of these. We'll get a chance to talk later. You are staying the night, I hope?'

Max answered for her. 'Wouldn't miss your mother's cooking for the world.'

'Don't let Robert hear you say that,' said Kay. 'He's desperately proud of his barbecues! Lauren, darling, just to warn you. Patricia Rutherford's knitted something for Tom.'

'How kind of her.'

'Yes, well, just try not to look too aghast when you see it. It is rather a curious thing. I still haven't quite worked out what it is yet. It appears to have three arms.'

As Lauren passed the wet, shrieking children, she caught her sister's eye. Sukie looked bored.

'I'm taking him up for a feed,' Lauren mouthed. 'Join me if you want to.'

Sukie nodded and resumed her moody smoking. Oh dear, thought Lauren, making her way back up to the house. She's probably got a raging hangover. She was knocking it back last night. God knows why: a few bitchy remarks about work but Lauren doubted it was that. For all her moaning Sukie liked her job. But today Sukie seemed to be making absolutely no effort to mix. Man trouble probably. Lauren could always gauge how Sukie's lovelife was going by the amount of shopping bags she came home with. There was a stack of them upstairs. After an early supper last night, Sukie had dragged her up to her room to show off all her new purchases. Three Nicole Farhi silk shirts, a wool jacket and a short skirt which must have cost a fortune.

'Well, they were in the sale,' Sukie had said defensively. 'Thirty-five per cent off.'

'That's just you trying to justify it.'

As Sukie didn't have that kind of money to spend, Lauren guessed she'd talked their father into giving it to her. Which made Lauren hopping mad. Her parents gave the impression of being financially very comfortable, but the truth was they were being taken to the cleaners by Lloyds.

The house was now in view. Lauren walked with discomfort, troubled by slow-mending stitches; thirty hours of labour and a ten-pound baby had left her badly torn – The Bayeux Tapestry had *nothing* on her. She felt amused, stunned, knocked out in turn by her new role as a mother. The experience had left her wondering why she had waited so long. Yet nothing could have prepared her for the earth-shattering change it had had on her life. A baby was unbelievably hard work. She hadn't slept for more than three hours in a row since Tom's birth. Even so, she felt incredibly blessed: a beautiful son, a happy marriage, her husband's career going exactly the way he'd planned.

James, the little boy Lottie had been playing with – no one was quite sure who he belonged to – dashed out of the front door as if being chased by some invisible monster and came hurtling towards her.

'Lunchtime! Lunchtime!' he yelped, his bandy legs racing frantically towards the pool. 'Yabbadabba*dooo*!' The baby squirmed crossly in his basket.

'Okay, Tom,' Lauren cooed, upping the speed of her walk, 'we're almost there.'

Already she could feel her shirt dampen with the sweet clear milk. Impatiently, she entered the main hall which smelt faintly of pot-pourri, and went up to her room. She wanted to feel her son's smooth little cheek against her breast.

Lauren wasn't the only one who had been keeping an eye on Sukie. The Canadian, Luke Falkner had noticed her the moment he arrived.

'Hi,' he said approaching her now.

Sukie lifted her head and lowered her sunglasses to get a better look at him. 'Hello.' Her voice was guarded.

'As it's pretty obvious nobody around here's going to introduce us, I'm going to do it myself. Luke Falkner, and you're Lauren's sister, Sukie, right?'

'Was that an educated guess or did someone help you?'

'Does it matter?'

Sukie shrugged. 'Not really.' Relaxing back against the chair, her face pale beneath the tinted sunglasses, she resumed sunbathing.

If the deliberately rude gesture was meant as a deterrent, however, it had absolutely no effect on Luke. He pulled up a nearby chair and sat down next to her. Light danced on the surface of the swimming pool.

'So Su-kie,' he said, tasting the two syllables, the slightly babyish sound of her name, 'you got a BF?'

'A what?'

'A boyfriend.'

She sniffed contemptuously. 'No. And I'm not looking for one either.' She scrutinised the cuticles on the nails of her left hand, implying lack of interest.

'Cool. Where's your pad?'

'If you mean my flat, it's in London.'

'London's a big place.'

'Notting Hill Gate.'

'That's where they have the Carnival, right?'

'Right.'

'I usually hang out at the St James Court when I'm in the UK. Not all that far from you.'

Sukie inclined her head towards him. 'Look, I don't want to be rude, but please go away. I'm feeling rather fragile.'

James flew past them still hollering 'Yabbadabba*doo*.'

'If he's not careful he'll fall into the pool,' muttered Sukie. 'Serve him right for being so disgustingly energetic.'

'I take it you're not the maternal kind.'

She drew her right eyebrow into a cynical arch. 'As it happens, I am, but I wear expensive shoes – I like to see my feet!'

It took him a moment to get the joke. A sleepy wasp buzzed past and landed on Sukie's leg.

'Shit!' She sprang up, shaking the insect off. It dropped to the ground. 'Eeech, I hate them!'

Luke calmly reached over with his foot and squashed it. 'There,' he said, 'gone.'

With a not-too-steady hand, Sukie lit up another cigarette. Then, as an afterthought she offered him one.

'Thanks, but I like my lungs clean.'

'Oh, here we go. The sermon. According to the health experts meat, butter, alcohol and sugar are all just as dangerous. Anything, basically, that's pleasurable.'

Luke gave her a Don Juan smile. 'Not everything.'

And in spite of herself, Sukie smiled back.

'Robert!' Kay's voice carried across the pool. 'Darling, I don't think we've got enough wine. Can you get some more from the cellar. Don't worry about the chops. I'll keep an eye on them.'

'Can I come? Can I come?' begged James. Robert swept him up onto his shoulders and carried him off, with the now towering James beaming like a beacon.

'Anyone ever tell you that you look like the actor Sam Neill?'

'You could say that,' Max replied wearily. He had been cornered by Patricia Rutherford, a robust woman with stiff black hair and a ruddy complexion. Her partially uncovered breasts had turned Spam-pink in the roasting sun.

'I must say,' she was saying, running a searching tongue across her front teeth as though something had got lodged between them, 'we're all jolly excited about tomorrow's tournament. Did Kay tell you that they're using our court as well?' Max shook his head. 'Well, you can imagine with thirty-two competitors, that's an awful lot of matches to get through. We thought we'd just have them playing one set for the first two rounds. Just to get things going, you know the sort of thing. Both my girls will be playing.'

'That so?' Max's eyes strayed. He spotted Tiffany talking to Lottie and Josh. One good thing about her was that he never felt he had to look after her at parties. Tiffany could hold her own at the White House.

'I see you're looking at young Charlotte over there,'

Patricia Rutherford continued. 'Such a little thing, isn't she? I believe she's playing tomorrow too. Attractive player to watch but her size really does let her down. Pity,' she paused thoughtfully, 'I suppose she still has a year or two of growth.' She made Lottie sound like a potted plant. 'Now Serena on the other hand – she's our eldest – is really frightfully good. Got the most marvellous forehand. Jeffrey and I expect great things from her.' She stopped at this point and looked at Max as though she expected him to say something.

'Er, can I get you another drink?'

'How awfully kind. Whisky thanks and not too much ice. I know you American chaps practically bathe in the stuff.'

'Coming right up,' said Max, taking her glass and his leave with all the relish of a just-released convict.

Sukie, shielding her light-dazzled eyes with one hand, joined him.

'Hogging the whisky again, Max?'

'Not me, sweetheart. Patricia Rutherford over there. Nice enough lady but she drinks like a fish, I shouldn't wonder.'

Sukie laughed. 'She also has the constitution of an ox!' She watched Max drop two chunks of ice into a glass. 'I'm surprised you've let your girlfriend loose. She's been chatted up by all the men here. Attractive, isn't she? Makes the rest of us feel quite plain.'

'If that's an attempt to get a compliment out of me, you're going about it the wrong way. What happened to Christopher or whatever his name was?'

Sukie's face fell into a sulk. 'Oliver,' she corrected. 'He went ages ago. It wasn't anything serious. More of a stopgap really.'

'Sukie, your love life is more complicated than the peace process between Israel and Palestine. Who is it now?'

'No one. I've been saving myself for you.' Max looked

dubious. 'Oh, I know. You've got your Texan. But really, I wish there *was* someone.' She moved closer, curving the corners of her mouth impudently. 'Come on, Max, you must know hundreds of devastatingly attractive men.'

'How about Luke over there? I saw you guys talking earlier. He's single.'

Sukie pouted. 'He's very young too. Looks like a seven-foot Tintin.'

Max laughed. 'Your problem is that you're too quick to rule the nice guys out. Luke's got quite a following on the circuit. Girls go nuts for him.'

'They do?' Lighting up her eighth cigarette of the day, she studied the Canadian with mild interest.

Max was amused by Sukie's predictability. 'I'll leave you to mull that one over. Oh, and do me a favour,' he handed her the replenished glass of whisky. 'Take this over to Mrs Rutherford. I've had my quota for the day.' Before she could refuse, he made a beeline for Tiffany.

Sukie watched him go, irritated by the fact that he never took her seriously. But then, unlike Tiffany, she wasn't rolling in money and like attracts like. She sipped her drink, wondering if the hair of the dog was ever going to work. Her head was pounding despite having taken four Ibuprofen. But she daren't take any more. Being out in this heat probably wasn't brilliantly clever either. She could feel the sun through her short cap of hair burning her scalp.

Having thrust Mrs Rutherford's whisky into her hand, Sukie was about to go in search of Lauren when her sister reappeared, Tomless. God, she looked radiant. As if she'd just been made love to. Her cheeks were flushed, her eyes sparkling. How come I never look like that, Sukie thought with an old stab of envy. Lauren had reached Josh who was deep in conversation. He circled an arm around his wife and although he didn't interrupt the flow of conversation, the instinctive gesture was clearly meant to make her feel included.

Sukie always looked intently at her sister, searching for configurations that matched her own. People said they could tell they were sisters, but apart from their laugh – a deep, bubbly explosion – and a few inherited mannerisms, Sukie could see no resemblance at all. She wondered if the dress Lauren was wearing could possibly be the one she had seen in the Marks & Spencer's sale last week. Surely not. But then Lauren had a knack of wearing any old thing and making it look wonderful. Sukie invested a large chunk of her hard-earned salary on clothes, once even paying a specialist to take her shopping – and she still got it wrong. Clothes always looked better on girls with height and Lauren had the advantage of three extra inches. But it wasn't just the height. Her sister was perfect, right down to her uninhibited enjoyment of life – and she wasn't. Although Sukie tried to hide it, she could never forgive Lauren for that.

Someone was breathing down her neck. Instinctively Sukie knew it was Jeffrey Rutherford. The pungent reek of whisky was an instant giveaway. He smelt as if he'd been marinated in the stuff. Cringing, she turned round with an insincere smile fixed to her mouth. Why me? Why is it *always* me?

On the other side of the pool, the atmosphere was less charged.

'Having a good time?' Max slipped a warm hand along Tiffany's arm.

'Actually, yes, I am. I like these friends of yours. Kay's asked me to go to an exhibition at the Tate Gallery next week and Josh wants us to spend some time with them in Wimbledon. Lottie's a bit introverted. Doesn't like to talk about herself much, but she knows a heck of a lot about tennis. What's her connection? I mean, she's not actually related to Josh?'

'Josh used to live with her mother.'

'No!'

'It lasted almost five years. When he moved in with Lauren there was a hell of a scene. It left Lottie pretty cut up. He was the closest thing she had to a father.'

'But what about her real father? What happened to him?'

'He should have died.' Tiffany's mouth dropped. 'That is, he found out he had a terminal brain tumour and was given as little as six months to live. The guy freaked out and one day just didn't come home. That was eight years ago. From what I hear, he's still going strong.'

'What's he do?'

'He was a doctor, but he quit shortly after the tumour was diagnosed.'

'Does he visit?'

'Your guess is as good as mine.'

Kay was handing round more plates of food. 'Fancy another chop, either of you?' she urged. 'There's masses left and they all need eating up.'

Tiffany shook her head. 'I couldn't eat another thing. Great food though, Kay.'

'Mrs Miller?' said a small voice. They all looked down at James who was looking very guilty. 'Tadpole's been sick on your carpet. There was bits of straw and pooey things in it.'

'Oh, God. Sounds like my hat. I left it in the hall. What did I say about accidents. Come on, James,' she said, taking his hand, 'you'd better lead me to it.'

At about five, Mrs Poole, the housekeeper, produced tea. Mounds of home-made scones and jam made with strawberries picked from the garden accompanied bowls filled with masses of whipped cream. Excitedly the children, hungry from so much swimming and rushing about, clustered around the table, piling their plates high. Max, who didn't want tea, went up to the house in search of

some strong coffee. He left a reluctant Tiffany talking to
Patricia Rutherford.

'I hear your father keeps horses. We stable a couple
of hunters nearby. Not that I get to ride as much as
I'd like,' she said, running her tongue across her upper
teeth. 'We're so terribly busy all the time. Mind you, the
occasional chase is always jolly good fun. How many does
he own?'

'Oh, we don't hunt. They're mostly polo ponies. I'm not
real sure of the numbers. We're always getting more in.'

'Oh, come now, dear,' Patricia crammed half a scone into
her mouth, catching some of the thick cream on the tip of
her chin. 'Surely you'd know a thing like that.'

'Well, roughly speaking, I'd say we have about two
hundred.'

Patricia choked so violently on her scone that part of it
flew out of her mouth and landed on Tiffany's silk shirt. Eyes
flooding, Patricia rapped her fist against her chest, trying to
clear her windpipe.

'Here,' offered Tiffany, passing Patricia her untouched
cup of tea, 'this might help.'

'I'm most *terribly* sorry,' Patricia said a few moments later,
when she had recovered. 'Your lovely shirt. Do let me get
a cloth.'

Tiffany smiled. 'It'll wash off with some soap and water.
Will you excuse me?'

'Yes, of course. I really am most *dreadfully* sorry.'

Back at the house Tiffany bumped into Jeffrey in the hall
carrying out a crate of champagne. Behind him was Lottie
clutching a large dish of sweets.

'Lottie, Jeffrey. You seen Max anywhere?'

'In the kitchen, I think,' said Jeffrey. 'We're all meeting in
the drawing room to toast the happy couple and watch them
open their presents. Shall we say in about five minutes? Pass
on the word, will you?'

Tiffany went down the hall and turned left into an oak-panelled dining room. Another door faced her behind which she could hear muffled laughter. Timidly she opened it.

With her back to the door, Mrs Poole's hair was pinned on top of her head in an enormous bun. Her plump arms were submerged in a sink full of washing up. Sprawled around the kitchen table, which was littered with empty Coke cans, mineral water and beer, were Josh, Luke and Max. To her amazement, Max was holding Josh's baby. And not just holding it either. Supporting the baby's bobbing head in one hand, he was jiggling him up and down on his knee as though he had been handling babies all his life. Tiffany felt a stab of jealousy.

'How long have you got?' Josh was asking Max.

'Until the end of the year, then they'll give me another.'

'I've had offers from both BMW and Jaguar. Don't know which to opt for.'

'Go for the Jag,' suggested Luke, pouring himself some juice. 'I would.'

Josh grinned. 'Only because you're a poser, mate. Hey, Mrs Poole, this smoothie's as good as I get back home.'

Mrs Poole blushed.

'I'd take the BMW.' Max swapped Tom on to his other knee so that his father was in full view, but the baby's eyes remained transfixed on Max. 'Solid German car and it won't let you down. What is it? 5 series?'

'535. They'll provide me with cars wherever I go,' said Josh. 'Watch your jacket, mate, he's burping a bit. Are you going to play in Kitzbühel for the Austrian Cup?'

'If I can get back from the States in time. My name's down.'

The baby farted.

'Say what?' said Max, holding the infant up.

Luke laughed. 'Reckon it's Pampers you should be looking to for sponsorship, Josh, not Jaguar.' He sniffed the air. 'Mmmm, not quite the same aroma as Mrs Poole's cooking.'

Mrs Poole cocked her head round and gave him one of her now-then-you-just-behave smiles.

Luke drained his glass. 'Listen, Josh. This Sukie chick. What's the scoop? She really footloose?'

'Sukie's always got some poor sod in tow,' said Josh, 'and most of them are married. I think it gives her a kick. But don't ever let me catch you telling Lauren that. As sisters go they're pretty close.'

Tiffany decided it was time to show herself. She opened the door more fully.

'This a private party or can anyone join in? Hi, honey,' she said, sidling up to Max. 'Do I get to hold him too?'

She lifted the baby into her arms and examined its round, perfect face. Bright blue eyes gazed curiously at her. Lauren's eyes.

'Jeffrey wanted me to tell you that they're serving champagne in the drawing room. They're going to make a speech or something for Robert and Kay. He wanted you all to be there.'

Luke rose. 'Guess we shouldn't miss that. Besides, you've got me intrigued now, Josh. I always did like a BOC, especially sexy ones.'

'BOC?' whispered Tiffany to Max as they followed Luke out.

'Bit of a challenge. Not that she's in your league, baby. Fact is, she doesn't even come close.'

As they had all eaten and drunk so much that afternoon, dinner was put back an hour to nine o'clock. The Rutherfords had returned to their house, keen to finish the preparations for tomorrow's tennis tournament. Lauren was helping Kay in the kitchen. While the rest of the men poured drinks in the library, Max went upstairs with Tiffany to change.

Their south-facing bedroom had a beamed ceiling and a fireplace. The floor was uneven and creaky, the walls had been painted a lemon yellow, the curtains festooned with flowers and birds. From the bed Tiffany, who was feeling the aftereffects of too much sun, watched him undress.

'Tired?' she asked.

'A little. It only seems to happen when I slow down. That, and being around guys like Luke Falkner.'

'He's not that young?'

'Eighteen's young.'

Tiffany held up a framed photo. 'Did you see this?'

Max approached her to get a better look.

'Cute, aren't they?'

The shot was of two young girls sitting on a rug in a garden, their arms round each other's shoulders, smiling into the camera.

'I guess this must be Sukie and Lauren?' said Tiffany. 'Hard to tell which is which.'

'That's Lauren,' Max pointed decisively to the girl in a striped jersey and bleach-blonde hair.

'Maybe,' said Tiffany, less certain. 'So is Robert a good attorney?'

'He's what they call over here a Queen's Counsel. Bright man. Good enough to be able to pick and choose which cases he takes on. Works on defamation, libel suits, that kind of thing.' Max pulled off his T-shirt. 'You've been awful quiet this evening. Got something on your mind?'

How well he could read her even after just a few months. 'Oh, you know,' she said airily, 'I was just watching you downstairs in the kitchen with the guys, noticing how good you were with that baby.'

Max grinned. 'He is a nice little fella.'

'Did you ever think about having one yourself?'

Max roared with laughter. 'Me, a father?' He looked at her more closely, realising that she was serious, then sat down on the edge of the bed. 'Hang on a moment. If I'm reading this right, then I'd have to say you'd had too much sun or booze or something.'

'Why?' she asked, her voice faintly huffy. 'What's so strange about it?'

'Oh, come on, baby. Where the hell would you and I find time to raise a kid? I mean, be serious for a moment. We're both constantly on the move. Have you spent more than a month in your house this year?'

'No.'

'Precisely my point.'

'But only because I don't have any commitments.'

'That's how you like it.'

She was stung by his immediate and vigorous condemnation. What was so ridiculous about having a baby together? Between them they had enough money to raise ten kids if they wanted. Max was thirty-two, after all. And she was . . . Well, pushing thirty wasn't exactly old but she no longer felt the timeless luxury of youth. These days the years seemed to speed by with a worrying momentum, piling on the pressure to settle down. For much of her life, she had sneered at housewives, contemptuous of their lack of freedom, wearily anchored to their breadwinning husbands and family demands. What kind of life was that? Whenever she raised this domestic question in her mind, she inevitably thought of her father. Not exactly a glowing role model. He was already on to wife number three who was younger than herself by three years. And after only six brief months the union was already showing signs of strain. Ah, but what the hell! She couldn't run his life for him.

So why this sudden domestic craving? Tiffany sighed. Over the years, she had gone through a succession of lovers. But none of them had challenged her or held her interest for more than a few weeks. None had curbed her restless outstretched wings.

Until Max.

Pressed against the down-filled pillows she watched him climb out of his Fila shorts, debating whether or not to push the subject further. She decided against it. Perhaps now wasn't the time. Max had a lot of things going on and she didn't want to be added to the list of problems. Best just to play it cool.

'I'm going to take a bath.' She slipped off the edge of the bed but Max grabbed her arm, stopped her.

'You haven't gone and done anything dumb like come off the pill, have you, Tiff?'

She looked hurt. 'Gee, thanks for the vote of confidence.'

'I didn't mean it to sound like that.' He kissed the tip of her nose.

'I know.'

'It's just that right now it wouldn't work.'

'Sure,' she murmured, smiling bravely to hide her disappointment.

5

Lottie's alarm woke her. Six o'clock. She sat up sleepily. A bright morning glare was already splintering the unlined curtains. She left them drawn and climbed with sleep-dazed eyes into her tracksuit. Sitting back on the bed, she yawned, then bent down and clumsily laced up her shoes. Her limbs felt heavy, protesting at the early hour. Against the edge of the bed was her tennis racquet. Lottie picked it up and tiptoed downstairs. No one was about, but she found Tadpole at the foot of the staircase. Pleased to see a familiar face he raised soft eyes and thumped his tail eagerly.

'Hello,' she whispered, stopping to stroke his golden head, 'are you going to wish me a Happy Birthday?'

Tadpole tilted his head to one side and whimpered.

The entrance hall had a sweet, musty smell and was decorated with a collection of muddy boots, Barbours, an old bicycle, wooden tennis racquets, walking sticks, and spiders' webs. The front door creaked as she opened it, the hall clock struck six times. Lottie stepped out into the already warm morning and made her way round to the back of the house. The first sound she heard was the farmer, Mr Poole, calling to the cows. He lived with his wife in a nearby cottage which was part of the Millers' estate. The Pooles had been there for almost thirty years and were now thought of as part of the family. Charged a modest rent, Mr Poole paid for their keep by tending the garden, while Mrs Poole cooked and cleaned at the big house four mornings a week. Lottie waved to him and gazed happily at the cows as they ambled by, their chocolate rumps swaying.

She passed Kay's treasured fruit and vegetable patch bursting at the seams with glossy-red tomatoes, thick runner beans, neat frilly rows of lettuces, onions and rhubarb. Birds chirped excitedly. Lavender-crowned chives stirred briefly as her legs brushed by. The sweet fragrance of strawberries filled her nose as she moved on to the raspberry patch. Further along was a rusty swing alongside the Millers' old milk barn. Now it was used to house gardening equipment, chopped-up logs and an old Morris Minor from Robert's student days. Whenever Kay bullied him to sell it, he would argue that the car held too many fond memories. Like the Morris, the barn was looking decidedly the worse for wear. A warped door was hanging off its hinges and part of the roof had caved in so that from inside you could see jigsaw pieces of sky. One unblemished wall remained intact round the back. It was the wall that had inspired Lottie's early rise.

Slipping the head of her racquet from its sleeve, she plucked a green ball from her pocket. She bounced it to test the firmness of the ground. It sprang up with reassuring strength. But the first vibrating thud of the ball as it struck the barn made such a noise that Lottie stopped immediately. Had they heard it at the house? She nibbled on a nail. She would *die* if anyone saw her out here practising. She meant to win today – she believed she could. But she didn't want anyone to know how much the winning mattered to her.

After Josh's spectacular visit to the school play, Lottie had enjoyed a brief interlude of fame. The new Wimbledon champion had come to see *her*. He had taken *her* out to dinner. No one else. She was special. For a week, Lottie had walked a foot taller, bathed in her new-found popularity, revelling in the gossipy, excited envy of the other girls as they surrounded her to ask questions. And then they lost interest, the exalted bubble burst. Lottie resumed her small and insignificant position and Arabella went back to calling her squirt. But having had a crumb-sized taste of what it must feel like to be Josh, Lottie craved to have it again. Today's tournament was going to provide her with that opportunity. But she had to concentrate, not mess up or make any mistakes.

After a few more cautious hits, she forgot about disturbing the sleeping household, forgot about the list of presents she was hoping to get. The only thing she concentrated on was the steady, methodical rhythm of the ball.

Two hours later, Lottie, red-faced and boiling in the heat, returned to the kitchen. Mrs Poole was making vol-au-vents and fillings for the sandwiches. She was humming a familiar tune while her plump hands worked swiftly.

She smiled at Lottie. 'My, you're an early bird. Been out running, have you, duck?' Mrs Poole started undoing another packet of sliced bread. 'Going to be a scorcher today. I expect you'd like some breakfast. There's some Frosties on the table and milk in the fridge. Best get it down you quick before the rest of the troops descend.'

Mrs Poole wiped the small beads of sweat that had collected on her brow. Her niece was getting married at two and she still had to go home and change. All this food to prepare, she thought glancing worriedly at the clock. She only had until noon.

By ten a cavalcade of Saabs and Volvos had arrived. A production line of Sophies, Lucys and Camillas scrambled from the back seats clutching sports bags and racquets and rushed off to trade gossip. Harassed-looking mothers followed, hoping to find a cup of coffee and somewhere to sit down. Kay showed the girls where they were to change and suggested to Lottie that some of them use her room.

Traipsing back up to her attic bedroom with three strange girls in tow, Lottie drew back the flowered curtains and let in some air. She was embarrassed that the room was so untidy, hot and stuffy. Amy, who was gangly and had a stubby nose, didn't seem to be fussed and threw herself onto Lottie's unmade bed.

'Anyone know Ursula Law-Billulp?' she said, reading from a slip of paper. 'I'm playing her in the first round.'

'Fancy being saddled with a name like that!' said Sarah Hicks, a busty brunette who constantly flicked at her long bouncy hair.

Amy fished out what looked like a programme from her sports bag.

'Check this out.' She waved the programme triumphantly. 'Gorgeous, isn't he! Look, he even wrote my name.'

'Gary Barlow!' shrieked Jane, who was very spotty. 'You lucky cow. How did you get it?'

'My elder brother works part-time at Wembley. He got it for me last week.'

Lottie frowned. Were they talking about a football player?

'Wow!' Jane looked really impressed. 'Did he manage to get Jason Orange's too?'

Amy glibly pointed to an indecipherable signature on the back page.

'Who is it?' Lottie asked, digging out her newly washed tennis gear from a bottom drawer.

'Take That,' said Amy, as if Lottie should have known. Lottie looked blank. 'Oh, you know. They're this really hot group. Don't tell me you haven't heard of them. *God!*' she gasped incredulously when she realised Lottie hadn't. 'D'you live in a convent or something?'

Sarah laughed. Lottie pulled self-consciously at a few wispy strands of fringe. Did they all have to stare at her like that? She contemplated blaming her mother for this latest predicament she had found herself in, but the truth was she never really listened to pop music. Most of her free time was spent in front of the box glued to Sky Sports. Clever Josh had

had a satellite dish installed shortly before he had moved out. Although her mother was always threatening to have it disconnected because Lottie's homework was increasingly neglected, she went on paying the rental.

'I'm into Bad Boys Inc,' said Sarah who was wearing Singing Pink lipstick. Her low-cut top jiggled as she talked and they all tried not to notice her breasts which were a fascination as they rose and fell. 'My boyfriend's practising to be a DJ and one of these days I'm going to be lead singer in a band of my own.' Sarah was a year older than the others.

A singer! Lottie hid her contempt. There were three high-ranked players staying in the same house and all they could think about was pop stars!

The conversation moved on to school and the girls got changed. Jane, sitting on the floor, had only to change out of her grey shorts and into a skirt. Over a pea-green swimming costume, skinny Amy was wearing a T-shirt long enough to pass as a dress. Lottie was still in the tracksuit she had put on that morning. Sarah Hicks, however, was altogether another story, what with her rows of noisy bangles and hip-hugging jeans that had rips in the back pocket. She wore earrings, multicoloured parrots, flying against her neck. They looked heavy. Lottie wondered if she was going to play in them. When Sarah removed her top they all stopped pretending not to stare. They gazed with unadulterated envy at her bursting bra. Lottie turned her back and her flat chest on the girls and faced a cracked blue bowl in which someone had arranged large white daisies. She caught a glimpse of herself in the mirror and scowled at her inflamed cheeks. Was she going to be plagued by them all her life? Undressing very reluctantly, she kept her back turned. But she could see the girls from the corner of one eye. Sarah gave her the creeps the way she sat on the bed just staring. Why couldn't she watch one of the other girls? Deliberately, Lottie left her shirt on until the last possible second, then quickly whipped it off while no one was looking. When she turned round Sarah had changed. Lottie could see the clear outline of her bosoms straining against her T-shirt. That was definitely the last straw. First thing Monday, she was going to make her mother buy her a bra.

Sarah was off again. 'My boyfriend's going to Portugal and wants to take me with him. But screwing's got a bit fiddly lately – I'm seriously thinking about going on the pill.'

There was a stunned silence.

'There's nothing wrong with it,' she said. 'They were handing out condoms in our sex education class last term.'

'To keep?' Amy's eyebrows had practically reached the spots sprouting in her hairline.

Sarah looked at her scornfully. 'You can't recycle them, Amy. What gets my goat is that they give you free contraceptives then go on about sex before you're sixteen being against the law. It's so hypocritical!'

'Which school do you go to?' asked Jane. When Sarah told her, all the rest of the girls swapped knowing looks.

Sarah began applying Punk Orange lipstick. To Lottie it was obvious she wasn't very serious about tennis.

In the front hall Robert had set up a large board with the running order stapled to it. Several girls had gathered round.

'Can you see my name?'

'Stop shoving!'

'Who are you playing?'

'You'll get your turn if you just wait.'

'It's all right. You're not on for at least an hour. We can go for a quick swim.'

'But I didn't bring my costume!'

There were a total of five rounds. To save time, one set would be played for the first three rounds. From then on the contestants would play the best of three sets. As there were just two courts, only two matches could be played simultaneously. Lottie found that she was playing in the first match, then couldn't decide if that was a good thing or not. Part of her would have liked to have watched some of the competition, but wasn't it better to make an early start rather than having to hang around with building nerves. The girl she was playing was a Rose Paterley. Lottie peered at the name hoping it would reveal some clue about her opponent but after a while the black capital letters began to blur.

'There you are, Lottie,' said Lauren, dark panda rings under her eyes. 'I think they want you out on court.'

'You haven't seen Josh anywhere, have you?'

'Still in bed. Neither of us got much sleep last night.' She smiled reassuringly, understanding the disappointment on Lottie's face. 'But I'm sure he'll be down soon and when he does appear I'll point him in your direction.' She held up crossed fingers. 'Best of luck for today.'

Rose Paterley, with her pale hair and pink eyes, was not much taller than Lottie, which came as a great relief. But she was already practising her stylish serve. Lottie hoped her smile hid how nervous she was feeling. Robert Miller, acting as umpire, was drinking beer from a can.

'Right then. Let's get going,' he said cheerfully, 'and may the best girl win.'

Lottie won the toss and opted to serve.

In the first three games both girls convincingly held their serve. To the gathering spectators it looked an even match. With only one set to play neither of them had the luxury of making early mistakes. During the fourth game, however, with Rose serving thirty-fifteen up, Lottie spotted a weakness in Rose's game. Her forehand was consistent but she kept on running round her backhand. Why? Lottie decided to test her. From then on she directed every shot to Rose's backhand. Her tactics paid off. She got the break she was looking for and took the lead by three games to one.

As they swapped ends, Lottie's eye roved around for

Josh. He had promised to watch, but there was no sign
of him anywhere. Mustn't worry about that now. Hadn't
he always told her to keep her mind on the match? At five
games to two, and forty-love up, Lottie had her first match
point, but she was distracted by a backfiring car during her
second serve. The ball overshot the serve line by a millimetre.
Robert called it out. The reprieved Rose then made a couple
of nifty returns and brought the match back up to five-three.
Furious with herself for letting such an easy opportunity slip,
Lottie poured all her concentration into the next game and
climbed back up to fifteen-thirty. This time it was Rose who
double-faulted. Match point to Lottie for the fourth time.
Rose delivered a shaky serve and Lottie swooped down on
it, taking the ball early. The quick, intelligent passing shot
wrong-footed Rose and won Lottie the match.

'Well done, Lottie!' said Robert in his rich, plummy voice
as he climbed down from his chair.

The girls shook hands at the net. 'Bad luck,' said Lottie
graciously.

'Oh, never mind. You played jolly well,' Rose conceded,
'and I've got a rotten backhand.'

After her first win, Lottie sailed through her next three
matches, dropping only seven games in all. In one of them
she played Sarah whose generous bosoms bounced with as
much spring as the tennis balls. She clocked up a humiliating
score of 1–6. So much for pop music, Lottie thought smugly.
Coming off court she passed a couple of boys bragging about
their conquests.

'Did you go below the neck?'

''Course I did, you big spazzo. Much lower than that.'

'Did she let you touch her tits?'

'Uhuh.'

Dorks, Lottie thought contemptuously, using one of Josh's
words. She didn't wish to seem ungrateful but she sometimes
wished that Josh had never met Lauren. Then he wouldn't

have had a baby to look after and could spend more time with her. She knew she was being selfish thinking like this. It was unkind to Lauren – and Tom who she already loved like a brother. But more than half of her birthday was already over. This wasn't what she had planned. During her fourth match she thought she spotted Josh walking by with a mug of coffee but he disappeared back into the house before she could get his attention. Had he forgotten after all? No one else had mentioned her birthday. She was beginning to feel extremely sorry for herself.

Josh was in fact recovering from a hangover. Tom had screamed his guts out throughout the night and had driven both him and Lauren into a state of utter despair. Unable to cope with his wailing son, Josh had finally staggered downstairs to the kitchen and made himself some coffee. He had then gone out for a swim to clear his fuzzy head but found the pool already saturated with energetic children. He got a nice view of Tiffany's bum though, who was sunbathing nearby in the briefest of G-strings. But in the end, even the leggy Texan's bum wasn't enough of a lure. Josh had fled back to bed. Mercifully, he found their room empty and had passed out on the bed.

Three blissful sleep-filled hours later, fortified by a cooked breakfast, he now felt able to cope with the world. He had a look to see who was playing on court. No one he knew. It looked a rather feeble match. Where had the boys got to? No sign of Luke or Max.

'Decided to join the land of the living?' Lauren, carrying Tom, kissed him on the cheek. She smelt of baby powder. 'How are you, darling?'

'Pretty crook. Shouldn't have mixed my drinks last night.'

'So what? You worked hard enough for it. I'm so proud of you – have I told you that lately?'

Josh grinned. 'Yes, but don't ever stop saying it.' He looked down at his sleeping son.

'Hello, monster. How come I still love you so much after all you put me through last night?'

Lauren laughed. 'The monster's just been fed so with luck he should stay like that for at least an hour. Have you been watching Lottie?'

'Is she playing still?'

Lauren dropped her shoulders in disappointment. 'Oh, Josh. She's in the final. You must go and watch her. She's been looking for you all day. She'll be devastated if you don't go.'

'I couldn't see her.'

'She's on the Rutherfords' court next door. Everyone's over there. I was just about to go and ice her cake. Mrs Poole had so much on her plate this morning what with her niece's wedding, I said I'd do it. Oh, *do* hurry, Josh. Or Lottie will think we've all forgotten about her birthday. Oh, and her present,' she urged as Josh took off. 'It's on our bed already wrapped with all the others. You give it to her, darling. She'll be thrilled to bits.'

By the time he reached the Rutherfords', Lottie was one set up and had taken the lead by three games to two in the second. She was playing against the Rutherfords' eldest daughter, Serena, who was a powerfully built girl. She obviously took after her father.

Christ, the girl could hit, Josh thought as the ball cannoned cross-court. It was a hell of a forehand. She walloped the ball as though she never wanted to see it again. He sat down on the grass next to two mothers who were discussing parking problems at Waitrose. As the match developed, he could see what an intelligent game Lottie was trying to play. What she lacked in power and size she made up for in speed and agility. As she walked back to the serve line he waved to get her attention. He felt more than a twinge of guilt at how transparently pleased she was to see him.

Lottie and tennis. A bit like—now what was it she used

to say? 'An apple without cheese, was like a kiss without the squeeze.' He thought about the time he had given Lottie her first child-size racquet. He had started seeing her mother so she couldn't have been more than four. The two of them used to go down to the local courts and play short tennis; he gently hitting over a production line of balls, Lottie pouncing on them with the mobility and keenness of a kitten. No matter how long they played, how hot or cold it got, Lottie always wanted to continue. Just one more minute, she would plead, one more ball. For a while Josh would humour her, but eventually he would try to tire her out, sending her little legs scampering from one side of the court to the other. It wasn't much of a deterrent. Wherever the ball landed, Lottie was right behind it, sweeping it relentlessly back over the net. It was this sort of tenacity that had first impressed him. But it was also what stopped him from developing such a natural talent too quickly. So many young players, especially girls, burnt themselves out even before they'd seen out their teens. He didn't want that happening to Lottie.

Lottie put the next ball away and Josh joined in with the clapping. Eleven today, he realised with amazement. Where had all the time gone? He thought back to the immediate aftermath of his Wimbledon victory. Even now he couldn't quite absorb what he had actually accomplished. How after striking that final triumphant ball he had instantly become a superstar, a face recognised all over the globe.

The immediate events that had followed remained only a blur in his mind: the Champions Ball at the Savoy; the speeches; John Curry toasting the Queen; dancing with the newly crowned ladies champion who was an inch taller than him. All the time at the back of his mind was Lauren, in hospital still, with their new son. *His* son. He could still remember the unbearable softness of Tom's newborn head; the miniature hands opening and closing with surprising strength on his calloused finger. Having a child was the best thing that had ever happened to him. Why had he waited so long? Why the hell had he been so afraid?

Absently he began to rub the small scar on the palm of his hand. He closed his eyes. Hot rays licked his skin, soothed him. So many mixed emotions. So many memories – some travelling towards a dark place he was unwilling, unable to go. Why go over what had happened? He shook his head. No. Not when he had worked so hard to remove the stain. Tom's birth had righted everything. His life was everything he'd hoped for. The future no longer carried any fears.

'You look as though you're miles away.' Max was smiling at him. 'Just came to tell you that we're off.'

Josh pulled his mind into gear. 'Mate you're not going now?'

'Got a business meeting back in London. No way of getting out of it.'

'Tiffany going with you?' Max shook his head. 'Good! She's fun to have around.'

'Say goodbye to Lauren for me. I didn't get to see much of her this time round.'

'Join the club, mate. She's become an obsessed mother.' He chuckled. 'But be sure to visit for dinner soon. We can afford to give you the works now!'

Max laughed. 'I'll hold you to that!'

Josh watched Max retreat to the Millers' house to collect his car. Years ago he had asked Max what was the easiest way of becoming a Wimbledon member and Max had said, 'By winning it.' Now he had and suddenly his life had been transformed.

Josh's contract with his management company had recently lapsed. Unhappy with the way they were handling him, Josh had decided not to re-sign. The company had done little to dissuade him as they couldn't have dreamt that Josh would soon turn into a goldmine. Even before Josh had the

Wimbledon trophy in his hands, Advantage International and IMG, the largest and most powerful management company representing most of the major names in sport, had stepped in offering cut fees and guarantees. Both companies were determined to get him to sign. While agents often worked with each other putting together tournaments and exhibitions, they fought like wild animals over a player, especially a big moneymaker. From Josh's point of view, loyalty to the company he'd been with for most of his career meant little to him. Quite simply he was looking for the best deal. As IMG already represented a player whose age and ranking was similar, and had ironically turned Josh down only last year, he signed with Advantage.

The role of an agent differs greatly from that of a coach. Whereas a coach is often as well known as his protegé, a personality in his own right in order to attract other players, an agent avoids the glare of publicity. The relationship between player and coach is closer and more emotional, although players will often work with a coach they don't trust – which is usually why the partnership doesn't last. Rapport and an ability to make the player perform is what's required from a coach. Trusting an agent, however, is crucial. Not only do agents handle finances, and all off-court endorsements, they are also responsible for shaping the player's career.

From Advantage's point of view it was vital to capitalise immediately on Josh winning Wimbledon. With so many other sporting distractions following on from the championship, the novelty of a new champion would soon wear off. Endorsement offers promoting everything from watches, racquets, mineral water, cars, even cereals, flooded in and most contracts were secured the following day. The tennis marketing director at Nike had already approached with a sponsorship deal worth millions over the next decade.

To Josh it was all still a bit of a joke. He hadn't yet fully understood that he wouldn't have to worry about money

ever again. What a change! All those years he'd spent
struggling to get his career off the ground, sometimes getting
close to success but never quite touching it. Now he was a
name player which meant he could command guarantees for
as much as $300,000 just to turn up for a match – even before
he had struck a single ball. In crude terms top players meant
'bums on seats'. And at the end of the day to the Association
of Tennis Professionals that was all that mattered.

Josh turned his attention back to the game. Lottie was in
trouble.

'Advantage Miss Rutherford,' Luke called, leaning forward
in his high chair. Kay had persuaded the Canadian to umpire
one match and he was thoroughly enjoying himself.

Serena, after receiving a fierce 'come on!' nod from her
mother who was watching eagle-eyed a few feet from Josh,
delivered a searing ace. It won her the game. With mounting
ease, she broke Lottie's serve in the next set, again taking
the lead. Lottie was suddenly looking tired. Josh winced.
Serena was using her stinging backhand not so much with
skill but with such dominance that Lottie hadn't a hope of
returning it.

In less than fifteen minutes she had lost the second set.

From then on it was a steady descent for Lottie. The
hopes of those cheering her on were diminishing and the
end seemed nigh when she put three weary volleys into
the foot of the net to trail 3–5 and 15–40. She's too small
to volley, thought Josh.

'Howdy.' Tiffany, looking cool and refreshed from her
second shower of the day, came and sat down next to him.
'Gee, it's muggy today,' she sighed. 'I've got all these little
bites around my ankles. See?' She showed him her ankle
which did indeed look very angry. 'How's Lottie doing? I
saw her play the last round. Great win.'

'Two match points for Serena, I'm afraid.'

'Now that's a shame.'

The first match point was saved when Serena uncharacteristically double-faulted. On the next point Lottie again squirmed to safety with a shaky return and an outrageous yet delicate drop shot. Deuce!

'Go for it, Lottie. Just take one point at a time,' yelled Josh, earning a black look from Patricia Rutherford.

But all the support in the world wasn't enough to get Lottie's grip back on the match. The prodigious strength of Serena's shots proved too much for her. After three nail-biting returns to deuce with Lottie fighting every inch, Serena finally secured the match.

As Lottie came off court, Tiffany put out an arm to stop her.

'Hey, honey, you played your heart out today. Don't be upset that you didn't win.'

'She's right, sweetheart,' Josh added.

But Lottie stood in a lather of fury, too embarrassed to look Josh in the eye, too choked even to speak. She had failed. She had bloody well failed! Her one chance to show him that she wasn't completely useless had slipped by. She swore never to forgive herself. Adding salt to the wound was the fact that she couldn't even skulk off quietly. There was the prize ceremony which took for ever to organise because Kay couldn't remember where she had hidden the prizes. They eventually turned up, after a great deal of searching, in the boot of Robert's car.

Both girls were given an enthusiastic round of applause as they went up to receive their awards from Kay. Luke gained a furious glare from Patricia when he gave a series of high-pitched whistles as Lottie took her turn. Serena got a new racquet and a silver statue that would have her engraved name added to the other ten previous winners. As runner-up, Lottie got a Miss Selfridge voucher valued at twenty pounds and a biography of Agassi which she had already borrowed from the library.

High above their heads, a huge black bird was circling the house in a sinister fashion.

'That,' said Serena, her upturned eyes squinting against the burning sun, 'means very bad luck.' But for whom she didn't say.

The moment the speeches were over Kay announced tea for everyone would be down by the pool shortly. Unable to face Josh, Lottie fled back to the house which was blessedly cool. She was so thirsty she could have drunk the Amazon. She poked her head round the kitchen door. As she had hoped, the kitchen was empty, but somehow the absence of Mrs Poole left the room looking incomplete. The housekeeper was as much part of it as the cosy Aga, the latched-open lattice windows and the great china sink that looked almost as old as the house. Lottie put down her sweat top and her book, the clothes voucher safely held between its pages. In the middle of the room, rows of mugs had been laid out on the big oak table along with large plates of sandwiches and a mouth-watering chocolate cake hiding under teatowels. The jugs of fresh lemonade had obviously just been made because big chunks of ice clustered inside their necks. A tray of bottles had been abandoned as if someone had been in a hurry on a second table under the window. Lottie picked one up and examined the label. Vodka. Her mother drank that when people came round for supper. The only alcohol Lottie had ever tried was red wine. French, according to Melanie, and *very* expensive. She had quite liked it and was disappointed that her mother hadn't allowed her to have more. She held the bottle in one hand. Go on. Have some, urged her wilder side. Oh, why not. It was her birthday. Defiantly, she unscrewed the vodka bottle top. The liquid spilled into the pretty glass she had found, clear and pure like water. As an afterthought she added some of the squash and drained the glass.

Having satisfied her thirst she now felt hungry. Would

anyone notice if she were to pinch one of Mrs Poole's sandwiches? She'd made enough to feed an army. Having swiftly devoured two, Lottie was just about to embark on her third when she heard a noise. Guiltily she replaced the vodka bottle on the tray then quickly whipped the teatowel back over the sandwiches. Was it Kay coming for the tea things? She grabbed her glass, now covered in grubby fingermarks and raced over with it to the sink. Her head spun. The drink seemed to have gone straight down to her stomach like a blade-swallower's sword. She felt serene, a floating sensation, like lying on her back in the swimming pool. Running the hot tap, she rinsed the glass with her fingers. The voices, there were two of them, were getting louder. Lottie swivelled her head round towards the door, willing it not to open. Hurry, hurry, her mind urged. How awful if Kay was to find her here, drinking her vodka, eating everyone's food. She would never be invited again. If only she didn't feel so strange. Her body seemed suddenly to have a mind of its own. Her limbs had seized up with stiffness.

There was a sudden crack. Lottie's eyes looked down in horror at her hands. The fragile glass had snapped into two pieces as easily as a potato crisp. Mortified, she now recognised it as part of the set Kay had been given last night as an anniversary present. The voices were almost upon her. Eyes skimming over the room frantically for somewhere to hide the evidence, Lottie spotted her sweat top. Grabbing it, she wrapped it round the glass.

Sounds of giggling.

'Hilarious! I've never laughed so much in my life.'

'Luke's nice, isn't he?' Lauren's voice.

'He's okay. What did Mum say about candles?'

'Said to try the kitchen drawer. There should be two new boxes. He likes you.'

'I know. The last thing I need . . . Oh! Hello, Lottie.'

Sukie and Lauren glanced from her to the table, then at each other. 'We didn't expect to find you here.'

'I was, um, just getting myself a drink of water.'

'Everyone's down by the pool,' Lauren said coaxingly. 'Why don't you join them. We were just going to bring out tea.'

'Can I help?' Lottie asked, wondering if she could get away with holding the jumper under one arm without the bits of glass slipping out, or cutting her.

'Oh, that's all right, poppet. We'll manage. You go on ahead. I think Josh was looking for you anyway.'

'She forgot her book,' Lottie heard Lauren say as she closed the kitchen door behind her.

Lottie slipped out into the back garden and up to the swing, safely out of sight of the party. She chose her spot carefully and began digging. But the hot sun was making it hard for her to concentrate. She pressed hard against the bone of her skull to stop the whirring and ringing in her ears, wondered if she was going to be sick. Her mind began to roll backwards to a time when a similar incident had occurred. She used to have a tennis ball which was bubble-gum pink on one side, acid green on the other. Like a mother with a newborn baby she took that ball with her everywhere, knocking up with it against the garage wall, bouncing it on the floor of her room. Melanie had forbidden her to play with it in the house after Lottie had come very close to smashing a treasured vase. Despite that she had ignored the warning.

Then one weekend while Josh was away playing a grand prix tournament, a terrible thing happened. Lottie was juggling two balls against the sitting-room wall when one of them misfired and hit one of Josh's trophies. In slow motion, she watched it topple precariously then fall and smash into different sized pieces as it hit the floor. Paralysed with fear and remorse, Lottie could only gawp at the damage. Melanie would go spare. She hated mess in the house. Everything always had to be neat and tidy. For a while she sat there fooling herself that she would be brave and own up to her crime. Then her mind began to run away with itself, imagining all kinds of horrors. She had let Josh down. He would be disappointed in her. Melanie might even make her go to the badly behaved children's department in Peter Jones. She couldn't do it, couldn't admit her crime. Instead, she had taken the broken pieces out to the back garden and methodically buried them under the apple tree.

When Melanie returned later, Lottie was so riddled with guilt that she didn't immediately notice how preoccupied her mother was. She seemed distant, agitated, hardly speaking a word over supper. Melanie even forgot to make her do the drying up, and she was always made to do that. When her mother finally told her, her eyelashes flickering angrily, Lottie had put her hands to her ears and squeezed them as hard as she could so that she wouldn't have to hear what Melanie was saying. Josh had done a terrible thing. He was leaving her mother for another woman. He wouldn't be coming back. Ever. And by the stiff, proud way in which her mother held herself, Lottie realised sickeningly that it was true.

Later on, her mother went up to her room with one of her headaches and had stayed there for two days; her mother, flat on her back in that dark room, with ice packs on her head, her eyes screwed up tightly as if she were suffering greatly. Lottie tried to be nice, tried to understand how her mother was feeling. But she couldn't help feeling angry with her. It was wrong to give up so easily. Why couldn't she be a proper mother and bring Josh home?

Once she heard Melanie crying. Really worried, she entered the bedroom and found her lying prostrate on the bed, looking more miserable and bereft than Lottie had ever seen her.

'It's because of my age,' Melanie wept piteously. 'It's because I'm so much older'.

She latched tightly on to Lottie and sobbed into her hair. Lottie wondered what she meant. When her mother was feeling better and the tears had stopped, she had said, 'We'll be much better off on our own. We don't need Josh, do we?'

She did. Lottie did. It was all she thought about. But she felt under pressure to reassure her mother. 'No,' she said, her voice small and lacking conviction.

In the days that followed, Lottie waited for Josh to return. She willed him to come and get her, take her away with him. She slept badly, waking in the middle of the night because her nightdress was soaked and the sheets were stuck to her back. In the mornings Melanie would peel the sheets back and change them for crisp cleans ones, opening the bedroom window wide to shoo away the lingering smell of urine and fear. She never said a word, but Lottie knew that she was cross because of the heavy sighs her mother gave while she worked. She remembered then how her mother took to cleaning with more vigour each time Josh went away on a trip. Diligently, she would scrub the bathroom floor with bleach, brush down the stairs, wash the lace curtains in Napisan, reorganise the cupboards – that took up a lot of time. Everything could have gone back to normal had Josh come home. But he didn't. And it was her fault. She was to blame. It was because of the broken trophy. In her heart she believed that Josh's leaving was her punishment.

'Hey, Lottie!'

At the sound of the familiar voice, her head shot round guiltily.

'*There* you are. I've been looking for you all over. What you doing up there. Landscape gardening?'

Her small hands burrowed more urgently into the soil, trying to cover up the evidence. But the sun had baked it so hard all she succeeded in doing was hurt her hands. Too late, anyway. Josh had seen. Gently moving her aside, he bent down and inspected the damage.

'What have you got here? One of Kay's glasses, hey?' He compressed his lips together as though he were disappointed.

'Oh, Josh, it was an accident,' Lottie said desperately. 'I honestly didn't mean to break it. *PLEASE,* don't tell anyone. They'll be so cross. I'll get into trouble and Mrs Miller won't let me come again.'

'Hey, you big dork,' Josh placed both hands on her shoulders, 'no one's going to punish you. It's just a stupid glass.'

Lottie looked close to tears. 'But you don't understand. It was part of the set Mr Miller gave her. It was very important to her. And I've ruined it all.'

'Don't you think you might be overreacting slightly?'

'No,' she said with force, her eyes dazzled and lost beneath the irregular fringe. 'I know what'll happen.'

Josh suppressed a smile. 'What?'

Lottie hung her head and tortured a blade of grass.

'Come on, sweetheart, it's me, Josh.'

She drew in a deep breath as if she were about to swim a great length under water and told him about breaking his trophy. All the time she spoke, she had her arms wrapped around her bent knees, her eyes fixed to the ground so that he wouldn't see how ashamed she was. She scuffed at the grass and noticed that one of the soles of her trainers was peeling away.

Josh put a hand out and tucked the mousy strands that were hanging over her eyes behind her ear.

'Want to know something?' he said gently. 'I never did like that trophy. You did me a favour getting rid of it. I'm serious,' his hand was stroking her hair. 'But you didn't do yourself any good by bottling up this secret for so long. That kind of stuff eats at you, Lottie. Accidents are part of life. We don't like them but we all have them. Don't you think it's better to own up and get it over and done with?'

He bent his head, trying to read the expression in Lottie's eyes. But she was too busy enjoying the expert tenderness flowing from the fingers stroking her head. Just like when her mother combed her hair. Only this time she was floating. It made her feel peaceful and sleepy. She was close and contained, feeling his heartbeat, smelling his special smell. She sat quite still listening to the rise and fall of his voice as though it were music, willing the moment to last for ever.

The sun was inching its way back down to earth, shedding some of its earlier heat. Little sparks of white light danced before Lottie's eyes. For a while they sat studying the grass, each lost in his or her own private thoughts. Then Josh raised his body from the ground and pulled out a small package from his back pocket.

'I almost forgot why I came to find you. Here,' he handed it to her, 'this is for you. Happy Birthday, star.'

He *hadn't* forgotten, after all. Impatiently she ripped off the paper and examined the small box. Inside was a delicate gold bracelet with eleven miniature tennis racquets dangling from its rim. She struggled to get it on, but the clasp slipped twice so Josh helped her. Holding out her arm, she twisted her wrist from side to side so that the little racquets spun and tinkled like bells. She gasped with joy. To Lottie it was the most beautiful thing she had ever seen.

'Oh, Josh, I won't *ever* take it off. It's going to be my lucky bracelet.' It glinted in the sunlight. She couldn't tear her eyes from it.

Josh smiled, enjoying her youthful, transparent pleasure. Then he took one of her excited hands and stilled it with his own.

'Listen to me, sweetheart. I know I'm not around much these days and that I don't see enough of you, but there's something you should know.' He tilted her chin upwards so that she was forced to look him in the eye.

'You don't need to prove a *thing* to me. Get that into your thick head. Don't you think I know you could have beaten that Rutherford girl? All right, she hits the ball hard, I'll grant you that. But I've seen you play enough tennis to know you're *streets* ahead of the kids around here. Christ, I was the one that gave you your first lesson. You just got a dose of nerves. You choked. We all suffer from that, even champions like me.'

Encouraged, she looked at him.

'Now, do you reckon that message has got across?' He tapped a finger lightly against her forehead. Lottie smiled, feeling light-headed and foolish for having made such a fuss. For believing that she had lost Josh.

'I just wanted to win it for you,' she admitted, 'I wanted you to be proud of me.'

'You big dilly,' he ruffled her hair affectionately, 'I'm proud of everything you do. You've got a real gift for tennis.'

'A gift?'

'Yeah. Reckon you have. Now,' his voice altered, sounding more stern, 'when do you go back to school?'

Lottie was still gloating over her 'gift'. 'The middle of September.'

Josh made a quick calculation in his head. 'Well, how'd you like to come with me to the Canadian Open in Toronto?'

She gazed at him incredulously.

'I'm flying out to Stuttgart tonight, but I'll only be gone a few days. We can talk more about it when I get back.'

Lottie's face fell.

'I thought you'd be pleased.'

'It's just that Mum will say we can't afford it or something. She's always worrying about money.'

'Not on this occasion, she won't. I'll be picking up the tab.

So don't worry about your mum. We sorted a few things out. I reckon she'll come round.'

For a moment Lottie couldn't speak. This is what it is to be happy, she thought wildly. Then she flung her arms around Josh's neck.

'Oh, Josh,' she sobbed, 'you're the most perfect person in the world.'

He laughed. 'My wife might have a few things to say about that. Especially if I don't get you back, pronto. You, my little mate, have got a birthday cake to cut!'

Lottie felt she would burst with happiness as they made their way back to the house. The sun warmed their backs as they walked hand in hand. High above their heads the large beetle-black bird squawked triumphantly.

6

Somehow things had got terribly behind. Lauren rushed home in a flap because she was late for the plumber, only to find that she had missed him, which was bloody annoying as it meant two, maybe three, more days without the use of the washing machine. The man had slipped one of those small curt 'We called' white cards through the letter box, which, reading between the lines, meant, 'And we're bloody pissed off you weren't in.' She would just have to ring them in the morning. It had been almost a week since visiting her parents and she was still trying to catch up. In the old days she would have taken a broken washing machine in her stride, but having a baby changed everything!

In the hall the answer machine was clogged with messages, the small red light frantically blinking. She pressed the replay button fast-forwarding the calls from the press. Since Josh's win at Wimbledon Lauren had been besieged with requests to appear in countless newspapers and magazines. She had politely but firmly turned them all down. Her husband was the one in the limelight now, not her. She'd turned her back on all that. None of the messages were from Josh. This irked Lauren. Her husband was pushing his luck. He should have returned from the Mercedes Cup in Stuttgart three days ago, having lost in the quarterfinals. Instead he had flown on to the Egyptian sea resort of Sharm-el-Sheikh for a break. 'The boys talked me into it. Couldn't resist, sweetheart,' his buoyant message had said on the machine, '. . . just for a few days because I miss you and Tom like crazy!' She was cross because she'd been out when he'd called. Crosser still because she had thus far been unable to track him down at the Hilton where he was staying.

'All right, all right!' she snapped at her devil child who was screaming blue murder. 'I know you're hungry. But *please*, Tom, a little bit of patience would go a long way with your mother.'

An unrepentant Tom merely upped the caterwauling. Marching into the kitchen, Lauren dumped the shopping on the table in a heap and poured herself a glass of apple juice. Thirstily she drained the glass then began shoving the frozen food into the freezer. She contemplated inviting someone over for dinner, but frankly, by the time she had dealt with Tom and waded through the list of household chores, she'd be too tired to cope with more than a quick soak in the tub then bed. When they were in England she and Josh entertained constantly. They loved nothing more than an evening dining with close friends. But since the birth of Tom there wasn't time for luxuries. All her energies were centred on his demands. This Lauren did without reproach, without complaint. Nonetheless, it somewhat galled her that Josh was off scuba-diving with his mates and not at home providing her with much needed support.

She inspected the sky. Several fat clouds had massed. It was a sweltering day. Tempers simmered in the muggy heatwave. But the forecast for heavy storms was as yet unfounded. Perhaps it would rain tonight. She wished it would. All the built-up pressure was giving her a headache.

'And you don't help,' she said, hauling the complaining Tom unceremoniously from his pram.

She lowered them both into the feeding chair. Her fingers moved deftly over her shirt buttons which slipped open with ease. She unzipped a cup of her maternity bra and guided

Tom's mouth to the exposed swollen nipple. Instinctively he latched on to it like the mouth of a Hoover, sucking with amazing strength and sureness. Lauren shifted gingerly in the chair, still painfully sore from the birth. A recent visit to her doctor revealed that some stitches not properly dissolved had become infected.

'A course of antibiotics will clear it up. Don't worry about young Tom,' the doctor had assured her, 'just watch him when you feed. He might find the milk tastes slightly bitter in which case you'll have to stop. But I would rather you gave it a try. Best to get these problems dealt with quickly.'

Twice she winced when Tom nipped her but he soon settled down. Lovingly, she explored his rapt face, the fierce concentrated workings of his mouth, his steady, watchful eyes as serious as a politician's. Already, after only a few days, Josh would find so many changes in his son. She thought about how lucky she was not having to work, the luxury of being able to stay at home and enjoy this precious time with her son. She smiled into his flawless face, revelling in the folds of silky fat on his thighs, his apple cheeks, the small dimple on his chin, exactly like his father's. She imagined him as a grown man loving not just herself but other women too. Would he choose wisely? Or would his sweet, trusting heart be abused? She tried to picture this unknown future woman that would take her place but failed.

So many people had gathered round after the birth. But it was Tom they had fussed over with their gifts, their cooings, their praise. Disorientated, exhausted after the ordeal, Lauren was left feeling pushed to one side. She had served her purpose. Tom was the one they wanted to see. And how could she blame them? He was so tiny, so perfect, so utterly delicious. One person knew exactly how she was feeling – Kay. Like a warm ray of sunshine her mother had cooked and cleaned, offered massage and soothing oils to heal her daughter's battered body. It taught Lauren a valuable lesson; that the sacrifices she was making for Tom, her mother had also made for her. Lauren was beginning to understand the inextricable bond between mother and child.

As Tom drank, she could feel the tug of him in her womb; powerful, sensual, slightly erotic. She placed a finger inside one of his hands which flexed and relaxed in rhythm to the sucking. The milk had the effect of a sleeping pill. Within half an hour Tom's eyes had closed, his body slumped in her arms. She rose slowly and caught the bluish white trickle seeping from his mouth. Hard to believe that just a few hours ago this blond cherub had produced decibels in M&S to rival Luciano Pavarotti. At the time she could have cheerfully murdered him.

By seven o'clock the house was as well organised and as quiet as an army barracks after lights out. Tom had been bathed and fed and was now sleeping and Lauren was enjoying a well-earned glass of wine in the kitchen when the doorbell rang.

'Keith!' It was Keith Cochran, Josh's agent from Advantage. 'This *is* a surprise.'

Keith's eyes were invisible behind black sunglasses. He gave her an apologetic smile. 'I hope I'm not interrupting anything.'

'No. Not at all. Come in.'

She beckoned him into the drawing room. He removed his glasses. Lauren thought he looked tired. A workaholic, he was famous for putting in five eighteen-hour days back to back.

'Can I get you a drink?' she offered. 'I've just opened a bottle.'

'Please.'

Disappearing into the kitchen, Lauren returned moments later carrying a tray. She handed him the bottle.

'How's Sally?'

'A bit shattered but I suppose that's to be expected,' Keith's hand trembled slightly as he poured himself some wine, 'only six weeks to go before the birth. Cheers,' he said with a false brightness and took a swift gulp of the pale liquid.

'I must look some things out for her. Tom's growing at such a rate that he's already getting too big for his baby-gros.'

Keith smiled ineffectually.

'Actually, I'm glad you're here,' said Lauren, sinking gratefully onto the sofa. 'You can tell me what that husband of mine has been up to. I've left countless messages for him at the Hilton but I've heard nothing. They're obviously having a whale of a time.'

Keith cleared his throat and studied his drink.

'Who's out there with him?' Lauren asked.

'Max Carter, Bill Knoll, John Cartwright.'

Lauren rolled her eyes, 'Cartwright! *That* lunatic. The last time Josh went off on a trip with him they ended up getting completely plastered and Bunjy-jumping off a hundred-foot cliff!'

'Look it's . . .'

'I know. Perfectly safe. But I still think you must be barking to do it. When did you speak to him?'

'Yesterday morning.'

'Don't suppose he remembered he has a son who would quite like to see him occasionally, not to mention his wife.' Lauren grimaced. 'Sorry, Keith, it's not fair to take this out on you. What did he say?'

'He wanted me to shift his tournament schedule in Toronto back by a couple of days. Lauren . . .'

'So that he could carry on scuba-diving?'

'As Wimbledon champion he has that prerogative.'

Part of the role of an agent was to make excuses when a player decided to cancel a tournament – often because they didn't feel like playing. The same applied to skipped interviews, an exhibition or a corporate appearance they wanted to pull out of even when there was money involved. Once you got to the top, passing up $50,000 for a day's work didn't amount to much.

Keith shifted uncomfortably in his chair and leaned forward. 'Lauren, this isn't an easy thing for me to say.'

'What? That my husband's about as responsible as a five-year-old?' She giggled to show that she was teasing. 'How about some more wine?'

Keith shook his head. Rising abruptly, he walked over to the window and gazed woodenly out at the garden. It was the sort of garden that seemed to be waiting for friends to carry out food and glasses, to spread rugs, delighted to be able to lunch outside. He fiddled with the neck of his tie as though it was too tight.

'I can't do this,' he said, shaking his head.

'Do what?'

He turned to her, his expression desperate.

Lauren's smile faded. 'What's wrong?'

'He's not coming back.'

She gazed at him. For a moment she was disorientated, unable to digest what he had just said. She felt the first fluttering of fear in her stomach.

'What do you mean he's not coming back?'

'Oh, God.' He rubbed his face tiredly as though he hadn't slept for days.

Lauren swallowed. '*Keith*. You're frightening me. What's happened?'

Keith exhaled a profound sigh. 'Josh died this morning.'

She realised she was trembling. A strange sensation inside her seemed to swell and sour.

'It's not *true*.'

'I'm afraid it is.'

She watched his face, waiting for the strained lines around his mouth to ebb, for him to smile, to tell her that this was just some silly prank Josh had dreamt up. Why then were his eyes so full of pity?

'Lauren . . .'

'No,' she held up a hand. 'Don't. Just tell me what happened. I want to know.' Her voice seemed far away. It was as though someone else had spoken. Keith walked over to the sofa and sat down next to her. He cleared his throat and began to speak.

'They took a boat out to Ras Muhammad on the southern tip of the Sinai Peninsula – it's about an hour-and-a-half ride from Naama Bay where they were staying. The coral cliff there is an eighty-metre vertical drop. They'd already made the trip twice before and as John's such an experienced diver they didn't bother to take an instructor.' Lauren watched Keith's thin mouth move as he talked, but it was like watching a silent movie without the subtitles. She couldn't understand what he was saying.

'They had reached a depth of about fifty metres when Josh got separated from the group. From what I understand he went down too far. It's very common with divers – even the really good ones. Josh suffered from nitrogen narcosis. It's like having an LSD trip underwater. You get careless, clumsy. Think you can fly, breathe without your equipment. Dumb things like that. Josh began to behave in a peculiar fashion. The regulator slipped out of his mouth, he lost control.' Keith shook his head as though even he himself couldn't believe what he was saying. 'He wouldn't have been aware of what was happening.'

Lauren buried her face in her hands for a moment, pressing her fingers tight against her skull, trying to think straight. The room felt chilly. She hugged the upper part of her body tightly.

'Cartwright found the body – it was Cartwright who called to tell me what had happened. I made arrangements for it to be flown back tomorrow. I hope I did the right thing.'

It Lauren repeated in her head. Had Josh already become an *it*? She gazed at the side lamp which cast a warm, buttery pool of light onto the desk. Keith's words recycled themselves in her brain; *Down too deep . . . nitrogen narcosis . . . flying . . . wouldn't have been aware . . .* Josh had taught her to dive while they were honeymooning out on the Barrier Reef. Vividly she now saw it, the sea, an impossibly beautiful and transcendental colour. How she'd loved it. She pictured Josh suspended in that magical world of fragmented light and colour, weightless, peaceful. She saw him hesitate as he glanced up at his flippered friends, drifting like fish a few yards above his head. Air bubbles rose from his tank, floated upwards and grew into silver spaceships. He watched with childish abandon, arms open to everything he saw; yellow-fin goatfish; explosions of red sea coral; bold Napoleons; electric clams; parrot fish; shoals of lunar fusilier; lyretail coralfish. Hands digging into water, he plunged headlong into the deepest dive of his life. Aware of the danger Lauren wanted to cry out, to stop him, but he was heedless of her warning. The deeper he went and with every suck of compressed air, the more euphoric he grew. She could feel what he felt; the driven need to go further, to explore. On and on he pressed, ignoring the cold, the thickening of the sea basin. And then, without warning, blackness. It engulfed him. In a matter of seconds he felt a drunken sickness. Some part of his brain told him to look at his depth gauge, check how deep he had gone, how long he'd been down. But he ignored the instinct, distracted by a large shape swimming under him. He wasn't sure what it was; a whitetip reef shark, a young whale perhaps? But he wanted to follow it, wanted to continue the beauty of the dive. *Don't*, Lauren urged, *go back*. She could feel panic crawl around inside her, rise like ivy through her veins to her neck and choke her. *Go back, go back*. But he'd lost all sense of time. He no longer had light to guide him. He felt the weight of water that enclosed him like a solid mass and he panicked. He started to claw at the tank on his back. The regulator fell from his mouth, beyond his grasp. His eyes, enlarged by his diving mask, were enormous globes of terror. Salt water filled his lungs. No air, couldn't breathe. He began to sink . . .

Keith reached out a warm hand and very gently touched her arm, 'I'm so sorry, Lauren,' he said quietly. 'It's a terrible tragedy.'

After Keith left she returned numbly to the drawing room. She wasn't sure how long she remained there, staring blankly into the deep, tiled fireplace. It was Tom's insistent cry that roused her from her dream-like trance. Tom, her son, her precious boy. She half-ran upstairs to the second floor, her need for his warm little body suddenly overwhelming. Rushing to his little cot, almost as if she were afraid she would find him gone, she peered inside. She felt knocked out with relief. He had kicked the blankets down to his ankles and had got himself all hot and bothered. She lifted him bawling from the cot and wiped his damp head.

'There, there,' she murmured, kissing and hugging him greedily. 'Mummy's here. Mummy's got you. Everything's going to be all right.'

Tom squirmed until his face had settled against the side of Lauren's chin. She could feel the soft heat from his head, the thin layer of perspiration on her neck, smell the sweetness of him. She carried him over to the small window, the only view point in the house from which you could see the common, and examined the warm airless night. The sky was dark and troubled with deep scarlet clouds. In the distance she could see the occasional flash of lightning followed by a low rumble. Once or twice she heard a muffled bang of thunder as if someone had let off a cannon. She wondered how far away it was. Weren't you supposed to tell by counting the seconds between? As another streak of lightning ignited the sky she put a protective hand up to her baby's head.

'Hush, my darling. Sleep now. I won't let anything hurt you.'

Recognising his mother's reassuring voice, Tom's little body began to relax, crying still but with less conviction now, less force. He was hovering on the brink of sleep. She gazed at the lights blazing in houses across the common, the black silhouette of someone walking a dog. She could hear the wind in the trees, feel the hills crowding around her like violent ocean waves.

In the gloom of the nursery Josh's photograph smiled at her. Lauren gently rocked her son back to sleep, waiting for the impact of the storm.

DROUGHT

I am inhabited by a cry.
Nightly it flaps out
Looking, with its hooks, for something to love.

I am terrified by this dark thing
That sleeps in me;
All day I feel its soft, feathery turnings,
its malignity.

'Elm'
Sylvia Plath

7

Hugo Butler stopped at the lights and gave an oily smile to the girl in the blue Vitara idling next to him. She smiled back, then quickly looked away, her expression puzzled as though she had recognised his face but couldn't quite place it. Hugo was used to strangers behaving as though they had seen him before. Women especially. He would look at them and smile with such assurance, with such ease that they were instantly wrong-footed; had they seen him on the box, was he a Hollywood director perhaps, or a sports personality? Of course they were always impressed by the Gold Jaguar XJS. Apart from the Belgravia flat it was his most prized possession. The girl in the Vitara was staring at him openly now. Hugo inwardly chuckled, enjoying the attention. It would be bugging her for the rest of the day. He thought idly about handing her one of the new personalised gold-embossed cards he'd just had printed but decided against it. After all there'd be other opportunities, other girls.

He reflected on what a good day it had been and began mentally totting up how much commission he would make. He gave the August air a satisfactory sniff. If only all sales could be this easy. Shame he wasn't a smoker because he felt the need to celebrate and a cigar would have been a good way of going about it. The reality was that he'd been cajoled into taking Philippa to see a production of *Don Giovanni*. He must have been mad when he'd agreed. Hugo loathed opera almost as much as he loathed disorder, or people being late.

He himself was a stickler for punctuality. Maybe they could leave early and nip back to her place for a quickie. After which he could escape to his pad.

Hugo had invested his savings in the Eaton Square flat because it was the very best address he could find. That it was the size of a postage stamp didn't bother him a jot, since it served his needs adequately. But he never took anyone to see his flat. It was important to Hugo that people imagined him living somewhere very grand.

The lights changed and Hugo pulled away, the girl in the Vitara now forgotten. As he gunned the powerful car across Wandsworth Bridge Road he glanced at his Cartier watch and smiled.

Bang on time, as usual.

'Come on, Mel! If we don't leave now we'll miss the start.'

'I'm coming. I'm coming!' a muffled voice called from upstairs. 'Just check that the cat's out, Gillian, and the back door's locked.'

'You asked me to do that half an hour ago. Your house has more security features attached to it than Fort Knox. So will you please stop worrying!'

Melanie Roach rushed downstairs, her right hand foraging around in her handbag.

Melanie's friend, Gillian Twist, gazed at her. 'God, Mel, what a transformation. You look gorgeous.'

'Do I?' Melanie checked her appearance in the hall mirror as if she herself had had doubts. She was frowning again. 'Keys,' she said, checking coat pockets, 'where did I put my house keys?'

'They're exactly where you left them.' From the hall table Gillian picked up the small bunch and dangled them between her thumb and forefinger. 'The sandwiches are safely tucked away in my bag, there's petrol in the car and, yes, I've got both tickets. Is there anything else you think you might like to worry about before we go?'

Melanie stood still and looked at her friend.

'You're right,' she laughed. 'Anyone would think I was going on a date with James Fox!'

They managed to find a place to park in West Side Common, just outside Cannizaro House. To get to the open-air theatre they had to walk through the tranquil grounds behind the elegant Georgian house. It was a balmy evening with a cloudless sky. They followed the winding path through the park past the Gothic aviary and down to the ornamental lake.

Gillian showed their tickets to the usherette at the black theatre gates and they meandered into the kitchen garden and down a tidy path bordered by dusky-pink heather.

'I can't believe I've lived in Wimbledon all these years and never once been to the festival,' said Melanie, trying to identify the classical music being played over the loud speakers.

'I can,' said Gillian with a trace of irony. 'How about a quick drink?'

Melanie looked at her watch. 'Do we have time? It's starting in five minutes.'

'Then we'll just take them to our seats. Make it a proper picnic.'

Melanie sniffed the air contentedly. 'I'm so glad we did this.'

'You don't get out enough, Mel. That's your trouble. Hiding yourself away in that little house, your whole life wrapped up in Lottie. Moping about Josh . . .'

Melanie straightened her shoulders. 'I thought we'd agreed not to talk about him.'

'Sorry.'

'Don't be. It's all in the past now. As from tonight, I'm turning over a new leaf. Take what opportunities present themselves.'

Gillian feigned an incredulous look. 'Can I have that in writing?'

'Oh, you!' They both giggled, enjoying the rare feeling of being young and silly.

Melanie caught the barman's attention, 'Two gins and tonic, please.'

'How's the art course going?'

'I *love* it. It was such a good idea of yours. Some evenings I don't feel like going but I never regret it once I'm there. Remind me to show you some of my new work next time you're round. Gillian?' she said, seeing her friend's attention had been diverted.

'Over there,' Gillian inclined her head of short copper curls towards a man at the main gates. 'Look at what the cat's just pulled in.'

The woman clinging to his arm certainly had a feline look about her; wild straggly mane, long shapely legs, the sort of prettiness that demanded continual attention. The man, who must have been twice her age, was tall and powerfully built. Early forties, she guessed, but he looked incredibly fit. Exactly Gillian's type. What made him stand out, apart from his height, was the way he was dressed – as if he were going to a Cartier polo match, not into the relaxed atmosphere of an outdoor theatre.

'I know that face,' said Gillian with conviction. 'He's an actor or something. Definitely seen him before. Where have I seen him before, Mel?'

'Don't know.' The man and his Catwoman had almost reached the bar. For some unfathomable reason Melanie wanted to flee. 'Come on. Let's go and find our seats.'

'Spoilsport,' Gillian muttered, grabbing her half-empty plastic cup.

The young usherette showed them to their seats, which were rather good ones four rows from the front. Gillian with her beady eye was quick to point out June Whitfield nearby.

Despite the fact that it would be light for another hour, the stage lights were already glowing.

'It's so pretty,' Melanie said, admiring the ivy-draped wall that acted as a backdrop.

'Jonathan and I used to spend many a romantic evening here.'

'Do you see much of him these days?'

'Occasionally. When he comes to pick up or drop off the children. But we don't communicate any more. At least he won't. I think he finds it all a bit too painful. Don't know why.' Gillian began fiddling with her handbag. 'It's been almost three years now. But that's men for you. They dump their dirty washing in your lap expecting you to forgive their silly, foolish ways. Then, when you don't they go around with a wounded look on their faces asking how you can be such a cold heartless bitch!'

The seats were beginning to fill. Gillian pulled herself more upright. 'How about a sandwich? All those barbecue smells have brought back my appetite with a vengeance.'

'Good idea.'

Gillian dished them out of a Sainsbury's carrier and helped herself to one. 'Pop them on the seat next to you,' she said, passing them over. 'Doesn't look like anyone's going to be sitting there.'

For a minute they munched in contented silence, the gin and tonic beginning to take effect. Then Gillian dug her elbow into Melanie's side.

'Don't look now,' she muttered, 'but Don Giovanni's heading in our direction.'

'Excuse me,' said a voice in Melanie's left ear.

She looked up in a daze. He had the sort of polished, George Hamilton complexion that had been expensively stained with lots of sun and very short wiry hair.

'Are these yours?' he indicated her sandwiches in tin foil parked on the seat. *His* seat evidently.

'Oh, I *am* sorry.' She swiftly removed them, embarrassed by the pungent smell of mustard.

Someone turned up the music and actors appeared on the stage. It was a magical evening. Throughout the first act Melanie was horribly conscious of the stranger's arm sealed to her own. Gillian whispered incessantly, polishing off both packets of sandwiches – Melanie found she had lost her appetite. During the twenty-minute interval Gillian, after a lot of unsubtle winking and nudging in the man's direction, dashed off to the portable latrine. Melanie stayed in her seat, hoping the stranger would move, but he too remained where he was.

'Hughie, darling.' It was the first time Melanie had heard Catwoman speak. 'I'm absolutely famished.' She licked her lips with a cat's precision, touching only the corners with the tip of her pink tongue. 'I know we're having dinner after the show, but I don't think I'll last the course.'

The man automatically withdrew a wallet from his breast pocket and handed her a fiver.

'Darling, you're an angel,' she said, kissing his cheek. 'Drinkie?'

He shook his head.

As soon as she'd gone, Melanie felt vulnerable. Should she try and make conversation? She was so out of practice at this kind of thing. It had literally been years since she'd tried chatting up a man. And yet she was physically drawn to him. She wanted to be interesting enough for him to want her. Only she feared that he wouldn't, saw what he would see were his eyes to make a tour over her neat, summery appearance: the prim, self-conscious face, her slightly anxious eyes, her sensible trousers and leather sandalled feet that revealed unpainted toenails. Damn Gillian for leaving her like this, for her campaigning matchmaking. Perhaps she should go and find her.

'Enjoying it?'

She turned to the man in surprise. 'Why, yes. Yes, I am,' she stammered. 'I've never been to an outdoor theatre before. It's really rather lovely.'

'You should try the Amphitheatre in Griffith Park. That's something else.'

'Really?' said Melanie helplessly. Where on earth was Griffith Park?

'Do you live around here?'

She nodded. 'Within walking distance. Just down the bottom of Wimbledon Hill.' The poor end, she almost added. 'What about you?'

'Belgravia,' he said with a touch of smugness. Well, that was obvious by the way he was dressed. 'I have a business near there,' he added, fuelling her curiosity.

She could see Gillian wending her way back towards them. Oh, well, so much for making the most of her moment.

'Horrible stink in the loos,' Gillian said gaily as she sat down. Melanie prayed for the opera to resume. Unabashed, Gillian reached a hand across Melanie towards Hugo. 'Hello there. I'm Gillian.'

'Hugo Butler. But I don't yet know your friend's name?'

'Melanie,' Gillian volunteered before Melanie had a chance to do so herself. 'This is Melanie Roach and she's single.'

Melanie glowered with embarrassment. She sat under his bold scrutiny and felt exposed, like a plain girl at a dance wearing the wrong dress.

Hugo gave her a half-lidded smile. 'And what do you girls do when you're not out on the tiles?'

The women looked at one another. Girls?

'My hands are kept constantly tied with three impossible children. Melanie's the lucky one. She only has . . .'

'I temp,' Melanie said firmly. 'I do temping work.' The

fierce look she shot her friend seemed to say: and if you say just one more word!

'Do you enjoy that?'

'Sometimes,' Melanie admitted. 'Depends on the company I'm working for.'

She knew Gillian was dying to find out more about him, as she was herself, but at that point Catwoman returned.

'Sorry I was so long, darling,' she said, sighing delicately. 'Frightful queue.'

The lights dimmed.

'Hello?'

'Mrs Roach? Oh, hello. It's Valerie at Office Angels here. Look, a job's just come in for next week. It's not your usual area, I know. But it's good money and they want you for the five days.' There was a rustle of paper. 'It's an estate agency on the Fulham Road. Only five minutes from South Ken tube. Would you be interested?'

Melanie hesitated. It was still the school holidays and she was worried about leaving Lottie on her own for so long. But on the other hand they badly needed the money. Perhaps Gillian could help the odd day. Lottie got on well enough with her girls.

'Mrs Roach?'

'Yes, I was just trying to work out my dates. I'll take it.'

After she had scribbled down the details, Melanie returned to her sums. This new job would mean she'd be able to cover the main utility bills. There was still the damp-proofing account to settle, of course. And that worried her. The builders had been very patient but she couldn't put them off for ever. It just seemed that no sooner had she got one thing fixed than something else gave in to old age or broke down, draining more money from the measly allowance she got. Still, the days of plaster patches, damp walls and the garden's overgrown wilderness had long since gone. She could take solace from that.

Melanie's eyes were drawn to the framed photo next to the phone of her only child, taken when she was six. Somehow she looked so much younger. Melanie could remember the day it was taken vividly: Lottie and Josh riffling through the dressing-up box, acting out well-known stories, appearing in more and more outlandish costumes that had them all in fits of laughter. Melanie sighed. Lottie had been so happy at that age. If only she could have found some way of bottling that happiness and keeping it for her daughter now. Now, when she could do with a good dose of it.

Soon after Josh's death, Lottie had complained of head-aches and neck stiffness. When it was discovered she also had a high temperature, Melanie called the doctor. She was shocked to learn that Lottie had contracted meningitis. Fortunately they had caught the infection in its early stages but a delay could have resulted in brain damage or death. They kept her in hospital for a week until the vomiting stopped, feeding her penicillin. When she came home Lottie's recovery was rapid. Once she was able to get out of bed, however, she mooned around the house with unwashed hair, refusing to take part in anything, hardly saying a word except to talk about Josh as though he were still alive. It was as if she couldn't accept his death. It left Melanie feeling helpless.

So when out of the blue Lottie suddenly declared she wanted to spend the day with a friend, Melanie was thrilled. Here at last, was someone to take her daughter's mind off the whole terrible business. But far from having a positive effect, Lottie had returned home worn and exhausted, picking birdlike at her food before disappearing up to her room. On her way up to bed later on, Melanie ventured into her daughter's room. The light was on. Still dressed, Lottie was curled up on the bed with her arms wrapped tightly round her rabbit, her anguished, tear-stained face softened in sleep.

They hadn't talked about the accident. Melanie had attempted to after the funeral, but Lottie had turned on her with such fury, such blistering rage, that she had quickly backed off. After that the occasion had never presented itself again. But she couldn't bear to see Lottie's small wretched form day in day out. In desperation she turned to Gillian for advice.

'She looks so forlorn, so sad.'

'Girls of her age are always sad. They choose to be. It makes them feel strong – here, have another tissue.' Gillian passed her the box.

'I feel useless. I don't know how to help her.'

'She'll come round, Mel. It's early days yet. It's only been a few weeks. What Lottie needs is time to heal. Josh was her world. He meant everything to her.'

'He meant a great deal to me too,' choked Melanie, tears gathering again in the corners of her green eyes. 'I never really knew how much until I watched him being buried.'

Gillian had done exactly the right thing. She had packed the kids off to the zoo for the afternoon with their father – he did, said Gillian waving them off, have his moments. In her bright Hygena kitchen which smelt of flour and cloves and burnt sugar, the cupboard doors covered with childish paintings, she had made them mugs of milky coffee. She was a good listener. As the belligerent tears flowed uncontrollably, Melanie had given free rein to her own unexamined grief, the loss she felt not only of Josh, but of what she had once had with him, what she might still have had. There was no justice in the world, she thought savagely. Men she had given her love to, men that had let her down.

She sometimes suspected that Josh had merely used her. That all she had been to him was a temporary convenience.

A warm body who provided free meals, board and lodging. He had been her life. But had she been his? He had refused to give her the child she so badly wanted – his child. For years she'd tried to persuade him but he never relented, never warmed to the idea. He'd once told her that families were for other people, not for him. He would only make a mess of things. But when she'd challenged this remark he said it was because she didn't understand him. Painfully, she contemplated this nagging possibility. God knows he had given her enough reason to believe it. Now it was too late. Josh had taken the truth with him to the grave.

After her emotional outburst she felt a great deal better. Gillian had given her a cuddle, told her that everything was going to be all right and Melanie went home to the house in Gladstone Road, the house where she had lived for almost fourteen years. She wanted to offer her daughter the same counselling, show her what an affectionate mother she could be – that Lottie was much loved. But this was about as likely as Melanie bringing Josh back to life. Lottie was being *impossible*. She had built an impenetrable wall around herself, and nothing, not even a mother's love, could pierce it.

Early on Monday morning, Melanie walked up to Wimbledon station and caught the tube to South Kensington. The train was stuffed with weary, grey-faced commuters, standing room only. Melanie found herself sandwiched between a stockbroker and an old tramp who smelt as though he'd been stewing in a bath of urine for a week. The tramp coughed chestily into her right ear. Shuddering, Melanie closed her eyes and tried not to think about her headache.

Hopkins and Co., squeezed between a Mercedes show-room and an expensive Italian pottery shop, had a slick glossy exterior. Displayed in the window were meticulously drawn-up particulars which represented some of the smart-est properties in the area. Most had been marked with a

SOLD sticker, and Melanie wondered, as she always did whenever she passed an estate agency, what the point was in displaying them at all? Didn't it make more sense to put particulars up of houses that had yet to find a purchaser?

With some trepidation she pushed open the heavy glass front door and approached the receptionist's desk just inside. An untidy blonde was on the phone. After a long wait, she finally hung up.

'Can I help you?' she said, her upper-class voice crisp to the point of stand-offishness.

'I'm Melanie Roach, your new temp.'

The girl frowned. 'No one said anything about it to me.' She looked faintly cross.

'I'm supposed to be here for the week. Well, that's what they told me . . .' The girl's dubious air was contagious. 'Office Angels are normally very reliable.'

'Yes, we use them a lot. Hang on. I'll call downstairs.' She picked up the phone, examining a broken nail while it rang in her ear.

'Rodders,' she said after a few seconds, 'Rodders, know anything about a new temp? Yes. Today. He did?' she expelled a long-suffering sigh. 'Good of him to tell me.' Another pause. 'Well, what shall I do with her?' She glanced up at Melanie disparagingly as if the task at hand was one she would rather not have had. 'Okay. I'll send her down.' She hung up.

'Rodders wants you downstairs,' she pointed to a staircase behind the desk. 'He'll meet you at the bottom.'

'Right,' said Melanie, feeling her neck muscles knot.

Rodney Tate, a senior negotiator with Hopkins and Co., had the sort of boyish good looks that must have been spectacular as a child but were already going to seed. He smiled at Melanie and showed her where she would be working.

'Damn' machine's been nothing but trouble,' he said,

switching on the computer; 'it's bloody well stumped me, that's for sure. Hope you know how to use this.' Melanie assured him she did.

He looked relieved. 'The girl we had last week was *hopeless*. Perhaps you could start off by typing up the details of these properties we've just taken on. See how you go.'

Melanie smiled reassuringly. 'Don't worry. I'll be fine.'

'Good,' said Rodney, gratefully. 'Right then, I'll leave you to it.'

And leave her to it he did. The morning whizzed by. The particulars were pretty straightforward and Melanie would have had them typed up by eleven had it not been for the constant stream of interruptions: could she take the post out; would she mind typing out a couple of letters; coffee would be lovely, two sugars but no milk. The pedestrian requests were endless.

At noon a perceptible change in the office atmosphere occurred. Everyone suddenly looked very busy. Rodney, who had been having a fag in the loo was, moments later, furiously scribbling away at his desk. Melanie could hear animated conversation going on upstairs, a male voice, deep and commanding. After a few minutes a pair of polished shoes appeared on the stairs, followed by a well-tailored suit. Melanie's mouth fell open. The man inside the suit was none other than the man she'd sat next to in Cannizaro Park. Hugo Butler.

'Rodney,' he said curtly, striding up to Rodney's desk, 'where are the keys to 149 Tate Street? Caroline thinks she must have left them with you. I need them for a viewing after lunch.'

'Got them right here. Actually, I showed some people round it this morning.'

'Any interest?'

'Doubt it. They're caught up in a chain and aren't likely to have their mortgage through for weeks.'

Melanie was confused, startled, rooted to the seat of her chair.

'No good to the Keeleys then. They're after cash buyers only. Anything else I should know?'

'Small pad I've just taken on in Cheyne Walk. Bit of a gem. Might like to skim through the details. They've just been typed up.'

Hugo cocked a thick eyebrow. 'You're never that efficient.'

'Not me,' said Rodney, tilting his head in Melanie's direction. 'Melanie's been a treasure. Don't suppose we could keep her on permanently?'

For the first time since he had arrived, Melanie felt Hugo Butler's direct gaze on her.

'Ah, yes,' he said, in a puzzling way, 'I'd almost forgotten. How are you getting on?' The question was asked so casually it was as if the interval of almost a week since their short conversation had never occurred.

'Um, fine, thank you,' she stammered, half getting up from her desk. 'Rodney's been showing me the ropes.'

Hugo looked at his watch. 'Has he fed you yet?'

'Well, no. Actually I was going to . . .'

'Then you can come and have lunch with me.'

'Lunch? Now?' said Melanie a little stupidly. A thousand expectations flew through her mind like a Rolodex.

He seemed amused. 'Well it is noon and I've got to be back for an appointment at 1.30. Come on,' he said decisively, 'it's too nice a day to waste entirely down here in the dungeon. Grab your bag.'

Not quite sure she liked the loaded wink she got from Rodney, Melanie nevertheless followed Hugo upstairs. She then had to wait while he reached across Caroline and fumbled for the petty cash.

Hovering awkwardly by the door, Melanie felt herself

scrutinized by the other staff members. She was confused
by the sudden glare of attention and put a hand to her left
temple where her earlier headache still lingered. Perhaps
she should have declined his offer, settled instead for a
sandwich and take-away coffee.

But seated five minutes later in the smart, bustling
restaurant across the road, she soon relaxed.

'So,' Hugo said to Melanie, leaning back in his chair as
the waiter gave them their menus, 'were you surprised?'

'Surprised?' It took her a moment to grasp what he meant.
'Well, yes, I was. You must admit it's quite a coincidence
you and I meeting again like this.'

'Perhaps not.'

'I don't understand?'

'Why should you? Let me come clean. Your working
for Hopkins and Co. was, shall we say, engineered. After
meeting you at Cannizaro Park last week I wanted to see
you again. So I took the trouble of finding out which temping
agency you worked for. Didn't take me long. Just one call.'
He smiled at her, a pleased, voracious smile revealing a
mouthful of strong white teeth.

Melanie was stunned.

'I've shocked you.'

'No. Well, yes, actually. I mean, I'm very flattered and all
that. But I thought . . .'

He cut her off. 'You thought correctly. Whatever my
personal interest in you I should not have let it affect
my business.' He was certainly blunt. 'We needed a
temp for the week and you came with excellent credentials. You got the job on merit and ability, nothing else.'

The waiter returned, pen and pad poised. They were both
quiet for a moment as they made a quick study of the menu.
Hugo ordered the food: two onion soups, to be followed by
steak and salad for himself, mushroom omelette for Melanie.

While he did this she contemplated this new and startling, but not displeasing situation she had found herself in. How long had it been since a man had shown interest in her? How long since she had permitted one to? Not since Josh – Poor Josh. How could she, how could anyone have guessed such a tragedy would occur. If only their last meeting had been a happier one. If she could just have told him how she really felt, made him realise that despite everything that had happened, she still loved him. Tears pricked her eyes. She looked down at her folded hands willing the effects of the still fresh memory of his funeral not to intrude on lunch. Not now. Around the room she could hear a volley of exchanges going back and forth like ping-pong balls, bright incomprehensible words. Pull yourself together, she told herself fiercely.

Hugo was telling the waiter how he liked his steak. She studied his green speckled eyes – the intensity of their colour enhanced by his tan, his capable broad shoulders, the firm jaw that bespoke strength and stubbornness. This man had actually gone to the trouble of engineering a meeting. In him she suddenly saw someone she could lean on a bit, someone who might erase some of the terrible weight of responsibility, the loneliness she had been feeling. He was smiling at her now, no doubt trying to guess what she was thinking. She grabbed the orange juice she had ordered, stalling for time.

Hugo told her he'd been with Hopkins and Co. for almost twenty years and was now a senior partner. He'd had considerable success and clearly enjoyed his work but had never married. She found this surprising. They talked about the changing housing climate in London, the desire of more and more people to move to the country. They discussed global warming and the increasing asthma problems cropping up all over the city because of poor air quality. They moved on to sport and tennis, in which it turned out they both shared a keen interest. Hugo admitted to having once hoped to make it a professional career, but for a number of reasons (which he seemed reluctant to go into), he'd never pursued. Melanie had mentioned her marriage briefly, but said nothing of Josh. Not because she had anything to hide. It was just that she didn't feel ready to put her feelings to the test with anyone new. Especially a potential boyfriend.

'In the end,' Hugo was saying, 'after a certain amount of soul searching, if I can use such a vulgar expression,' he smiled at her apologetically, 'I discovered I was rather adept at selling houses. Of course I still play when I get the time at Queen's, my club.' He said this proudly.

Melanie was impressed. 'How on earth did you get into Queen's? I hear they have a twenty-year waiting list.'

'Contacts,' said Hugo significantly.

She returned to the office alone – Hugo was anxious not to be late for his appointment and had gone on directly. Not, however, before he had extracted a promise from her to have dinner with him during the week. There was no sign of Caroline and none of the sales staff were at their desks. Must be a busy afternoon. She was about to descend the staircase when she paused. There were people downstairs talking in low conspiratorial voices.

'Up to his old tricks.' Caroline's voice.

'Careful, Caro, the claws are showing.'

'Well, come on. You know what he's like. We all do.'

'Yup,' a snigger. 'He's had more temps than Office Angels.'

Their hysterical laughter came to an abrupt halt the moment they caught sight of Melanie.

'Good lunch?' Rodney asked smoothly.

'Yes,' said Melanie colourlessly, ignoring the slight smirk on Caroline's face.

'Right,' said Rodney, sliding off his desk and pulling at his crooked tie. 'Yes. Righto then. S'pose we'd better get back to work. Caro, you'd better leg it back upstairs or we'll both cop it.'

'Well, you know what they say,' Caroline remarked, her eyes on Melanie as she climbed the stairs. 'No rest for the wicked!'

Melanie kept her head bent, refusing to rise to Caroline's silky insinuations and bitchiness. Whatever it was they were implying, she refused to be part of it. They could, after all, have been talking about anyone. She wasn't going to let them spoil her afternoon. Her mind drifted back to when Hugo said goodbye.

He'd kissed her cheek. A bold gesture, perhaps, from employer to employee, particularly as they hardly knew one another. But he had smelt so good, clean and sweet like fresh laundry. Standing there in the street under the warm sun it was his close maleness after such an eternity since Josh that she had found difficult to resist.

Even now it threatened her.

8

Annabel's, the smart teashop, was packed with afternoon shoppers. Ingeborg Bohakari, née Klinsmann, sat nursing a cup of Assam tea deep in thought. Although a resident of Putney she preferred to shop in Wimbledon. She liked the intimacy of the village, the select choice and quality of things it provided, the gentle street charm and the sprawling common which petered out only yards from the high street. Having inherited her German mother's sweet tooth and passion for exotic infusions she also enjoyed sampling the local teashops. Having tea and cake was one of the great pleasures in her life. Mindful always to choose a seat by the window, Inge loved to gaze out at passers-by. As always, the high street was teeming with shoppers. Four-wheel drives and BMWs obligingly crawled to a halt as two horses and their riders tentatively crossed the road – one of the horses stopping halfway to take an untimely shit. Pedestrians stepped cautiously round.

Inge shifted in her chair. She was restless, brimming with a rare sense of excitement. Her period, always so punctual, was twelve days overdue. Tucked amongst the contents of her basket was a home pregnancy kit bought in Boots. She planned to do the test in the morning but it would be more a formality than confirmation. In her heart Inge already knew. She was quite, quite sure she was going to have a baby.

At first she had worried about how Wolff might take the news. They had been married for such a short time. He might feel threatened by a new addition to their relationship, having to share her suddenly. But to Inge it made sense. The life of a professional tennis player was such a precarious one. Everything about Wolff was crying out for stability, the love and security of a family. She felt sure that once he got used to the idea fatherhood would be the making of him.

Shifting more comfortably against the unyielding back of her seat, her eyes explored the tearoom interior. Her attention was caught by a young mother trying to comfort an irate infant. The woman was striking not only because of her flawless good looks, but because she seemed so familiar. Inge blew on hot tea trying to place her: had they met at a party? did she work in Putney? was she connected to the local school? And then Inge twigged. Of course, Lauren Kendall. Wolff had pointed her out in the players' airport-style canteen at Wimbledon shortly before Josh Kendall had destroyed him in the second round. A furious Wolff had irrationally blamed his defeat on poor line calling and blatant distractions from the crowd. But all that had seemed trivial once they'd heard the devastating news. They had read about it while they were on holiday in Bali. For two days Wolff had talked of little else. Who could have predicted that within weeks of winning the Wimbledon title Josh Kendall would be dead. It was a dreadful thing to have happened and the tennis world was still reeling from the shock.

Curiously Inge studied his widow with closer attention. Lauren had spread an assortment of coins from her purse onto the table, soundlessly moving her mouth as she counted out the money. A slab of carrot cake with one bite out of it sat neglected on one side, together with a folded copy of the *Guardian*. The baby was crying more strenuously now and it seemed to Inge that all Lauren wanted to do was escape the attention her baby's cries had attracted. Slightly flushed, she rose and collected several shopping bags lying at her feet, able to fit only two under the pram. The rest she clasped awkwardly together in one hand.

Poor, poor woman, Inge thought. To lose a husband in such a way and with a baby so young. What if something were to happen to Wolff? Inge shuddered. It was no good thinking like that. To take her mind off morbid thoughts she consulted her 'things to do' list: jacket from Matches; drop off Wolff's watch at the mender's; order quiche from the Pie Man; pick up Livarot and Parmesan from the Real Cheese shop. She glanced at her watch. Time to go. A woman who had been sitting with her wide mohair-clad back to Inge, hauled herself up from the flimsy little chair. Inge paid her bill and followed her out.

She wandered next door to Matches. Divided into three boutiques in Wimbledon, Matches stocked exclusive designer clothes for men and women and customers came from as far away as Surrey. Inge closed the door behind her. A pram and clutch of shopping bags were parked close to the cash desk. To Inge's surprise, Lauren Kendall was methodically going through a rack of dresses.

The young assistant smiled professionally at Inge. 'Would you like any help?'

Inge handed her a shop receipt. 'I brought in a jacket last week to be altered. Can you see if it is ready for me?'

'Ah, yes,' said the girl, 'it came in yesterday. Won't be a tick.'

While she waited, Inge inspected a selection of paisley scarves displayed next to the till. Pretty, she thought fingering one of the delicate silk squares, but expensive. Her attention moved on to the pram and she couldn't resist taking a quick peek inside. The baby, blond like its mother, was lying asleep on its back. Plump, sausage-shaped arms lay close to its head, tiny hands curled upwards into half-fists. As if aware of Inge's scrutiny, the infant stirred and crumpled its eyes then drifted back to sleep with a deep shuddering sigh.

'Your baby is quite beautiful.'

'He is when he's asleep.' Lauren was holding a long coffee-coloured dress against herself. She smiled at Inge. 'The poor darling's had colic so he's been a bit grumpy today. My fault,' she explained. 'Too much fruit.'

Lauren's eyes suddenly widened with recognition. 'We've met, haven't we? You're Wolff Bohakari's wife?'

'Please, call me Inge. I like the dress.'

Lauren's gaze returned to her reflection in the mirror. 'I've been coveting it for days,' she said wistfully, checking the sale ticket again as if she were hoping she had misread the ruinously expensive price.

'It suits you,' Inge encouraged.

'It does, doesn't it. Oh, why not? It's been a long week and I deserve it.' Folding the linen dress decisively over one arm Lauren joined Inge at the pay desk.

Moments later the sales assistant returned with Inge's jacket.

'I'll put it in here, Mrs Bohakari,' she said, her voice fading as she vanished for a second to hang it up in the small changing room.

Inge slipped on the MaxMara jacket that had been a birthday present from Wolff. She had asked them to remove the substantial shoulder pads as she had enough shoulders for two. Wolff detested shopping, so she had picked it out herself. He claimed he always bought the wrong things. Inge understood this. She wasn't the kind of woman who expected or needed romantic gestures. In sixteen married months she could count on one hand how often Wolff had told her he loved her. It was unnecessary. She didn't need jewels or soft words to know how he felt. She could read the commitment in his eyes when he looked at her, feel the trust when they held each other at night.

She turned and examined her reflection in the mirror. The jacket now fitted perfectly. It occurred to her that before too long she would need to make alterations to most of her clothes. She touched her belly with wonder. A baby was growing inside her – *Wolff's* baby. She prayed it would be a boy.

Back at the pay desk, Lauren was having problems. Inge waited her turn.

'It can't be,' Lauren said. 'Try it again.'

'I did, madam, twice.'

'But I don't understand. This has never happened before.' Lauren's voice was beginning to show signs of strain.

'Haven't you got anything else? We'll accept a cheque with a banker's card.'

'No,' Lauren withdrew another credit card from her handbag, 'you'd better put it on my American Express.'

The high-pitched tinkle of the bell above the shop door disturbed the baby's slumber as two women entered. They cast a quick beady eye over the racks of expensive designer clothes and made their way over to the same silk scarves Inge had been admiring earlier. While the first woman investigated prices, the younger woman found herself drawn to the sharp restless squeaks coming from inside the pram.

'Is someone waking up then? Yes, you are, aren't you. Here, Mum,' she gushed, 'looks the splitting image of little Jamie, doesn't he? Don't you, pet?'

She picked up a rattle and gave it an energetic shake. 'What's this then, you little love? Oochie, coochy, *coo*.'

The baby opened its mouth in protest.

'You are funny,' she giggled. 'Aaah, look at him, the angel. Aren't you a little angel?'

'He's hungry,' declared the older woman, abandoning the scarves. 'Seems to me he wants feeding. I always know a hungry child when I see one,' and without further ado, she stuck a fat manicured finger into the baby's mouth.

'Please, I'd rather you didn't do that,' said Lauren, rather more sharply than she meant.

Offended, the elder woman withdrew her hand.

'Well,' she said huffily, 'I was only trying to help, dear. I've got four grandchildren of my own, you know.'

'Yes. Of course. And thank you. But he'd only just gone to sleep.' Four pairs of eyes fastened themselves on the pram as the furious cries increased in volume.

'Hush, darling, hush,' Lauren soothed.

'Wants feeding,' the woman muttered under her breath.

As if she hadn't enough to worry about, the assistant handed back Lauren's American Express card and said, 'I'm afraid it's expired.'

'Are you sure?' Lauren looked at the card in exasperation and saw that it had indeed expired three days before. 'Oh, for God's sake, this is absolutely ridiculous!'

The two women, sensing a scene, quickly moved over to the dress rail where they could watch from a discreet distance. Inge, gently rocking the pram, noticed Lauren's shoulders sag as if the weight of the day had suddenly become too much for her. Time to intervene.

'I think Mrs Kendall will leave the dress for today. For the time being, could you put it to one side? This,' Inge said handing back her jacket to the assistant, 'is fine now. I just need a bag.' Then she turned back to Lauren.

'My car is parked just across the road. I live close by, in Putney. Why don't you come back with me? Then you can feed and change the baby.'

Faced with the grim prospect of going home to a house full of waiting chores and about ready to collapse from weariness and the heat of the day, Lauren gratefully accepted.

'Doesn't look like a fit mother to me,' muttered the older woman as she watched them leave. She was still smarting from Lauren's rebuke.

'Don't let her get to you, Mum.'

'Too right I won't.' She threw a brief patronising smile at the hovering assistant. 'It's just that to my mind the young girls today don't know the meaning of hard work!'

In the end they took both cars, as Lauren hadn't wanted to feel dependent on Inge in getting home. The Victorian house in Lower Common South had kept its name, the Vicarage, but there was no stout clergyman propped against a mantelpiece reflectively smoking his pipe, no bosomy housekeeper kneading dough in the kitchen. The once poky downstairs rooms had been knocked through to create a large open-plan area. The house had Inge's own personal stamp all over it – bright with warm saffron walls and a few choice pieces of furniture. Lauren liked it immediately and stopped to admire a French wall clock in the hall. As if sensing an audience, the clock's ornate central doors flapped open. Three cherubs emerged and put their tiny gilt trumpets to their lips and tooted out five shrill notes one after the other. Having announced the hour they slipped back into the dark enclosure, the flapping doors snapping shut behind them.

Lauren was captivated. 'Where did you get it?' she asked.

Inge's pale grey eyes, strengthened by a pair of strong eyebrows, crinkled at the corners. 'It was a wedding present from my sister. I wanted it here in England. The rest of our more precious things are in Monte Carlo.'

'Monaco?'

'Yes. We have an apartment there.'

While Inge made tea, Lauren settled herself on the huge sofa from which she could view the garden, with Putney Common beyond. She could hear the familiar sounds of cutlery clinking against china as Inge moved around next door humming softly to herself. The sitting room emanated a gentle calm. It was a room designed for friends to gather and relax in. Lauren savoured the peaceful moments she had to herself, registering with a shock how long it had been since she'd had time to relax. For a moment her heart swelled with gratitude. Inge had been absolutely brilliant, taking charge of the wailing Tom with the efficiency of someone used to handling small babies.

Now he was asleep in the shade of the garden. She could see the blue hood of the pram through the sliding glass doors that Inge had earlier unlatched and pulled apart. It was a little cold, but the early September breeze helped to clear her head and Tom was well wrapped up. Beyond, was a long narrow stretch of uneven grass with bald patches trimmed with various wild shrubs and bushes. Wild roses and the tail end of some honeysuckle climbed along the west-facing wall of the garden. The end wall by contrast was bald and patchy and crying out for something to adorn it. The garden had potential. Lauren's expert eye could see that. But it would need a lot of work. It seemed an ambitious house to take on for just two people and Lauren wondered if they had any children. Her eye roamed across the room but she couldn't see any of the usual telltale signs. Everything was too clean, too tidy. Pretty jugs had been filled with flowers. On the wall above the fireplace was a Patagonian photograph of Wolff taken just as he was about to serve. The shot was sepia-toned, with the exception of the tennis ball which had been tinted a luminous orange to attract attention to the brand label. Wolff's expression was one of intense concentration, angry veins highlighted on one side of his neck.

'It's my favourite picture of him,' said Inge, emerging from the kitchen with a wicker tray. 'He has so many pictures it was difficult to choose, but I didn't want the house to look like a tennis museum, so I just put up the one.'

'It's very powerful.'

'I think so.'

'How did you two meet?'

Inge put the tray onto the coffee table, inlaid, mosaic-like, with shards of broken pottery, and sat down.

'At Roland Garros during the French Open. I had brought along some of my pupils for *Les Enfants* day – Wolff being a hero to so many French children. After his match, well, two of the children asked for his autograph. He was very rude to them, telling them he didn't have time for it. So I spoke my mind to him. I think he was so surprised by my indignation that he asked me to have dinner with him. I made him ask six times before I finally said yes.'

Lauren smiled. 'Is that why you're so good with babies? Through teaching? Tom rarely responds so quickly to strangers.'

'I was a primary school teacher for five years,' Inge explained. 'But I learned most things from my older sister. She has three children of her own.'

'Still early days for you though?'

'Oh, it's not so early, I don't think so,' Inge smiled enigmatically.

The bright china cups and saucers, none of which matched made a successful mélange. There was a plate of biscuits and a home-made cake which Lauren guessed was coffee and walnut. At Annabel's her appetite had failed her. Relaxed now, her hunger returned.

'You're not too cold?' Inge asked, 'I can close the doors.'

'No. Keep them open. Winter will descend on us soon enough. It's not the cold I mind; it's the relentless dark afternoons.' Lauren's smile seemed to be full of foreboding. 'They can get a bit depressing.'

'Yes,' said Inge, understanding.

'You don't look remotely French.'

'No. Physically I am more like my mother. She's typically German looking; blonde hair, big bones, big nose.' Inge laughed, and her eyes widened and sparkled. 'My father is French. A very practical man. Demanding and sometimes difficult. But after twenty-five years of marriage my mother knows very well how to handle him, you know? They were in France for six years but my mother didn't like it. Now they live in Rheinberg, a small German town.'

Lauren shrugged, indicating she hadn't heard of it. She sipped her tea, steam warming her face as she held the cup to her lips.

'Of course, Rheinberg is only famous for producing the supermodel Claudia Schiffer. Did you ever work with her?' Inge asked the question politely, remembering that Lauren had been a successful model, but the fashion industry wasn't an area that interested her much.

'We did a show together but I wasn't in her league. She seemed nice enough . . .' Lauren trailed off. Lately she had lost the knack of making frivolous conversation.

She took one of the wafer-thin biscuits Inge offered her. It tasted of almonds and had a soft, chewy centre. A pale sun was breaking through the threatening rain clouds as Inge poured out more tea with strong capable hands. Watching her, Lauren considered the possibility of their becoming friends. For the first time in weeks she felt an urge to talk, to confess. No, that was the wrong word. And yet, and yet, she wanted to unburden herself, speak truthfully about the awfulness of Josh's death, how difficult she had found it to bear, alone and unable to express even to her closest friends what she really felt. She had carried around her grief, corked like some rancid fluid in a bottle. Not once had she cried but she realised that she'd make no progress in healing herself until she did. Looking at Inge, Lauren saw someone with whom she could reveal her feelings. It was just that here in the foreign intimacy of Inge's home she didn't know where to start. In the end she was helped by Inge herself.

'I would like now to say something. I never knew your husband but we felt his loss very much and I want you to know how sorry I am for you.'

The unexpectedness of her words was a shock. Most of Josh's friends, apart from Max, had skirted the subject of his death, afraid of what they might unleash. Their kindness, the concern they had shown at the start had all but vanished. Now they hardly ever called. It was as if they found being around her too painful. The period of mourning was over. She had reached the point where she was expected to get on with her life as before. Here, however, was a complete stranger who was prepared to take a risk. She was willing to talk about it because she wanted to be kind. Blood swam to the surface of Lauren's face and suddenly she was sobbing. Appalled, she brought her hands to her cheeks as if by doing so she could stem the violent onslaught of tears. But having started she found she couldn't stop. Not even the presence of Inge watching her could prevent them. It was as if within her an emotional dam had burst. Time ceased to exist. Lauren had no idea how long she cried. But when it was over she lay back against the fat cushions and felt an overwhelming sense of relief. Inge offered no conciliatory arm, no comforting words. She watched benignly, detached yet also gentle. Lauren was grateful for this.

Inge dug out a bottle and two small fine-cut glasses from one of the sitting-room cupboards.

'Let's have some schnapps,' she said gently.

Lauren blew into a man-sized Kleenex. She wiped her cheeks, licked her lips and tasted salt.

'I'm so sorry. I'm being absurdly emotional— You bring me to your lovely house, put my baby to sleep, make me tea and all I can do is—' She sniffed, using the tissue to tidy the corners of her nose. 'You must think I'm a wreck.'

'I think that it is wrong for you to go through this on your own.'

'Oh, it's not been that bad really,' Lauren said hastily, loath to sound melodramatic. 'I've just bottled things up.'

The schnapps tasted bitter but left a warm comforting

glow inside her. Lauren blew her nose again, then didn't know what to do with the used tissues. She ended up stuffing them into a pocket.

'Don't you get some help with Tom?'

'Yes, my sister Sukie – when she can, but she has a full-time job. My parents have been brilliant but they live in Sussex and both lead busy lives. I can't expect them just to drop everything.'

'But we've *masses* of space, darling,' Kay had stressed on her last visit to London, 'and we'd love to help out with Tom. We so rarely get to see you these days.'

Lauren took a sip of lukewarm tea wondering why she was admitting so much to a stranger.

'Is it cold?' Inge asked, indicating Lauren's tea.

'No,' Lauren protested, worried Inge would make some more, 'you've already done so much. You don't know how grateful I am just having someone to talk to.'

'I understand. Perhaps if you had some professional help—' Lauren glanced up sharply. 'A nanny, I mean.'

'No.'

'Why not? Do you have problems with money?'

Lauren winced. Inge was nothing if not direct. 'There have been . . .' she began, 'complications.'

Having been raised by a man who had always handled money so effortlessly (or so it had seemed until the Lloyds fiasco), it was hard for Lauren admitting even to herself what had been one of her husband's chief deficiencies. When Josh had signed with Advantage, he had been strongly advised to take out TTD, insurance cover in case of Temporary or Total Disablement. The premium of £5,000 would have meant a pay-out of £4,000,000. But with all the hype following Wimbledon and the changeover in management, the company had overlooked the fact that Josh had neglected to pay it. Which was unfortunate because only a few weeks before his death, and without telling her, Josh had bought almost three thousand acres of land in Telluride, Colorado. According to their lawyer, unless Lauren could offload it quickly, the payments would clean her out. In the case of Josh's endorsement deals, the money owed from the weeks Josh had been alive didn't amount to much. Letters of agreement had been exchanged with Advantage but nothing had been signed. As a result, the companies were dragging their feet about settling up.

'Josh died so suddenly,' Lauren said with a stoical shake of her shoulders. 'None of us could have foreseen what would happen.'

Some of the relief she had felt earlier now shifted to a sense of unease. All the problems she'd managed to blank out during her short visit with Inge now returned in their droves. She must stop talking about herself. She would only regret it later. Not that Inge seemed the type to gossip but you could never tell. Even the most genuine people sometimes behaved out of character and the tennis world was a small one. After all her efforts to keep things on an even keel it would be intolerable if word were to get out about how bad things really were.

'I've been admiring the way you've done this room,' Lauren said. 'So many people would have made the mistake of adding too much. You haven't done that.'

'We had very little furniture to start with,' Inge admitted, 'but anyway I don't like busy rooms. It is the garden that is a problem. Wolff has no interest in such things.'

'Oh, but I love gardening,' Lauren enthused, relieved to have something else to talk about. 'I could give you a hand.'

'I would like that very much.' Inge shifted in her chair and leaned forward so that her arms were supported by her knees.

'You know something, Lauren? You could maybe get a job. It might help things.'

A job! Lauren was shaken. 'And leave Tom? I couldn't possibly.' Automatically her eyes shot to the pram in the garden. 'Perhaps when he's older,' she said, half to herself, 'but it's much too soon now. These first few months are precious – they grow so quickly.'

But it was a shabby excuse. A job was exactly what she needed. She couldn't continue pretending that the money due from endorsement deals would be enough to live on. Going through Josh's desk a few days after the funeral she had found a blizzard of unpaid bills; credit cards, gas, water, electricity, H.P. It was clear from his bank statements that his spending had far exceeded his capital. Even so, Inge's sound advice wasn't what Lauren wanted to hear. She was still coming to terms with her bereavement. It was unthinkable to lose Tom too, even if it only meant for a few hours each day. There were other contributing worries. She was afraid to go back to work. What if she was now too old? What if she couldn't do it? Sustained breaks away from any career had their drawbacks, but from the fashion industry three years was a lifetime. The life of a model was brutally short-term and Lauren had witnessed far too many of her contemporaries attempt a comeback only to be greeted with a barrage of rejections. Those who had managed it lived on a financial roller coaster, one day earning £1,000, then nothing for the next three months. She drained the contents of her cup and carefully replaced it on its saucer.

'Listen to me harping on about all my silly problems,' she said brightly. Inge opened her mouth to protest. 'No, really, it's time we got going. Apart from anything else your sofa's so comfortable that if I don't move from it instantly you'll have me camped here for the night!'

The joke rolled over Inge's head. 'Of course you are very welcome to stay. There's plenty to eat and I am sure Wolff would enjoy meeting you.'

But Lauren had already reached the garden. 'Come on,

scallywag,' she said to her sleeping son, snapping free the pram brakes with her foot. 'Time you were in bed.'

Before she left, Inge handed her a piece of paper with her number scribbled on it.

'We will be leaving for New York in two days' time, but when we get back . . .' she shrugged her broad shoulders as though she didn't know what else to say, Lauren's new overly bright mood affecting her too. 'Well, I'm a good babysitter if you ever want one.'

'Thank you. I hope Wolff does well in the Open.'

When Lauren finally got back to the house in Somerset Road, Inge's sad departing smile lingering in her mind, the day's tension had been replaced with an almost mindless fatigue. She felt drained. She put Tom down, afraid he wouldn't sleep after having napped for so long at Inge's, but he drifted off immediately. Studying him, she noticed how each day he grew more and more like her. This saddened her because she longed for signs of Josh. Not a day went by when she didn't constantly think about him, long for him to be alive and with her. Sometimes the longing became so agonising she wondered if she had the strength to go on. Then she remembered Max's words the day they had buried Josh.

'You're so much stronger than you give yourself credit for, Lauren. And you are going to get through this. Not just for Tom's sake but for your own. Don't let Josh's death destroy what you two had or your chance of happiness. You found it once with him, one day you'll find it again. You've gotta believe that; hang on to it.'

"I am the resurrection and the life; he who believes in me, though he die, yet shall he live . . ."

Quite simply she couldn't have got through those first earth- shattering hours without Max. Later that night, after Keith had brought her the terrible news, Max appeared. He'd caught a flight back from Sharm and come directly

to the Wimbledon house. Quietly and effectively Max had
taken charge. He had wrapped her up in a blanket and
made her take a sleeping pill. Too upset to argue, she had
done as she was told and lay down on her bed like a child,
drowsy and feeling cared for. Even so, she was awake in
time to watch the milky dawn seep round the edges of her
bedroom curtains.

After the first breathless shock of the news, which made
her gasp and clutch for air as though someone was holding
her head under water, she remembered feeling a desperate
finality, an end of all she had ever known and understood.
Her life no longer made any sense to her.

Max had coped with the deluge of calls from the press
with the efficiency of a switchboard operator. He had even
organised the funeral. That same afternoon, her parents
drove up from Sussex – Max had had to fly out to Los
Angeles. He'd done what he could to get out of the match
(and for that she would always be grateful) but he had been
paid a guarantee of $250,000. Max was legally bound. Yet
he was back in time for the funeral having 'tanked' in the
first round.

Max, she thought now. Who would have believed it?

Mostly Lauren carried distorted memories of what had
taken place, but some things lingered; the vicar's kind and
sympathetic words, the neglected graveyard, the wilting
heat, the hundreds of flowers sent by fans, the ITF, the ATP,
the All England Club, who in a carefully worded statement,
said that 'the unique spirit of Josh was a tremendous loss to
the world of tennis'. Kay's voice shepherding everyone. 'You
come with us, Sukie. Robert can take one more. Frank, John,
can you go with Max?' The flat clack of car doors, rattling of
teacups and cake being passed round, the light bleeding out
of the sky, until finally she could stand it no longer and had
excused herself, locking herself in the upstairs bathroom to
be sick.

Then Josh's parents. Throughout her marriage Josh had said little about them, fobbing off her curiosity about his childhood with peculiar stubbornness. Why? Coming from such a happy family she found his behaviour entirely foreign. What had happened to make him so closed? To make him cut all ties with his past? With nothing to build on, Lauren began to imagine his parents as monsters. It was a surprise, therefore, that when she did finally meet the Kendalls (while on honeymoon in Australia) Lauren had instantly warmed to them. They were older than she had expected but very kind and touchingly devoted to their son. It seemed extraordinary to her that Josh had made so little effort to keep in touch.

The Kendalls had caught the first flight out from Sydney. Lauren drove to Heathrow to collect them, leaving Kay and Robert to babysit Tom. Mr Kendall was the first to emerge from arrivals. He reminded her so painfully of Josh; the same limber walk, the freckly arms, that disarming smile that had so captivated and won her heart. But some of the astonishing optimism that Josh had inherited from him was now missing. The change in Mrs Kendall was more startling. She seemed diminished as if grief had worn her down like water dripping methodically on a stone. The gold hair that she had once been so proud of now showed signs of thinning and was spattered with silver.

They spent just two nights with Lauren. Robert Miller did his best to keep everyone's spirits up, but Mrs Kendall seemed utterly lost, haunting the rooms her son had spent the last few months of his life in, a strained smile on her fragile face.

The night before their departure, Lauren had passed their bedroom on her way up to bed. The door was ajar and she could see Mrs Kendall sitting on the side of the bed, her husband's arm wrapped supportively around her shoulders.

'Both my babies gone,' she had sobbed in a voice so

wretched that Lauren could hardly bear to listen. 'It's my fault. It's *all* my fault. I'm being punished. I know I am. Oh, Doug, what now? How am I going to have the strength to carry on without them?'

It was the same question Lauren had been asking herself over and over. How to go on without him? It was only later, lying alone in the large double bed that she was struck by the implication of what Mrs Kendall had said. *Both my babies gone.*

Josh was their only child!

With Tom asleep, Lauren returned downstairs to the kitchen but couldn't be bothered to cook. Instead she made herself some hot milk which she laced with a drop of brandy. She ignored the pile of ironing, her vitamin tablets that she was supposed to take twice daily, the clean washing that needed to be taken out of the machine and hung up to air. She went into the sitting room. Several people had left messages, including Max, but they could all wait until the morning. It was a peculiar manifestation of death; suddenly everyone was overcome with grief; people whose names she had never heard were talking about Josh as if he were their best friend, wondering how they were going to survive without him. All of them hypocrites. They knew as much about the private Josh as the sporting magazines that wrote about him did.

Lauren gazed at their wedding photo on her writing desk. Captured on film, Josh's unmistakable grin shone into the room. A vibrant, gleaming animal he looked incapable of death, of such stillness. It was a face she thought she had known so well. Yet, already in her mind his features had become blurred. It seemed inconceivable, but she needed the photo to remind her what he looked like.

She let the frame fall onto its front, obscuring the picture. Then flopped on to the drawing-room sofa with her drink and a packet of shortbread and flicked the remote control on-button hoping to catch the news. On BBC2 they were showing a six-part documentary about the Royal Navy. ITV were running a repeat of *The Singing Detective*. The last thing she wanted to see was a middle-aged man suffering from psoriasis. She switched channels again just in time to hear the headlines.

They were all grim: more atrocities in Bosnia, a tube strike scheduled for the end of the week, a three-year-old girl's body found battered to death on a council estate.

Finding herself on the brink of tears, Lauren reached in her bag for the remaining tissues Inge had given her. Her hand touched a foreign object. Intrigued, she pulled it from the bag and examined it slowly. Odd how it had slipped her mind. Odder still had been her complete lack of fear when she'd taken it. Using her teeth she ripped off the Matches price tag and reread the price. Thirty-four pounds. A great deal of money for something so small, so light.

Lauren dozed. She had been conscious of swimming slowly to the surface, like a fish coming up for air, then sliding heavily back into slumber. When she finally woke it was with a jolt, having dreamt that Tom had been taken from her by bailiffs. Half-drugged with sleep she squinted at the television which was no longer showing programmes but was still flickering in the background. Fumbling between the cushions she found the remote control and switched it off. Then she tried to stand up and get herself to bed, but her limbs, like her eyes, felt so heavy. Giving in finally, she slid back into unconsciousness, holding the rich, silk scarf against her cheek as though she were afraid to let it go.

9

Melanie lay in the bath contemplating the early evening sky. She could see it through the slanted sky light, flushing from a pink eight o'clock sun. She felt a strong desire to paint it, capture its impossibly subtle rosiness, streaks of vibrant orange staining the horizontal clouds which promised another glorious day tomorrow. Dreamy and romantic, adjectives that lingered in her mind. Ideal for watercolours. Closing her eyes she planned the composition in her mind, the size, her starting point, how to capture the constant forming and reforming of the clouds. How clearly she saw it now. But to reproduce successfully what constantly shifted and changed onto paper was very different. She still had a great deal to learn and her work often frustrated her. But, oh, how she loved it. If it wasn't for Lottie still being at school she might apply to go to art college full time. But she was letting her thoughts run wild.

The phone rang in the hall. She contemplated not answering it. On the other hand she could never resist a ringing phone and it might be something important. She grabbed a towel and tiptoed back to the bedroom, trying not to get too much water on the carpet.

'Melanie?' said the voice on the other end.

Her heart skipped a beat. 'Hello.'

'Bad time to call?'

'Not at all. How are you, Hugo?' she said, testing his name like a child might, allowed for the first time to call a revered teacher by their Christian name.

'I'm well. Very well. Rushed off my feet at work but I'd be lying if I said I didn't enjoy it.'

Men and their work, she thought.

Hugo cleared his throat. 'I was just wondering how you were fixed for tomorrow night?'

'Tomorrow?' Oh, it wasn't *fair*! 'I have a class.'

'I didn't know you were a teacher.'

'Oh, I'm not. But I'm taking a one-year art course at the Wimbledon School of Art. I've already missed two nights, otherwise . . .'

'I *quite* understand,' said Hugo, rather more understandingly than she would have liked.

She wavered. 'What had you in mind?'

'Oh, just a cosy dinner for two at Quaglino's. I managed to get a table.'

Quaglino's! With Hugo Butler! Immediately she weakened.

'I don't suppose – I mean, if I were to miss one more night—Well, it wouldn't make that much difference.'

'I was hoping you'd say that. Give me your address? I'll come and pick you up.'

After she had hung up, Melanie sat on the floor gazing into space. Then she stood up again and returned to the bathroom turning off, on her way, a light Lottie had left burning in her room. Recklessly she crumbled the last of the Body Shop bath cubes into the water and immediately the faint smell of dewberry filled the steamy air. Lowering herself back into the hot water she could feel the gritty residue against her bottom. Melanie relaxed and closed her eyes.

'*Fuck*!' Wolff Bohakari slammed his racquet down in a fury, glaring at the spot were he was convinced the ball had landed. 'It was out!' he shouted. 'Any dumb-arsed fool can see that the ball was *OUT*!'

His eyes appealed to the umpire but Gil Boyd, chairing the

US Open's men's quarterfinals and one of the best umpires in the game, did not take kindly to Wolff's language. Nor was he about to indulge him. Solemnly shaking his head, he made a note on his score sheet indicating that the matter was closed.

Wolff stood resolute, his hands clamped mutinously against his hips as the hot swirling September wind of Flushing Meadow whipped around the court. He seemed to be struggling with himself, trying to overcome his churning emotions. Was he going to appeal? Bored by his unsportsmanlike behaviour, the intolerant crowd began a slow clap, with a few boos and whistles infiltrating the noise of an overhead plane.

Pacing the other end of the court to keep his muscles supple was Luke Falkner. He seemed remarkably calm. In fact, he looked altogether amused by Wolff's ungovernable rage. But then Luke could afford to be. He had already blasted one hundred and five aces past his four previous opponents during the last fortnight and now his deadly serve had effectively earned him the first two sets, putting him in the lead by three games to two in the third. Wolff losing his cool gave Luke an additional advantage.

Wolff realised that Gil wasn't going to relent and have them replay the point. Shaking his head, the French Algerian took up his position to receive serve and immediately found himself the unfortunate recipient of two blistering consecutive aces. Luke, smelling victory, punched the air.

'Game Falkner. Falkner leads by four games to two and by two sets to love.'

The pervasive volume of support from the crowd showed in no uncertain terms on which side of the net their loyalty lay. One row of fans hoping to attract the television cameras had on T-shirts which together spelt out *Luke the Duke*. Two young men waved FAULTLESS FALKNER boards, a young girl with cropped hair had painted the Canadian flag on her face. Angrily, Wolff stomped back to his chair making no attempt to hide his contempt for Gil. He clearly held the umpire responsible for his losing the game.

Wolff covered his head with a towel, blocking out the distracting crowd and beady-eyed press. He leant forward so that his elbows were resting on his knees and began muttering to himself. He was in despair. What else was there for him to fall back on? He had tried *everything*, every trick in the tennis bible but Luke just kept on attacking. The match was slipping away from him and he felt powerless to stop it.

Wolff learned to play tennis on clay. Throughout his career it had proved his winning surface, culminating with his first grand slam win on the red clay of Roland Garros. A powerful baseline player, he had one of the best returns of serve in the game, but his serve was unreliable and he rarely volleyed. Wolff only liked to approach the net to shake hands at the end of the match. Luke, on the other hand, was a natural serve volleyer and produced some of his best shots at the net. He had the additional advantage of four extra inches in height. No matter how hard Wolff pounded each ball, driving it hard and deep, the Canadian was still able to find a way to come in on the returns.

Pulling the towel off his head, Wolff used it to wipe the sweat from his hands. He only sweated in two areas; his feet and his hands. As a shy teenager his clammy hands had caused him a great deal of embarrassment with the opposite sex. But these days the only thing that concerned Wolff about his hands was the grip on his racquet. He glanced briefly round the court while one of the ball boys got him some more water. The US Stars and Stripes were everywhere; how the Yanks loved their flag, he thought contemptuously.

Adjusting his baseball cap, Gil Boyd called time. A final wipe down and the players changed ends, studiously avoiding eye contact with one another. As Luke sauntered towards the baseline he stopped suddenly and smiled at a pretty girl in the crowd. The press leaned forward in their seats, smelling an incident. With Luke, anything was likely to happen. He didn't disappoint them. Ignoring the increasingly frustrated Wolff waiting to serve, Luke ambled over to where the blonde was sitting and sat down next to her. Some spectators giggled, others glanced at the umpire to see how he would handle the situation. Wolff was one of them.

Luke was given a warning, but it seemed to have absolutely no effect. He whispered something to the girl who blushed furiously and handed him a slip of paper. Luke casually slipped it into his pocket, then ambled back to the baseline shrugging his shoulders at Gil as if to say, what's all the fuss about?

'Code violation to Mr Falkner,' announced Gil, delivering his punishment in a crisp voice. The crowd began to slow-clap.

Fiddling with the strings of his racquet, Wolff waited for the noise to die down before he resumed play. Then a funny thing happened. Luke completely misjudged the first serve. The second he hit wide, the third landed in the net. When Luke lost the next point it seemed as if his game had gone completely to pieces. His fans were stunned into silence, the fabulous-looking blonde gnawed at white knuckles. He missed several easy shots which cost him his own serve – the first time in the match Wolff had broken him. Baffled, Wolff nevertheless took advantage of his 'purple patch', snarling at Luke as he easily put away the next shot. But infuriatingly, all Luke did was grin stupidly at the girl in the crowd as if his only interest now was in her.

'Talk about flirting with danger!' said someone in the crowd.

With growing impatience, Wolff again complained to Gil

when Luke once more delayed play to do up his shoelace. 'Tell him to stop fooling around. He is stopping me from concentrating.'

And because he was so angry, Wolff misfired his next serve completely and hit one of the ball girls in the thigh. Despite the fact that he immediately rushed over to see that the girl was all right, several spectators booed. From his seat in the players' box, Wolff's world-weary coach, Ostoja, wearing futuristic sunglasses and a chain bracelet, contrived to look impassive.

'You are okay?' Wolff asked the ball girl, ignoring the noise. Stoically the chubby teenager nodded and resumed her position at the end of the net.

Then everything changed. Crouching like a hungry cat, Luke seemed to pull himself together and was suddenly a daring eighteen-year-old again, cruising through the next game without conceding a single point. Luke kept up the pressure and a self-destructive Wolff missed two backhands, the latter a mis-hit that brought giggles from the crowd. There were other distractions: one or two stray fans trying to bait the frustrated Wolff by whistling when he threw the ball up to serve; a baby crying; catcalling.

'Uuuaghh! How am I supposed to *concentrate*?' Wolff wailed. Which naturally brought more giggles.

Sensing Luke was only moments from victory, the cameras homed in on Wolff's face. The dropped shoulders, the resigned look he wore spoke volumes. It was one thing to fight a man who was on such burning form, but when you had the crowd against you – Wolff returned Luke's serve straight into the net.

'Game, set and match to Falkner.'

'He choked!' gasped Andrew Castle, Sky's resident commentator. 'I don't believe it. He let it go!'

The crowd thundered their approval. The lovely blonde, spilling out of her tight dress, looked like the cat who'd got the cream. Ostoja got up from his seat and left the court shaking his head. Wolff, who only two and a half hours ago had walked out convinced he would win, was so angry he couldn't even summon a smile as the two men briefly shook hands. It was no secret that they could hardly stand one another. Studiously ignoring Gil Boyd, Wolff grabbed his things and stormed off court without bothering to wait for Luke. Probably just as well. The Canadian was besieged by fans wanting their programmes signed.

'If you ask me, that's just darn right rude,' complained an American spectator. 'What kind of attitude is that? Darn well deserves to lose.'

'That's Krauts for you,' mumbled a man sitting next to him, his lips wrapped around a bulging hot dog.

The American looked confused, 'I thought he was French Algerian?'

'Yer, well, says it all, dunnit? Any chance of one of your beers, mate?'

Inge Bohakari was watching her husband play from her room at the Summit. She had meant to be there to support him, as she had been for all his other matches. But over the last few days, with the hectic schedule, the heat and so much to organise, she was now desperately tired. This morning she had been alarmed to find herself bleeding. Nothing serious, the hotel doctor had been quick to reassure her – just a slight haemorrhaging which was very common in the early months of first pregnancies. He had nevertheless advised her to take it easy for a few days, prescribing complete rest and no excitement. No excitement! The man didn't know her husband.

Only last week she had heard that one of the players' wives had miscarried in her fourth month. A gruelling schedule was blamed. Of course she hadn't voiced her fears to Wolff, but the sight of her bloodstained nightdress when she had woken this morning really had frightened her. Long after Wolff had gone, she had continued to check herself, dreading what she might find. But her worries were unfounded. The bleeding had stopped. She seemed to be over the worst.

Inge slumped back against the pillows, watching the television set as her husband left the court, muttering to himself with an almost perceptible black cloud over his head. Oh, Wolff, *mein Herzblatt*. Always the same. It was hard enough seeing him lose. But today's vitriolic display had upset her more than usual. This year alone Wolff had been fined four times at ATP tournaments, running up a total penalty of $6,000. The money itself was irrelevant to Wolff but the fact that he'd been fined in five of the eight tournaments he had played in indicated a pattern. And that was worrying. Inge knew precisely what her husband had invested into preparing for the last of the year's grand slams; hours toiling away in the gymnasium, training with his coach Ostoja, studying opponents' shots on the VCR. If he could just have kept his concentration and put behind him the errors of the second set. But he had lashed out at the ball, hitting it in a blind rage instead of using the game plan Ostoja had worked so diligently on with him. He hadn't won a title since the French Open last year which meant his world ranking had dropped from eight to twenty-three. His dream of winning this year's Wimbledon title had been crushed. And now the US Open was gone. How, she wondered uneasily, would this latest setback affect him?

In some ways, Wolff was experiencing something almost every good young player went through and Inge understood this. The early days of playing on tour often felt intimidating. Players were excited, but much like a pupil's first term at school, they took time to settle in. Then a year or two down the track and friends and contacts had been established. Wolff began to feel comfortable. There was no real pressure. No one expected him to do much. Not until his third year as a pro when Wolff's ranking jumped from two hundred to the dizzy heights of thirty-four in the world. Quite suddenly the spotlight was on him; he was under everyone's scrutiny. It was no longer just a question of making points, but protecting the ones he already had.

Restlessly Inge turned on her side careful not to cover her good right ear – she was deaf in her left one. Maybe it was being cooped up in this stuffy hotel room with windows you couldn't open that unsettled her. Or the fact that she was so far from her adopted England. Inge was a natural home bird and yearned to set her energies loose on their new home, her nest. New York with its skyscrapers that cast whole neighbourhoods into darkness and vulgar neon signs did nothing for her. There were no villages, no towns, no sense of community. It was disorientating. But right from the start of their relationship Inge had made a conscious decision to accompany Wolff abroad. The alternative was not to see him half the year. She hated the angry brawling chaos of Flushing Meadow; the hot menacing winds, the planes that roared overhead. The equally disrespectful spectators who paid no attention to the stewards half-heartedly trying to get them to sit down. How the players were able to concentrate baffled her.

She knew Wolff would be castigating himself. If only he could somehow learn to curb his temper. But Inge had known what she was taking on when she married him. Difficult men held no fear for her – hadn't she been raised by one? The irony was that the private Wolff, the Wolff she had grown to know was so different from the sullen man the fans saw on court. She had been drawn to the dark suspicious gaze that made him look like a stray dog that had been badly hurt and kicked around. Wolff rarely talked about his experiences as a boy in Algeria, but she could guess. It was in his eyes. It didn't take a degree in psychology to understand the need in him to beat other players all the time; the destructive element which shut out anyone who attempted to get close – until she had come along, determined to prove to him how rewarding the love of a family could be.

They flew back to England the next day, after being given a reluctant okay from the hotel's doctor. Still brooding over his embarrassing defeat and from having been given an earful by a furious Óstoja, Wolff hardly said a word during the flight. Vengefully, he paced the aisles of first class. Being cooped up in a small confined space for several hours was not something Wolff took kindly to. His black mood hung in the air like a migraine. But recognising that there was little she could do when he was like this, Inge sensibly kept her distance.

Back in the Putney house, their suitcases littering the hall, Wolff checked his post.

'Good,' he said, holding up a tournament registration form, 'I'm in. The Cologne Open,' he said to his wife's questioning expression.

Wearily, Inge collapsed onto the sofa, worried about a new dull ache throbbing in her lower abdomen.

'When is it?'

'In three days.' He looked at his watch. 'I should check flights.'

'Wolff,' Inge had slipped back into her native German, 'didn't we agree we would spend some time together at home?'

'That was before the US Open,' Wolff had picked up the receiver but when he caught sight of Inge's expression, he hung up.

'Darling, Cologne is an opportunity because so many of the top players are still out in New York. I could win this one.'

Inge raised her shoulders good-humouredly. He was right. He needed some good results. According to the ATP rules a player could play as many tournaments as he wished but only his best fourteen results (which were added up) counted in the rankings. Thus far, it had been a disastrous year for Wolff.

He sat down next to her and took her hand.

'Ostoja's fixed it. Six days. It's not so long. I promise to take it more easy when I'm back. *Tiens, chérie,*' he said more gently, noticing for the first time how pale his wife was. 'Maybe this time I should go alone?'

She inspected his hand, frowning. Wolff wasn't good on his own. Who would be there to calm him down if he fell into one of his rages? Ostoja was worth every penny they were paying him – despite Wolff's current poor form. The long term the changes they were making to Wolff's game would soon be worth the current sacrifices. But Ostoja couldn't provide the emotional support that was crucial to Wolff's psychological welfare.

Wolff swung his body round and stretched out on the sofa, his head pillowed in Inge's lap. She put a loving hand to his long face, exploring the still surprising edges. It was a face that could in no way be described as handsome but then she had never been drawn to handsome men. There was something shallow about male beauty, particularly in the tennis world; a commonplace which devalued it. Wolff's face was gaunt and sketched with too many lines for a man of his age. It was a face with lots of contradictions; a commanding nose, a mouth that was full and feminine, eyelashes thick like a child's fringing enormous Bovril-coloured eyes. She loved his face – all the tempestuous expressions that flooded across it. And when he smiled, very occasionally as he did now, the effect was miraculous.

'You are sure this is what you want, *mein Schatz?*' she murmured, raking the hair above his ears with her fingertips.

'You heard the doctor in New York. You are supposed to be resting.'

'I know.'

'Then it is decided.'

Despite threatening rain clouds, Wolff disappeared for the afternoon to play golf at the Roehampton Golf Club. He had only been playing for three years but it was already becoming an obsession. Inge gathered her strength at home with a cup of coffee and a quick read of the paper. Then wished she hadn't. On the back page of the sport's section was a picture of Wolff smashing his racquet to the ground:

> *Tennis personalities prevail, but are these the sorts of role models we want for our kids? Doubtless it was galling to be ousted from the quarterfinals of the US Open in straight sets by long-term rival Luke Falkner, but Walid 'Wolff' Bohakari's behaviour yesterday over one of many clashes with umpire Gil Boyd was inexcusable. In a match that featured more fits of pique than glimpses of brilliance, Bohakari was beaten as much by his own irritability as by the faultless play of Falkner. Though he had reason to be annoyed with Falkner for showing off to the crowd, Bohakari let his six-five lead in the first set slide, and from then on was never really in the game. After being warned for an audible obscenity, he was penalised a point for ball abuse, and was fortunate to escape further punishment for throwing his racquet at the ball box next to the umpire's chair. According to the tennis code of conduct he could have (some say should have) been defaulted.*

Unwilling to read any more, Inge folded the paper and slipped it into the bin. With luck Wolff wouldn't have had a chance to see it. She unpacked Wolff's kit: plasters, strappings, dirty socks, and loaded up the washing machine. She contemplated going out to do a food shop, but at about four

the heavens opened and discharged a furious downpour.
The shopping would have to wait. Next to the phone she
noticed two letters addressed to her. One from her mother
– she recognised the bold, neat writing instantly. The other,
typed, looked like a bill. This she opened first. She blanched
as she read the contents. It was another of those hate letters.
How could someone *do* this! Since marrying Wolff she had
received countless letters accusing her of, amongst other
things, being after Wolff's money. She had also suffered
racist slurs. Not that Wolff had escaped unscathed. North
Africans in France were not popular. Of course, the police
had been informed. They had been quick to point out that
nine times out of ten it was just some harmless crank. The
recurring threats, however, had eventually persuaded them
to sell up their Paris home and move to England. They kept
the Monaco apartment as a base. Inge frowned at the letter in
her hand. Why would people write such things? What harm
had she done anyone?

When Wolff got back he was soaked to the skin, his shoes
squelching across her clean kitchen floor.

'Here,' he murmured, handing her a bedraggled bunch
of daisies. 'For putting up with me.'

Trouble flowers, she thought with a smile as she searched
for a vase. Wolff only ever bought them when he had stayed
out too long, forgotten a social event or had behaved badly.
She buried her nose in the white, dripping scentless faces.

By the time she had remembered the anonymous letter
it was too late. Wolff left early the following morning
immediately after breakfast. As with all his meals he ate
with the concentration and speed of someone afraid his
plate would be snatched away before he had finished.
Inge had insisted on driving him to the airport, but when
she got home she felt jolted and sick. The bleeding had
resumed. Just a few spots of blood, but enough to launch
her straight back to bed. Cradling one of the pillows in her

arms, she glanced out at the watery blue sky and the tops of limes that lined the street, shivering and swaying in the wind. The forecast had promised an afternoon of sun, but it didn't look very likely. For the first time since she had arrived in England, Inge felt a stab of loneliness. If only she knew someone she could ask round. There were one or two friends she had made at the community centre when she sometimes helped out, but she had little in common with either of them. It was to be expected, she supposed, joining the travelling caravan of players, wives, girlfriends and coaches that jetted around the world circuit. Unless you had an outgoing and trusting personality, it was hard to make new friends. Wolff was so utterly absorbed in his tennis that it excluded everyone apart from a handful of people either directly or indirectly involved in the game. And most of them she quickly discovered were fairly colourless. Inge was quite content with her own company, but sometimes she found the instability of her married life quite hard. Like today. She yearned for another female to confide in, who could understand how she was feeling.

Then she thought of Lauren Kendall. They hadn't spoken since that day she had asked her round for tea, but Inge sensed that if she were to call, Lauren would welcome it. Perhaps Lauren had gone through the same thing when she was pregnant with Tom. It would help to talk about it, ease her mind. She decided to try. When she dialled the number, however, all she got was a recording. She almost hung up, then changed her mind and left a brief message. Oh, well, she thought a little despondently, she had tried.

She decided to make herself some tea. She hadn't eaten all day, but for some reason her appetite had gone. At least she wasn't still feeling sick. That was one thing about being pregnant she wouldn't miss.

Halfway across the bedroom, she was suddenly gripped by a blinding cramping pain in her stomach. She stumbled towards the en suite bathroom, clutching at pieces of furniture to steady herself. The next spasm brought her crashing to the floor. She had never known pain like it. Sobbing, she tried to haul herself up.

Breathe, she told herself, concentrate on your breathing. But even as she thought the words, she was filled with an icy terror. The level of pain was intensifying. She didn't know what to do. She had reached the bathroom now and gripped the sides of the loo seat. Perhaps she should just stay still. Wait for the pain to subside, then call her doctor. She tried to remember what he had said. Surely, this wasn't right. She focused on her breathing. Slowly, in and out, in and out, pushing oxygen all the way down to her thorax, all the time trying to steady the terrific beat of her heart.

The phone was ringing in the bedroom. Should she try to answer it or stay where she was. She decided to risk it. The pain had eased slightly. Perhaps she was going to be all right after all. If she was, she vowed to spend the rest of the week in bed, even if she had to go without food. Gingerly, she crawled back to the phone on her hands and knees, praying illogically that it would be Wolff.

'Hello,' she croaked.

'Inge?' Lauren's voice. 'Hi, I'm sorry I wasn't in when you called. I had to take Tom down to the surgery for one of his jabs. Screamed blue bloody murder, I can tell you.'

'Please,' Inge sobbed, her voice cracking.

'God you sound terrible. What is it? What's wrong?'

'Help me . . .'

'I'm on my way.'

But Inge didn't hear any more. The pain had returned with a renewed force, ripping through her like a piece of jagged glass. She groaned, feeling saliva swirl in her mouth and dropped the phone to the floor. Lauren was coming. Lauren was going to help her. Over and over she kept on repeating this to herself. She was suddenly consumed by a need to empty her bowels. As she stumbled back to the bathroom, she vomited into the bath.

Less than a minute later, sprawled on the floor, she watched helplessly as fat crimson clots slithered from between her thighs and onto the floor.

Wolff returned in a victorious mood after his convincing win of the Cologne Open. It seemed as though the six days he had been away had rolled by so quickly they felt more like three. Perhaps because they'd been such good ones. Tucked safely inside his bag was the trophy and a cheque for his share of the $300,000 prize money. Both went a long way to salvaging his bruised ego. For once he had kept his head, playing with some of his old verve. Ostoja had been ecstatic, voicing his desire to get to work immediately on a new strategy he'd formulated. Wolff had twice called Inge during the week and then again from the airport to say when he'd be home. He didn't want her to worry about picking him up as he was going to get a lift with Ostoja. But he kept getting the machine, so he left only a brief message – he had never been good with phones.

By the time he reached the Vicarage it was plunged in darkness. This surprised him. Had Inge gone to bed already? Almost eleven, he noted, peering at his digital watch. It was quite late. But riding high on a cloud of victory, Ostoja had insisted on stopping off for a celebratory pint and a Chinese takeaway. Wolff knew Inge wouldn't mind. She was good like that. Didn't nag at him like some of the women he had known before her.

As he slipped his key into the lock, Wolff smiled to himself. He couldn't wait to see the look on her face when he told her the news. His first win in months! Opening the front door, he switched on the light and called his wife's name, his buoyant voice breaking the silence. Nothing. He waited a few moments. Strange. Inge always made a point of welcoming him home. And although he was reluctant to admit it, he had grown used to her demonstrative affection.

Wolff was about to race upstairs when Inge suddenly appeared on the top landing. Light seeped from the half-open door of their bedroom casting a sherry colour on the carpet. He could see the generous outline of her body through the thin nightdress she wore.

'Hi,' he said, wondering why he was whispering, 'I tried to call you.'

Inge stood motionless, her eyes wide and vacant, arms limp against her sides as if she had just woken from a deep sleep.

'Inge?' he said hesitantly.

No response. He felt the first flicker of fear. 'Inge, you're worrying me. What's wrong?'

She took a faltering step towards him, her right foot edging over the top step. Afraid she might fall, Wolff leapt upstairs and caught her in his arms. She looked so unusually pale, so fragile.

'What is it?' he demanded, shaking her rather more forcefully than he meant to because he had never seen her like this before.

Inge looked at him. What Wolff read in her eyes triggered off a sudden terrible alarm.

'We lost it,' she said, her voice soft and scratchy with fatigue, 'Wolff, we lost our baby.'

He couldn't speak, couldn't find any words to comfort his wife. He just knelt there with a wounded puzzled look on his face. Inge smoothed her fingers across his eyes, wanting to shield him from the pain she knew he was experiencing.

'I'm sorry, I'm so sorry,' she sobbed. 'Forgive me.'

Somewhere in the distance an owl hooted. Through the banisters Wolff could see his sports bag at the foot of the stairs. Just a few hours ago he had proudly held the Cologne trophy up for the cheering German crowd. Now it meant nothing to him. With terrible composure, he pulled himself up, his wife in his arms, and carried her back to their bed. When he was certain she was asleep he went to the window and opened it. He stood perfectly still, the wind ruffling his dark hair, rain, like sharp grey splinters stinging his cheeks. It fell in long, steady slants throughout the night, illuminated by the occasional passing car.

It wasn't until seven the following morning when Inge woke up and spoke to him, that Wolff realised how long he had been standing there.

10

'Ah, but you're a sweet little t'ing. You have your mummy's eyes, so you do.'

'You think so?' said Lauren.

The saleswoman bent her grey head towards Tom for a further inspection, then looked up and said decisively, 'The little fella has you written all over his face. It's as plain as daylight, there for all to see, so it is.'

She handed Lauren her receipt. 'That there now has your delivery date on it. They should be with you between seven thirty and noon on Friday. I doubt if you'll have any problems but if you were to, be sure to give us a call on that number there that I've circled.'

'Thank you.'

'Miss,' the woman said, letting a motherly hand rest on Lauren's arm just for a second, 'I get this feeling that I've seen you before. It's your hair, you see. You have the most beautiful hair.'

'Oh, now . . .'

'You do so. I'd kill to have hair like that. D'you mind if I ask you where you get it cut? It's just that I have this niece, you see.'

Lauren, anxious to put a stop to this already prolonged conversation, shrugged as if she couldn't remember. In her modelling days, she used to be able to stroll into Vidal Sassoon whenever she liked and get it cut free. These days she trimmed it herself. How times had changed.

She wheeled Tom's pushchair through to the lighting

department which blazed with hundreds of bulbs. Nothing of much interest here. So she took the lift back up to ground level and found herself in books. Mmmm. She needed a new road atlas for the Discovery. Their old one was falling apart. Theirs? No. Hers now. Just hers. She hunted round for maps then found herself drawn towards the hardback section. She picked up a copy of *French Antiques* and opened it. The thick, glossy pages smelt faintly of chemicals. The aroma lingered in her nostrils. As she flicked through the lovingly compiled illustrations, Lauren suddenly thought what a nice gift it would make for Inge. The poor thing could do with a bit of cheering up.

She would never forget that awful afternoon: Inge's uncharacteristically weak voice on the phone that had driven Lauren next door, pleading with her neighbours to look after Tom for just an hour or so. Then shooting off down Roehampton Lane towards Putney all the time wondering what on earth could be wrong. By the time she had reached the Vicarage there was no answer. Three times she rang. In a panic she had finally broken in through the back kitchen window praying that she wouldn't set off any alarms. When she found Inge lying inert on the upstairs bathroom floor, her immediate thought was that she was dead. Until, that was, she had seen Inge's blood-stained thighs and then worked the rest out for herself. There followed a nightmare journey to the hospital – Inge, who she had managed to get up from the floor, was adamant that she was all right, but Lauren had insisted on taking her to Queen Mary's. Never in her life had she witnessed such a production line of appalling injuries as had poured through the doors. A waiting room that reeked of pain and death. One poor little boy had lost all four fingers on one hand. Good God! What if it had been Tom!

'Excuse me,' said a man, reaching across her to get a book on the bottom shelf. Lauren noticed he wore shoes rather like a pair Josh used to have.

She turned to the inside front cover. Forty-two pounds! She couldn't afford to spend that on a gift. Oh, but it was a pity. She'd already decided on getting it for Inge. But the washing machine had cost a fortune and all those outstanding bills lying ignored on her desk—

'Sorry.' The man with Josh's shoes leaned across her, swapping the book he'd picked up for another one. 'Can't decide.'

Lauren stepped further back from the cloying odour of his cologne. Tom, making whiny disgruntled sounds, was beginning to wake up. She had only fed him an hour ago. He *couldn't* be hungry again so soon. Reluctant to give up the book, she glanced casually around the busy department. She caught the man eyeing her up. She ignored him. Go away, she thought irritably, go and find someone else to annoy. Adrenaline bubbled up and churned through her veins. Go on, a voice inside had said. Do it now. With her eyes fixed on the two overextended sales assistants serving at the nearby till, Lauren casually slipped the antique book in Tom's pram then quickly picked up another book – one on fly fishing – and flicked through it as though she were undecided. The moment the man wearing Josh's shoes left with his book, she returned the one she had in her hand to the shelf, grabbed her bag from the floor and placed it in the pram so that the antique book was hidden.

Immediately this was done Lauren wheeled Tom away from the department, losing herself in the crowd of weekend shoppers. She walked briskly, though not too fast, passing through stationery, then scarves, one of which she idly stroked, then through to cosmetics where she had stopped earlier to buy some face cream, her eyes glued to the exit signs. Everywhere she looked there were mirrors. It was difficult to judge who the multiple reflections advantaged; her, the thief, or the security guards that must surely be hovering, watchful.

Tom's face was scrunched up in anger now. He was wiggling around, agitated, kicking out with his legs, working himself into a state. She *must* get him out. Lauren felt a fog settle onto her head. Her ears were beginning to hum. It was insufferably hot. She longed to remove her coat but dared not attract attention to herself. The main exit doors took days to reach. She was almost there when she heard a voice behind her say,

'Excuse me, miss.'

As if on cue, Tom opened his mouth, wide, wide, wide and began to wail. The humming in Lauren's ears intensified. Not now, Tom. Not now, *please*. She continued walking.

'I say, *EXCUSE ME*,' the voice was sharper now, clear and loud like an intercom. Oh, God.

'Could someone stop that woman for me before she leaves.'

A knife of terror plunged through Lauren's heart. They had seen her take the book. Somehow she had known they would. She felt a strong desire to be sick. Slowly she turned round, blood draining from her face.

'You forgot your purse.' The girl behind the counter was smiling. Only it wasn't Lauren she was smiling at. It was another woman.

'Oh, you sweetheart,' the woman said, clucking, 'I'd forget my head given half a chance.'

Weak with relief, Lauren threw her weight against the store's heavy glass doors and pulled Tom's pram after her into the bright sunlight. She'd done it!

She was amazed by how easy it had been.

The sun was warm on her face and the back of her legs. She slowed her pace, relaxing her shoulders which had been hunched practically up to her ears. Now that they were in the fresh air Tom had settled down. Unable to resist, she slipped a hand under her bag and rummaged for the book. It felt like a prize.

Three blocks on she passed a wretched-looking 'new age' beggar holed up in the doorway of a café and read the sign at his feet:

'HOMELESS AND COLD. HAVEN'T EATEN IN TWO DAYS.'

Impulsively, Lauren snapped down the pram brake and entered the café. Minutes later she re-emerged with a steak and kidney pie and a cup of tea. She offered them to the young man.

'What's this?' he asked, peering suspiciously at the food.

'Steak and kidney pie. And some hot tea.'

He looked at her indignantly. 'But I'm a vegetarian!'

Lauren laughed. So much for charitable impulses. She made her way back to the car, dumping the incriminating book deep into the boot with the rest of the shopping. Not that she feared the lawful hand on the shoulder – it was just a precaution. She realised that had anyone intended arresting her they would have done so as she'd left the department store. She strapped the groggy, half-protesting Tom into his car seat, then slipped the Discovery into drive.

By the time they got home she was still trembling, but from a sense of triumph. There was an agreeable shifting in her gut, an excited tightening of muscles as she considered the prospect of stealing again. The moment she had fed Tom, she would call Inge and arrange to go round. The matter felt urgent to her, as if the high of what she had done was not in itself enough. She wanted to see Inge's face when she handed over her 'gift'.

She was still deep in thought as she unloaded the shopping and pram from the boot. Thankfully Tom had decided he was much too tired to scream any more and had gone back to sleep. She had just put her key in the front-door lock when she heard a voice behind her.

'You're here. My luck's in.'

She spun round.

'Hello, Lauren.'

'Max!'

Her eyes dropped guiltily to the bag of shopping which now held Inge's book. She had some absurd notion of the book becoming suddenly animate, leaping from the bag and denouncing her. A plane roared by overhead, invisible above the clouds.

'Did I catch you at a bad moment?'

'Not at all.'

'Been shopping?'

'For a washing machine. My old one blew up yesterday. Oh,' she said, dismissing Max's expression of alarm with a wave of her hand, 'nothing remotely exciting happened. More of a pop than a bang really. One of the main parts blew up and as it had already been fixed once I was advised to get a new one.'

'Here,' said Max, grabbing the bag, 'let me give you a hand.'

'Thanks. I'll get Tom.' Her son stirred as she picked him up. 'Sorry if I seemed startled just now, only you're a bit of a surprise.'

'A nice one, I hope.' Max put a finger to Tom's nose. 'Hey, Tom, how're you doing? I got here half an hour ago – been sitting over there on the wall enjoying the sun. Told myself I'd give it another five minutes then head off. I'm catching an eight o'clock flight.'

'When did you get in?'

He grinned. 'This morning.'

'Same old Max. Elusive as always.' Lauren gave him one of her Mona Lisa smiles then reached up to kiss him on the cheek, 'Of course, it's good to see you. Come on in.' She nudged open the door with her foot. 'I'll make us some tea.'

'Not like you to forget the alarm,' he said, following her in.

'It's on the blink. Can't figure out what's wrong with it.'

Max frowned. 'You should get someone to fix it, Lauren. A big house like this. You and the kid on your own— Where d'you want this?'

'The table will do.'

'You look well,' she said a little later when Tom had been put down and the two of them had settled themselves in the snug kitchen. Max's dark glossy brown hair had grown to his collar and the recent tan he had picked up made his whole face come alive.

'And you're always telling me that living in the fast lane is bad for me.'

'Well, there are exceptions, Max. And you seem to be one of them. You'll probably outlive us all.' There was a slight pause as they both digested what she had just said. 'Why are you here, anyway? You were playing in the US Open. I watched your third round on Sky.'

Max tapped the side of his right ankle, 'Tendonitis. It went on me in the fourth. God, I was pissed! Felt I was on really good form – hard court is my best surface. But there wasn't a damn thing I could do and I didn't want to risk a more serious injury by forcing it. My fault. I've had this problem before. Too many exhibition matches. All I can do now is rest up.'

'For how long?'

'A month. Maybe less if I'm lucky.' He glanced down at his mug. 'Luke's doing well – you remember the Canadian?' Lauren nodded. 'Good chance of winning, that guy. He's on really top form.'

'Do I detect a trace of envy in your voice?'

Max shrugged, 'It'd be nice to have another title. But it's a new game out there and it's not just down to racquet technology. Players are younger, faster and a hell of a lot fitter too.'

'You're one of the fittest people I know.'

'It's the mental state that counts – remember that dry period with Josh? Sometimes it's hard not letting things get to you when the press start referring to you as the "Old Master". Makes me sound like a total has-been.' He looked at her challengingly, as if to say and don't you dare feel sorry for me. Lauren tactfully changed the subject.

'Tell me about Tiffany?'

'She's good.'

Lauren's eyes filled with exasperation. Max wasn't known for expansive chat. 'Why isn't she here with you? I thought you two were inseparable?'

Max pointed a finger. 'And you can cut the romantics right out. Tiffany had to go back to Florida. Her dad's having a few domestic problems.'

'Oh?'

'Wife number three's about to walk out. Guess Tiffany thought she could help.'

'You don't look convinced.'

'Not at all. When it comes to her dad, Tiffany and I don't have much to agree on.'

'Parents-in-law can often be tricky,' said Lauren sympathetically.

'I'm not married to her, Lauren, nor am I looking to be.'

That surprised her. 'Oh, but I thought this time it was serious?'

'Hey, Tiffany's a great girl; beautiful, smart and independent. We have a good time together. Why spoil that?'

Unconvinced, Lauren got up and walked to the sink, picturing the tall woman: delicate, a pale freckled face, that lovely reddish-brown hair.

'Sounds like a big cop-out to me. More tea?' she asked, refilling the kettle.

Max looked at his watch. 'Okay, but just a quick one. I should be heading off pretty soon. Tell me, have you seen much of your sister lately?'

'Sukie?'

He came clean. 'Luke's been hassling me. Seems like she made a bit of an impression. My personal advice was to stay well clear but he's not going to listen to me.'

Lauren returned his smile and got out a packet of biscuits. 'Funny you should bring her up. Sukie's coming over for supper later tonight. Shame you have to leave, otherwise I'd have asked you to join us.'

'Next time.'

The phone rang. While Lauren spoke Max got up with his mug of tea and wandered into the drawing room across the hall. He took a sip of the hot, sweet Earl Grey, puzzled by the fact that the only time he ended up drinking the stuff was when he visited Lauren. Lauren and her English ways. He walked over to the large sash windows, pausing to study a wedding photograph of Lauren and Josh. He picked it up. Christ! And they looked so much in love. What a mess. What a goddamn mess. He glanced towards the light, memories clicking at random like a slide show: the first time he saw Josh, a brash, overly keen teenager with a blush of spots scattered across his cheeks; the day Josh yelled at some kid fooling around with a knife. The boy hadn't been doing anyone any harm but Josh had gone berserk, put the fear of God in him; slogging it out at SW19, Josh robbing him of his second win of the title; the antiseptic smell of the hospital waiting room and Josh's astonished face as he emerged to announce the birth of his son; Lauren in blue-black, inscrutable behind her dark glasses, dangerously calm. Her gloved hand tossing the tiny bouquet of sweet peas on to the lowered coffin; and then, inexplicably, an image of his own mother leaning down to do up his shoes.

He blinked, focusing again on the photograph he held. After only three brief months his recollection of the Wimbledon final had become distant and blurred (selective amnesia?). Yet now, it returned in sharp focus burning

indelibly on his optic nerve. He turned his head sideways
and glanced across the hall at Lauren, still talking on the
phone. She was in jeans and wearing a fisherman's sweater,
its bulk unable to disguise the fact that she had lost weight.
Too much, he thought. There was subtle evidence of fatigue
too, and strain in the slope of her shoulders. How was she
coping? She hadn't talked about it yet but he guessed that
the heavier stuff would come later, when she had got used
to having him around again. He felt slightly irritated by their
conversation. Not that talking to her about girlfriends had
ever bothered him before, but he sensed that she no longer
accepted his cavalier behaviour in quite the same way. Was
it disapproval? Well why, damn it? He'd meant what he'd said
about Tiffany. He had been with her for almost a year now.
Didn't that count for something?

As he returned the photo to its spot next to a silver
bowl of roses, his eye rested on a pile of bills. Lazily,
he glanced through some of the top ones, most of which
seemed to have been outstanding for several weeks. One
letter in particular caught his attention, a letter from Visa
threatening court action if the account for nine thousand
pounds wasn't immediately settled. Was it possible Lauren
was having financial problems? Surely not.

Back in the kitchen, Lauren was replacing the receiver.

'Bloody press!' she muttered.

Max eased himself back into his chair.

'Hassles?'

'Oh, probably nothing. It was just some sports journalist,
a Colin Banks, claiming he's writing a biography of Josh.
He wanted to come round and interview me.'

Max narrowed his sherry-brown eyes. 'What did you
tell him?'

'I told him no, of course. It's too soon for anything like
that. Hard to tell his age but he sounded very pushy. The
sort that likes to get his own way.'

'Know the type well. Guess he lucked out today.'

'Mmmm,' said Lauren thoughtfully, 'probably lied about which paper he worked for too. Oh, well,' she poured boiling water into the teapot, 'don't suppose I'll hear from him again.'

Before he left, Max made her promise to get the alarm fixed. Then he had put his hands on her shoulders and her face had grown solemn.

'Lauren,' he said gently.

'Don't, Max.' He could see her eyes brimming with tears. 'I'll fall apart.'

'Hey, this is me, remember?'

'No, I can't.'

'Okay. I understand if you don't want to talk about it, but I'm here if you need me. Just a plane ride away.'

Her quivering smile didn't convince either of them.

'Josh was lucky to have a friend like you, Max.'

'*You* got me too.'

She let him hold her against his six-foot-two-inch frame, then squeezed his arm gratefully. 'Go on now or you'll miss your plane.'

As he went down the drive he turned and gave her one final wave. The house was now golden in the sunset. He looked at Lauren thinking she would say something, anything. But she didn't. She went into the house and shut the door behind her. Then he thought about the bills he had found in the drawing room, the washing machine that had packed up, the broken alarm and he felt, for the first time that day, his tiredness. In three days he'd had less than twelve hours' sleep. A decade ago he wouldn't have given it a moment's thought but after years of relentlessly chasing tennis balls, his body was beginning to rebel.

A black cab cruised into sight and he hailed it.

By the time it had reached Heathrow, Max was fast asleep in the back.

*   *   *

After Max had gone, Lauren went upstairs to check on Tom. He was sleeping peacefully but she felt a sudden urge to pick him up and feel the comfort of his tiny body. She resisted it. Some nights when she awoke from a bad dream she would go into his room and hold a mirror in front of his face to check he was breathing. She couldn't shake off the fear that one day Tom would be taken from her too.

Stepping back out onto the landing, she closed the door gently behind her and glanced across at the room that had been Josh's study. All his things had been stored there. For weeks she had been putting off going through them. She couldn't go on delaying it for ever. The time had come. Time for her to let a small part of him go. Taking a deep breath, she approached the door and opened it.

She is lying on the bed with one arm wrapped around his sleeping torso, the palm of her hand flattened against his chest, pulling him, her honeymoon man, closer to her. Her nose is pressed against the strong indent of his neck. She breathes in the sweet smell which has become as familiar as her own, then sucks the skin like a baby. From the half-open window she hears the purring of a kookaburra, cicadas buzzing their relentless, pulsing song, the faint rustling of warm wind in the jacaranda trees. Leisurely, she slides her hand downwards along the wiry, thickening path of hair until it reaches his flaccid penis. She cradles it, enjoying the fleshy warmth it exudes. As it thickens and grows beyond the bounds of her fingers, he swivels round. And when, in half-sleep his mouth opens to meet hers, she finds the peace she has been looking for.

When Lauren re-emerged almost three hours later, she had sorted through most of the stuff; clothes and shoes that were going to charity had been placed in dustbin bags, other things that she had packed into a suitcase were to go back to his family in Sydney. In the back of the wardrobe she'd chanced upon an envelope stuffed into one of Josh's old boots – a pair he'd always refused to throw out even though he'd long since stopped wearing them. Inside was a photograph of a baby. Propped up in a pram in the middle of an unidentified garden, its eyes were squinting into the sun. Lauren studied it curiously. She'd never seen it before. At some point the photograph had been folded carelessly down the middle. The crease ran along the infant's face slightly distorting the features. The infant had a sickly look about it. Sellotaped to the back was a lock of blond hair but there was no inscription. Lauren was puzzled. Why did Josh have it? And why keep it in an old boot?

She put the envelope, its contents and a few precious things to one side for herself. Some photos and a couple of letters from Josh she kept for Lottie. It seemed only right. The child, after all, had been very close to him. Lauren wanted her to have something to remember him by.

As she dialled the Roaches' number she felt a twinge of guilt. She hadn't spoken to Lottie since the funeral. Which was her fault. She should have made an effort earlier. But the truth was she hadn't been much good to anyone, least of all herself. She had merely existed.

It was Melanie who answered the phone.

'Hi. It's Lauren Kendall. I was hoping to speak to Lottie. Is she around?'

'I'm afraid not.'

'Do you know when she'll be back?'

'She didn't say.' Melanie sounded embarrassed – well, it was eight o'clock, an hour when most eleven-year-olds should have been at home. 'Perhaps I could get her to call you?'

'Would you? I'll be in all evening.'

Lauren kept the conversation deliberately brief, afraid

of the bitter recriminations she might hear seeping into Melanie's voice. During the few times Lottie had spent with them it was clear to Lauren that Melanie neither liked nor approved of the relationship.

By the time Sukie arrived it was dark and raining; a heavy, relentless downpour that blurred and drowned the road. Typically, Sukie had come without an umbrella and because she was feeling poor (and had no need to worry about her appearance as it was only Lauren), she had opted not to get a cab from the tube but had walked instead and had arrived absolutely soaked. Her hair was slicked flat to her head.

'Here,' said Lauren, taking her drenched coat, 'I'll put it on a radiator. It'll be dry by the time you leave. How about a drink?'

'Love one, I'm gasping.' And without waiting to see what she was offered, Sukie pulled a bottle of Sainsbury's white wine from the fridge. 'Are you joining me?'

'Please.' Lauren checked to see that everything was in hand: ratatouille, sliced lamb, baked sweet potatoes. The lemon brûlé tart could go in later.

'Smells good,' Sukie said hungrily. 'Hope you haven't cooked anything *too* fattening. I put on four pounds last week.'

Lauren refrained from answering. Like most people who didn't have to worry about their weight, she had difficulty comprehending the love/hate relationship her sister had with her body. Sukie's diets were so habitual that Lauren had begun to suspect she went on them as much for the attention they attracted as for the desired pounds shed.

Sukie was regarding her sister's figure enviously. 'You look like you've lost a bit.'

Lauren laughed and reached for two glasses from a cupboard.

'You're always saying that. Come on. Let's go next door.

You can tell me about Dad. I'm dying to know about this big case he's been working on.'

Sukie's eyes gleamed proudly.

'I take it that means he won?'

'Lo, he was *bril-liant!* If they'd put Myra Hindley up there on the stand he'd have made her look like Mother Teresa. The prosecution never stood a chance.'

'Good for Dad. I must call and congratulate him.'

'You won't get him tonight. He's out celebrating with Mum and a few friends.' Sukie lit a cigarette with a yellow Bic lighter. 'I had hoped he'd have time to take me shopping – he's usually more generous with money when a case goes his way, but this Lloyds business has changed all that.'

They walked through to the drawing room. By the window stood an immense weeping fig in a terracotta urn. Knowing how much her sister disliked smoking, Sukie eased herself round the foliage and opened the window. Her eyes fell on the small writing table nearby.

'Didn't know you were into antiques?' she said, picking up Inge's book.

'I'm not. It's, er, for a friend. A birthday present,' Lauren lied.

Sukie ran a hand across the glossy cover. 'Must be a close friend.' She put the book back and sat down, kicking her shoes off. 'Christ, I'm shattered! I'm working for a bloody *monster*. Frankly, since all that franchise business, things haven't been the same,' she took a slug of wine, waving a hand from side to side as if to say, hang on a minute, 'not now that Graham's gone.'

Graham Tate, who worked for Central, had hired Sukie for a year as freelance script editor. Until, that was, Carlton had made a takeover bid for the franchise and won it, throwing a great many noses out of joint. Graham was one of the casualties and had been replaced by an ambitious whiz kid. Sukie was luckier, holding (no, clutching with both hands)

onto the remaining seven months of her contract. But one of
the problems contributing to the friction-laden relationship
she had with her new boss, Simon, had less to do with her
new workload as the fact that he refused to sleep with her.
And Sukie liked to keep her working relationships cosy.

'Simon's *so* moody,' she complained. 'Piles on the work
too, expecting me to put in all kinds of antisocial hours but
won't pay me anything extra.'

'Have you tried talking to him about it?'

'Won't listen. I tell you the man's a beast,' she sighed
again. 'My life would be a lot easier if I had a car or a
boyfriend who could run me in occasionally. It takes me
almost an hour to get in to work each morning – assuming
the tubes are running on time.'

'Nobody new on the scene?'

'You're *joking*. I don't even get time to look!'

'What about Luke Falkner?' said Lauren, remembering
what Max had said earlier. 'He seemed very keen at Mum
and Dad's barbecue.'

'If it has to be a tennis player – I'd go for Carter.'

'Max?'

'Some of us think he's a very sexy man. Trouble is I
don't seem to be his type. He likes very tall Texans!
I thought she was rather loud. What did you think
of her?'

'I liked her. A lot of fun and good for Max.'

'Shouldn't think it will last long,' Sukie said dismissively.

'Cynic.'

'If only Max didn't know quite so much about my sexual
history. I'm sure that's what puts him off.'

'He was here just a few hours ago.'

'Sod's law.'

'He dropped by for tea.'

'Damn.' Sukie pulled on her cigarette then ejected the
smoke from her mouth as if she were blowing out a candle.

'You know, Lo, you've no idea how lucky you are not having to work.'

'That may soon change.'

'You!'

'Don't sound so surprised.' Lauren was unable to keep the small defensive note from her voice.

'Well, why would you?' Sukie stubbed out her cigarette, glancing around the room. 'You've got this gorgeous house, nice car parked in the drive, a small baby, megastars like Max dropping round in the middle of the day . . .'

Lauren laughed out loud. 'Your regular suburban house-wife. Thanks, Sukie.'

'Then why did you give up such a lucrative modelling career?'

'You know it wasn't that straightforward. There were other considerations.'

'Like Josh?'

'Josh was one of them,' Lauren said carefully.

'Yes, well . . .' The atmosphere in the room had become suddenly charged. Sukie helped herself to more wine.

'What?'

'Seems to me you gave up rather too much for that man.'

'What's that supposed to mean?'

Sukie ignored the dangerous tone that had edged into her sister's voice.

'Don't get me wrong. You were obviously really happy with him. We could all see that. But the moment you met him you put your own life on hold.'

'That's not true.'

'Oh, come on!' Sukie looked at Lauren patronisingly. Not having eaten a thing all day, she was quickly feeling the effects of the wine. 'First your career, then letting your flat go – oh, and don't look like that. You *loved* that flat. All the work, the money you spent on doing it up. You swore you'd never sell it.'

Lauren kept her face rigidly neutral. 'That was before I met Josh. We needed the cash.'

But Sukie was off again, 'You *lost* money. You sold at the worst possible time, Lo, with a collapsed market. And why? Because Josh was intent on having this house.'

'Mum and Dad gave us that money to do with as we saw fit. Josh and I bought this house. You chose a mortgage and a trip to the States. I don't see what you're getting at?'

'I'm talking about Josh having made absolutely no compromises in his life after he met you. His tennis, his needs, they all came first. For a year you danced to his tune while he toured around the world. Then,' she paused dramatically, 'when you were offered the chance of a lifetime, he got you pregnant.'

'Oh, and I didn't have any say in the matter? Sukie, why are you attacking him like this? I always thought you liked Josh.'

'I do. I mean, I did. But he *changed* you. We all noticed it, not just me.'

Lauren, roused now, snapped, 'Who's we?'

Sukie wouldn't say.

'I suppose you mean Mum and Dad?'

Sukie had the grace to look embarrassed. 'Well, you'd have eventually seen it for yourself too.'

Lauren jumped to her feet in a sudden rage. '*Shut up*, Sukie, just *shut up!* How *dare* you talk about my marriage like that. Josh meant everything to me. I *loved* him. But what the hell would you know about love! You're so busy manipulating men into bed – men who aren't worth the time of day – or banging on about your pathetic problems. What problems do you really have, Sukie, other than the ones you create yourself? How can you just sit there and criticise me for sacrifices I've willingly made when your whole life has been one long compromise?'

Sukie sat rigid with shock, an unsightly flush spreading across her face.

Lauren's voice sounded more wretched now than angry. 'There's so much you don't know. Things—' Lauren drew in a deep breath to control her emotions, 'that happen between two people that you'll never understand. How could you possibly? I didn't ask you here to lecture me. I want my life back the way it was. I WANT MY HUSBAND!' Exhausted, she collapsed, sobbing into her chair.

Appalled by the savage misery in Lauren's voice, Sukie rushed to comfort her.

'Lo, I'm so sorry,' she murmured, hugging her sister tightly. 'Please, *please* forgive me.'

Lauren's sobs struck Sukie like hammer blows. Then very abruptly they stopped. For a moment the room was silent. Sukie's eyes explored her sister's wet face.

'It's hard being without him, Sukie,' she began. 'The pain—the—sometimes I actually hate him. Does that shock you?' Sukie shook her head. 'I'm *furious* with Josh for dying and leaving me alone to cope with Tom. I want to know why he did it. What made him go down, be so bloody irresponsible?' She rubbed the back of her neck with one hand. 'He fills my dreams. I imagine him under the sea, weighed down by all that water . . .'

'Don't,' Sukie's hand flew to her sister's mouth to block the words. 'Don't do it to yourself. I was bloody insensitive. I should never have mentioned Josh. Forgive me. It's just that you seemed to be coping so well. You seemed so strong.'

Lauren sniffed, impatiently wiping away her tears as she got up. 'I need a tissue and then I think we should eat. The ratatouille's probably burnt to a frazzle by now.'

But to her surprise it wasn't. The meal was delicious. They ate in the kitchen on the oak refectory table. Not another word was mentioned about Lauren's explosive outburst. But by the deliberate way they avoided all but the lightest of subjects, it was clear that it had shaken them both.

After Sukie had gone, her coat dry and toastily warm, Lauren went back to the drawing room to turn off the lights. The window was still open and a gust of cold wind was blowing against the curtains. Inge's antique book carelessly left nearby was splattered with rain, some of which had leaked onto the pages. Fretfully, she rushed it over to the still-warm radiator wiping off what rain she could with her jumper.

As she held the book against the heat, something tugged at her, the same sinking feeling she got when crossing the steep curve of a bridge at speed. Like an echo it was too faint for her to identify. But it was there, nagging deep within her.

Three days later Lottie came for lunch. She arrived half an hour late but Lauren made no mention of the time. She pulled Lottie into the house and told her how pleased she was to see her again. Then she stood back and inspected her young friend. Lauren was appalled. The effect Josh's death had had on Lottie was startling. Sullen and bone-pale with lank hair, Lottie's clothes hung off her: she seemed to retreat into them. Her face was puffy and her skin was sprinkled with spots. A breath would blow you away, Lauren thought, aghast. More noticeable and more worrying was the change in her character. Gone was the impetuous, giggly schoolgirl Lauren remembered so vividly. Here was a solemn adolescent who spoke little and wore a constant frown.

Lauren did her best to hide her shock, keeping the conversation light and producing all the things Lottie most loved to eat for lunch. But Lottie showed little interest in the food, requesting only things to drink.

'When did school start?' Lauren asked, serving up a Marks & Spencer blackberry crumble.

'Two weeks ago.'

'Are you not enjoying it?'

'Not really,' said Lottie, rejecting the jugful of double cream Lauren passed her, 'but there's not a lot I can do about it.' She held up her empty glass. 'Could I have some more juice?'

'Of course. I'll get you some.' Lauren took out the carton from the fridge and was surprised to find it empty. Surely Lottie couldn't have drunk two litres since she'd arrived? 'I'm afraid we've run out of apple juice,' she said, returning with a bottle of fizzy water. 'Will this do?'

'Thanks.' Lottie poured herself a glass and drained half of it.

'How's your mother?'

'I think she's got a new boyfriend but I haven't been allowed to meet him yet.'

Lauren tried to hide her surprise. 'Do you think she's happy?'

'Must be, I suppose. She doesn't talk about him – I don't think I'm meant to know. Not that I care. I mean, he's not Josh. No one's like Josh and he was the only man Mum had any real feelings for.'

Lauren bit into her crumble.

Throughout the meal Lottie remained moody and distant, answering Lauren's questions monosyllabically. Lauren made allowances – she'd heard about the meningitis, and the child was obviously hurting. Perhaps being here in Josh's house brought back too many painful memories. She now questioned her wisdom in asking her here.

Afterwards they played with Tom in the drawing room. He was in a good mood and Lottie seemed to enjoy holding him. She even laughed a couple of times. But once Lauren had fed him and put him down for his nap, the seriousness in Lottie's face returned.

'You miss him, don't you?' Lauren said when Lottie came back from the loo, knowing that at some point they would have to stop skirting round the real issue that had brought them together again. 'It might help to talk about it.'

Lottie's features were pinched, closed off; she glared at Lauren as though she thought Lauren was trying to trick her in some way.

'It won't bring him back.'

'No,' Lauren said gently, 'but it can make the feelings seem less intense.'

Lottie debated this. 'Have *you* talked about it?'

'A little. I'd like to talk more though – with you.'

Lottie seemed to relax her guard. 'I just keep thinking over and over about the old days. About how it used to be when we were a proper family. Sometimes I pretend that Josh is still living with us in Gladstone Road. Only he doesn't leave, he doesn't die and everything's normal again. I make up stories about how we'll spend our lives together. Then I get stuck. I don't know how it's going to end.'

'Maybe there won't be an end?'

'Everything comes to an end. Don't you know that?'

Lauren was taken aback by the flat tone in Lottie's voice. She reached across and put her hand on Lottie's. 'Look, I understand how unhappy you must be feeling.'

No reaction.

'I miss him too, you know. But he loved you very much, as much as if you had been his own little girl. No one can take that away from you.'

Lottie withdrew her hand and began to pick at one of her spots. 'Do you believe in God?' she asked finally.

Lauren decided to answer honestly. 'Religion is something I struggle with. It always seems so intent on punishment. We're told we should be grateful for whatever time we've had with loved ones, but I'm not that accepting.'

Lottie's eyes latched on to Lauren's. 'Mum says that going to church will make me feel better. That I should talk to God. But all I want to do is smash things.'

'I can understand that.'

'I'm angry and I don't know what to do with the anger. Praying doesn't help at all. I've already tried.'

Lauren chose her words carefully. 'Perhaps if you found a more constructive way to channel your anger – like a hobby or something.'

Lottie seemed pleased with this idea. 'Yes,' she said, pouring herself some more water. 'I've thought of that.' Lauren noticed she'd finished what was left in the bottle which she had brought with her to the drawing room.

'One of the reasons for this lunch,' said Lauren, 'is that I've been going through some of Josh's things and I found some old letters. Some of them are about you, about how he felt. I thought you'd like to keep them, along with some of his old photos.'

'Can I see them now?' Lottie's voice sounded greedy.

'They're upstairs with all his other things in his study. Come on, I'll take you.'

But Lottie was already on her feet. 'If it's okay, I'd like to go by myself.'

'All right,' said Lauren, trying to suppress the niggle of anxiety and doubt she had started to feel. 'You know where the study is.'

An hour later, when Lottie still hadn't re-emerged and the house had grown too silent, Lauren went upstairs to investigate. She found Lottie sitting cross-legged on the floor. In her arms she was holding a tennis racquet that Lauren had put aside with the few things of Josh's she planned to keep for herself.

'I see you've got his racquet.'

Lottie pulled it closer to her chest as if it were a shield. 'He won Wimbledon with this. See,' she pointed to a mark engraved on the side, 'he put his initials on it.' There was a pause.

'Lauren, do you think I can have it?'

'I, er, Lottie that racquet . . .'

'I know what you're going to say, but I'll grow into it one day, and I promise I'll look after it. Honestly.'

It was the first time in almost two hours that Lottie had expressed any emotion. For an instant her face had come alive. How could she deny Lottie? Lauren didn't have the heart to say no.

'Did you find the letters?'

Lauren could see that she had. Lottie had them tucked partially under her bottom as though she was afraid someone would take them away from her.

'Well, if your heart's really set on having it . . .'

'Oh, *yes*. I want it more than I've ever wanted anything else.'

Lauren's eyes creased with worry as she tried to read what was going on in the girl's mind. She thought about how drained and tired she looked and wondered if Lottie was ill. Somehow she had expected things to turn out differently. They had both loved Josh. It seemed only natural that his death would bring them closer together. But instead, it had drawn Lottie back into her past, back to a time when Lauren and Tom hadn't existed. She seemed fixated on it and Lauren found this almost unbearable. She hoped that Lottie would say something but she just stood there, staring resolutely at the carpet, every cell of her thin body screaming to be gone from the room now that she had what she wanted.

Finally, Lauren could stand it no longer. 'Come on, Lottie, I think we could both do with a hug.'

Lauren approached her. Gently easing the racquet from Lottie's grip, she pulled the stiff little body to her and folded her in her arms. But if she had expected tears none came.

Lottie's grief raged on in silence.

11

The noise caused him to twitch and burrow further down under the sheet. He felt hot and vaguely nauseous but decided that if he stayed very still the feeling would go away. However the shrill, insistent tone continued; he groped for the receiver and held it limply to his ear.

'Yeah?' he mumbled, wondering as he opened his eyes why he couldn't see out of them.

'Luke Falkner?'

'Yeah?'

'Colin Banks for *Sports Illustrated*. Commiserations on yesterday's match. In my opinion you were the better man. Wonder if we could fix up an interview while you're here?'

Shit! Who fucked up at reception? Luke struggled for vision trying dazedly to remember how much he'd had to drink last night. He discovered an arm draped over his eyes and removed it gently.

'Look, man, you're going to have to talk to my manager about that. He fixes my schedule.'

'It wouldn't take up much of your time. Say, a quick half-hour? I could meet you at the hotel.'

'Like I say, you'll have to talk to ProServe. Number's in the book.'

But the journalist's voice was persistent. 'Let me ask you one thing then; how close to Josh Kendall were you?'

Luke sat up stiffly.

'Hey, what is this? Look, buddy. It's—' he peered at the

digital clock built into the bedside cabinet, 'it's goddamn eight a.m. and I only went to bed five hours ago. Do me a favour. Go bug someone else with your questions.'

He hung up. The room smelled sour and stale. Next to the phone was a wine glass with cigarette butts floating inside. Gross. His body felt stiff and bruised and there was a pain in his right shoulder. He hoped he hadn't done anything serious to it. Sheepishly he glanced at the still body lying next to him. So he had wound up bringing her back after all; the blonde he'd made such a play for in his earlier match against Wolff. Sure it had been fun at the time, working the crowd, getting his fans (and Wolff) really worried when he'd deliberately hit a few duff shots. As to her! By the end of the match she had been eating out of his hand. It was so easy. But then they all were, the tennis groupies, creaming their panties at the thought of getting close to you. Nothing, he had learned early in his career, attracted women more than fame, money and success.

Shifting upwards against the pillows, Luke gave a gargantuan yawn. As his brain fused back into life, he went over every point of yesterday's final he'd come so close to winning. Goddamn. He'd battled his way from behind until the final set when he had suddenly turned the match around. He had built up a three-two lead and in the next game had the number six seed running all over the place. At four-two he had felt sure the match had swung permanently in his direction, but then had unwisely grown complacent, losing his concentration and the match. The hard-serving Croatian's winning streak prevailed. But this was the closest he had ever come to clinching a grand slam title and he had taken heart when Donald, his coach, had afterwards described his performance to the media as 'nothing less than a triumph'.

Donald Phipp, once an American Davis Cup player, had been Luke's coach for six years. He was almost fifty, but looked much older, living each day in a fixed state of urgency. Although it was a partnership which worked well, Luke sometimes questioned whether Donald had his best interests at heart. Like many coaches, Donald was in the game for ego, to prove himself. A big personality, he was more widely recognised by the public than many of his protégés. But unlike an agent whose role was to remain strictly anonymous, coaches depended on a high profile. Donald was known on the circuit for being able to pick winners. It was this reputation that kept him in constant demand.

The blonde stirred, revealing a pale thigh as she sluggishly kicked away the sheet. Luke contemplated her. She was very pretty, the bright-eyed, effervescent type he always went for. Last night he couldn't wait to get her warm and exciting body into bed – he could still taste her lip gloss, reminiscent of bubble gum. But this morning? This morning he couldn't even remember her name.

He just wanted her out of here.

Luke eased himself from the bed, suffering from a terrible thirst. What time had he said he'd agreed to meet Donald? He had a vague idea it was lunchtime. As he crossed the room he tripped on an empty bottle of wine and stubbed his toe. Jesus. The room looked like a junk-food convention. How many people had been up here last night! In the bathroom he filled the tooth mug with water and drained it. He refilled it three times. To wake himself up he splashed his eyes with cold water, then peed counting up to forty seconds. Close, he thought, smiling to himself, but not his record. He flushed the toilet, then walked back into the bedroom. The blonde was up.

'Hi,' she murmured, giving him a sleepy half-smile, half-grimace, 'guess you must be feeling pretty bad today, huh? I mean getting so close an' all.'

'I guess.' He began hunting amongst the wreckage of

last night's party for his clothes. Now where had he put his watch?

The girl studied his naked form for a moment, running a hand through her long hair. Then she took a slow avid pull on her cigarette.

'You know, they were right.'

'About what?'

'About you,' she said, stubbing her half-finished cigarette in one of the uncleared plates. Luke hated people doing that. Where the hell was his watch? 'Wanna do it again?'

He arranged his features into what he hoped was a suitably rueful expression. 'I seriously don't think I've got it in me. Catching an early flight back to Florida.'

'You said. I was thinking maybe we could go together?' She slipped into her dress. No underwear, Luke noticed.

'Look, er,' he struggled for a name, 'er, I've got to go back with my coach. He doesn't like me hanging around with girls too much. Know what I mean? Says it breaks my concentration,' he added, not wanting her to get any wrong ideas about the kind of relationship he had with his coach. 'Maybe we could drop you off before heading on to the airport. What's your address?'

She stopped dressing and looked at him.

'You asked me that last night.'

'I did?' He shrugged apologetically.

She looked hurt, 'You didn't take in a word I said, did you?'

He was getting a nasty sense of déjà vu. Definitely time to leave. Luke grabbed his change from the dresser and to his relief found his watch under a sock.

'Honey,' he said, not quite catching her eye, 'I've left you some bills on the side. Should be enough to get you wherever you're going.'

'I'm not a prostitute.' Her voice sounded bitter.

'It wasn't what I meant. Look, I'll call you.'

The moment she was alone the blonde's doleful expression vanished. She sprang across the bed and picked up the phone. The connection was made after only three rings.

'Paula? It's me. Guess where I am?' She smirked catlike into the receiver. 'Uh-hu. That's right. Honey, we went all the way to heaven and back again. Yeah. And you know how none of us were believing what you said the other night? Well, honey, you were right about that too. The guy's got testicles the size of tennis balls!'

Colin Banks swore as the receiver clicked in his ear.

'The bastard hung up on me!'

'Well, what did you expect?' said John, his spectacled colleague facing him on the other side of the desk. 'Giving him the third degree at this time of the morning, you just got his back up.'

'I only asked for an appointment.'

'He probably thought you were one of the tabloids after a murky story.'

Thoughtfully, Colin slipped the receiver back onto its cradle.

'I *am* after a murky story.'

'That's as may be but why not tell him what it's for – that you're writing a biography of Josh Kendall.'

'Because no one'll let me get my foot through the door. They're all so bloody cagey.'

'He hasn't been dead all that long. People are still grieving.'

'Are you suggesting I'm insensitive?'

'No, just impatient.' John ignored the look of frustration on his friend's face and resumed tapping information into his word processor. 'Look,' he said finally, 'I know how keen you are to do this book but my advice would be to leave it a few weeks. Concentrate on writing the Linford Christie story you were asked to do. Because when Ed

finds out how you've been spending your working hours
he'll do his *nut*.'

Colin snorted. 'Ed's a miserable git – wouldn't recognise
a story if it was jammed right up his pig nostrils.' He leaned
back in his chair and smiled. 'You know your trouble, John?
You're not ambitious enough.'

'Sure, Colin.'

'When I've made it to the best-seller list, you'll still be
whinging about the mortgage, sitting in that chair with the
broken leg in your conservative Marks & Spencer suits,
drinking the same foul instant coffee.'

'I like the coffee!' John said genially, 'And you're a fine one
to talk about appearances. When was the last time you took
a good hard look in the mirror?' They both glanced at Colin's
shapeless grey jacket, frayed at the elbows with sleeves that
didn't meet his wrists. It still reeked of the whisky he had
spilt on it two nights before. 'You should never have let
Jenny go. Your trouble is you don't know a good thing
when you've got it.'

Colin was fumbling for something in his drawer. 'You
seen my smokes anywhere?'

'Underneath your notepad,' John indicated. 'On your
left.'

Colin pushed back his chair. 'I'm off out for a bit. Fancy
joining me for a swift one over the road?'

'No thanks, mate. Bit early for me.'

'Suit yourself.'

As Colin stuffed his wallet, Dictaphone and a grubby
pack of Benson & Hedges into his already bulging jacket
pocket, someone from the other side of the room yelled
out his name.

'Yup,' he shouted back.

'Ed wants a word in his office. Now!'

John grinned. 'Guess that drink'll have to wait after all.'

But Colin was already off, his fists in his pockets,

the patchy red of his socks exposed and vulnerable like flesh.

Luke landed in Florida just after two o'clock and was home within an hour. Unlike many of his nomadic contemporaries, he felt a strong attachment to his ocean-facing apartment. He had put a lot of time and money into it. A gadget man, he had a cinema-sized TV hooked up to the music system with quadrophonic Dolby stereo; a stack of videos; a pool table that had got trashed one night and now had several beer stains spoiling the rich baize cloth. A ball was missing and Luke suspected one of the girls he had brought home had kept it as a souvenir. In the kitchen was a pinball machine that made space-age sounds and a fridge large enough to accommodate food for a family of six. Its meagre, bachelor contents consisted of a six-pack of Coke, a mouldy slab of cheese, mayonnaise, two eggs, some Budweiser and three rolls of unused Kodak film. In the bathroom (his favourite room) he'd had installed a volcanic Jacuzzi with wall-to-wall mirrors.

After chucking his keys onto the avant-garde sofa it was the stereo Luke made a beeline for. In seconds, Crowded House was belting out 'Kare Kare'. For a while he wandered around in his boxer shorts, unpacking, checking his mail, gazing out at the view, getting used to being home again. For some reason he felt out of sorts. The apartment seemed too small and he contemplated going to a downtown bar he often frequented. It had pool tables in the back and a wide-screen television that played baseball and MTV videos. There would be no shortage of company – he knew most of the regulars. A modelling agency, sponsoring a bash for muscular dystrophy at a new club, had sent him an invitation. But for some reason his usual prescription of night clubs and getting laid held no attraction for him today. Besides, he thought moodily, rummaging through his laundry bag for something that would pass the sniff test, he had nothing to wear!

From the fridge he got himself a can of Coke which spat at him as it clicked open. Then he ordered in some pizza and called his manager to go over his schedule. In just under a week Luke was scheduled to play an exhibition match in Florida. But this conflicted with the Australian Indoor Tennis Championship in Sydney. Luke wanted to play in the latter but the deadline for pulling out of the next week's tournament without incurring a stiff fine was Friday midday.

Luke had signed with ProServ two years before. The agent assigned to him was responsible for contracts, guarantees, all off-court financial negotiations to do with his tennis career. This in return for a twenty-five per cent slice of everything Luke made. He was now answering Luke's list of questions about the Australian Championships; how efficient was transportation to and from the airport and the hotel? How many practice courts were there? What was the food like? What were the players' gifts like?

'Jesus, Luke!' wailed the agent into the receiver, 'I can hardly hear myself think down here there's so much noise. What the hell's going on?'

'Good ol' fashioned R and R. Can't beat it. What's the scoop on my Florida match?'

'I wangled it. But you know how they get – threatening to have you fly out there, get you examined by one of their medics. Don't keep putting me through that. Even an alley cat like you only has nine lives. As to that gig of yours, there are a couple of loose ends but nothing to worry about your end – that's my job. Beats me why anyone would pay good money to hear you lunatics play, but if it's helping your career, then it's okay with me.'

'It's for a good cause.'

His agent laughed gruffly, 'Yeah, the Luke Falkner

cause. Let's speak Friday. I should have it tied up by then.'

Luke's pizza arrived. He paid the delivery boy then settled himself on the black leather couch, flicking through magazines as he ate. He skimmed through an old *Sporting Life* article about Max, captioned 'The rise and rise of Carter', who was the only player apart from Jimmy Connors, Mats Wilander and Agassi to have won Grand Slam tournament titles on three different surfaces. A piece about the international attraction of carnivals followed, with a big section devoted to Europe's biggest carnival in Notting Hill Gate. It looked crazy but fun. The last carnival he'd been to had been in Rio – what a party that had been. Luke stopped eating. Notting Hill. Hey. Wasn't that where the snooty English chick lived? The one that acted like he didn't exist. Somewhere he had her number that Josh had jotted down for him. Where the hell had he put it? Shoving the last wedge of pizza into his mouth, Luke began a furious search through his things until at last he found what he was looking for. He glanced at his watch. He calculated the time in London. Late, but she hadn't struck him as the kind of girl into early nights. He dialled the number.

'This had better be an emergency,' a fuzzy but familiar voice mumbled.

Luke smiled into the receiver. 'Hey Su-kie. How's life in London?'

'Who is this?'

'I'm hurt you don't remember. Luke Falkner. The man of your dreams.'

He could hear her yawning, 'Do you have any idea what time it is?'

'I figured it wasn't too late to call.'

'It's bloody well twenty past one in the morning and I've got to get up for work in four hours.'

'Hey. That's cool. I'll call back.'

'No. I'm awake now,' she said grudgingly. 'What's the matter?'

'Nothing at all. Just wanted to hear your voice. Guess you heard I made it to the final?'

'Of what? The egg-and-spoon race?'

He laughed. 'That's one way of describing the US Open.'

'And you woke me up in the middle of the night just to tell me that?'

Christ! Was she ever in a good mood?

He wondered if calling had been such a good idea. 'I've got this tournament in Sydney next month and I wondered if you'd like to come along?'

He could almost hear her mind ticking. 'How long for?'

'About a week. Longer if you like.' Silence. 'Hey,' he added, panicking, 'no strings. Strictly platonic, okay?'

'I can't,' she said finally, 'I have to work – you sound as though you're calling from a bar.'

Luke used the remote control to turn the CD volume down. 'Can't you get out of it?'

'No.'

All the same he was encouraged by the slightly less glacial tone of her voice. 'Well, how about I give you my number in case you change your mind.'

'If you want,' she said noncommittally. He could hear her yawning again, the slight rustling movement of sheets. He had a sudden yearning to be wrapped up inside them with her.

'Look, Luke,' it was the first time she had said his name, 'I've got to be up in a few hours . . .'

He was struck with disappointment. 'That's cool. I'm sorry I woke you.'

'Good night then.'

'G'night,' he repeated. But the line had already clicked in his ear.

*   *   *

Sukie was having a bad day. In fact it could be said the entire week had been something of a calamity. She was a month behind with her mortgage, her phone bill for the last quarter was almost three hundred pounds (she had nearly fainted when she had opened it), she had been late for work four times and caught by her boss on all of them. Then Massimo, a swanky Italian she'd started dating who was into computers and blondes, suddenly went cold on her. No explanation. Just a curt little note through her letter box one morning saying, 'I can't see you no more.' And only last week he'd been talking about her being the mother of his future children! That was Italians for you.

She meandered out to the drinks machine which hummed at the end of the hall and pressed the espresso button. The machine burped, a plastic cup dropped onto the metal grid tray and with a noisy squirt, steaming liquid filled the cup. Not that you could call what came out coffee but she needed her morning fix. She'd put on a tight pair of jeans and pseudo riding boots in the hope that they'd make her feel tough and jaunty. But she was now having second thoughts; the jeans dug into her stomach, strained against her bottom. From her bag she pulled out a Vicks inhaler.

'Sinuses still playing up, Sukie?'

It was Tony, the office gossip and one of the commissioning editors that Carlton employed full time. He chewed gum compulsively and used the company phone lines to keep up with his complex social life. 'I hate to be the one to say it but you're not looking your rosiest this morning.'

'No one asked for your opinion,' she snapped, taking the piping hot polystyrene cup from its slot. 'Some idiot chose to make his calls in the middle of the night. By the time I'd got rid of him I couldn't get back to sleep.'

Tony feigned surprise. 'You mean no one was at home

tucked up in your bed keeping you warm? My, my! Sounds
to me like your technique's getting a touch rusty.'

She scowled at him.

'Ah,' said Tony with an infuriatingly smug gleam in his
eye. 'Have I hit a nerve?'

Tony and his crass, predictable sexual innuendos. She
might have felt flattered were it not for the fact that he
behaved in exactly the same way to all the girls in the office.
Before he could say any more, Sukie escaped back to her
desk. There was a stack of pre-production calls awaiting
her and several new scripts that she was supposed to wade
through. But she honestly couldn't face it. Instead she put
her feet up on the desk, pulled the latest copy of *Hello*
magazine out of the top drawer, delved greedily into her
stash of fudge, and cupped the hot, sweet coffee in her lap
like a tiny hot water bottle. There was something shaming
about rushing out to buy the latest issue of *Hello*. Its pages
contained mostly rubbish. But the rich and famous held a
morbid fascination for Sukie, and it was worth reading if only
to snort at the often appalling taste in clothes and interior
decorating.

She was just in the middle of Rachel Hunter banging on
about how happy she and Rod were after the birth of their
second baby girl, when Simon Kilby, bully of the year, man
with no heart, or more precisely, her boss, stormed in.

'Sukie. In my office. *Now*!'

Shoving the *Hello* magazine into a side drawer, she
followed him, wondering what Simon was doing here
when he was supposed to be having a lengthy meeting at
Shepperton. Panicky thoughts rose like milk coming to the
boil. Had she stuffed up somewhere, forgotten something?
If so, what? She was never very good at lying convincingly
when put on the spot.

Simon walked behind his desk and sat down. He looked
very cross.

'Close the door,' he barked.

'Bad morning?' Sukie tried, installing herself in the chair facing him.

'You could say that,' he said in a tone of voice that made her blood curdle. 'Now just what the *bloody hell* do you think you're playing at?'

'I don't know what you mean, Simon?' Sukie stammered, her bright smile dimming a wattage or two.

'Don't you now?' he mimicked her voice. 'Well, let me spell it out for you. We start filming in under three weeks. Part of your job – which seems to have slipped your tiny mind – is to liaise between the script writer, the director and myself. A bit of communication tends to go a long way around here.' Sukie bit the inside of her cheek, wondering where this sarcastic monologue was leading. 'One of our leads came down with bronchitis last week and you were supposed to tell Lynn to rewrite the character. I just got off the phone to her and she says today's the first she's heard about it.'

'I can explain . . .' she started.

'Oh, I'm sure you can, young lady. You seem to have an answer for absolutely *everything*. Only I don't want to hear any more. I've had it up to here with you,' he raised his hand to his forehead like a salute. 'How the hell you've survived in television this long defies all reason. You arrive late most mornings, your work is sloppy, you never follow things through and you have the memory of a five-year-old. No, I retract that,' Sukie's hopes rose then immediately sank again when Simon completed his sentence, 'I'd be insulting a five-year-old.'

She gave him her best indignant look.

'In all fairness, Simon,' she said defensively, 'if I've been getting in late it's only because I've been working until well past eight each evening.'

Simon clucked his tongue like a disapproving nanny. 'You

know perfectly well that during filming, you put the rest of your life on hold. We all do. Why should you get special favours?'

Sukie leant forward in her chair. 'Look Simon,' she tried, her voice silky smooth, 'I'm sure we can work this out. There's just been a misunderstanding. I'll talk to Lynn, explain . . .'

But Simon wasn't listening. 'If you wanted a nine-to-five job, Sukie, you should have joined a building society.'

'But I . . .'

'No. Don't say another word.' Simon's face was set. 'It's too late. You're sacked. I want your things cleared from your desk by the close of play today.'

He picked up the phone and turned his back, giving her no opportunity to retaliate. *Sacked*. He had to be joking. He couldn't sack her after all the hard work she'd invested in the company. And what about staff loyalty? Fuming, she glared at his hateful profile, trying to think up some suitably scathing words to avenge herself, but none were forthcoming. Simon was speaking now in low whispers, so she got up and left the room, slamming the door with as much venom as her five-foot-seven frame could muster. Everyone in the office looked at her. She glared at them scornfully. Marching to her desk she collected her few possessions, stuffed them into a scruffy Sainsbury's shopping bag and walked, head high, out to the lifts.

'What kind of flowers do you want on your grave?' Tony had a habit of popping up at irritating moments. 'I'm rather partial to daisies but perhaps the situation calls for something more dramatic. How about roses – red ones?'

'Fuck off, Tony.'

He feigned a hurtful expression. 'Heard you got it in the head.'

Sukie smiled as cryptically as possible. 'Why ask me? Thought you knew everything that went on around here.'

All the same she allowed him to light her cigarette. Her hands were shaking badly.

'Actually, I was in Simon's office while he was on the phone to Lynn,' he admitted. 'I was going to warn you earlier, but you weren't in the mood for conversation.'

'Well, good riddance, I say,' said Sukie, as the lift doors pinged open. 'I never did like it here.'

Tony circled the air with his arm in farewell as she stepped resolutely inside.

Ten minutes later, with a burning sense of indignation, she was on her way to Harrods. Men might take their frustrations to the pub but Sukie was of that other breed. Shopping did wonders for her morale.

When she reached the main doors of the department store, however, she found her entry blocked by the uniformed doorman, built like King Kong.

'Sorry, madam, but I can't let you in like that.'

Sukie blinked uncomprehendingly.

'Your jeans, madam,' he gestured to a large sign above the door which said that along with vest tops and backpacks, 'rips and tears' were unacceptable.

'You mean to say you're not going to let me in because my jeans have holes in them?'

The man looked away.

'Have you any idea how much these cost? They're *designer* jeans. I bought them from your bloody store!'

The man ignored her. His eyes were fixed on an Ivana Trump look-alike clutching the arm of a middle-aged businessman. The scanty candyfloss-pink skirt that grazed the top of her bottom and the adornment of jewels she was swimming in declared her his mistress. The door to Harrods' cavern of expensive treasures was instantly opened.

Sukie's eyes narrowed. 'I don't believe this. She's flashing her bum to the world and you're worried about me showing half an inch of *knee?*'

The doorman looked at her blankly. 'Madam, I'd rather you didn't make a scene. I'm just doing my job.'

I'll hit you, she thought furiously, if you call me 'Madam' one more time. She glared at the gold military-style buttons on his jacket battling with a rising sense of injustice. 'You're supposed to encourage people to spend money, not turn them away. Now let me pass.'

Towering above her, the man stepped forward and blocked her path. 'You're not going anywhere. I've already told you . . .'

'I'm going to speak to someone about this, you can be sure of that,' Sukie said angrily, shaking a finger at him. 'You're not getting away with this outrageous fucking discrimination.'

'Here, here,' piped someone from the crowd.

'All right now, that's enough. There's no call for that sort of language,' snapped the doorman.

'Up yours!' Sukie turned on her heel in disgust. She would never, *ever* shop at Harrods again!

On her way home she stopped off to buy two packets of Marlboro. Her rule was never to smoke more than twenty a day, but today she'd been sorely provoked. Frankly she didn't care. By the time she got home depression had set in. No job, no money, not even a man to take her out to dinner and cheer her up. She contemplated calling Lauren but ever since their dinner, she had felt reluctant to make the first move. She could try her mother but what would be the point? All she'd get was the usual indulgent 'Never mind, dear, you'll get another job soon enough.'

She riffled through her filofax and called up an old boyfriend who had made so much money he'd announced his retirement at the grand old age of thirty-five. She had once contemplated marrying him, but didn't think she would ever get used to his unfortunate looks – Keanu Reeves he wasn't – or the fact that he was a committed scientolgist. He was probably swanning it in the Seychelles or somewhere equally glamorous. But to her surprise he answered after a couple of rings.

He took her for a slap-up tea at the Ritz and ordered everything from peach champagne to tiers of crustless cress sandwiches, tiny butterfly cakes and mouth-watering scones, all of which they polished off with a wanton abandon – well she had already blown the diet with the fudge. Afterwards they saw a Spanish film in which all the characters seemed to be obsessed with ham. By the time they got back to her flat, Sukie had drunk sufficient to numb all her financial worries. The alcoholic effects had worked so well, in fact, that she had begun to find her companion's bulbous nose rather attractive. She even forgave him for having a hairy neck. They went straight to bed, ignoring the phone when it rang, where they remained inebriated for two days.

The following Monday, anxiety returned with the force of a raging hangover. Nasty brown envelopes clogged the front-door mat and her building society had written to say that if she didn't pay her mortgage soon, they would repossess the flat. Having hoped that Simon would call and ask her to forgive all and come back, she was furious that he hadn't. She'd worked bloody hard. Good script editors weren't all *that* easy to find. She deserved better.

As she sifted through the rest of her post in the bath Sukie wondered if the bank would give her a loan? Probably not, now that she'd joined the ranks of the unemployed. What a mess. A cream envelope slipped through the pile and landed in the bath. She scooped it up and shook off the worst of the bathwater then examined the front. Didn't look like a bill. Maybe it was something nice like a cheque. Curious now, she consigned the rest of the post to the floor, and ripped it open. Inside was a complimentary tournament pass and an open return to Sydney. A note was stuck to the top. Water had blurred the cramped, spidery,

unmistakably male writing which she had difficulty in
reading;

> Sukie. My invitation was a genuine one. Even if you don't
> come out for me you should do it to see Australia. Second
> to home, there's nowhere quite like it. October is the start
> of their summer so the weather will be FAB. If you change
> your mind you can get me at the above number. Oh, and
> there's a machine in case I'm out.
>   Here's hoping. Luke

Sukie carefully put the letter on one side then submerged
her head briefly under the warm water. A trip to sunny
Australia. She could unearth her spaghetti-strap dresses,
her Laura Biagotti sunglasses, those strappy sandals she
had bought in the autumn sale but hadn't had a chance to
wear. She would look good with a tan. Mmm. Long sultry
evenings sampling Sydney's nightlife, trying out her green
polka-dot bikini under mango trees – did they have mango
trees in Australia? She reached for the shampoo and poured
a small syrupy pool into the palm of her hand. An exotic
wave of coconut hit her nostrils. It smelt good enough to
eat. Closing her eyes she massaged her scalp with the tips
of her fingers, imagining herself on the other side of the
world. She leaked a smile.

Things were suddenly looking infinitely more cheerful.

12

Having never flown further than America, Sukie found the twenty-four hour flight an endurance test. For most of the journey she kept herself topped up with sleeping pills, dreaming fitfully of her approaching arrival in Sydney, now so close it conjured pictures of the opera house in her mind. She didn't bother with the movie or the trashy novel bought at the last minute in Terminal One. The glossy cover far excelled the weak, predictable storyline. She fell into conversation with her neighbour and together munched their way through her bag of Bassett jelly babies. An architect, he was on his third business trip to Australia that month and was thinking of moving his family out permanently. Why? she wondered with all the ignorance of someone who had never been to Australia and thought of it purely as a male chauvinist domain where Aussies dangled corks from the brim of their hats, called their wives 'mate' and kept possums and iguanas as pets.

Luke had sounded over the moon when she called to say she was coming.

'You'll love it here, Sukie. You won't want to leave.' No doubt he expected her to find him irresistible too.

After customs, she spotted a man holding up a placard on which her name had been written in capital letters. He introduced himself as Wayne, took hold of her bags and escorted her from the terminal. Outside he held open the door of a white Mercedes. Luke *had* pulled out the stops; long-distance phone calls, club class air ticket, the car. She paused, momentarily disorientated by the glaring sun-blistered pavement, the thick sweetness of the Southern Hemisphere air, the stupefying heat. October meant autumn, dead leaves, central heating, yet here she felt like she'd stepped straight into July. She felt suddenly very remote from England and the people she knew there.

Wayne, a heavily built blond from Brisbane, pumped her shamelessly about her visit to Sydney. Sukie wasn't about to be slotted in the tennis groupie category so she took the easy way out and answered his questions enigmatically. By the time Wayne pulled up at the hotel in William Street, jet lag had set in. Bleary-eyed, Sukie stepped out of the car and watched two towering transvestites wrapped in hip-hugging skirts sashay towards them in stilettos.

'Hey, big boy,' one of them called out to Wayne who was collecting Sukie's suitcases from the boot, 'fancy a trip to the stars?'

Wayne scowled, waving them off as though bothered by nothing more than an irritating fly. 'Hop it, Tinkerbell.'

There was a hold-up at reception and she was made to wait for almost half an hour before checking in. To counteract the boredom she smoked four cigarettes and chatted to a man who had a cattle ranch in Texas. Finally a key appeared and then a porter. Sukie stubbed out her cigarette, longing for a bath and a bed she could put her feet up on.

'Excuse me,' she said in a huffy voice when she was shown to her room, 'there's been a mistake.'

'This was where Mr Falkner said to put you.' The porter had already unloaded her bags.

'I'm sure he did,' she muttered, eyeing up the double bed he no doubt expected to find her draped across on his return, the unquestionably male articles strewn around the room. Bloody cheek! All those remarks about it being strictly platonic. Oh, but then what had she expected? There was no such thing as a freebie.

She turned to the porter. 'You can put that lot back. I'm not sleeping here.'

He looked put out. 'No one said anything about it to me.'

'I just did.' She gave him a sugary smile, 'Now, am I going to call reception and tell them or will you?'

Having secured a rather pretty room on the next floor up which looked out on to St Mary's Cathedral and the Cross, Sukie ran herself a bath. There was a generous selection of sweet-scented towels and expensive smellies displayed on a shelf above the sink. Sukie turned on the radio that had speakers in the bathroom and settled into the water with a KitKat she had forgotten to eat. When the phone rang she ignored it. She knew who it was. Do him good to wait, she thought, squeezing warm water from her flannel onto her half-submerged breasts. Cool down some of that eager testosterone. Sukie was on the bed rubbing cream into her legs when it rang a second time.

'Hello?' she said coolly, leaning back against the pillows.

'Hi. It's Luke.'

'I didn't expect it to be anyone else.'

He laughed, a little nervously, she thought.

'Look, sorry about the mix-up with your room. That should never have happened.'

'No, it shouldn't have.'

'Believe me, I gave them hell downstairs.'

'Oh, I'm sure you did.'

There was an embarrassed pause. 'So,' he said finally, 'how was your flight?'

'Boring,' said Sukie, then decided to let him off, 'but I've come armed with a trunkload of duty free! By the way, thanks for sending the car and everything. I got my first taste of Aussie T.V. Watched a programme about fat models,' which reminded her of the extra three pounds she had gained. 'How did your match go?'

'I won in straight sets. Say, maybe we could go for a drink – just a quick one,' he added. 'I'd like to see you tonight.'

Sukie debated. It seemed that since her bath all her tiredness had swum to the surface. Right now the only thing that attracted her was to remain in bed and sleep for three days. But she was his guest and she didn't want to get off on the wrong foot. She asked him to give her twenty minutes.

She found him in the twenty-ninth floor bar which had a staggering view of the city. He was wearing jeans and a white baseball cap. Sukie immediately felt overdressed.

Rising hastily from his seat, he gave her an admiring glance.

'What can I get you?'

'Whisky. No ice,' she said to the hovering barman.

'And I'll have another of these fruit things,' Luke shook his empty tumbler.

'About the room business,' he said, once their drinks had arrived, 'I'd hate for you to get the wrong idea. It wasn't what you were thinking.'

She aped his expression, stern and jowly. 'No, of course not.'

'No, I mean it,' and he grinned. His strawberry-blond hair flowed in loose waves under his cap. 'What changed your mind about coming?'

'One of the advantages of working freelance. We finished filming early.'

'Lucky me. What were you shooting?'

'A six-part thriller about a widow who keeps finding dead bodies and suspects that her son may be the killer.'

'Sounds cool.' His voice had a staccato edge to it much like a Californian. The Canadian twang only re-emerged in odd words. What little time Sukie had spent with tennis players had taught her that regardless of where they were from in the world they all spoke a uniform language; a sort of American slang.

'Actually it is,' Sukie conceded, with what was for her a rare honesty. 'Its strength lies in the script which is really good. Hard to come by these days.'

'So what now?'

Sukie drained her glass. 'I look for another job.'

'You could come and work for me any time,' Luke said, turning frivolous in his nervousness. 'Hey, just kidding,' and he held up his hands to show he was joking.

'Something will come along. It usually does. But I wouldn't mind being in my sister's position of not having to work.'

Luke's face fell. 'That was a real bummer. Me and the guys were talking about it. Some of them are still pretty cut up. I mean Josh, of all people. Last thing any of us expected.' He ducked his capped head and let it swing a little, dolefully. 'How's she been doing?'

'Having Tom helps. He keeps her so busy she hardly has time to grieve. Mum and Dad have been brilliant. But then they always are – I'm not sure if that's always a good thing?'

'I liked your folks.'

'Lauren's not one to brood or let things get on top of her. She's quite level-headed, unlike me.'

The barman came over and Luke ordered them both more drinks. Sukie glanced out at the shimmering city sprawled below. A moment of disorientation engulfed her. Was she crazy to have come? To cross the world on a whim, when what she should be doing was sorting her life out – looking for a job. She reached for another cigarette and allowed the waiter to light it for her.

'So,' she said, when they were alone again, 'were you one of those boys that thought, when I grow up I'm going to be a tennis player?'

Luke smiled. 'No. My true love was baseball. It's just that

I wasn't as good at it as I was with tennis. When I turned thirteen I had to make a decision. As I've never liked being second best, I stuck with tennis. Then I got this call from Nick – Bollettieri – asking me if I wanted to come to the academy full time. That sort of clinched things for me. That, and the fact that my folks were prepared to move closer to Bradenton so that I could get to go visit them each weekend.'

'How admirable of them,' said Sukie unable to keep the envy from leaking into her voice. Atomic bombs wouldn't move her parents from Willow. 'They obviously thought you'd go far.'

'Yeah,' Luke agreed modestly, 'but that wasn't their only reason for moving. They wanted to support their kids. Guess they knew how tough it would be.'

'Tell me how you and Josh became friends.'

'He and I were at the Academy together. But we were never real close. I was only thirteen when I joined. Josh was a bit older. But we'd hang out together, hit a few balls.'

'What was he like then?'

'Pretty wild. We all were. But I think a lot of Josh's cockiness was for show. I can't really explain it but it was like he had something to prove besides playing good tennis. He'd fool around to get attention, but if he got on the wrong side of someone it would bug him like crazy. You know, like really get to him – sometimes for weeks on end. Kinda weird when you think about it. I mean, why bother?'

Sukie stifled her third yawn.

Luke put his drink down. 'Want to call it a night?'

'If y u don't mind. I suddenly feel absolutely shattered. Must be the booze.'

'Any idea what you'd like to do tomorrow? Afraid I've got to play most of the afternoon but I could take some practice time off, show you the sights in the morning?'

The idea of an early start didn't remotely appeal to Sukie.

'Or,' Luke ventured, when she showed no enthusiasm, 'you could come down to the courts and watch for a bit. Donald, my coach'll be there. You can sit with him.'

'Okay. You've persuaded me. What should I wear?'

'You're asking me? Sukie, wear what you like. You look great in everything!'

Sukie slept through her wake-up call and the knock on her door from room service. By the time she surfaced her breakfast (parked on a tray in the corridor) was cold, so she ordered some more. Back in bed, studiously ignoring the late hour, she mulled over the previous night's conversation, trying to imagine Josh as an arrogant teenager. She thought of her parents whom she hadn't seen for almost a month and imagined herself back at Willow; the apple orchard, the pool house converted from eighteenth-century stables, the familiar row of poplars, the smell of stacked hay in her parents' barn, Mr Poole and his treasured cows. The drone of an occasional tractor. Idyllic environment for kids to grow up in – only it had never felt that way to her. She thought about Lauren and how well she was coping with Josh's death. Funny thing was, Lauren had always been able to cope with traumas. Even as a child. Perhaps that was why she had been so shocked by Lauren's sudden outburst the night of their dinner. Sukie could remember the time when her mother's beloved red setter Pharaoh, a temperamental beast that Sukie had never liked, had returned home one afternoon from a fight covered in scratches and a bleeding nose. Within minutes the house was in chaos: Kay trying to get through to the vet, Sukie screaming like a piglet getting in everyone's way, poor Pharaoh frenzied and wild, flicking his head from side to side and getting blood on everything. It had been seven-year-old Lauren who had finally taken control. Calmly, she had locked herself and Pharaoh into the tiled bathroom. There she had stayed for almost three hours.

When she re-emerged, blood on her face and hands but triumphant, Pharaoh was lying on the floor in an exhausted sleep, his congealed but now dry nose propped between his front paws.

When Sukie stepped out into the glary sunlight wearing a knee-length, engine-red dress, Wayne was waiting for her with the car. They reached the tennis complex after lunch – too late for Sukie to meet Luke, but as his match wasn't for at least an hour, she made her way to the players' hospitality area and flashed her pass at the security guards. They immediately let her through and for a moment she felt like royalty. Special privileges. She could get used to this. Upstairs was a lounge full of people having drinks. There were no empty tables, so Sukie boldly approached a suitably good-looking man and asked if she could sit down.

He glanced up briefly from his magazine. 'Sure. I'll be moving on shortly.'

Sukie looked around. Suspended from one wall were two television screens showing play on court and the latest match results. She watched for a few moments then got bored and searched for a waiter. Her eyes rested on a dark-skinned man with a wedding band shining conspicuously on his left hand. She wouldn't describe him as handsome exactly, but there was something, something about his keyed-up energy, the cold insolent way he was returning her gaze that made her shiver with excitement. She liked the bullish confidence of his size and the challenging fact that he was looking at her so dismissively. Very few men did that. She held his stare, willing him to come over. Then her vision was blocked by a fair-haired woman with a large bottom. Squeezing past her table Sukie gave the woman a brief once-over, brief because big bottoms reminded Sukie of her own none too small one. By the time her eyes strayed back again she saw that the woman had sat down next to the stranger. Surely she wasn't his wife? Then Sukie caught sight of an identical gold band that flashed from her wedding finger. Well, she thought cynically, he must have married her for money.

'All yours,' her dark-haired companion was rising from his seat. 'If you want a drink, you'll need to get it yourself from the bar.'

'Thanks,' she said, admiring his tanned legs that stretched all the way to Albuquerque.

At the bar she ordered herself a gin and tonic. An empty stool had become available, so she sat on it and made small talk with the barman.

'So,' she said, surveying the room, 'who's famous in here?'

'Well, you couldn't get much more famous than the bloke you were just talking to. That was Pete Sampras.'

'Oh,' said Sukie, immediately regretting not having made more of her opportunity. 'Is he playing this afternoon?'

'He's done for the day. Won his match in straight sets this morning. It's all up there, everything you need to know,' he pointed to the monitor.

'What about Luke Falkner? Don't suppose you've heard of him?'

The barman laughed. 'Right,' he said and walked away.

If there was one thing Sukie wasn't prepared for it was the barrage of fans, seemingly all female. Their loud and enthusiastic support for Luke made her wonder if she hadn't inadvertently stumbled into a rock concert. Luke's easy, clownish command of the indoor court fuelled the screams of delight from his fans. He was playing a young Bosnian whose name no one, including the umpire, could pronounce. According to Donald, Luke's coach, whom she had joined, he had leapt from being an unknown straight into the top one hundred rankings after his shock victory over the number four seed. It should have been a close match. The Bosnian had started off well, taking the first set, but had gone to pieces in the second.

Sukie was enjoying herself. The combination of Luke's weighty support and the frequent glances he cast in her direction (which did not go unnoticed by the local press) affected her like an aphrodisiac. Suddenly she could see what it was about Luke that made him so attractive. Not his looks so much as his athletic prowess on court. Donald, whose flesh had been tanned to leather, explained that part of his job as coach was to structure Luke's tournaments throughout the year, choose which countries to play in, arrange accommodation. She listened with one ear as he went on to point out Luke's winning characteristics; the deep and consistent serve which players found hard to read because he brought his racquet so far back; his quickness to the net and winning volleys; the almost poetic skill of his game that reminded many of Edberg. Some of this she grasped but Sukie was too busy lapping up the glamour surrounding Luke to take any of it too seriously. Luke, she decided, was like a magnetic field of fame within which she had been included.

Getting within a mile of Luke afterwards was impossible. Two security guards kept the fans at arm's length while Luke smiled and scribbled autographs. Sukie waved helplessly, trying to attract his attention but there was too much pushing and underhand shoving from the other women battling to get closer.

'Watch it!' Sukie snapped indignantly after someone had stepped on her toes for the third time. 'I'm trying to get to my boyfriend. Do you mind!'

'Not if you don't,' sneered a girl wrestling past her. She couldn't have been more than fourteen.

In the end, Sukie gave up. Special privileges only seemed to apply when Luke was with her. She had never been out with a celebrity before – not that she bracketed Luke with the likes of Martina Navratilova or Jimmy Connors. He had a long way to go before he reached their legendary heights. But it certainly seemed that wherever he went people recognised him, clamouring for autographs, offering assistance, free entry, the best table in an otherwise booked-up restaurant.

She made her way back to the courtesy car waiting room tugging at her short skirt and literally, bumped into the same dark-skinned man she'd been eyeing up earlier.

'Oops, sorry,' she said, enjoying the feel of strong hands gripping her waist as he steadied her.

'My fault,' said the man letting her go. He had a foreign accent.

'I, er, didn't we meet earlier?' He had turned to leave, and for some reason she didn't want him to.

Slowly he turned round. His lips formed a bow like a lion's grin. 'No,' he said, insolently, 'but that is what you wished.'

Sukie snorted. 'You're very sure of yourself, aren't you?'

The man shrugged. 'Why not?'

At that moment Luke walked through the door. He had changed into his own clothes but was still sporting his white baseball cap.

Sukie jumped because he had approached her silently.

'There you are,' he said, stopping short when he saw who she was talking to. Silence hung between the two men. Luke nodded curtly, 'Wolff,' then to Sukie, 'you all fixed to go?'

'Ready when you are.'

The stranger's squid-black eyes flickered from her to Luke then slowly back to her again. In them Sukie was shocked to read contempt. Turning abruptly, the man left the room.

'Who was *that*?' Sukie asked, feeling a little tremor inside, a not unpleasant fluttering of fear. There was something very powerful about him.

'Walid Bohakari. Known as Wolff. He and I don't get on.'

'That's obvious. Why's he called Wolff?'

'Because he's got the hairiest legs on the circuit.'

'Oh.'

Sukie was wondering if at one time they'd both been after the same woman. 'That's not a reason for disliking someone.'

Luke jangled keys in his pocket. 'Wolff doesn't like to lose. Eight out of the ten matches I've played against him have gone in my favour.' Luke shrugged. 'The guy's a moody s.o.b., what else can I say.'

Time to change the subject. She lit a cigarette. 'I hadn't realised I was going to participate in a rugby match.'

'Oh, you mean back out there. Yeah. Sorry. It can get kind of heavy.'

Sukie exhaled smoke. 'Goes with the territory I suppose. I enjoyed the match but you weren't very nice to the Bosnian. Talk about an assassination job!'

Luke rubbed fiercely at his bloodshot green eyes. The apathy, the anticlimax after a win had already begun to set in.

'You don't get to where I am by giving away points,' he said bluntly. 'That guy lost it out there. Most of us reckon he's a bit of a fluke. Happens all the time.' He was studying a piece of typed paper. 'Looks like I'm playing Kafelnikof in the next round. He's PDG.'

'I'll hazard a guess that means pretty damn good.'

Luke flashed a grin, 'Fuckin' A, Sukie. You catch on fast.'

They stopped off at Doyles, a sort of posh fish-and-chips restaurant that overlooked Watsons Bay and had queues half-a-mile long. Luke wasn't prepared to wait and instead took her to Lucio's, an Italian restaurant he'd already sampled in Paddington.

It was packed. Sukie, who hadn't eaten since lunch, was worried they wouldn't get a table. But as luck would have it, Lucio himself whisked them upstairs, fussing over their orders, checking to see they had enough to drink, issuing endless compliments to Sukie who (he said) reminded him of Jennifer Jason Leigh.

'Who?' whispered Sukie, after he'd gone. There was so much noise coming from neighbouring tables and Lucio's accent was so thick, she couldn't understand a word he said.

'You ever see *Backdraft*?'

'I missed that one.'

'Okay. Well, she was in that.'

Lucio produced a feast; slender home-made green noodles in a sauce laced with blue swimmer crabmeat. Luke had calf's liver with bacon and melted onions, followed by pieces of chicken grilled with garlic, rosemary and chilli. They washed it all down with a deliciously cold Chardonnay. Still thinking about Wolff, Sukie asked, 'Do you get very competitive with one another?'

Luke puckered his bottom lip thoughtfully, wiping the juice on his plate with some bread. 'There aren't too many egos off court. Don't get me wrong – they exist, and when you're out there playing you're trying to kill one another. But once the game's over we'll go share a couple of beers. Sure.'

Their plates were cleared and they both ordered dessert. Sukie leaned forward onto her forearms and explored Luke's eyes which were a pale green and fringed with blond stubby eyelashes. She could imagine exactly what he'd been like as a child. Impish, fidgety, utterly unselfconscious.

She lit a cigarette. 'Does that cap ever come off?'

'Nope, not during competitions. My dad gave it to me when I turned pro. Worn it ever since. I'm superstitious. Yeah, I know, and you're probably not into that shit, but it's my lucky charm. It gives my dad a real kick to see me wear it. They gave up pretty much all they had for Kelly and me.'

'Kelly's your sister?'

'Right. She's pretty good – ranked 120 on the WTA. We play mixed doubles together. My parents went without a vacation for six years saving money wherever they could to finance our careers. Dad had his own building company and worked like crazy to raise money. They were *unreal*. Travelling with us, booking houses to cut down on hotel costs. All our meals together were spent talking about tennis; arguing, questioning, finding ways to improve our game.' He plunged his spoon into his tiramisu which seemed to consist almost entirely of cream. 'I can honestly say that it was their love and support that got me where I am today. The circuit can be a real lonely place. You need all the support you can get.'

On the way back to the hotel she let him kiss her. But she refused to let him into her room. She decided to take a bath. Recklessly she filled the tub with all the complimentary bottles of bath oil, then she poured herself some champagne from the fridge. She burned herself as she stepped into the water, but she endured it, shifting sideways, so that her strong, well-shaped legs dangled over the edge. The radio was on. Some psychologist was discussing ways in which parents might handle difficult children. Sukie thought of her father who had never learnt to recognise her own deep need of him. All the controversial things she had done in her life, the tobacco habit she knew he hated; the rejection of school; losing her virginity at thirteen, were all desperate attempts to get his attention. But to no avail. Lauren was the example. She was and always would be his favourite. Sukie swore. Why was it that everything came back to Lauren?

She hauled her legs back into the bath and inspected them. She counted four ingrowing hairs. One more week and they would need waxing. Starting to feel like a stewed prune, Sukie gingerly got out of the slippery bath, towelled herself down, then retrieved the flimsy lingerie she had packed – just in case. In the mirror she examined her reflection. She had established the beginnings of a tan which was offset by the bra and knickers – cream with just enough green to do something for her eyes. Her face looked curiously vulnerable without her usual armour of make-up, her hair chaotic, but the overall effect pleased her. She had a sudden image of Luke kissing her in the car, his lips incredibly soft and giving, his earlobes fleshy. Beneath his thin cotton T-shirt his back felt like warm marble. Her clitoris throbbed with a sudden urgency.

Sukie made one small adjustment to her face. With careful deliberation, she painted her mouth crimson. Then she walked over to the phone and dialled his room.

'Yeah?' his voice sounded tired. 'Who is this?'

'The door's unlocked,' she murmured, then hung up.

13

In a way Lottie's going back to school had made all the difference. If, on the spur of the moment, Hugo wanted to have lunch with her, she was free to say yes without having to worry about who would keep an eye on her daughter. Melanie was concerned by the growing evasiveness and rebellion in Lottie. Half the time she had no idea where Lottie went or what time she could be expected home. Melanie wasn't happy either about her spending so much time at Lauren Kendall's house or about what Melanie saw as interference from Lauren – ringing up to say how worried she was about Lottie: the weight loss, lethargy, the excessive urinating. Bloody cheek. Of *course* Lottie was run down, a defensive Melanie had snapped, having first told Lauren where to get off. Lottie's system was obviously still taking time to get over the meningitis. She was quite capable of taking care of her own daughter without any outside interference. However, she *was* concerned by how thin Lottie had become and other things like the demands for money. It seemed that each time Lottie stepped outside the house she was asking for more; a school trip had been planned, materials were needed for a project she was working on, new clothes, new shoes. After a while the excuses had worn thin and Melanie had begun to suspect she might have a boyfriend.

Or even something worse.

Two nights before, Hugo had taken Melanie to see *The Madness of King George*. She had already seen it with Gillian – she didn't tell him this, but found herself enjoying it as much the second time round. There in the dark intimacy of the theatre, relaxed and close, Melanie marvelled at how it was that this man holding her hand had so quickly installed himself in her life. She just prayed it would last.

The doorbell rang snapping her out of her speculations. He was early. Her hand reached up automatically to touch the side of her hair. Casting a quick nervous look at her appearance in the bedroom mirror, Melanie flew down the stairs, mentally checking that everything was as it should be. At the bottom, she grabbed Lottie's filthy denim jacket draped over the banister and hung it up in its rightful place in the hall.

When she opened the door, she felt an unexpected thrill at the sight of him, poised, elegant, a man very much in control. She'd forgotten how big he was. Wicklow shot outside and stopped to sniff Hugo's shoes.

'I'm early, I know,' he said smoothly. 'My last appointment didn't turn up, so I came straight here.'

'Come in,' she beckoned, taking from him the roses he held out to her. 'Thank you. They're lovely.'

He bent to kiss her cheek but in her nervousness she moved her head and he got her small nose instead.

She scurried off to the kitchen. 'What would you like to drink?' she called as he followed her. 'There's a bottle of white wine in the fridge – or some fizzy water, or a Coke if you'd prefer something non-alcoholic. I always buy it in bulk – Lottie gets through so much.'

'Lottie?'

'Yes,' she said, with as much casualness as she could muster. She had wanted to wait until she felt more secure about him before introducing Lottie into the conversation. She pointed to one of the better photos stuck on the fridge. 'My daughter.'

For once it was Hugo's turn to look surprised. 'You have a daughter?'

She shrugged ruefully. 'She's really a very good child.'

Hugo's composure had been re-established. 'How old is she?'

'Eleven last July. Quite grown-up now.' Melanie wished he'd stop staring at the photo. 'She takes after her father.'

'Evidently.'

The phone rang. Handing him the chilled bottle of wine to open, Melanie excused herself. She picked up the extension in the hall.

'Hello.'

'Is this Mrs Roach?' said a male voice. Unfamiliar, mild northern accent. Something about it put her on guard.

'Who's speaking?'

There was a slight pause, a clearing of the throat. 'Colin Banks. I'm doing a story on—'

Melanie interrupted him. 'I'm sorry, Mrs Roach isn't here,' and she hung up.

Hugo raised a questioning eyebrow as she returned to the kitchen.

'It was a wrong number,' she said, wondering vaguely if she should go ex-directory. She looked at Hugo, still studying Lottie's picture. There was an aura about him that made everything in the room appear dingy in comparison with his suave elegance.

'So, am I going to meet her?'

'Not today. She's at school. Went back two weeks ago.'

'I see.'

'You don't have any children?' she asked, testing him.

'No.' He made a noncommittal sound and turned towards her. 'No, I never got round to it.'

She had roasted a chicken (a faithful Delia Smith recipe), believing him to be a traditional man. In this area, at least, she was successful. Hugo made several enthusiastic noises as she pulled the sizzling bird out of the oven, placing it carefully on a carving board while she made the gravy. They ate the meal in the small dining room which hadn't been used for months – she and Lottie usually ate in the kitchen.

'This is wonderful,' Hugo finally announced, lining his knife and fork neatly in the centre of his empty plate. 'Melanie, you can really cook.'

'It's just a chicken.'

'But it's what you've done with it.'

'There's plenty more,' she said, looking pleased.

Hugo held up a hand.

'Coffee then,' she said, rushing to collect the plates. 'We'll have it next door.'

Hugo made no offer to help, and she left the room, relieved – it gave her a few private moments to collect her thoughts, work out how the afternoon was going.

'Which are you?' asked Hugo, when she appeared in the sitting room a few minutes later. He was standing next to the bookshelf inspecting the titles. He held two in his hand, *Women Who Always Say 'No'*, or *Women Who Always Say 'Yes'*?'

Melanie blushed. 'Those aren't actually mine,' she lied. 'A friend from America spent a few days here and left them behind.'

'Really,' said Hugo, resisting an urge to smile.

They were sitting together on the sofa, Hugo stirring his tea – he didn't drink coffee, while Melanie talked about a holiday she had taken in Portugal last year. She regretted wearing the cream shirt and Liberty-print skirt of tiny blue flowers. It wasn't an outfit that made her feel empowered, sexy. Not that she should be thinking such things. She knew she was babbling but she couldn't help it. All she could think about was the thin thread of distance that separated them, and that with just the slightest of moves she would be touching him. She was itching to. All her senses, dormant for so long, were now alive with expectancy. She was like a spring bubbling inside with rising urgency. Couldn't he feel it too? He must! And yet he did nothing. Made no move towards her. At least he seemed in no hurry to get back to his office. She had that in her favour. Prudently she glanced at the clock above the fireplace. Two fifteen. Lottie wouldn't be back for another three hours.

'Hugo, why did you never marry?'

'Didn't believe in it,' he said with candour. 'That and the fact that I'd never met anyone I felt would fit into my lifestyle – sex you can get from anyone. A woman who accepts her true role in a marriage these days is rare. So many go chasing after careers when what they should really be doing is solidifying the relationship with their spouse. It doesn't work having both partners working. Maybe you think I'm selfish saying that?'

'No, I don't at all. I actually agree with you.'

'The fact is I'm old fashioned. I come from a background where the men provide a roof and an income and the women look after the home.'

It suddenly occurred to Melanie that if she were to marry Hugo she would never have to worry about money or having to work again. She edged closer to him.

'I've never thought of myself as a career woman.'

'No,' said Hugo, anticipating the direction her thoughts were going, 'but had you been, I wouldn't be here now.'

There followed that inevitable moment when he moved towards her, his thin but perfectly formed mouth so impossible to resist leaning towards hers. She felt as bashful as a schoolgirl, dropping her head as his hand sought the inside of her thigh.

'Hugo, look, I . . .'

'I haven't slept with a woman for months, Melanie.'

'It's been a long time for me too,' she admitted.

'Then don't deny me.'

'It's too late for that,' she whispered, quelling the last vestiges of self-consciousness.

'You're cold,' he said, running a hand along the raised goose-bumped surface of her arm. He pushed her skirt aside, then slid his hand inside, ferreting around for the elastic of her knickers. Somehow they had both ended up on the floor and all Hugo's shirt buttons had come undone. His hand had found a way into her knickers. Rigid with shock, she tried not to think about what he was doing. She was embarrassed by how wet she was.

'Turn over,' he instructed. 'No, not like that. On all fours.'

She obeyed him, feeling the weight of his large body cover her like a thick blanket as Wicklow bounded into the room. At first she couldn't believe he was inside her. But then he began to thrust, one hand clutching at her hanging breasts, swinging like bells.

'Melanie,' he groaned. 'Oh God, that feels so good.'

She turned her head and kissed him awkwardly on the mouth, his tongue forcing its way into her mouth then sucking on her tongue. She shut her eyes, trying not to think about how heavy he was or how much the carpet was hurting her knees. She could hear Wicklow whining, feel him twine around her legs until Hugo pushed his little body away with an impatient shove. He was moving faster now, his breathing wild and heavy. Opening her eyes again she glanced through the gap in her legs and could see that he was balancing on the balls of his feet. This excited her enormously. He was like an animal in his demands of her. Primitive, dangerous. She could smell the faint, vinegary smell of his sweat, the now familiar scent of his piny eau de cologne. When he suddenly stopped, pushing her away from him, she almost howled in frustration. She'd been so close. When she turned around she expected to see that he'd come, but he was still erect.

'Take it in your mouth,' he muttered, the lids of his eyes half-closed.

Melanie hesitated.

'Go on, Melly. Do it for me,' he urged.

She tensed, then gingerly took the shaft between her hands. It jerked into life, the foreskin rolling back proudly to reveal shiny pink flesh. She held it steady then placed her lips around the tip of it, trying as she did so to remember all the things she had read about oral sex. It tasted faintly sour and rubbery, with traces of soap (she took some comfort in this). Part of her reluctance came not just from a dislike of the act, but because she felt she wasn't very good at it. The last thing she wanted to do was make a fool of herself. Hugo, however, had closed his eyes and was moaning sonorously with pleasure. Encouraged, she began to suck him, taking his member into her mouth as far as she dared. After a while the muscles in her jaw began to ache but she continued sucking. He put his hands against the back of her head, dictating the rhythm. Faster and faster, deeper and deeper until she thought she would gag.

'Oh, yes, baby, oh, *yes*,' he murmured in a feverish voice, 'I'm coming. I'm *coming*!'

Hugo's head twisted; his face had a strained look as though he was trying to listen in on a faint conversation. Instinctively, she tried to pull away but he was too strong, holding her there as his syrupy semen spurted into her mouth. As Hugo sank back against the sofa, she looked vainly around for a repository to put the sperm she still held in her mouth. She could go straight up to the bathroom. And yet what would that look like? She might hurt his feelings. Hugo had opened his eyes. He smiled triumphantly at her as she swallowed.

'Come here, darling,' he said, opening his arms.

And like a child she went to him.

*   *   *

Later, upstairs in the bed she had shared with Josh for five years, he made love to her again. No rush this time, taking it very slowly and (to her relief) in the conventional way. It wasn't that she didn't enjoy sex. She liked being held afterwards, just as she liked being caressed and kissed and told that she was beautiful, which was what Josh used to do when they had sex. Perhaps if they had done it more she might have learned to relax and cast aside her insecurities. Sometimes, like now, she would cry. She didn't know where the tears came from or why they chose to flow after sex, but Hugo didn't seem to mind. His acceptance filled her with gratitude. Because if he had asked for an explanation she didn't think she would be able to give him one. Cocooned within the plump muscular curve of his arm, blissfully debilitated, Hugo stroked Melanie's hair while she finally told him about Josh.

'We were devastated but Lottie took it worse. They'd been so close, you see. Josh was the nearest thing she'd had to a father.'

Hugo was watching her with an intense concentration, as if he were weighing up whether or not to say something of the gravest importance. It suddenly occurred to her that he might be feeling jealous.

'Look, Hugo . . .' her fingers continued their exploration down his wiry thatched chest, 'I did love him very much but it's been over for a long time and there's been no one since. No, truly. No one,' her voice was insistent because she could read the scepticism in his eyes.

'Three years is a long time to be on your own, Melanie.'

'Yes, it is,' she said sadly, then burrowed her face against his chin, tickling his earlobe with her tongue, 'but I'm being paid back with interest now.' She felt the wet, sticky sperm slide from her. 'Oh, God. The sheets.' She sprang from the bed, 'Hang on, I'll grab a tissue.'

She was on her way back from the bathroom when

she heard the front door slam. Lottie! She sprinted to the bedroom, signalling frantically for Hugo to get dressed. He'd anticipated her, however, and was already belting up his trousers. Melanie hunted wildly round for her pleated skirt then rushed back to the door as she zipped it up from the back.

'That you, darling?' she called.

She could hear running water and the clattering of plates in the kitchen as she struggled with the buttons on her shirt. Hugo had followed her out and was giving her a hand.

'MUM!' Lottie's voice hollered, 'What's going on? Has someone been round for lunch?'

'I, um,' Melanie, struggling for a reply, looked helplessly at Hugo. 'Darling, Gillian stopped by unexpectedly. I'll be down in a minute to make you some tea. I'll tell you all about it.'

'What shall we do?' she whispered. Wicklow had sprung up the stairs and was weaving between their legs.

'Come clean?'

'But she's only eleven!'

'Okay, I won't stay. But she's going to have to be told sooner or later.'

Worried as she was, Melanie's heart gave a small flurry of delight at the permanence of this last statement. She looked at him for guidance.

'What do you want me to do?'

'Go down and keep her occupied. I'll let myself out.'

'But what about your jacket? You left it in the sitting room.'

'I was distracted,' he said meaningfully, tweaking her cheek. 'Don't worry. She won't see me.'

As she reached the bottom of the stairs, with Wicklow tucked under one arm, Melanie paused to see that the coast was clear.

'Okay,' she mouthed, urgently motioning to Hugo with her free hand. He slipped in and out of the sitting room, his blazer over one arm. When the front door shut silently behind him, Melanie giggled. How long it had been since she had felt so alive, so exhilarated. She felt *wonderful*. Walking into the kitchen, she was unable to stop herself from smiling.

'So, darling,' she said lightly, blind to the appalling mess her daughter had made within minutes of coming home, 'How was your day?'

'I think she's taking drugs.'

'Don't be ridiculous.'

'No, really, Hugo. I'm serious. Over the past few weeks she's changed so much. You don't know her, how – reliable she's always been. It's just so out of character.'

'She's eating, isn't she?' said Hugo, who'd had little experience of children. 'She's not sick or anything?'

'Well, no.' Melanie stopped to think. 'But she's so thin and pasty looking, and her skin's terrible.'

'It's called puberty, I believe.' Hugo moved his arm from under her head. 'Pins and needles,' he explained. 'Shift on to my other side.'

'But how do you explain her fatigue and all the demands for money? Never a word of thanks,' she added irritably. 'What can she be spending it on if not drugs? She's always been scrupulously honest. And yet I caught her lying twice last week. Once when she'd told me she'd been to see her nana, which I later found out couldn't be true as Esme was away in Ipswich. Far more seriously, Mrs Garrett – she's one of her teachers at school – called to see if she was feeling better. Apparently Lottie had left at lunchtime after fainting in geography but didn't come home until seven. Hugo, I'm really worried. What if she's fallen in with a bad crowd? You hear this sort of thing happening to youngsters all the time.'

Hugo cast a surreptitious glance at his watch. Melanie had been harping on about her daughter for almost half an hour now. This wasn't how he'd planned to spend his lunch break. He had hoped to squeeze in fifteen minutes at the tanning salon before getting back to the office. If there was any hope of that he'd have to leave now.

' . . . that boy on the news who went into a coma after taking speed at a party. He wasn't much older than Lottie.'

'You're probably not being firm enough with her,' he said unthinkingly.

Melanie smiled away her hurt. 'I do try. But it's not easy raising a child on your own.'

'No,' he said immediately contrite, 'I don't imagine it is.'

They were having what had become one of many clandestine meetings in one of Hopkins's smaller unoccupied properties. Hugo had recently taken on the furnished Boltons flat as a rental, but as the tenants weren't due to move in until the end of the month, it was a convenient place for both of them to meet; in five minutes he could be back in the office should anything unexpected crop up, and Melanie didn't have to worry about her daughter putting in another untimely appearance.

He was surprised by the speed with which the relationship had developed. Not that he'd actually sat down and analysed it – at least, not until recently. It was Rodney who had first brought it to his attention last Wednesday afternoon while they were out valuing a house.

'So who is it this afternoon?'

'Melanie.' Hugo was driving.

'Again! Careful, Hugo. Sounds dangerously like you're getting involved.'

'You've got it all wrong.'

Rodney gave him a sideways smirk. 'Is that right, old boy? Just wait till Philippa hears that you've been rogering the same woman for weeks now. Remember the last time she caught you out. She went absolutely ape.'

'Drop it, Rodney,' Hugo warned.

'You can always put me down as chief usher. Five of my mates have got married in the last six months so I've had plenty of practice.'

'I suggest that if you fancy keeping your job you'll shut the hell up. And get rid of that cigarette. You know I hate smoking in my car.'

Curbing a smile, Rodney rolled down the window and flicked his cigarette butt into the road.

'Anything you say.'

Melanie was getting dressed. Lazily, Hugo observed her from the bed. It wasn't just her surprisingly erotic body that pleased him, it was her tidy, economic movements. She was both graceful and feminine with an almost silent approach to her routine. Had he so wished, he could have quite happily gone to sleep in this room and felt in no way irritated or threatened by her presence.

She came and sat on the edge of the bed while she reapplied lipstick, using a small compact to see what she was doing. This allowed him to study her more closely. Her small features had a sense of order to them which again pleased him, the high cheekbones, the tidy angle of her nose, the unblemished skin – he was very particular about that. His cock stirred appreciatively. Her tiny wrists bespoke fragility and there was a small mole on the right side of her neck that he hadn't previously noticed. Mostly she wore her hair down.

Melanie was using a dark-coloured pencil to fill in the corners of her mouth. His mother had only ever worn make-up for weddings and funerals – and then just a discreet application of lipstick, a thin film of powder to cover up the red and blotchy tinge of her skin, the snake-like thin veins on the sides of her prominent nose.

Having inherited his mother's nose Hugo warily watched throughout his twenties for the same veins to appear on his nose. When finally they had, he went straight to Harley Street and had them zapped. Some returned later but not enough to bother about – yet.

Hugo scratched his stomach, frowning. What on earth had made him think of his mother? He hadn't seen the old dear for more than six years. The one tenuous link that remained these days was the occasional call from Matron. That and the cheques he sent to the home each month for her upkeep and for someone else to shoulder the wearisome responsibility of looking after her. Mother. Poor old, weak mother with her thin body and thin lips, who just once in her pitiful life had made a stand against his father by walking out on him. Hugo could have loved her for it, only by then it was all too late. By then his sixteen-year-old heart had toughened. He'd had enough of the arguments, the slum his parents called home. Nothing would induce him to follow their miserable lives. He was determined to *make* something of his.

'Do you mind me doing this?' Melanie said, interrupting his thoughts.

'No. I enjoy watching you.'

'Not too much?' she said, meaning the colour of her lipstick.

Hugo shook his head. 'Look, about your daughter—'

Melanie instantly lowered her compact, giving him her full attention.

'Perhaps it's time she and I met,' he said with an effort, shifting his eyes.

'Do you think so?'

'Well, some male influence on the situation might help,' he continued vaguely. 'I don't know.'

She looked so pitifully grateful. 'Oh, Hugo. I'm sure it would. You'll like her, you really will.'

'Then why don't you go ahead and set something up?'

The meeting, however, was a disaster. Temping that day in Kingston for a marketing company, Melanie had been forced to stay on and do overtime, then had been further delayed by rush-hour traffic. By the time she arrived back at the house, hot and in need of a bath, she found both of them in the sitting room, Hugo hunched in moody silence, Lottie lying on her front, a half-empty bottle of coke in one hand, flicking through the television channels – a wildlife programme, men playing rugby, a quiz show, Oprah.

'Sorry I'm so late,' Melanie said, her cheerful voice breaking the silence. 'Lottie, darling, haven't you offered Hugo any tea?'

'He didn't want any.' Lottie switched channels again and the screen was filled with teenagers chatting in a coffee shop.

Melanie looked at Hugo, but he merely shrugged. Oh, dear, she thought. He's angry.

'Lottie, you're being incredibly rude. Turn that television off this instant.'

'But *Mu-um*. I want to watch this.'

'This instant!'

Lottie dragged herself up from the floor and flicked the remote control.

'Can I go up to my room then?' she asked sulkily.

'Don't you want to have tea with us?'

'I'm not hungry.'

Hugo rose. 'Look, I think, under the circumstances, Melanie, I'd better be off. There are a few things back at the office that need my attention.'

'But it's almost eight. You can't mean it.' Melanie was crestfallen. She had been so looking forward to this evening.

'I'll get your coat,' said Lottie, springing to her feet, 'then you can leave right away.'

'How dare you speak to Mr Butler like that! Apologise.'

'Why should I?' Lottie shouted. 'If he wants a bloody shitty apology then he should apologise to me first. He's *not* my bloody father!'

'*Lottie!*'

But she had already slammed the door shut. Pictures on the wall shuddered, then angry footsteps could be heard stomping upstairs.

'Hugo—'

'I don't think now's the time, frankly,' he said, tight-lipped.

Melanie was almost in tears. 'But what happened?'

'Our meeting wasn't a very successful one.' He said it almost as a recrimination. 'Let's just leave it at that.'

'But what did she say to you? I must know.'

For a moment, his eyes softened. 'It was too soon, that's all.'

She couldn't bear it. 'Will I see you again?'

'Of course,' he gave her arm a brief squeeze. 'I'll call you – soon.'

The moment he'd gone Melanie marched straight upstairs to Lottie's room. The usual music was hammering away inside.

'What did you say to him?' she demanded, angrily switching off the radio. On the floor lay the familiar trail of her school clothes, a crumpled copy of *Me* magazine, a French textbook, covered in graffiti-like doodles.

Lottie was lying on her bed gazing at the ceiling, hands tucked behind her head. She was wearing the stubborn set look that always drove Melanie mad. It made her want to goad her daughter, to wipe the look off her face.

'*Answer* me.'

'I didn't say anything.'

'Don't give me that, young lady. And look at me when I'm talking to you.'

Lottie's face suddenly became animated. 'How come I

always get the blame for everything that goes wrong around here? It's not my fault if he didn't want to bloody stay.'

'I'm not leaving this room until I get a satisfactory answer.'

'Oh, Mum. How can you go out with him? He's *gross*.'

'I won't have you say that about Hugo.'

'He's so *old*! He must be at least fifty.'

'That's enough!'

'Well, it's true. I can't believe you talked about me to a stranger.'

'Hugo's a friend.'

'Not one of mine,' Lottie mumbled. 'He got all preachy, telling me about how I should be more responsible, how I wasn't to take your money for granted, that I had to do better at school because you were getting upset and everything. He went on and on about boys too. It was *so* embarrassing!'

'Oh, now that's silly,' Melanie sat on the end of the bed. 'I'd be lying if I said I hadn't been worried about you. You haven't been yourself since Josh. Hugo was only trying to help. If he went on a bit about responsibilities, it's only because he cares about me.' She looked at the suspicious Lottie trying to make her understand.

'Hugo isn't used to dealing with young people,' she said gently. 'As an only child he had quite an isolated upbringing. He's had to sacrifice a great deal to get where he is now. Hard work – that's all he's ever known. But he's a good man, he really is, and once you get to know him better you'll see that for yourself. Don't be cross with me for confiding in him. I need support too and he means well.'

'I just don't want you talking about me like that,' Lottie said sulkily. 'I don't like people knowing . . .' she rolled on to one side, facing the wall.

'No, come on. Don't turn away from me. Let's discuss it. Why, for instance, weren't you at school last Tuesday afternoon?'

Lottie glanced sharply at her mother.

'I was bound to find out eventually.'

'It was just some poxy biology test. What use is knowing how leaves breathe to anyone? I wouldn't have passed it anyway.'

For a while Melanie sat there and contemplated her thorny and unapproachable daughter. The impossibility of hugging her hit her forcefully. Was she wrong about Hugo? Would he, in the end, make a good substitute father figure for Lottie or was what had happened this evening a sign of things to come? She went back over their previous conversations, straining to remember exact words, any subtle clues about his character she might have missed. But how could she be wrong about someone who stirred within her so many dormant emotions – someone, worryingly, frustratingly, she was beginning to feel she had known for years? She could feel the first nigglings of a headache creeping up the back of her neck as if she were wearing a hat that was too tight. She'd take something to catch it before it got worse.

As she reached the door, Melanie's foot knocked against something hard. It was an empty bottle of Perrier – the one she'd put in the fridge only this morning to have with supper. She refrained from saying anything about it. 'Hungry?'

'Not really.'

'All the same, I'll make something light – in case you change your mind.'

And as she searched downstairs for some Panadol, Melanie realised that she was overreacting. Once Hugo and Lottie grew to know each other, the way she knew them, things would improve. It was just a stage Lottie was going through. She would soon grow out of it.

14

Tiffany had insisted on Max coming shopping with her. He had protested strongly – nothing induced a thumping headache faster than the inside of a department store. But they hadn't been together much lately. He felt he owed it to her.

They had spent last night at an apartment her father rented for her in Beverly Hills. The view was fantastic and the interior had been lavishly and painstakingly furnished. But somehow the large airy rooms had lost some of their integrity. Though not slovenly, Tiffany bordered on untidy. Magazines were stacked on every available surface (she claimed she didn't have time for books). Months after moving in, packing boxes remained stacked and untouched in the hallway making it impossible for more than one person to pass through it at a time. In her bedroom, expensive clothes carelessly littered the floor, the curtains remained closed irrespective of whether it was day or night, the dressing table was strewn with half-empty glasses, dead flowers in a porcelain vase, lidless jars of designer face cream. Twice a week a maid arrived to restore a sense of order and cleanliness, but Max was never entirely comfortable staying there. The place was too impersonal, too much like a hotel. And God knows he'd spent enough time in those.

They had just surfaced from a ruinously expensive jewellers on Rodeo Drive with a new glittering Cartier watch flashing on Tiffany's wrist. It had cost a great deal more than the sum paid out by the insurance company, but as she'd said, her father had enough money to buy her fifty Cartiers. Max suspected that it was knowing she was spending Tony Forbes' money, *not* what she was buying that was so satisfying.

'How about some lunch, hon?' she suggested, linking her arm into his. Neither of them had had breakfast.

'Now *that* I like the sound of.'

'Oh,' she teased, pushing her shoulder-length toffee-coloured hair from her shoulders, 'it hasn't been all that bad. You got a new pair of cuff links out of it.'

But he wasn't happy about her paying for them. Normally he would have refused point blank but Tiffany had made such a fuss in the shop he hadn't wanted to attract any further attention. Max had relented but it had left a bad taste in his mouth. He'd make sure that it never happened again.

'Let's go there,' he said, steering her across the road, 'they do great seafood and I'm in the mood for tuna.'

As they entered the popular Art-Deco restaurant, the blond maître d' breezed across the room towards them.

'Hi there,' he said with a Californian smile. 'You have a booking?'

'No,' said Max, glancing round the busy room, 'but I'd appreciate it if you'd fit us in.'

The maître d's eyes widened with recognition. His index finger skimmed professionally down his table register, then with one hand he reached up and plucked a pencil from the back of his ear.

'There's a table available in the front room. I could put you there, Mr Carter?'

Max rewarded him with a dazzling smile. 'That'd be great. I knew I could count on you.'

The maître d' blushed. 'We try our best.'

While they waited for their food they discussed a forest fire that had started during the night and continued blazing like a raging holocaust eighty miles south of the city. Already thousands of acres had been blackened, driving families in droves from their homes. Tiffany was worried about her aunt who lived in the area. She hadn't been able to get through to her on the phone. Their food arrived swiftly and Max ate with the abandon of a very hungry man. Tiffany, however, defeated after only a few bites of her Szechuan noodles, merely picked at the rest.

'Not hungry?' said Max, glancing at her untouched arugula salad.

'Guess not.'

Max popped the last of the cornmeal bread into his mouth. He thought she looked pale – more so than usual with bruised circles under her eyes. And she had been restless last night despite complaining of fatigue. All telling signs of PMT. As she turned to examine the room he inspected her hooked nose. It made a refreshing change from the carefully remodelled Californian profile. The slight sharpness added interest to her otherwise tidy features.

'Maybe I'll have some coffee,' she said, pushing her plate to one side. 'Feel kind of dopey today.'

'I'll join you.'

As he signalled for the waiter Max thought he heard his name being called. He glanced around but couldn't trace the owner.

'Over here, buddy.'

Four tables away he spotted Bob Hallaway. Bob had a long past in advertising and marketing, most notably for the many lucrative deals he had pulled off for Sergio Tacchini. The two men had become friends during the early part of Max's career when Bob had managed to persuade Max to endorse the Tacchini label. Max had just switched from ProServe to IMG and signed a three-year clothing contract for $500,000. Over the years they had lost touch but Max had heard that Bob's wife Frances had been admitted to the Betty Ford Center for alcoholism. Max waved him over.

'Hey,' he grinned, as Bob sat down next to Tiffany, 'not like you to be eating on your own.'

'I wasn't. Had a meeting with a client. It just finished.'

'Tiffany, this is Bob Hallaway.'

'Hi,' she said sweetly.

'Bob and I go back quite a way. You still with Tacchini?'

'Hell, no. Left four years ago. Got my own marketing setup now.'

'No kidding,' said Max, tucking into Tiffany's salad. 'Moving up in the world, hey?'

Bob nodded modestly. 'It's doing good. Actually we're currently working on a new range of casual wear for Tuff.'

'I thought Tuff was a sportswear company?' said Tiffany.

'Right. But they wanted to branch out. They've devised a new range. I think it's going to be a winner. Just got to come up with a great-looking package to sell the product.'

'Which is where you come in,' Max used his index finger to help a stray ribbon of alfalfa into his mouth.

'Yeah. But we're running into a few problems.'

Tiffany could see this was turning into more than a quick exchange of pleasantries. Decisively she grabbed her bag.

'Seems like you need some time to catch up. I've still got a few things to purchase so how about I leave you guys for a while?'

Max looked questioningly at Bob, 'Got time for a quick one?'

Bob relaxed back into his seat, 'Sure. But I don't want to break anything up here.'

'You're not breaking anything up,' insisted Tiffany. 'Max'll thank you for it. He hates shopping almost as much as I loathe football.' She winked at Bob, 'I'll get things done much faster on my own.' She glanced at her watch. 'What say I meet you back here in forty minutes?'

Max nodded at her gratefully. After she had gone, they ordered two beers and a packet of Marlboro for Bob.

'I thought you'd given those things up.'

Bob grinned as he ripped off the Cellophane with his teeth. 'That was before I started working for myself. It's been kind of a tough year.'

'Yeah,' said Max, thinking about Bob's wife, 'I heard.'

Bob lit his cigarette and inhaled deeply. 'What the hell. We all have to deal with these things in life. In some ways I've fared better than most.'

Max shifted in his seat. 'So go on telling me about this campaign you're working on for Tuff.'

'Ideally, we wanted Josh Kendall as our main man. We'd already started negotiations with Advantage when the poor son-of-a-bitch was killed.' Bob stopped himself suddenly and held up a hand. 'Jeez Max, I'm sorry. He was a buddy of yours.'

Max briefly lowered his head. 'You could say that.' Bob was looking so uncomfortable Max made it easy for him. 'Any idea who else you might use?'

'Luke Falkner's a hot contender for the menswear. He's got the kind of image we're looking for; clean-cut, easy-going. He's doing *real* well on the circuit.'

Max nodded. 'Good choice. Luke's got the makings of a champion, no question about that.'

'The target group is primarily fashion-conscious young men and women between twenty and thirty. Finding guys to fit the bill isn't the problem; it's the ladies' range that's proving hard work. There's just no one out there suitable. Okay, so we want real-looking people, faces the public can identify with but they've got to have that something extra too.'

'Steffi?' Max suggested.

'*Way* out of our league. Besides, we don't want anyone with too high a profile. With her kind of schedule it'd be hard to organise anything for more than a couple of hours at a time. Top players aren't into personal appearances – as you know.'

Max grinned. 'Does she have to be a player?'

Bob frowned quizzically. 'I don't get you?'

Thoughtfully, Max swilled the beer in his glass. 'I was just thinking. If you're targeting a wider market and you want someone without work-related ties elsewhere, why not endorse someone *linked* to a player.'

Bob's sharp eyes narrowed against the smoke from his cigarette. 'Got anyone in mind, Max?'

'As a matter of fact, I have. Mrs Josh Kendall.'

'You're kidding me.'

'Think about it for a moment,' Max pushed, warming to his idea. 'When she quit modelling she was at the peak of her career.'

Bob interrupted him. 'How come she quit if she was so good?'

'Because she wanted to be with Josh. She couldn't have both.'

Bob began to look interested. 'You seem to know an awful lot about her.'

'Like you said, I was close to her husband.' Max leaned forward. 'Bob, everyone knows she's Josh Kendall's widow. She's got the kind of looks that would have international appeal. She has a son but no other commitments. She'd make the perfect endorsee. I don't see where you could go wrong.'

'What's she up to now?'

Max contained his smile. Bob had taken the bait. 'Guess you'd have to find that out for yourself,' he said carefully, 'but do me a favour.'

'Name it.'

'Don't let on that it was me who suggested her. Brits,' he said lightly, 'they get awful proud. Know what I mean?'

Bob laughed. 'Sure do.'

Lauren found the approaching winter both gloomy and solitary. Trees that had been swathed in green leaves turned yellow, then brown, then dropped very suddenly. It rained a great deal and lights shone in people's homes long before children returned from school. Everyone seemed to have been taken by surprise, as if the vengeful weather was a new and unexpected experience. Flimsy bright-coloured clothing was shed, stored away in cupboards, replaced by sombre coats, dark boots and thick ribbed tights. Lauren watched the change with regret. Everything became so much more of an effort in winter. She hadn't expected the mourning to consume her for so long. The effects of Josh's death would be around for years, but somehow she had hoped the misery she felt would have lessened.

She loved Tom with an intensity that sometimes frightened her. This morning she had held him curled into her breasts and carried him from his cot to his nappy table. But the moment she had placed him down on the cool plastic to change him (the smell of milky shit wafting up punchily), he became purple with rage and misery. And when he wouldn't stop she grew frightened that he would choke on his own cries. It took her almost thirty minutes to calm him down. She blamed herself for his fractious moods. Not that she wasn't a good mother. She gave Tom masses of love and attention, but he picked up on her anxiety and this affected his behaviour.

Nine o'clock in the morning and she was already exhausted.

The miscarriage had accelerated her developing friendship with Inge. Keen to put her own troubles to one side, Lauren took to dropping round at the Vicarage and soon their tea rituals had become routine. They spent a lot of time working on Inge's garden, cultivating the patchy lawn, planting a Virginia creeper to cover the uninspiring back-end wall which had been built with unsightly grey bricks. At a village fair they had paid fifteen pounds for four massive terracotta pots and had filled them with nasturtiums, lavender and busy Lizzies. Inge was delighted with the results. Already it looked transformed. Even Wolff had joined in their enthusiasm. He had erected a trellis on either side of the garden which he had painted white, successfully blocking out their inquisitive neighbours – a middle-aged couple who had heard that a famous tennis player had moved in and had since been bending over backwards to get an invite, thus far unsuccessfully.

It was a funny thing about Wolff. He wasn't given to much self-expression. To strangers he showed a distinct wariness but when he was around Inge he became a different person, warm and voluble with a sharp sense of humour. He wasn't in any way handsome, but his wide mouth and dark eyes acted powerfully together. It was a face that continually defied definition. Just as Lauren had decided on disdain, she would see it was actually humour. When he was angry she often saw bitterness. She had noticed that people never seemed to recognise him off court, which was odd given the amount of publicity his temper tantrums and racial threats provoked, if not his ability to play top-class tennis. She had tried to work out why, concluding in the end that it was because he didn't want to be recognised. He had an uncanny knack of making himself invisible, a bit like Superman's Clark Kent – amazing what a pair of glasses can do. Off court, Wolff wore featureless clothes, wandered round with his head dipped, blending anonymously into crowds. She had commented on this to Inge.

'Oh, it's his way. He just doesn't like much attention.'

The antithesis of Josh: party animal, generous host, always happiest being the centre of attention. But Lauren and Inge found that they had more in common with one another than had at first seemed apparent. Although neither of them showed more than a healthy interest in the shape of their bodies, they felt strongly about what they put into them. Whenever possible they bought unprocessed food, favouring health food shops and organic butchers. They took a responsible attitude to the environment and were careful about waste. They liked the occasional drop of whisky which they sometimes drank when they had tea together. The real bond, however, was that they had both made considerable personal sacrifices for their husbands, both felt ambivalent towards the tennis circuit, both had been recently bereaved.

Inge talked bravely about the miscarriage and stressed her eagerness to try again but it was obvious to Lauren that her friend was hurting. Inge had not looked well on their last meeting. Her face was pinched and tired although her manner had been as kind as ever. Privately, Lauren questioned whether Wolff fully understood what his wife was going through. He could be so distant – it was this that often made him hard to read. She noticed that they had this peculiar way of communicating with one another, switching from one language to another and speaking very rapidly – between them they spoke four languages – French, Arabic, German and Spanish. Sometimes they used their code in front of her. But it was done so instinctively, so unselfconsciously that Lauren doubted they even realised they were doing it. She never said anything to Inge.

The two women met twice a week now and as Lauren had stopped breast-feeding, Inge had persuaded her to take time off for herself. Gratefully, Lauren made the most of her free hours.

This afternoon she planned to have a facial and get her legs waxed. It had been so long since she had indulged herself. She was looking forward to her treat. Leaving Tom gurgling happily on Inge's double bed, Lauren pointed the Discovery back through Putney High Street towards Tibbet's Corner. Recklessly she ejected Tom's baby tape and slipped in a Ray Charles favourite. Immediately the car filled with the jazz singer's rich, syrupy voice. Lauren joined in, humming bars from 'Everytime we say goodbye'. At a zebra-crossing she stopped for an old woman with a shopping trolley. A woman with a small child followed, then three suited businessmen holding an animated conversation and a schoolboy. She didn't mind the hold-up. The afternoon was hers to do with as she liked.

Smiling at the schoolboy, Lauren's mouth suddenly froze. Josh had just stepped onto the crossing, his arm fixed around the shoulders of a striking woman. Josh – alive! Was it true? A car behind her honked impatiently but Lauren was rigid with shock. She couldn't move. The couple drew closer, their young happy faces tilted towards her. She could see them better now. It wasn't Josh at all. He just looked so much like him. Her body sagged with disappointment.

'Come on, for *Christsakes*,' yelled a voice, 'some of us have work to get back to!'

Motivated by further insistent honking, Lauren's foot hit the accelerator and the car shot forward. Out of the corner of one eye, she saw the couple enter W.H. Smith's. Instinctively Lauren pulled abruptly into a side street. She parked the car and retrieved her shoulder bag from the boot.

Minutes later she had followed them into the newsagent. The shop was very full. She quickly lost sight of them. After ten minutes of searching, Lauren gave up. What was the point after all. He hadn't been Josh. Josh had drowned in the Red Sea. His body might still be down there had it not been for John Cartwright. It was due to his bravery that they had been able to bury Josh. She blinked, pushed the image of her husband's cold stiff body from her mind. At the magazine stand she picked up a copy of *Vogue*. Suddenly she wanted it. Instead of returning it to the shelf she dropped it into her shoulder bag and moved away. By the time she had left the shop she had also taken a stapler, a hardback sketchbook, three greeting cards and a pair of scissors.

Three doors along she entered a smart boutique. Lauren's eyes quickly took in the security brackets on either side of the front door. No cameras, she noted, glancing up at the ceiling. No customers either. Not so good: no one to distract the two hovering saleswomen. She was outnumbered by two to one. Feigning interest, Lauren casually ran her hand along a rack of clothes, biding her time, planning her attack. Her eyes drank in the price tags but she was disappointed that they weren't more expensive. Then she spotted a duck-egg blue cashmere sweater. Its label boasted a price of three hundred pounds. She felt her fingers tingle, her mood lift. Deliberately, Lauren let her hand brush past the sweater. Instead she picked up a trouser suit.

The saleswoman, taking her cue, pounced. 'Nice, isn't it? We've just got that range in. Would you like to try it on?'

An elderly woman entered the shop and approached the second sales assistant at the counter.

'Why not?' Lauren said lightly. 'I might also get one or two other things to go with it,' she smiled impishly. 'I'm feeling reckless today.'

The woman beamed. 'Take all the time you need. I'll pop this in the changing room.'

As the girl walked away with the trouser suit, Lauren glanced briefly at the second saleswoman still occupied with the old lady. Lauren's hand snatched the cashmere sweater from its shelf then grabbed a coat and a trouser suit hanging underneath and threw them over her arm, barely concealing the sweater before the saleswoman returned from the changing room.

'Just go in whenever you're ready,' she said eagerly.

Lauren slipped into the changing room, first making sure the sales assistant had seen that she was carrying two items. The moment the curtains were drawn, Lauren dropped the coat and suit to the floor. The security tag had been stapled to the hem of the sweater. She tried to prise it off with her hands but the plastic was too hard. Riffling around in her shoulder bag, her hand sought the scissors. For general use, the label read. Careful not to make any noise she eased the security tag loose, wrenching the scissors from side to side until the plastic warped and finally gave way. She shoved the incriminating alarm into the coat pocket then crammed the sweater into the bottom of her bag.

'How are you getting on?' the saleswoman was hovering on the other side of the curtain.

Coughing in order to cover up the noise as she zipped shut her bag, Lauren then quickly shrugged off her jacket and swept the curtain aside.

'I'm afraid it's not quite me,' she said, indicating the coat. 'A shame because I like it.'

The woman looked disappointed. 'What about the suit?'

'I'm afraid not,' Lauren put on her jacket and threw her bag over one shoulder, 'but it's probably just as well. I spent a fortune last week.'

Three more customers had entered the boutique and one was looking at an identical coat to the one Lauren had just tried on. With any luck the saleswoman wouldn't have time to check the coat pockets while she was busy serving. After all, how would she know who took the cashmere in all the confusion. Heart pounding with illicit pleasure Lauren opened the front door and stepped out into the street and freedom. An attractive man in his thirties smiled hopefully at her; Lauren ignored him. As she walked back to the car her hand delved into her bag and touched the silky wool.

It got easier and easier.

Back in Wimbledon village, Lauren sat in her car and examined the spot where she had inadvertently nicked the cashmere, as she had prised off the alarm device. She rubbed the area with her finger, irritated by the small hole but satisfied that the offending mark wouldn't show if it was worn tucked in. The price tag was pinned to the label inside the collar. Removing it, Lauren tore it up into little pieces. She dropped it along with the little envelope that contained spare thread out of the window. The car was double-parked outside the post office. Lauren scanned the street for signs of a lurking traffic warden. They were notorious in Wimbledon. Three builders were sitting on an opposite wall having a tea break. Just to be sure she asked them to keep an eye on her car.

'You'll be all right, luv. They don't usually bovver to come dahn 'ere.'

'Thanks,' she said, smiling gratefully.

'Anything for a lovely bird like you.'

Inside was a long queue. Lauren waited impatiently and watched as an agonisingly slow exchange took place between a post-office assistant and a Polish woman who couldn't speak any English. It appeared she wanted to make a long-distance phone call but wouldn't believe the post office didn't provide such a facility. The queue shuffled forward. A video was being played on a TV screen which had been placed at the front of the line. Lauren watched it mindlessly, debating whether or not to check her car and lose her place in the queue.

In her hand was a letter. For weeks she had been haunted by the memory of grief-stricken Helen Kendall. Lauren felt guilty for not having made more of an effort with her in-laws, particularly as Josh had been so neglectful. His offhand behaviour particularly towards his mother had always puzzled her. Josh's old excuse about them living on the other side of the world hadn't washed. Not with the amount of travelling he'd done. Not with the evident willingness the Kendalls had shown to be part of his life – particularly with a grandchild on the way. There had been sporadic signs of real affection towards his father, but whenever Josh mentioned his mother the tone of his voice changed. It had a peculiar, unfamiliar quality about it, flattened out, monochrome as though the very effort of talking about her cost him a great deal. He never spoke of her with compassion or with feeling. 'We didn't get on,' she remembered him once saying. When Lauren suggested that solid foundations within a family were each member's strength, he had looked at her oddly and said, 'Why do you think I married you?' Part of Lauren was loath to dig up buried feelings about Josh: she continued to feel angry with him for leaving her, for dying so senselessly. But since his death the Kendalls had grown old with grief. She owed it to them at least to make an effort. Her letter had taken most of last night to write and had left her exhausted. Now that it was finished she was keen to see it on its way.

Back outside, she found a traffic warden taking down details from the back of her car. Oh, she thought in a panic. Not a ticket.

She rushed over to him, '*Please*! I haven't been more than a minute.'

The man, a massive Greek with a hairy neck, gave her an officious look then continued writing. 'Sorry, missus, but you been gone more than ten minutes. I know. I patrolling this street.'

'But I can't afford this,' she said irrationally.

'I just doing my job, missus.'

'I know. I know. I do realise that,' she said, biting the inside of her lip with frustration. 'It's the first time I've been away from my son and I had *such* a lot of things to get done.'

He raised his eyes and looked at her huge pleading ones. 'You have one son?'

'Yes,' she murmured, sensing weakness. 'My husband recently died and I've been finding it quite difficult,' her voice trailed off.

The man lowered his pad.

'Isn't there *anything* you could do?'

'I cannot to do it. It is, you know, very difficult. Once ticket is already written.'

'But what if you just said it was a mistake, that I'd broken down or something?'

He looked undecided, his left hand scratching his dark thatch of curly hair. 'I can getting into trouble for this. Lose me my job.'

Her heart leapt. 'But I'm sure you wouldn't.'

'I telling you,' he said eventually, turning to the back flap of his pad. 'I file this as one mistake but because maybe it comes back to me you give to me your address. Okay? Then they can sending you your ticket if there is any problem.'

'Oh, thank you. *Thank you!*' she gushed, reciting her details. 'No, it's spelt with two L s. Yes. Like that. You're really very kind to do this.'

'Mmmm,' he gave a manly sniff. 'You lucky you getting me is all I can say. The others, they would not letting you go so easy.'

She decided to go for a walk. It was a cold, bleak day, but the earlier threatening rain clouds had begun to clear and she could see patches of blue sky. Having dumped the car in the Rose and Crown's car park, her bag (and the cashmere) safely locked in the boot, she set off at a bracing pace across the common. From time to time she stopped to admire the golden trees and watch owners playing with their dogs. Having grown up in a house full of them it was something she missed terribly. But with Josh's career they had moved around so much. It would have been both burdensome and unfair on the animal, had they had one.

Lost in thought, she found she had walked quite a way. She turned back towards Parkside and headed down the high street, taking a brief respite in Fielding's cosy bookshop to warm her gloveless hands. Further down the hill she passed the bustling Centre Court Shopping Centre and Wimbledon station, the entrance as ever littered with black cabs. When she reached the theatre, Lauren stopped and gazed up at its great height. What, she thought, had brought her all the way down here? Instinctively, she turned right, following the elbow bend until she was in Gladstone Road. This was where Lottie lived, she realised with a jolt – Josh's home until he had met her. Ever since their lunch together Lottie's health had been preying on her mind. Surely there was no harm in stopping by to see how she was. She followed the line of houses until she reached the one she was looking for. She was filled with an inexplicable curiosity. As with his parents, Josh had rarely talked about Melanie. Yet he had spent almost five years living with her. This reticence had created an enigmatic and intriguing portrait of Melanie in Lauren's mind. Josh hadn't liked any kind of personal examination. How odd that it had never occurred to her until now. Other things about him sprang into her mind; his constant need of approval, the drive to succeed, his fear of failure, of criticism – even from people he hardly knew. When asked personal questions, Josh ran round them the way he used to run round his backhand. He didn't like people making judgments about him. If there were judgments to be made, *he* wanted to be the one making them.

Lauren approached the door. With trepidation she pressed the bell. It emitted a penetrating scream from within, unnerving her further. What could she say if Melanie answered the door? She didn't expect her to become her friend, but she hoped for something. Forgiveness? Understanding? She contemplated running off but reproved herself for such cowardice. I'm doing this for Lottie, she thought firmly. It's what Josh would have wanted.

Melanie answered the door. Lauren was surprised by how petite the dark-haired woman was. Somehow she had imagined Melanie to be tall and strong.

'Don't you worry about Mel. She'll be fine. Tough old

boot, that woman,' Josh once said a few days before he left her. 'Probably won't even notice I've gone.'

Had he just said that to lessen her feeling of guilt? Or had he said it to cover his own?

'Hello,' Lauren said gently.

'What do you want?' It was clear by the guarded expression in her dark-fringed eyes that Melanie recognised her visitor.

'I hope you don't mind my turning up like this. I thought we could talk.'

'Where did you leave my daughter?'

'Lottie?'

'She was spending the day with you.'

Lauren was unable to conceal her surprise. 'I haven't seen or heard from Lottie for weeks. Not since September when she came over for lunch.'

For a moment Melanie stared at her. Then she pulled back the door and said gravely, 'I suppose you'd better come in.'

When Lottie put her front-door key in the lock two hours later, she found her mother in the sitting room. The wintry sun, coming in at a slant through the window, pinpointed her face giving it a frozen, precisely detailed look.

'Hi, Mum,' Lottie said, breathing heavily as though she had been running. One foot was hooked behind the door.

'Did you have a good time?' Melanie asked pleasantly.

'It was okay.'

'Well, come in then. Unless you plan to hover behind the door like that indefinitely.'

'I was just going up to have a quick bath. Is the hot water on?'

Melanie ignored the question. 'How was Lauren?'

'Fine.'

'Just fine?'

'We took Tom to the park.'

'Did you now?' said Melanie evenly. 'Lucky it stayed dry. The forecast said it would rain. What time did you leave?'

'Oh,' Lottie said vaguely, ready to bolt, 'about an hour ago.' Wicklow sidled into the room and jumped up onto the sofa next to Melanie.

'Then perhaps you'd like to tell that to Lauren. She's been here all afternoon.'

Lottie pushed open the door which had been obscuring Lauren from her line of vision and turned white. She contrived to look angry and guilty all at once. Lauren raised her shoulders helplessly. Sorry, she mouthed.

'I think, missy,' Melanie snapped, crossing her thin arms, 'you have some explaining to do.'

Unrepentant, Lottie stood her ground.

'Where have you been?'

'Out.'

'Where out?'

'With some friends,' Lottie said peevishly, fiddling with her fringe.

'That's not what you told me this morning.'

Lottie scuffed the toe of her shoe against the carpet. 'I said I was going round to a friend's house. Look, can this wait until I've got myself a drink?'

'No, and don't do that to the carpet with your dirty shoes. You'll wreck it. I think you owe Lauren an apology.'

Lottie slid Lauren another quick look, bit her lip then glanced back at her mother. She seemed confused by the glare of attention.

'I'm sure it's just a simple mix-up,' said Lauren gently, who could see how upset Lottie was. The girl seemed to be using the door to support herself. 'There's no need.'

'But I think there is,' Melanie said. Agitated, she got up and walked over to the window.

'I'm off to my room,' said Lottie.

Melanie swung round.

'Don't think you're going anywhere until you tell me what's been going on. All these lies, these fabricated stories to get money. Getting home late at night, tired all the time, not doing your homework. If you've got yourself mixed up in drugs I'll . . .'

'Drugs!' Lottie glanced at her mother startled as a deer. Then an angry flush began to spread from her neck upwards. 'Is that what you think?'

'Well, what am I *supposed* to think with you always sneaking around, refusing to let me in on any part of your life.' Melanie threw her hands in the air. 'I feel I don't know you any more.'

'That's because you're never around enough to find out. And *you* can talk about being sneaky,' Lottie held her mother's gaze, her eyes candid and clear. 'You're *always* off out seeing that gross OAP boyfriend of yours. You think I'm too *stupid* not to notice what's been going on. I've seen him sneaking out of the house. I've . . .'

'That's *enough*, Lottie. I won't have you speaking to me like that.'

'Why? It's the truth.'

The phone rang. Lauren glanced nervously at Melanie. She was poker-stiff with rage.

'Yes?' Her voice was sharp as she raised the receiver to her ear. 'Oh, Esme, how are you?' She listened for a minute. 'I'm sure it can be fixed. Yes, look, I'm in the middle of something. Can I get back to you later? I will. Okay. Bye.'

She turned to Lottie. 'Your nana sends her love.'

'What did she say?'

'Oh, don't worry. Nothing's wrong.' Melanie said it in a very cold way as though with Esme there never was. She stopped as though she were struck by something. 'Does *she* know what you've been up to?'

For what seemed like for ever, Lottie wouldn't answer.
When she eventually said yes, Melanie was further enraged.

'I want you to go to your room,' she said icily, 'and when
you come down we'll discuss this calmly and rationally or
I will . . .'

'What Mum? Stop me seeing Nana? Giving me money?
Lock me in my room like a prisoner?' Lottie pushed the
fringe away from her blazing eyes. 'You've never trusted
me, ever! I don't care what you do to me. It won't make any
difference because I'm not telling you anything. I hate you!'
And she ran from the room, slamming the door behind her
with such force that one of the prints fell off the wall. The
cat flattened itself against the wall, its back a fierce arch.

Lauren studied Melanie with a sideways glance. She
shouldn't have come. She was crazy to have even contemplated it. But she could hardly just get up and leave
now. So she waited and they both sat there listening to
the melodic tick of the hall clock loud against the wall
of silence. Eventually, Melanie spoke. Her voice sounded
cracked and tired.

'I'm sorry you had to listen to that. Lottie's behaviour was
unforgivable. I just can't think what's got into her. She never
used to be like that.'

Lauren leaned forward in her chair. 'I think she may
be sick.'

'There's nothing wrong with that girl that a good night's
sleep won't cure,' said Melanie defensively. 'I do know my
own daughter.'

'Yes, of course. And I don't mean to interfere. It's just
that there are certain things that don't add up.' Lauren
was quite sure the problem wasn't drugs. 'I wondered
if you'd like me to go up and talk to her. Perhaps if it
came from someone she's not quite so closely involved
with?'

'I appreciate your help, Lauren, but this is a family matter,'

Melanie said, a fussy little smile on her face. 'Lottie and I can sort it out ourselves.'

Lauren recognised the snub. Unable to do any more for Lottie, she rose and reached for her bag. 'It's getting dark. I still have my son to collect.'

Melanie rose with her. 'It was good of you to come. I just wish it could have been a more agreeable visit.'

'Next time,' shrugged Lauren lamely, quite sure there wouldn't be a next time.

Later, when she had given herself and, she hoped, Lottie time to calm down, Melanie made her way upstairs to her daughter's room. Without knocking she opened the door and found Lottie lying on her bed. Her eyes skittered across the room. As usual, it looked like a tip, with clothes, shoes, a half-empty schoolbag and sweet wrappers littering the floor. She bit her lip to stop herself from saying anything about it.

For a moment they glared at one another. Then Melanie closed the door behind her and approached the bed.

'Right,' she said, folding her arms, 'talk!'

When Lauren got home, still worried about Lottie, she found a message from her old booker asking her to return her call. Jane Copeland had left her home phone number in case Lauren got in after six.

'Jane, I can't *believe* it's been so long. Are you still with Models One?'

'Where else would I be?' She laughed. 'In fact, it's work I was ringing about. I know you're officially "retired" but I got a call this morning from a Donna Ford. She works for the American company, Tuff . . .'

'The sports company?'

'Exactly. It seems she has you in mind for a campaign they're going to be running some time next summer.' Lauren could hear sounds of shrieking going on in the background.

'Hang on a moment, can you?' said Jane. '*Benjamin*! Leave your sister alone and put that jug down this instant. It's very expensive. *No*,' the shrieks subsided. 'Don't you dare,' a child's whiny voice. 'No, not there. Honey, give it to Daddy please. There's a good boy. Sorry,' she said, her voice returning.

'Look, Jane, I . . .'

'I know. You're probably going to say you're not interested, and if I were in your shoes I wouldn't bother either. They don't seem very clear about what they want. But you were the only one this Donna woman requested.'

'I don't understand. Tuff is a sportswear company. I wouldn't be right for them.'

'I wondered about that. But apparently they're planning to move away from their sporting image. They're not interested in our younger division. Sounds as though they're going to do something like The Gap. Still sports-orientated but stuff that people can wear on the street. Look, I'll get to the point. They'd like to do a test.'

Lauren leaned against the wall, toying with the telephone cord, 'A test?'

'We couldn't supply any up-to-date pictures of you and it seems they want to try you out with a male model – not one of ours,' she added a bit frostily.

'How many girls are up for this?'

'Don't know. I tried to wheedle it out of her, but she was a bit cagey. Could be worth your while. Not that you need the money, but were you to get the campaign you'd stand to make quite a tidy sum.'

Money, thought Lauren wildly. All those bills mounting in the top drawer of her desk. Oh, to clear her debts!

'When do they want to shoot?'

'Next week. I know it's not much notice, Lauren, that's why I wanted to speak to you today. Shall I tell them no?'

Lauren took a deep breath. 'No,' she said finally, 'tell them I'll do it.'

After hanging up, Lauren scrutinised her appearance in the large drawing-room mirror. What would they ask her to do? What kind of look were they after? She tried to guess, simulating sporty poses without looking too affected, standing on the coffee table so that she could see herself full length. Instantly she was a model again, drawing her lips together into a pout, distorting her body shape into familiar poses that came back to her instinctively. It pleased her to see how her body had shrunk to its old shape. Her breasts were still on the large side but for someone who rarely exercised she had little to complain about.

Tom's wails broke her concentration. She got down from the table, and as she did, Lauren could have sworn she saw someone watching from the window. Deeply embarrassed that anyone might have seen her frivolous display of vanity, she fled from the room and collected Tom who was still in his pram in the hall.

Changing him upstairs, she was amazed at herself for falling back into old habits. How could she think of herself as something she was not? As a model, Lauren had grown to despise herself for choosing a career that was based exclusively on appearance. Because beauty, as Kay had always taught her, unless backed up by something more meaningful, would always be superficial. Lauren didn't belong to the crew of waif-like creatures that stalked the international catwalks. Nor did she suffer their 'looks' anxieties. Hers was an athletic build and one that she had always been proud of. The perpetual demands from editors, agents, to keep slim, to conform, to be seen but not heard, had felt both hard and alien. As a model nothing was required of her except the way she looked and moved, which was why she had packed it all in. By letting go she had felt liberated, free again to take control of her life. Sukie, of course, hadn't been able to understand this, even when Lauren sat her down and explained it. Fame and money were Sukie's main interests in life. She honestly believed these two ingredients would make her happy; Lauren was a fool to turn her back on it, Sukie had declared, she would regret it later. But Lauren wasn't convinced. What was left once the excitement of a press show, the national TV commercial or *Vogue* cover had gone? Close friendships, self-fulfilment, gratification perhaps? More often than not just a collection of celluloid lies and a residue of worthlessness. This was because somewhere amongst the glamour and speed and flawless images, the inner self had been so ruthlessly ignored it sometimes felt as though it was not there at all.

Lauren had just finished changing Tom when she heard the crunch of footsteps on the front gravel drive. Who could it be at this time of night? She wasn't expecting anyone. She waited for a minute, wondering if it might be Sukie – she had sounded pretty depressed on the phone last night, but the doorbell remained silent. Then she remembered. Hallowe'en. It was probably some of the local kids Trick or Treating. Somewhere downstairs was a large bag of mini-chocolate bars she had been saving to give them. Propping Tom against one hip, she went downstairs to investigate.

But when she opened the front door all she was faced with was the chilly night.

The test was arranged for the following Wednesday, Guy Fawkes day. Having worried about the impending event all week Lauren woke up feeling strangely calm and made herself a large cooked breakfast. Thankfully, she wouldn't have Tom to worry about. Inge had already agreed to look after him.

She dressed with care, choosing a long double-breasted black jacket to go over her Levis and a thin cashmere sweater.

As a finishing touch she added a Hermès scarf which she used as a belt and brown ankle boots. She couldn't decide how to wear her hair so in the end she left it loose. They would have their own way of fixing it at the shoot. Jane called to make sure she knew where to go (more likely checking that Lauren hadn't changed her mind), then came a call from her mother who asked so many questions about the test that Lauren began to feel nervous again. She hung up. Grabbing her bag and cashmere shawl, she picked up Tom and his things she'd prepared for Inge, and banged the front door behind her.

The green Discovery was opaque with dew and all the windows had steamed up. Turning the heating on full, she got Tom settled in the back seat, then clicked in her seatbelt. As she checked the rear mirror she noticed a man on the opposite side of the road watching her. He looked like the Greek traffic warden. In her surprise, her foot slipped on the accelerator and the car shot forward. She slammed on the brake, halting the car with a jolt. But by the time she turned her head to take a better look, the man had gone. Oh, well. Perhaps she had imagined it.

She put the car into reverse and carefully manoeuvred it out of the drive, Tom gurgling happily in the back.

'Hello there, little man,' she murmured, turning briefly round to caress his bright red cheek. 'You feeling less grouchy now? Eh?'

It was a clear, smoky-smelling day with the occasional brown leaf floating down to join others rapidly collecting in the road. Frost had stiffened the grass and crystallised the branches. Lauren wound down her window and gave a satisfactory sniff. It was an extraordinarily beautiful morning. She felt suddenly as though her life, which had seemed so recently dead to her, buried along with Josh, was now indescribably precious and sweet. She had no right to feel sorry for herself. There was so *much* to be grateful for.

Having driven a short distance, she again noticed the traffic warden. He was issuing a ticket to a Ford. It *was* him, she thought, slowing down to have a better look. The man glanced up from his notepad and she waved to him as she drove by but he made no response. He merely stared at her in a way that made her feel uneasy.

The traffic had been hell, cars and buses clogging the roads. By the time Lauren reached home, she wished she had taken public transport. She so rarely had to drive into central London that she had forgotten what a nightmare it could be. She was looking forward to seeing Tom again. The test had gone well but the client's representatives had been so offhand it was as if they had already changed their minds about her. Were they just going through the formalities out of politeness? Had it been a waste of time? She thought not. People in the fashion industry rarely did anything out of politeness. To work with her they had chosen a blond, chisel-jawed model who had based his look on a modern-day Brando. He couldn't have been more than twenty and acted like a three-year-old – little Tom had more dignity. They made an incongruous pair, she felt, but the photographer had leapt around them with the kind of feverish energy and excitement usually found in Chris Evans in *Don't Forget Your Toothbrush*. They must have been doing *something* right.

'You look fab.' The make-up artist wore a skimpy T-shirt, baggy shorts held up with braces and bovver boots. His cropped hair was peroxide blond and his right ear had been pierced with six startling diamonds. Lauren asked him if they were real. 'Hon, you think I'd wear *diamante*! I worked for these babies, worked my butt off—head up—You got great lips, you know, hon—most of the time I have to fake it on girls, but not you—look up for me, hon, that's good—you ever have lipo? No? Well, take it from me, it hurts like hell—' Lauren tried to relax under the deft touch of his hands, the slightly scratchy feel of a blusher brush against her cheeks, the thin line of cold eyeliner against her closed lids, '—a little to the right—head up, hon—that's good. Now, don't go taking this the wrong way but I wanna say your husband was a real hunk . . .'

And on and on for almost five hours. She was relieved it was over.

Out of her bedroom window Lauren watched her neighbours building a bonfire. Their children had made a guy – rather a good one – and were being helped by their father to hoist it onto the pile. She thought fondly of her parents who were holding a party of their own at Willow. They had invited her but she couldn't face the drive, or all those people. The last party her parents had given had been their anniversary. Josh had been with her then. This made her think of Lottie, who only this morning had rung up in floods of tears. After she had calmed down, Lottie had asked if she could come round. She had something important to discuss. Because of school they arranged to meet on Saturday.

Lauren had just finished washing her hair when she heard the doorbell. She glanced at the bedside clock. Inge was early. She wasn't expected with Tom for another half-hour. Wrapping a towel around her hair, Lauren raced downstairs pulling the belt of her towelling robe as she answered the door.

'I tried to call you but . . . oh!' Her voice trailed off. Outside was the Greek traffic warden.

'Excuse me,' he said clumsily, 'I hoping you no mind, but I having accident.'

That was when she noticed his shirt. All the buttons had been ripped off. He had them in the held-out palm of his hand. She could see his grubby singlet vest underneath.

'This lady she have problems with her shopping, see, so I helping her. I getting my buttons stuck in her railings and they coming off,' he gave a rueful shrug.

Lauren bit down her anger. For a moment, she was quite unable to say anything.

'Is no very much. Maybe you don't mind to do it?'

Lauren made her voice cold. 'Take off your shirt and hand it to me,' she said curtly. He did as he was instructed. 'Now you wait outside. I have friends arriving any minute. Do you understand?'

The man nodded, dropping his eyes to where she had carelessly tied her robe. It was gaping slightly, revealing part of her breasts. Angrily, Lauren slammed the door then collapsed on the floor. Fool. You bloody little fool! What was she thinking of giving him her address? Of course, he was the one that had been prowling round her house. How long had he been watching her? Seething, she rose and went into the kitchen exploring the contents of the bulky breast pocket. Inside she found an ID badge. She quickly noted down his name and official number, then felt better for doing so. Should she call someone, she wondered, have them come round in case he tried to do something?

There was a loud piercing whine followed by a bang that sounded like a gun going off. She went to the window and looked out just in time to see glittering sparks of green and silver and blue explode in the air. Her neighbours' bonfire was blazing away, flames spitting and crackling hungrily as they devoured the defenceless guy. People were shouting and laughing, waving sparklers at arm's length. Their voices reassured her. She had nothing to be afraid of. If he *was* to try anything she could always go running next door. She got out her sewing box. One by one she sewed the buttons back on, her hands pulling roughly at the thread. She tried not to breathe in the pungent stench of his sweat-stained shirt. How *could* she have been so careless? What if he had hurt Tom? She brushed the thought away. Gingerly she returned the ID badge to the breast pocket.

When she opened the door she found him smoking on the front wall.

'Here,' she said coolly. 'It's fixed now.' She looked directly into his eyes. 'I think that makes us quits, don't you?'

He had the grace to look embarrassed. 'Okay, thank you, missus.' Head hung, he turned and made his way back up the drive.

Lauren closed the door on him shaking like a leaf.

15

It had been almost two weeks and still nothing from Hugo. Melanie was going out of her mind with worry. Since meeting him, her life had been measured by the times they had spent together and in some ways, now that she had time to think about it objectively, this made her resentful, aggrieved that he had so deeply, so easily ingratiated himself into her life. Already she had a collection of memories: Hugo sending her armfuls of roses on her birthday; walking, arms linked, on Wimbledon Common; their first lunch at the Fulham Brasserie; Hugo, after a long day at the office, squatting on his haunches as he contemplated how to mend her blocked dishwasher.

She was in love with him. Not in the way she had been with Josh: those uncertain but heady early months they'd spent together had transformed her life. Hugo was far less romantic, selfish too – she could see that. He lacked spontaneity, was ruled always by a need to control his surroundings. But this in part was what drew her to him. That and his sexual hold over her. No one had made her feel so – stirred, so inflamed in bed. She tried not to dwell on why he hadn't called. She put him out of her mind by taking on whatever temping work was available (there wasn't much), ignoring her unexplained fatigue at home by cleaning obsessively. But questions buzzed incessantly in her mind: Had he lost interest? Had he been put off by Lottie's rudeness? Or was he seeing someone else? She knew about his history of girlfriends; flaxen-haired, sporty, blue-eyed creatures that looked as though they'd just stepped off the pages of a glossy magazine, according to Caroline at the estate agency. She couldn't cope if it was another woman. Not again. Not after what Josh had put her through.

The first time it had happened with Josh she had felt devastated. Her small world had collapsed around her leaving her feeling worthless, sexless, useless. Later on she had gathered strength and vowed to give Josh his marching orders. Only by then his affair was over, and he had returned to her on begging knees. How could she resist – that face, that body, that, oh, so persuasive smile of his. Like a fool she forgave him, took him back into her home and wrapped him up in love. Until the next time it happened, and the next. And then one day he left for good. For Lauren Miller. How she had hated her for that. For being beautiful – and different.

Things might have been easier to cope with if Lottie hadn't become so impossible. It was getting to the point where Melanie was glad to have her out of the house. Gillian said it was a phase all kids went through, but Melanie, depressed and suffering from a cold, took little comfort in this. It was hard always being so understanding.

When the phone rang, her heart did a little dance. She grabbed the receiver certain it was Hugo. It was a shock, therefore, to hear Lauren Kendall's voice on the line.

'Something's happened,' she said hurriedly, 'to Lottie.'

Melanie's mouth went dry. 'Tell me.'

'She's in hospital – she collapsed. We're not sure why yet. I'm with her now.'

'Where is she?'

'Kingston hospital. I'll stay with her until you arrive.'

Melanie put the phone down then instantly picked it up again and dialled Hopkins and Co. Caroline answered the phone and Melanie almost hung up. But the secretary, suffering from a cold herself, hadn't recognised Melanie's nasal voice and she was put straight through.

'Rodney Tate.'

'Rodney. It's Melanie Roach.'

'Our much lamented office angel!' he shrieked in such a loud voice that Melanie's cheeks burned. 'You sound dreadful. Whatever is the matter?'

'I need to speak to Mr Butler. It's an emergency.'

'Afraid he's not here,' Rodney sounded concerned. 'Anything I can do?'

'Just tell him to get over to Kingston hospital as soon as he can.'

Melanie's head was pounding as she ran up to Wimbledon station. She barely gave the snow, falling around her in tiny flakes, a second glance. Her nose was completely blocked, which meant she had to pause every few yards to catch her breath. Then she realised she didn't have enough cash and had to make a frustrating detour back to her Midland branch.

The hospital heating was blazing. At reception there was some confusion about which ward Lottie was in. She was asked to wait and collapsed into a flap-down chair next to a black woman with wild, bulbous eyes.

'All right?' the woman said, folding her hands protectively against her stomach. She was pregnant.

Melanie smiled weakly, her stomach in knots. She still had a stitch from the last sprint from the station.

'Blood test, is it?'

Melanie shook her head, reluctant to encourage conversation. All she wanted was to hear that Lottie was all right.

'I'm back for one – can't think what the hold-up is. They don't normally take this long. I don't mind needles myself, but you get some in here who pass out at the sight of one. One lady came back eight times before she'd let them have a go. Gum?' She held out a packet of Wrigley's.

'No thanks.'

Fretfully, Melanie grabbed her last clean tissue from her coat pocket. Her nerves were in shreds. She still couldn't believe it: Lottie had collapsed. What from? Was it something to do with the meningitis, she wondered, blowing her nose so hard that her ears popped. And what had she been doing at Lauren's? She glanced at the receptionist, scribbling something down. Oh, for heaven's sake, why wouldn't they tell her what was going on?

The black lady was still rambling. 'They had me in here for weeks after the op. I've got an overactive thyroid,' she said, chewing manically on her gum. Melanie didn't think she could stand it another moment.

'Mrs Roach?' Melanie sprang to her feet, blood hammering in her temples. 'She's in ward 11B,' said the receptionist. 'Follow the corridor to the end until you come to the lifts. Go to the second floor and turn left. You'll go through two sets of double doors. Her ward's second door from the end.'

As the lift doors opened Melanie found Lauren Kendall standing next to the public phones. She was holding a plastic cup of water.

'How is she?' Melanie asked, forgetting her personal feelings for this woman.

'Awake – and *much* better. So you mustn't worry yourself. I told her you were on your way.'

Melanie glanced along the corridor. 'What happened?'

'I'm not sure. She'd only been with me for about ten minutes when she started complaining of blurred vision, feeling dizzy. She blacked out soon after.'

Melanie clutched her handbag tightly in both hands. She tried to appear friendly. 'Look, you've been very kind and I'm really grateful that you phoned but I'm sure you must have things to get back to. I can cope from here.'

Lauren nodded, understanding. 'I'll call later to find out how she's doing.'

Melanie wasn't sure what she'd expected. But to see her daughter propped up against the pillows, looking washed out in a hospital gown, her thin arm attached to a drip, oh, so vulnerable looking, but alive, *alive* and well enough to be reading a magazine, brought tears to Melanie's eyes. Her relief was so colossal that her already weak legs gave way and she had to support herself against the end of a patient's bed.

'You a'right?' asked the old woman whose bed it was.

'I'm sorry. I just need to sit down a moment.'

'Take as much time as you like. Don't normally get visitors on a Tuesday.'

All around the big ward, small clusters of people were talking to patients. Next to Lottie's bed was a young woman with long hair parted in the middle and gaunt cheeks. She was clutching a man's hand and sobbing. Melanie put a hand to her head as she approached her daughter's bed. She felt choked, her skin tingling with a rising temperature.

'Darling?'

At the sight of her mother, Lottie burst into tears. 'Oh, Mum,' she wailed feebly.

'It's all right. I'm here now.'

Lottie sniffed, lost in Melanie's embrace. 'I hate it here,' she sobbed. 'You've got to make them believe there's nothing wrong with me.'

'Of course, there isn't, silly,' Melanie soothed. 'Now come on, sit up a bit and try and tell me what happened. Lauren said you'd had a blackout.'

Lottie cast a weary glance at her mother. 'You're not cross with me for having been round there, are you?'

'No, I'm not cross. I just want to get you home. Are you really all right?' Lottie nodded quickly. 'Then why don't I try and find someone who'll tell me when we can get you discharged.'

The girl in the next bed was wailing, 'I'm sorry, darling, I only did it because I thought there was no hope for us.'

'Leave it out, Pizz,' her boyfriend was wearing a fake leopard-skin waistcoat. 'You can't go trying to top yourself every time you and I have a barney.'

An Indian nurse had come to inspect the colourless drip bottle suspended above Lottie's arm that looked like a skinny reading lamp. 'All right, love?' she said cheerily.

Melanie introduced herself. 'Is there any chance I could speak to the doctor – just for a moment?'

'Why don't I take you to her office? I know she wanted to see you.'

Dr Green, an attractive woman in her mid-thirties, got up from her desk as Melanie entered the small room.

'Mrs Roach,' she said, 'I'm sorry if I've kept you waiting. We've got our hands rather full today.' She indicated a chair for Melanie to sit down. 'We'd like to keep your daughter in overnight, if that's all right?'

'Why? What's wrong with her?'

'She's had a hypo.'

Melanie blinked uncomprehendingly. 'I don't understand.'

'Mrs Roach, your daughter has Type 1 diabetes.'

'Diabetes!' Melanie sat up in her chair. 'How?'

'Lottie's body has lost the ability to produce insulin because the cells in the pancreas that produce it have been destroyed. Without insulin her body cannot use glucose which is essential for creating fuel for the body. What happens is the blood glucose level rises. The excess glucose leaks into the urine causing frequent passing of urine and increased thirst. You may have noticed Lottie complaining of these symptoms.'

Lauren had. Perhaps if she'd listened to her, Lottie wouldn't be where she was now. The room was beginning to swim. Melanie's head was burning up. She was finding it very difficult to follow what Dr Green was saying.

'I'm sorry to sound so dim but just what does all this mean?'

The doctor smiled understandingly. 'Well, the hardest part of having Type 1 diabetes is that Lottie will be insulin-dependent for the rest of her life.' Melanie paled. 'I know this must come as a shock. It always is for people coping with diabetes for the first time. But if treated correctly there's no reason why Lottie can't lead a perfectly normal life.'

'You said insulin-dependent.'

'Yes. Lottie will have to be given insulin injections twice a day. As she gets more used to it she'll be able to inject herself.'

Melanie was making a huge effort to keep calm. 'I thought diabetes was hereditary?'

'It can be triggered by one of many things: heredity as you say, shock, a traumatic event usually followed by some sort of viral infection. Chances are she'll have had the condition for a while.'

All the pieces were now beginning to fit. 'Has she been told?'

'I've outlined the basis of her condition but I think it will take time for her to understand fully that things will never be quite the same again. It's not unusual to feel angry and cheated. Many patients go through a period of denial.'

'Oh, God,' Melanie rubbed her temples, 'this is awful.'

'It doesn't have to be, Mrs Roach,' Dr Green insisted. 'You'll get plenty of help and support through your local diabetic clinic. And Lottie will be entitled to free prescriptions. Once you realise how common this condition is, it'll no longer seem quite so overwhelming.'

An hour later, Melanie finally emerged from the hospital entrance, still feeling dazed and shocked. It was snowing harder now. Above, the sky was a uniform steel grey. Pulling her scarf more tightly around her neck, Melanie bowed her head and dashed across the car park. She thought she could hear someone calling her name. Whirling round she blinked against the waves of snow.

Standing a few feet away was Hugo.

'I was worried about you,' his voice sounded unfamiliar. 'When Rodney gave me the message I didn't know what to think.'

Melanie made no attempt to move towards him. 'They say she's got diabetes.'

'I know. I overheard the nurses talking about it.'

'I thought—' She looked down at her hands, not wanting him to see how upset she was by it all.

He took a step towards her. 'It's going to be all right.'

'Is it?' She was close to tears.

He was looking hard at her. Too hard, she thought, aware of how dreadful she must look. With no one to look nice for these past two weeks she had let her appearance go. And now with him turning up feeling the way she did, after giving up hope of ever seeing him again, she couldn't think of a thing to say.

'Look, Melanie, now's probably not the time to say this . . .'

She swallowed. He's come to tell me it's over. She thought: I don't think I can stand it.

'About us. I did have thoughts about ending it,' he said awkwardly. 'I wasn't sure if I could handle – all that responsibility.' He meant Lottie. He couldn't cope with her having a daughter. Well, he definitely wouldn't want to get involved now. She bit her lip. She felt like a piece of seaweed about to be washed away.

'It's all right,' she said flatly, 'you don't have to explain.'

'Oh, but I do. I must. You see I thought something had happened to *you*.' She threw him a look. 'Faced with the possibility of losing you, I realised what I had, what I wanted to keep.'

It was all Melanie could do to keep herself standing upright. 'You mustn't play games with me. I couldn't bear it if . . .'

This time when he stepped forward he grabbed her arms, pulled her towards him.

'This is no game, Melanie. Quite the opposite.' He looked at her very gravely. 'I'm asking you to be my wife.'

It was three weeks before Christmas and the unexpected sunshine had melted the thin crust of yesterday's snow. Later it would fall without mercy, silent and swallowing, burying indiscriminately the contours of buildings, trees, cars, land. Lauren and Inge had taken advantage of the reprieve and were walking Tom in Wimbledon Park. There was a surprising turn out. Fathers teaching their warmly clad boys how to fly kites, others jostling for a football, shouting, shrieking with the energy of youth. Toddlers parked on shoulders, gleefully waving mittens that were attached to string and threaded through the arms of their jackets. The scene reminded Inge of a Brueghel print she used to have pinned to the wall of one of her classes. They pulled away from the throng of people and settled themselves on a bench down by the tennis courts. For a moment they listened to the rhythmic pat, pat of balls.

Inge peeled a tangerine and handed half to Lauren. 'Have you heard any more from Tuff?'

'Not for a while. But things always quieten down before Christmas. My option's still on with the agency, so I'm hopeful. Should hear something in the New Year.'

'What will you do in the meantime?'

Lauren made an impotent gesture with her hands. 'Give in to one of the tabloids that have been hounding me all these weeks and sell my story – only joking, Inge. All the

same,' she sighed wistfully, 'I can think of a lot of things
to spend the money on.'

'I just don't want you to depend on Tuff. It might not
happen.'

'There's nothing wrong with a bit of healthy optimism.'
Lauren smiled wryly at her serious friend. The tip of Inge's
nose was a singing red. It looked as though she had dipped
it in tomato sauce. Lauren shifted against the wooden bench,
watching the players, 'You sounded very cagey on the phone
this morning. Are you going to tell me why you wanted to
meet today?'

Inge looked at her hands. 'I went to see my doctor.'

'You're not sick, are you?' The worried expression on
Lauren's face suddenly turned to joy. 'Oh, Inge, you're
not!'

The German smiled. They both smiled.

Lauren was jubilant. 'You are! That's *wonderful* news.
How far on are you?'

'Almost three months.'

'But that means you must have . . .'

Inge interjected, 'Yes. I thought it too – that the body
would take longer to heal. But it seems not so with me.'
Her radiant face was both proud and incredulous. 'You are
the first to know – except for Wolff, of course. I wanted to
be *really* sure before saying anything.'

'He must be over the moon.'

'I've never seen him so happy. Of course, we talked about
his schedule and Wolff sees that I should stay at home at least
for the early months.'

Lauren squeezed Inge's hand, 'He's right – just to be on
the safe side.'

'You know that when I met Wolff I'd never been out
of Europe. I was so hungry to see the world. It seemed
so exciting, travelling to all these new countries. I wanted
so much the experience. Now it is different. I feel content

to stay at home. I have my husband, my home – a baby coming.'

Inge wiped her nose which was running. She rather liked winter. Liked to wear substantial clothes, to come out of a tearoom and find it suddenly dark, inhale the smoky, frosty smell of the London air. Unwittingly the day of her miscarriage flashed into her mind. She put a protective hand to her stomach, urging the baby silently growing inside her to live. She was quite determined to be very careful, to take absolutely no risks this time. The morning sickness, despite its label, often lasted through the day. Not that she cared. She embraced the feeling. For as long as she had it, there was life in her womb.

Deep in thought, she watched a young girl playing on one of the courts. She was throwing herself with furious determination at a tennis ball. Inge smiled. Just like Wolff; the same gritty determination, the same intense concentration as though nothing else in the world mattered. She couldn't believe the change in her husband since she'd told him the good news. Lately he had become so moody and depressed about his game. It had even begun to affect their relationship. He was arguing with his coach and agent – even with sponsors. She remembered the most recent fracas.

Wolff was under contract with a French company to drink their mineral water. At each tournament the promoter may sell the rights to advertise on court to a company in one of three categories; a Lucozade-type liquid replenisher, soda and water. If the rights are sold, a player cannot use a different company's logo on court, although he may drink another company's product so long as it's in an unmarked bottle. In one tournament, Wolff had appeared on court carrying his sponsor's product, even though the tournament rights had been sold for all *three* categories to Pepsi. A terrific row had ensued with the ATP brought in to mediate.

Inge sighed. Another black mark against her husband's

name. She glanced at Tom in his pram, her face softening. Did any of that really matter now? Seeing the amazement on Wolff's face when she'd told him she was pregnant had meant everything to her. She could still hear him murmuring, '*Meine Inge, meine wunderliche, wunderliche Inge!*'

Lauren sat up abruptly.

'Gosh.' Her gaze was fixed on the tennis court nearest to them. 'So *that's* what she was trying to tell me. *Well, well.* Who'd have thought it!' Inge looked at Lauren inquiringly. 'Oh, Inge. Sorry, it's just that I've spotted someone I know.'

Inge's eyes drifted back to the girl on the tennis court. 'Who is she?'

'Lottie,' Lauren murmured, 'it's Lottie Roach. And it looks like she's got herself a coach. So this is the drug she's been taking.'

'Drugs?' Inge repeated. 'This young girl is taking drugs?'

'No. Oh, no, not drugs. No, Inge. I didn't mean that.'

Lauren watched the girl thoughtfully. The last time Lottie had been round to see her – the day of her collapse, she'd started to tell her something. A secret, she'd said, that no one else must know about. Had she told Melanie about the tennis? She must have done. With the diabetes there would have been no way round it. On the other hand, Lottie had become so introverted, built up so many walls. Lauren quite understood why, after all she'd been through. On the far side of the net a middle-aged man was lobbing a series of balls. Lottie had just sent one of them into the net and was cursing herself. Such fury. Josh always said that Lottie had talent. He took pride in drawing it out of her, developing her confidence with the game. Had this passion started after his death? Or long before? Was this a way of keeping Josh alive in Lottie's mind? If so, why be so secretive about it? Why hide it from her mother for so long? What did Lottie fear?

At three o'clock darkness was already settling over the

city. Lauren threw a cautious eye at her son sleeping in his pram. In his quilted coat and little hat, the blankets tucked snugly around him, Tom looked like a bound Russian doll. His cheeks were bright pink, his mouth opened and closed as if he were experimenting with some interesting new taste. Funny little thing, she thought lovingly, my darling little man. When was the last time *she* had been able to drift off with such contentment? Last night she had slept badly again, sporadically, her head filled with wild, urgent dreams.

Hand in hand they are running beneath a canopy of trees, branches cracking, leaves rustling, the long, rasping sound of things creeping, scuttling along the forest floor. Through the tunnels of green gloom they reach a waterfall pitching down a steep, crudely made shoot. Instinctively he leaps on, whooping with childlike fearlessness as he descends. She shouts a warning but he doesn't hear her. Down he goes sliding from side to side, the grin on his face switching to surprise, then shock as he is swept away, crashing into sharp bends, his head smacking against the wooden sides as vulnerably as a soft fruit until it no longer resembles anything human. She feels herself pushed by an invisible hand. NO! she screams, tumbling head first into the shoot, falling, plummeting to death. Miraculously, she reaches the bottom unhurt. She steps off and feels something sharp puncture the sole of her foot. She inspects the damage. Pulls out a piece of live coral. A sudden distant cry alerts her. She swings round, fearful of the mad noise, sees the raging waterfall.

Then she turns and runs from the furious wave of blood.

Inge was talking. 'Do you want to invite her for tea with us?'

'Who?'

'Your young friend,' Inge nodded towards the court. Now lying on her back, Lottie was facing the coach who was about two feet away. He kept throwing a football at her, making her do sit ups as she caught the ball and threw it back.

'She's busy. I think I'll leave it today.' Lauren shuddered, feeling chilled suddenly. Stupid not to have brought a hat. 'Are you ready to go? My ears are getting cold.'

Inge cast a glance towards the darkening sky. 'Anyway, I think it's going to rain.'

'Come on, then. I've got some Pandoro cake a friend brought back from Italy.'

Lauren energetically pushed Tom's pram on, suddenly desperate to be by a hot fire drinking hot tea. At the park entrance was a man in a faded suit that was too small for him. Wiping his mouth with stained fingers, he tugged out a cigarette from a crumpled packet and placed it between his lips.

'Got a light?' he asked Inge.

'I am sorry, but I don't smoke.'

As he wandered off, Lauren caught a strong whiff of whisky. She was struck by the oddness of his red socks.

They were married in the New Year. No fuss. No church, not even a reception. Just a low-key registry office ceremony with Rodney and Gillian as witnesses. Esme, who had kept ominously quiet about what she was going to wear, had been the first to arrive, making her grand entrance in an explosion of violet and orange stripes.

'She looks like a bloody deck chair,' muttered Hugo, as Esme took a seat at the front. 'I'm only surprised she didn't dye her hair orange to match the suit. My God, she's even brought her knitting!'

Hugo had ordered himself a new Italian suit made of dark brown wool. The colour brought out the green flecks in his hazel eyes and any doubts Melanie had had evaporated the moment she gazed into their depths. Hugo loved her and that was enough security she needed to build their future on. If she had been honest her romantic side would have liked to have made more fuss of their wedding; be blessed in a church, involve more people, wear a white gown. But she had already done that as a young woman. And as Hugo sensibly pointed out, the money they'd save could be put to better use elsewhere. She'd contemplated who to invite but there weren't many names to add to her guest list. A distant cousin who she rarely saw, mad Aunt Hilda who was staying with friends in Scotland. Hugo appeared to have no family, bar his mother now infirm and dotty in an old people's home. His father had been dead for years – a fatal heart attack. She could have invited friends she had made from her time with Josh, but none of them could be deemed close. It saddened her to think that so many people had crossed the path of her life and so few remained.

Coming to terms with Lottie's diabetes had at first been a struggle. It was hard for Melanie not to blame herself for what had happened. There seemed to be so many rules about when and what Lottie could eat and the importance of routine; the blood tests; administering the insulin injections which Lottie showed a great unwillingness to do for herself. One day, Lottie had come home from school, taken her insulin then gone upstairs for a quick bath before supper. Sometime later Melanie had found her in it unconscious. She had become hypoglycaemic because the hot water had warmed her injection site and absorbed the insulin too quickly. It was a terrifying scare for them both.

On the plus side Lottie's health had improved dramatically as had her weight and energy levels. As Dr Green had promised, they received a great deal of information and help both from the British Diabetic Association and their local GP clinic which they attended one evening every

fortnight. As both Melanie's and Lottie's confidence grew
and worrying questions like: would the diabetes affect her
career prospects? Would she still be able to exercise? Would
she develop complications? were answered, the intensity of
the initial turmoil began to fade.

Hugo accelerated the Jag along the M4 towards Bath and the
Priory hotel. It was where they had decided to spend their
honeymoon, somewhere they could enjoy the surrounding
countryside but near enough to the city as Hugo had to be
at work on Monday. Already the landscape was changing
to rolling fields covered in hard, sparkling frost. Two days
together wasn't much, but Melanie was grateful for them
and planned to make the most of their time alone. She
turned to look at her new husband almost as though she
couldn't quite believe what they'd just done, and thought:
you're strong and capable. You won't collapse and have a
breakdown like Andrew; you won't expect me to support
you financially then disappear for weeks at a time the
way Josh did. You're too proud, too settled in your ways
for that.

'I like it.'

'What?' said Melanie dreamily.

'The dress. Definitely your colour. It makes you glow.'

He had bought the red dress for her in Browns, South
Molton Street. She was horrified by the price but he
had insisted she should have it. So she had worn it
for him today.

'Feel strange being married to me?' Hugo asked without
taking his eyes off the road.

'A bit. But nice strange. Very, very nice,' and she leaned
across and gently pressed her lips against his cheek.

If Melanie had been concerned about anything, it had been
Lottie. She'd been through so much lately: the painful loss of
Josh; the meningitis; contracting diabetes. How would she

take to having Hugo as a stepfather? The two of them had discussed it a few nights before the wedding.

'Mum, I can't say he'd be my choice for you, but if he makes you happy then I suppose it's okay.'

'Do you mean that, darling? Do you really?'

'If he loves you, I do. We should all have someone to love. And I know that when you want something badly enough no one should stop you from having it.'

Something in her daughter's voice made Melanie look at her with suspicion.

'Now why do I get the feeling you're about to announce something?'

Lottie chewed on a nail. 'Promise you won't get cross if I tell you.' Melanie waited. 'I want to play tennis.'

'TENNIS!' Melanie almost laughed she was so relieved. 'Is that what all this sneaking around has been about?'

Lottie looked offended.

'Why didn't you tell me before? You knew how worried I was.'

'I was afraid of what you'd say. Things have finally started to work out. I thought you'd try and stop me.'

'Because of the diabetes?'

'No. I didn't think you'd mind about that. Dr Green said it was fine to exercise. It might even improve my blood glucose control.'

'True,' Melanie said cautiously, 'just so long as you're *extremely* careful. But why tennis?' Her face fell. 'Because of Josh, I suppose?'

'Oh, come on, Mum. From the start you never approved of what he did. The expense of everything, him away so much of the year, not knowing when he'd be back or anything.'

'And you blame me for that?' Lottie shook her head but Melanie seemed not to notice. 'Do you have any idea what I went through with that man?' The lines on her forehead pulled together into a frown, making her look much older.

'Oh, *Lottie*, I know you thought of him as some sort of god, but let me tell you he had a few flaws.'

Lottie bit down on her lip. 'I don't want to fight about Josh. I just want to tell you about me, about *my* future.'

'Look,' Melanie chose her words carefully, 'you're still very young.' Lottie sighed heavily as though she'd expected this. 'And there's plenty of time to decide on your career. In a few years from now . . .'

'Mum.'

'. . . when you finish school.'

'MUM! You're not listening to me.'

Melanie sat back and folded her arms. She had a wounded look on her face. 'Go on then,' she said defensively. 'What else do you want to tell me?'

'I've been getting free coaching down at the courts. Mark – he's the local park coach, got in touch with the county development officer and had him come down and watch me play.' She shuffled her feet. 'He wants me to try for the Starter tournaments and if I do well I can go on to play in the County Closed tournament next year.'

Melanie's frown deepened. 'That seems like an awful lot to take on.'

'It's not. Really, it's not. Mark's entered me in the Starter tournament at St George's College next weekend.' Melanie raised an eyebrow. 'Mum, I need someone to take me.'

'Where is St George's College?'

'Weybridge. I need to get myself on to the ratings system and the only way to do that is by beating other players. Mum, I've got to do it. I'm already eleven.'

Melanie pulled a face. 'Oh, so *old*!'

'You don't understand how hard it is getting noticed. Some of these kids have been playing since they were six. I've got to catch up, win as many tournaments as I can to get the points.'

'And where does school fit into all these elaborate plans, do you suppose?'

Lottie looked exasperated. 'Most tournaments take place during half-term and school holidays and I can keep my practising to weekends and evenings. I'll still be able to do all my school work.'

'And the diabetes? It's hard enough sticking to a routine at home. How do you think you'd cope taking on all this extra work?'

'I just *will*. It's what I want. But I can't do it without your help.'

Melanie recognised the commitment behind her daughter's words.

'No,' she said, half to herself, 'I can see that.'

Watching Lottie pick at a stain on her skirt, strands of hair straining to escape from her messy plait, Melanie couldn't help but despair at how dishevelled her daughter was looking; scuffed shoes, a stain on her school shirt, her knees red and puckered as though she had been kneeling on gravel. Her hair could do with a wash too. And she thought; how different we are. She thought about all the ambitions she'd had at Lottie's age. Most of them unfulfilled. She remembered the early pressure employed by her parents for her to get married and settle down; her father's kind but dismissive reaction to her telling him she wanted a career; her subsequent frustrations that had somehow got pushed aside and ignored yet had continued to prod and nag at her over the years. What a lot she had missed out on. Was it really fair to deny Lottie her chance when she had finally found happiness for herself?

'Mum?'

'Mmm?' Roused from her thoughts, Melanie shook herself and glanced at her watch.

'Gosh, is that the time! Hugo'll be back soon. I'd better get supper started.' She walked to the door. 'Chops all right?'

Lottie was frowning at her. 'Whatever. Just tell me I can do it. *Please!*'

'Tell you what, we'll talk about it over supper.'

The door closed and Lottie listened to her mother's footsteps going downstairs. Very quietly, with lumps of duvet stuffed into her mouth to muffle the noise, she began to cry.

GROWTH

Things out of darkness incline to the light,
colours flow into music and ascend,
and in that act consume themselves, to burn
is both a revelation and an end.

The Sunflower
Taken from *The Coastguard's House*
by Montale & Reed (Bloodaxe Books, 1990) Ltd.

16

'Charlotte.'

She was a child. Lying snug and warm in bed. Holding her breath, she shuffled further down into the bed, keeping her body as flat as possible so that not even a strand of hair would give her away.

'Hey, you little monkey,' he was laughing, 'your mother wants you downstairs. Pronto.'

She could feel strong but gentle hands tickling her through the duvet. Stifling giggles, she wriggled and squirmed until she could feel the duvet slipping off the bed. Immediately she grabbed the corners and pulled them back with all her might. It was all part of the game. There was a pause, then:

'Okay. You've got ten seconds to come out. One—two—three—'

Of course she waited until he'd reached nine.

'—nine, nine and a half. Ten. *Right*! You asked for it. Here I come.'

Shivering with excitement she threw the duvet back.

'*Charlotte!*'

She opened her eyes to bright sunshine spilling through undrawn curtains. For a moment she lay there confused, groping to make sense of the time and the day. She tried to grasp the shreds of her dream because it felt important, but already they had dissolved into the light, far beyond her reach.

'I'm not standing here all day!'

'I'm up,' Charlotte croaked, her body stiff and resistant as she hauled herself out of bed and staggered to the door.

Melanie was hovering on the landing. She looked pointedly at her watch.

'You've got five minutes, then I'm leaving. You're not going to make me late a second time this week.'

Charlotte's face was set in dull, early morning concentration. 'Sorry,' she said, 'the alarm didn't go off.'

But Melanie was already halfway downstairs, '*Five* minutes.'

Wicklow had sneaked into her room and installed himself on the end of the bed. Over the last eighteen months he had grown very fat and now dedicated most of his time to sleeping. His tiny black nose sniffed the June air experimentally. Through half-shut eyes he watched Charlotte throwing on clothes, already fatigued by the morning stir.

Little about the bedroom had changed. Josh's poster, frayed round the edges, still hung on the back of the door. Rivalling it on each of the walls were posters of the 1995 Australian champion Mary Pierce, 'Pistol Pete' and the fiery Spaniard Sergie Bruguera. Dimble, demoted from his throne on the bed, was now parked on the bookshelf. The bed had shrunk, of course, and there weren't quite so many bottles of cream on the dressing table. The most discernible difference about the room was its improved neatness. That, and a card Blu-tacked on the wall next to the bed. Charlotte read it every day.

Belief

If you think you're better – you are
If you think you dare not – you don't
If you'd like to think you can't
It's almost certain you won't.

If you think you'll lose – you've lost
For out of this world you'll find

Success begins in a person's will
It's all in a state of mind.

Charlotte inspected the upper side of her right thigh. The injection site was bruised where she had accidentally punctured a small blood vessel. She'd be better off using the other one. From a drawer she removed a preloaded syringe, removed all the air bubbles and stuck the half-inch needle into her left thigh. She then pumped the plunger several times and replaced the cap on the needle. She gave her hair a few vigorous tugs, strands flying up to meet the brush as it filled with static. A few weeks ago in a moment of rebellion, and egged on by her new friend Fran, she'd had it cut. Now the brown tresses curved inwards just below her chin. The style accentuated her large soft brown eyes but added weight to her already round face. She still couldn't decide if she approved of the change. She chucked the brush on her bed, giving up. Style or no style, her hair was beyond redemption. But for once she didn't care. One more week of school and she had the whole of the summer holidays to look forward to!

'You look a mess,' said Melanie when she walked into the kitchen.

'Oh, *thanks*, Mum. Same to you.'

'Well, if you'd just give yourself a bit more time to get ready instead of bolting your cereal and flying out the door in a mad frantic rush each morning . . . I can't think what it must be doing to your sugar level. Have you taken your shot?'

'Yup.'

Melanie handed her a cup of tea. 'Here, drink this. It's all you have time for.'

Charlotte took a grudging sip of the tea then put it down on the tablecloth – green with a bold strawberry pattern – and jammed her hair back with an Alice band. 'Who's picking me up tonight?'

'Hugo.'

'Why not you?'

'Because I want to see the Monet exhibition at the Royal Academy and it's the last day. And *please* don't make Hugo hang around, Lottie.' She flinched at her mistake – '*Charlotte*. You know how he is about time.'

'A real stickler.'

Melanie frowned. 'That's not fair. Hugo's gone out of his way to help. All those weekends and evenings he's given up for you, ferrying you around the country to your matches. You have a lot to be grateful for, young lady.'

Charlotte pulled up her socks. 'You know how hard I've worked to get my points. It's just that Hugo can be . . .' she slumped slightly in her chair as though the effort to explain was too much.

Melanie looked at her sharply. 'Can be what?'

'Oh, look, let's not argue. I was up half the night catching up with my homework. I don't know how I'm going to pull through today.'

'This was your idea, remember?' Melanie glanced at the clock then put her mug in the sink and filled it with water. 'We'd better go.' She handed Charlotte a lunch box. 'You can eat some of that in the car. Have you got everything else?'

Charlotte smacked her forehead. 'My racquet! I'll be *one* sec.'

'You haven't drunk your tea.'

But Charlotte had already flown from the room.

'Your entry forms for the National went off this morning.' Hugo turned the car radio volume down. 'Just as well you still qualify for the under-fourteens, given your current form. Can't think what was the matter with you tonight – your serve was all over the place.'

'My grip needs changing – it kept slipping.' Charlotte was

eating a banana. The car stank of it. Hugo wound down his window to let in some air.

'And what's all this I hear from Chris. He tells me you fainted. That true?'

'It's not what you think,' she mumbled, her mouth full. 'I got my period. The first day is always the worst.'

'You should have mentioned it.'

'I didn't want you to fuss.'

'Surely there are pills you can take for that sort of thing?'

'Yes, but they make me feel odd.'

'Then try a different brand.'

'These are the only ones that have any effect.'

'Well, we can't have you fainting every time you go out on court.' Hugo checked his rear mirror, making a mental note to look into the matter further. 'Tell me what you have lined up for tomorrow.'

Charlotte dropped the banana skin into her now empty lunch box and closed the lid. 'Squad training with Chris.'

'Time I had a word with Chris about that. Seems to me you're not getting enough one-on-one.'

'I get the same as everyone else.'

'Precisely my point. How are you supposed to move up in a squad of twenty-nine, tell me that? If Chris can't see your potential then it's my responsibility to tell him.'

Charlotte inwardly groaned. Hugo was always getting on his high horse about something. She hated him stirring things up with the LTA, drawing so much attention in her direction. On the other hand, without his help it would have been unlikely she'd have made it even this far. One thing about Hugo was that he got things done. She helped herself to a biscuit from the stock he always kept in the glove compartment along with her insulin and disposable syringes.

Hugo overtook a Golf convertible. 'The National's only seven weeks from now and before that you've got the cement/acrylic tournaments in Basingstoke, Bracknell . . .'

'Sheffield. I know.'

'Something's got to be done about your fitness level. You shouldn't be getting so tired after a straightforward match – I counted seven double faults tonight.'

Charlotte looked out of the window. 'Chris has been making changes to my serve. I'll get it – eventually.' If you stop nagging me, she thought moodily. *Failure, Charlotte, is proof that the desire wasn't strong enough.* Sometimes she wished they could just skip the post-match lecture.

'I also want you out on the practice courts more. I'm not letting all these months of training go to waste. Nottingham's the most important tournament of the year. That's where we're most likely to pick up sponsorship.'

'So you keep telling me.'

There was a moment of strained silence. Charlotte picked up his newspaper and hid behind it.

Hugo's requests for sponsorship had been repeatedly turned down. None of the sports manufacturers had shown even a flicker of interest in Charlotte. She needed a big win to convince them that she had a glowing future in tennis.

'Tell you what,' Hugo said finally. 'You get good results in the National and I'll take you and your mother skiing for Christmas. Now, how does that sound?'

'I don't ski,' she said ungraciously, running her eye over a crossword Hugo had started. 'Neither does Mum. She hates snow.'

'Then she'll just have to *learn* to like it,' Hugo retorted.

When Charlotte was four, Josh had taken her tobogganing on Hampstead Heath. The snow made everything bright and light with future. The toboggan Josh rented was red and made of plastic. They hauled it to the top of the hill and waited for the slope to clear. It seemed that everybody was out that day; groups of screaming children and grown-ups hurtling down on toboggans, sleighs and some on thick squares of cardboard. Many of these hit bumps and were upturned. Some of the children cried. But this didn't deter Charlotte. Josh would look after her. Just being with him intensified the pleasure of the day. They sat down in the small toboggan with Charlotte in front, her feet carefully tucked up inside.

'Ready?' Josh had cried.

Eyes sparkling with anticipation they were suddenly whizzing down the snow-encrusted hill. They flew through the air at an astonishing speed. Twice the toboggan threatened to upturn. Her little hands gripped the sides, mouth clamped down on a scream. But Josh kept on telling her to relax and on they sped. On and on until she thought she would burst with excitement. When they reached the bottom, she clambered out and begged to have another go. It had been the most thrilling moment of her short life and she wanted more. She wanted to fly down again and never, ever stop.

Charlotte looked down at the incomplete crossword. 'Can I finish this for you?'

Hugo glanced sideways. 'I doubt you'll have much luck.'

'Examine, seven letters,' she read, chewing a nail thoughtfully, trying a few ideas out.

Hugo threw her an amused sideways glance. 'You're wasting your time.'

Rising to the challenge, she counted the boxes, then finding a pencil on the dashboard wrote, ANALYSE. 'It fits. There you go,' she said smugly. 'Feel free to ask next time you get stuck.'

Hugo, who had spent twenty minutes grappling with the crossword, clamped his lips together and reached for the radio volume button.

Melanie inspected her half-finished landscape and let out a satisfied sigh. Not quite Monet but not bad, she mused. Not bad at all. Reluctantly, she checked her watch. Eight o'clock.

Hugo and Charlotte would be home soon. She should think
about getting supper.

As she washed paint from her hands in the kitchen, she
wondered if she'd been naive in thinking her daughter could
combine school work and tennis without her studies or her
health suffering.

Charlotte had ventured first into Starter tournaments but
rarely got past the second round. As she improved, however,
she entered the under-twelve County Closed Tournament
and to everyone's surprise she upset the number two seed,
managing to reach the semifinals. Picked up by the County,
Charlotte was invited to county training at the Sutton Junior
Tennis Centre.

It had taken Hugo quite a while to rectify his bad start with
Charlotte. Both of them, Melanie suspected, had tolerated
one another for her sake, but it wasn't until Charlotte's tennis
began to show real promise that Hugo's relationship with
his stepdaughter warmed. If it took tennis to bring them
closer together then that was fine by Melanie. All she had
ever wanted was for the three of them to get on, to be
a family.

It wasn't long before Hugo began actively supervising
Charlotte's career. When Charlotte joined the Sutton Junior
Tennis Centre it was Hugo's idea she switch from her school
in Wimbledon to Cheam. To help with the runs Hugo
bought Melanie the Fiat. No more hanging around waiting
for buses in the cold and rain. The car had transformed
Melanie's life.

Cheam, a sponsor of the Sutton Tennis Centre, was
one of the few schools that allowed its pupils time off
to play alternate mornings and afternoons. Pupils were
also permitted to play in tournaments although the head
made it clear that educational standards must be maintained.
Charlotte threw herself into her work and as promised kept
up her grades. But her growing obsession with tennis

worried Melanie. It was all very well Charlotte saying she loved playing. But what *possible* future was there in it for her when such a small percentage of girls made enough to survive on? And the constant ferrying around the country was beginning to take its toll on all of them. Tournaments ate into evenings, weekends and holidays. With the exception of school, Charlotte seemed to have no other life. Worried, Melanie discussed it with Hugo.

'She's given up so much already. Now she wants to discontinue her piano lessons. Has she mentioned that to you?'

'As a matter of fact it was I who suggested it. If you're going to make it to the top then you've got to be prepared to make sacrifices,' he reasoned, 'grab the opportunity while it's there. She can always return to her education at a later stage.'

'But can it really be good to push her so hard?'

'No one's forcing her to play. Charlotte pushes herself. I know you worry about her condition, but it's not healthy being too overprotective either. Charlotte's a strong girl with real talent – talent that shouldn't go to waste.'

I wonder, thought Melanie, popping fat potatoes liberally covered in salt and olive oil into the oven. What if Charlotte wasn't good enough? What if she failed? During her years with Josh, Melanie had seen countless players give up in despair. It was so hard for them to get anywhere. Would Charlotte have the discipline to recognise when the time had come for her to stop? Would she then be able to make a life for herself outside tennis? The pressure to succeed was immense. At matches, Melanie had watched parents pt very aggressive pressure on their children. Hugo was guilty of it too.

'That was useless!' she would hear him yell, as Charlotte came off court red with shame and anger. 'What the *hell* did you do that for? You weren't thinking!'

His philosophy was never to praise her for what she had
done right, only to criticise where she had gone wrong.
Melanie felt that when a child had lost, often all they needed
was a hug and reassurance, not bullying. Hugo remained a
loving and devoted husband. The problem lay in his attitude
to Charlotte. It was as though he saw her not as a child but
as an instrument to success, to money. No matter how hard
Charlotte worked for him, Hugo always wanted more from
her. He was never satisfied. No thirteen-year-old dealing
with so many physical and emotional changes should have to
cope with such pressure. But perhaps she was being unfair.
Hugo had been an incredible support. They relied almost
entirely on his income now. She must be more grateful for
the efforts he made.

They got back at nine, both looking fraught and tired. The
traffic had been dreadful. With supper over, Charlotte retired
to her room to do her homework. Hugo made a few calls
then settled down with his wife and a cup of tea to watch
the evening news.

'You've got paint in your hair,' he observed, switching
off Suzanne Charlton reading the weather.

Melanie stirred her tea. 'I got carried away. Finally finished
that painting I've been working on for so long.'

'Good, darling.' Hugo seemed deep in thought. She knew
he was under pressure at work. The property market had
nose-dived and sales in the last year had almost halved.
He'd never admit there were problems but she'd seen the
latest tax assessment. Over £10,000 had been put towards
Charlotte's tennis. Money that paid for coaching, kit, travel,
accommodation, court hire. Each year the costs increased.

'Something's troubling you, Hugo. What is it?'

He blew into his cup. 'Just been a long day.'

'It's money, isn't it?'

'You worry too much.'

'I can't help it if you don't tell me.'

Hugo lifted his shoulders in resignation, too tired to continue the pretence.

'If you must know, we've had a *disastrous* week. Negotiations collapsed on two substantial properties. And now Rodney's threatening to leave.' He rubbed his eyes, blinked, then focused his gaze back on her. 'It goes without saying that it couldn't have come at a worse time.'

Melanie put her hand on his. 'Oh, darling. I hate to think of you shouldering all this responsibility on your own.'

'We'll get there. It's just going to take a bit of time.'

'Perhaps I *can* help,' she said, an idea still embryonic in her mind. 'Gillian had a good look at my work yesterday. She says I've got something.' Hugo smiled half-heartedly. 'Darling, she thinks I could make money.'

'And why not? If it's something that will amuse you.' He yawned so widely that she could see the pink dangly bit at the back of his throat. 'Christ, why am I so *tired*?'

Melanie tried again. 'Hugo, Gillian knows this gallery owner in Kensington. She thinks he could be persuaded to exhibit some of my paintings . . .'

He gave a derisive snort. 'Then I'd say get right on to the Tate. I'm sure they'll snap you up.'

Melanie bit her lip.

He was immediately contrite. 'Hell, I'm sorry. That was insensitive of me. I think your paintings are very attractive, really I do. But frankly, darling, what I need right now is support, not you cooking up wild, hair-brained schemes with Gillian. I'm sure she meant well when she suggested an exhibition but I wouldn't call Gillian much of an expert on anything – least of all on art.'

'She seemed very . . .'

He took her hand. 'I think she was probably just being kind, don't you?'

Melanie cast her eyes downwards. 'It's just that Charlotte's tennis is costing you a fortune. I hate to think you're losing money because of it.'

'Isn't that for me to decide?' He squeezed her hand affectionately. 'Just you let *me* do the worrying. We're a long way from calling in the bailiffs.'

Later Melanie having packed Hugo off to bed, washed up supper and laid the table for breakfast. She fed the cat, made a shopping list for the next day and put sheets in the washing machine ready to do in the morning. She didn't regret their earlier talk. Better to get things out in the open, even though a tiny part of her felt aggrieved that Hugo had skated so blithely round Gillian's idea of an exhibition. Rashly, Melanie had allowed herself to get carried away by her friend's enthusiasm; it could work; she had talent. But Hugo was probably right to have said what he had. Better to find out now than to have her hopes crushed further down the line.

She walked into the sitting room and began turning out lights. Something jutting out from behind the sofa caught her eye. It was one of her watercolours, the one Gillian had liked so much. Curiously she went over and inspected it. The overall effect was quite pleasing but no one would pay money for it. She was an idiot even to have contemplated it. Looking at it now, she could see that the painting was really quite crude. Decisively, she carried it back upstairs to the small room where she worked and stacked it in the corner with the rest, its face to the wall.

'Wolff! Come in. Miriam's been such a sweetheart. My sister's been teaching her how to dance – I think they've exhausted each other.' Smiling, Lauren led him through into the drawing room. 'Have you two met? I can't remember.'

Sukie Miller was lying across the sofa pleading with a young howling infant. The child had her head buried in one of the cushions. *Thomas the Tank Engine*, Lego pieces and toys littered the floor. Gipsy Kings was playing in the background.

'Sukie?'

Self-consciously, Sukie sat up and straightened her short skirt.

'She hit her head,' she stammered, clearly embarrassed by the situation. 'I turned my back for a second to change the music – she must have tumbled off the sofa. She's fine now though. Really. More shock than anything.'

Wolff crossed the room in four paces and swung his daughter up into his arms. '*Qu'est-ce que ça, ma petite chérie?*'

The sound of his voice immediately arrested her tears. Huge blue eyes fringed with wet lashes blinked at him in recognition.

'It's okay,' he reassured Sukie. 'Don't worry. Miriam can be a handful – she's a very active child.'

'Sukie, this is Miriam's father, Wolff Bohakari,' said Lauren, turning down the volume.

'I know,' Sukie smiled impishly. 'You thrashed my friend, Luke Falkner in the French Open. Revenge must be sweet.'

'I'm sorry,' he said absurdly, kissing Miriam. The child gurgled with joy, and tweaked the end of his nose, tears and bumps on the head miraculously forgotten.

Lauren opened a window. Sun streamed into the room. 'How's Gretal? – Inge says the poor little thing's suffering from asthma again?'

'She's much better. The cough's almost cleared up.'

'You must be relieved. That kind of thing can drag on. Can I offer you some tea? There's plenty in the pot.'

Wolff eyed a tray of used cups and a half-eaten cake on a side table.

'I think not. I should be getting this little girl home to her mother.'

'Mrs Kendall.' A meek-looking young woman had appeared in the doorway.

'Are you off now, Pippa?' asked Lauren, collecting a tiny shoe from the floor which she placed on top of a miniature truck full of toys.

'I won't be back late,' the young woman said shyly, recognising Wolff. 'Tom's supper's all prepared. It just needs heating up.'

'Where is Tom?' asked Wolff, once she'd gone.

'Sent to his room in disgrace,' said Lauren. 'He's at that age when he wants to possess everything.' She gestured to the strewn toys with her arm. 'This mess is all his. He managed to pour most of his tea down the back of the sofa. It all ended in tears, of course. I think he was a bit overexcited with Miriam being here.'

The front door banged shut behind the departing nanny. 'So how's this new nanny working out? Pippa whats-her-name?' Wolff asked.

'Head's a bit in the clouds but Tom seems to like her. At least she doesn't go out raving until four in the morning every night like the last one.'

Sukie pulled herself to her feet. 'Lo, I should be making a move too. I promised I'd meet Luke at six.'

'Where's he taking you?'

'The Hard Rock to meet up with some of his sporting friends. I'd invite you along, but with Stella Artois about to start it'll just be endless boring tennis talk.' She threw a glance at Wolff as she said this.

'You're not going to lug that suitcase back on the tube,' said Lauren as her sister tested its weight with both hands. 'Oh Sukie, you'll break your back.'

Sukie was still looking at Wolff. 'It all depends on whether Mr Bohakari's prepared to give me a lift?'

He cleared his throat. 'Well, it . . .'

Miriam was trying to pull one of Wolff's shirt buttons off. 'Su-key,' she sang.

Sukie beamed. 'That settles it then.'

Lauren walked Sukie to the front door while Wolff collected the case. 'Why don't you bring Luke round for supper one night while you're both here? Pick any night – except Saturday,' she lowered her voice. 'I've got a date.'

'Who with?'

'Someone I met through Tuff. I hardly know the man, Sukie. So don't go buying a hat quite yet.'

The two sisters hugged one another. 'At last! I want to know *all* the gory details,' Sukie whispered. 'Promise to call me. And thanks for the things.'

'Clothes,' explained Sukie to Wolff as the two of them trooped out to his car. 'Lauren's been having a clear-out.'

Wolff was carrying the heavy case in one hand, his daughter supported by his free arm. His temples throbbed slightly, threatening a headache. He hoped he hadn't caught Inge's cold; he didn't need it. Not with Wimbledon approaching. They reached the car. Inside it was boiling. Wolff opened all the windows before strapping his daughter into the child's seat in the back.

'This is really very kind of you.' Sukie threw her cigarette butt out of the window. 'It's too hot to be lugging that thing around.'

'Seatbelt,' reminded Wolff, as he put the car into gear.

Miriam was playing with her doll in the back of the car when Wolff pulled up outside the hotel where Sukie was staying with Luke. The engine idled. For a moment neither of them spoke.

'You've decided to play in Manchester rather than Queen's?' said Sukie eventually, watching a young man hose down his car.

'I leave tomorrow.'

'I see.'

'With Gretal sick, it would be too difficult for Inge to come too.'

'Of course,' Sukie said quickly.

'We already talked about it.'

'Yes.' She collected the bag and case nestling at her feet and turned to Miriam.

'Bye then, sweetie.'

Miriam held out her doll.

'No, Mirry,' said Wolff. 'Sukie has to go now. Say 'bye 'bye.'

'Bye,' the child said in a hushed voice, 'Bye.'

Sukie opened the car door and was about to step out when she swivelled back round. She quickly slid a hand between Wolff's legs and wrapped it round the tip of his penis.

'I'll be dreaming about you,' she whispered, and vanished.

Inge sneezed against her sleeve then resumed spooning honey onto another triangle of toast. She handed it to her daughter Gretal.

'Want,' Gretal's twin whined in perfect German.

'Miriam, I already gave you two.'

'*MEINE.*'

Miriam was throwing her usual tantrum over tea. First there was too much jam on her toast, then there wasn't enough Perrier to make her apple juice 'go fizzy'. Inge, making herself a cup of strawberry tea, wondered if her daughter would ever tire of testing her. She might have felt more able to cope were it not for this ridiculous cold she had picked up.

'Come on, Gretal, eat it up for Mummy,' she urged her more gentle-natured child, sneezing again.

Miriam banged her plate in protest.

Wolff walked into the warm, bright kitchen with a copy of *Serve and Volley* in one hand.

'What is going on in here? Miriam, you already had tea at Mrs Kendall's. Don't be greedy now.'

Miriam picked up her empty plate and gnawed the edge of it with her teeth.

'And I don't want any complaining from you or I won't take you there again.'

Gretal gazed at her father with respect.

'Drink?' said Inge gratefully.

'Please.'

She poured him a glass of wine then returned to the pasta sauce she was making for supper. Neatly she snipped pieces of bacon into a frying pan of sautéed onions, sniffing as she worked. Because her nose was blocked Inge couldn't smell anything, but the air was rich with the aroma of cooked garlic. Wolff sipped his wine. He held its sweet, slightly carbonated taste in his mouth, contemplating his children, the bright primary colours of the room, toys, crayons, books littered across the yellow gingham tablecloth. It all felt reassuringly familiar and welcoming. He put his glass down on the table and approached his wife from behind.

'Smells good,' he said, wrapping his arms around her ample bosom, fitting her body tight against his. 'I've got quite an appetite. How are you feeling?'

'Better,' she pressed herself against him. 'It won't be long now.'

'No? Pity. We could have slipped upstairs for a while.'

'Wolff!' Inge gently chided, switching to German. 'The girls.'

'Is it wrong that your husband wants you so much?'

Behind them Gretal giggled.

'Dada,' smirked Miriam, 'bad.'

And Wolff turned to look at her, guilt written all over his face.

*   *   *

Sukie stood in the bathroom doorway and scowled out at Luke.

'What's up, baby?'

'Can't you ever remember to put the loo seat down? It's so irritating.'

'Hey, slapped wrists. Bad boy, L.F.' He put down the fountain pen he was writing with and grinned at her.

'It's not funny, Luke.'

'Who's laughing?'

'You. You're smirking.'

'Would you rather I cried? Hey! Don't go getting sulky on me, baby. Come over here.' He reached for her hand and pulled her to him, 'What is it? I noticed you didn't eat anything last night.'

She patted her stomach. 'I'm fat.'

'You're *gorgeous*,' he corrected, giving her a squeeze.

'I've put on at *least* half a stone.'

'Where?'

'*Here*,' she said, grabbing at flesh on her hip so that it hurt.

'It's all in your mind. I keep telling you.' Luke kissed the end of her nose. 'Okay. Now that we've established how gorgeous you are, d'you want to talk about what's bugging you?'

'You'll take it the wrong way.'

'Maybe not.'

She lay back on the bed and gazed up at the ceiling.

'If you really want to know, I'm *bored*. Tired of the travelling, the hotels, the tournaments, sightseeing tours and one-day golf events the sponsors always feel obliged to organise for us girls. It's as though they think us incapable of drumming up our own entertainment. I don't want to be a groupie. I want a *normal* life, Luke.'

He was thrown. 'It was your idea to lease your apartment.'

'Not much point in letting it just sit there. We're away half the year and I have a mortgage in case you've forgotten.'

'Which I offered to pay for you.'

'That's not the point,' she snapped irrationally. 'It's all right for you. You've got plenty to keep you busy. All I seem to do is hang around watching you play matches. I need more than tennis in my life.'

He gave a tolerant shrug. 'So what *do* you want? For me to give up my career?'

She pouted. 'That's a stupid thing to say. It's just that I don't think you quite appreciate the sacrifices I've made for you, Luke.'

'You think that? You really think that I take you for granted?' He looked hurt.

'That's not what I said.'

'No, but it's what you meant.'

She wandered over to the window and regarded the traffic moodily.

'I've been thinking about spending some time with my parents.'

'After Wimbledon?'

'No,' she said carefully, 'I thought I might go on Saturday.'

'You'll miss the finals at Queen's.'

'Luke, you don't know what's going to happen.'

'You mean I might lose, right?'

'No, that's *not* it. And don't snap at me!'

'I'm not snapping!'

They glared at each other for a second. Luke groaned in exasperation then joined her at the window. He put a hand on the nape of her neck and stroked it. Sukie sniffed and stiffened, then relaxed.

'I'd just like to get away for a couple of days, that's all,' she said finally. 'Can't you see that?'

Luke's expression softened. 'Can't you see that I'm jealous?'

Her eyes darted nervously to his. 'Luke, do you . . .?'

'Yes. I'm a selfish bastard and I don't like it when you're not with me.'

She hid her relief well. 'It won't be for long. I'll be back in plenty of time to see you win Wimbledon.'

'I *will* miss you,' he ran a finger down her tiny nose. 'I'll miss this,' he kissed the corner of her mouth, 'and my friend down here,' he said, sliding his hand up her skirt.

'Luke, I've got my period.'

'So?'

She turned her face away. 'It's hurting.'

'Okay.'

For a moment they gazed out at the flawless blue sky in silence, Sukie yearning to be with Wolff. At this very moment he would be packing for Manchester. In less than twenty-four hours she'd be there with him. Could she bear to wait that long!

Luke was thinking about the second half of his draw at Queen's. He knew how well he was playing. Only three players could really threaten his game now. One of them was emotionally wiped out after having been plagued for months with injuries. Then there was Pete Sampras. Luke respected the guy but with reoccurring shin splints and shoulder damage, he didn't fear him. The third man was Patrick Rafter. The Australian had beaten him in the Australian Open but that was on hard court. Grass was Luke's surface and of their two matches played on grass, Luke had won them both. Beyond a shadow of a doubt, if he could stay at this level he could win Queen's. After that? He would go on to claim his ultimate dream; the Wimbledon crown.

He reached for Sukie's hand. 'Christ,' he said softly, 'that's something, isn't it? Have you ever seen a sky quite like it?'

17

In the two years since Josh's death, Lauren had lived in a bubble. She had kept busy – having Tom meant that she had little time to herself. And she was glad of it. His tiny but incessant demands kept her from acknowledging the turmoil simmering inside. There were days when she felt some sense of normality. There were other days when she didn't really know how she was going to get through the next hour. A hole would open up in time and she would disappear into it. Only a ringing phone, the sound of someone's voice, a car backfiring would bring her round. She wasn't always thinking about Josh, but of some inconsequential memory; the indistinct voice of her father reading to her as a child as she drifted off to sleep; the smell of the kitchen at Willow; running through a field of daffodils aged six pretending she was a horse. Part of the Lauren she had grown up with was now absent.

Over the days and weeks and months she had noticed subtle changes in her appearance: new lines around the eyes, a brittleness in her lovely hair, a deterioration in her energy level – details so small to the eye that they were lost on even those close to her. But to Lauren they were all too apparent. The image of Josh in her mind however, remained the same. Exactly as he had been the last time she had seen him. Same age, same impish smile, same lolloping bounce to his walk. Sometimes he grew fainter, but he was always there, like the grey-blue haze of cigarette smoke lingering in a room long after the cigarette has been put out. At times when she was alone she would feel her loss so savagely she would bang her head with her palms trying to wipe it away.

By March, four months after her test with Tuff, there had still been nothing concrete, although the company continued to express interest. Lauren's financial state had reached a critical point. Unwisely perhaps, she had counted on the contract materialising. Well, Jane had sounded so *confident*. The red bills that Lauren had blithely put to one side secure in the knowledge of future work now screamed at her with a new sense of urgency. Inge was right. She couldn't go on waiting for ever. She had to start taking control of her life again, move on.

Scanning *Yellow Pages*, Lauren made an appointment with an employment agency. She was seen by a jovial woman wearing John Denver glasses and although it was clear Lauren's clerical skills were well below average, a small marketing company was looking for a Girl Friday. She was sent along for an interview.

The firm was on the second floor of an orange-brick building that smelt of tobacco and industrial ammonia. Mr Baldwin, the man she had been told to see, greeted her with oily hair, a too-tight polyester jacket, plum trousers and matching tie.

'Very nice, yes. Do sit down, Miss—?' he squinted myopically at her CV in front of him.

'Mrs Kendall,' Lauren volunteered.

'Oh. So you're married? I see. Right, well, *Mrs* Kendall. Tell me how much experience you've had in the marketing business?'

'Not much,' she admitted. 'But as you can see on my résumé I spent a year working for a QC' – no need to mention the QC was her father. 'My typing's good,' she added lamely, all too aware of how inexperienced she must sound.

'A QC eh! Well, you won't have to worry about doing anything so complicated around here.'

It had obviously been the wrong thing to say. 'I pick things up very quickly, Mr Baldwin.'

'Oh, and I don't doubt that for a moment, Mrs Kendall.' Lauren laughed uncertainly, fixing her gaze on his daisy-patterned tie that had a tomato ketchup stain on it.

'And it's Mike.'

'Sorry?'

'The name's Mike.' He held her résumé up to the light. 'I see here you've done a fair bit of modelling.' His eyes left her face and moved downwards as though he were appraising a prize pig. 'Those legs of yours could be an asset to the company. Aye, very nice too. We could use a bit of glamour about the place.' Lauren resisted the temptation to cross her legs. She didn't want to give him the satisfaction of knowing he'd put her on the defensive.

Mr Baldwin shuffled some papers on his desk, 'But it's loyalty I'm after. D'you understand?' Lauren nodded, disliking him more and more. 'We keep a cosy atmosphere. Pay's not bad either. I do a fair bit of travelling, mainly in the UK, mind, but I'd need you to accompany me. I'd be expecting you to start on Monday.'

Lauren was flustered. 'The agency mentioned nothing about travelling.'

He began to chew on the knuckle of his index finger. 'Not a problem is it, Mrs Kendall? Because I do need to know I can count on you.' She could have sworn he winked at her. 'Like I say, we keep things cosy around here. You scratch my back and all that kind of thing. D'you catch my drift?'

Lauren rose to her feet. 'I think there's been a mistake.'

'Now there's no point in jumping to conclusions, Mrs Kendall. Let's not be hasty. Perhaps I haven't explained myself properly.'

'I think you have.' You nasty little man, she thought contemptuously, picking up her bag.

Mr Baldwin's cheeks were inflamed. 'Not good enough for the likes of you, eh? Well, it's all the same to me.' In a show of defiance he ripped up her carefully typed-up CV and dropped it disdainfully into the bin. 'You can tell the next girl to come in on your way out.'

'Tell her yourself!' snapped Lauren, and marched regally out of the office.

She applied for six other jobs but nothing materialised. The two she was after expressed initial interest but had in the end decided she lacked the necessary credentials. Then with the advent of spring came hope and a riot of flowers; her Wimbledon lawn burst into a carpet of daffodils and purple crocuses; tiny birds squabbled in the trees. An ecstatic Jane called with news that Tuff had reached a decision. They wanted Lauren for the campaign.

'$500,000 dollars!' Lauren gasped when Jane told her how much they had agreed to pay.

'That's per year – with a three year guarantee. Oh, and you get two per cent royalties on sales of $600,000 and over.'

'I can't take it in, Jane. That's *brilliant* news.'

'Not bad for just twelve annual appearances. The down side is they want you to fly out to the States to begin shooting by the end of this week. I said you could. Usual last-minute panic. They sit twiddling their thumbs for months on end, then when they make a decision they expect everyone to jump. Oh, but who *cares*? For the amount of money involved I could forgive them anything.'

It had been a hard battle for Bob Hallaway to persuade Tuff into choosing Lauren. What had eventually clinched the deal was not so much her association with Josh but the fact that the American-based company could be more creative with her *not* being a player. A top-ranking player had so little time to set aside from the game it put severe

restrictions on marketing ventures. The decision to go with
Luke Falkner, however, had been instant and unanimous.
Later on, Lauren was to learn that his agent had insisted
on a guarantee of a million dollars of advertising to ensure
his client maximum exposure. She also discovered that
Luke was to get bonuses for tennis performance. She
begrudged him none of it. She was just so happy to be
working again.

After the trip to America, her next assignment was a four
city tour to Paris, Munich, Rome and Atlanta. Suddenly
Lauren's life went from the mundane to the dizzy roller
coaster of fittings, photo calls, press meetings, publicity
functions. Committed to tournaments, Luke was able to
join her for only part of the tour. During those times Lauren
was glad to have him around. She immediately responded
to the Canadian's relaxed, off-beat personality. His immense
public popularity was apparent wherever they turned up.
During the hours they spent hanging around, Luke kept
them all amused. It seemed his flamboyant Leconte-style
showmanship wasn't restricted to tennis courts.

Lauren's shop-lifting persisted. This character flaw had
taken hold of her, shackled her to a secret existence. She
felt powerless to break free. At first it had only been small
things, things that could be put away and excused. Then
there hadn't been time to consider her actions. She took
things instinctively. But gradually, no longer a novice, Lauren
became increasingly trapped in internal arguments, suffered
palpitations, panic attacks. Security guards that she had
always so successfully outmanoeuvred suddenly became a
real threat. The odds of getting caught were narrowing. She
felt both amazed and appalled by her audacity, taking bigger
and bigger risks; clothes, fabrics, books, food, household
goods. Yet the longer she got away with it, the bolder she
became. The more she took, the more habitual her need. It
was like a terrible fix. She kept telling herself that she would

stop but the promise she gave herself lacked conviction. It was almost as though the risk-taking was happening not to her, but to someone else. Again and again items seduced her. They burned in her mind until she was compelled to take them. She took huge risks. She binged on material things. But like bulimics who stuffed their bodies with food, then purged themselves by vomiting after the 'high' had worn off, Lauren was similarly a victim.

She developed side-effects: clawing headaches, eyestrain, forgetfulness, depression, a feeling of fatigue and lethargy that became apparent even before she entered a shop. The excitement was no longer there, yet the compulsion remained. Most of what she took she gave away or consigned to the back of a cupboard and instantly forgot. Some she threw out or returned, looking for a refund or exchange. She thought about how it would jeopardise her contract with Tuff were she to get caught. She worried about what her friends would think if they knew. But the fear wasn't enough to make her stop. Would they reject her? pity her? Their complaints that they didn't see enough of her were justified, but scared they might sense her guilt, she had begun to avoid people who knew the old Lauren. Lately she had begun to avoid lots of things.

She had little time for men, but that didn't mean she didn't get lonely. At night lying alone in the vast wedding bed, a gift from her parents, she frequently ached for a man's body, to feel it pressed against her skin, anchoring her to the bed, to life. There were the inevitable match-making parties given by friends. But their unsubtle albeit well-meant introductions to a long line of single men failed to have the slightest effect on her. Why was it that men attached to other women were always so much more attractive? Because they were safe, probably. Hadn't that always been Sukie's problem?

Lauren once overheard her live-in nanny on the phone

talking to a friend about ways to pick up men. Clubs, bars, dating agencies, the back pages of *Time Out* were apparently no longer in vogue. Supermarkets had emerged as the singles' new stamping ground and were apparently proving to be a roaring success. A lot of dross, Lauren thought, when one night she stopped off at the supermarket to do the weekly shop.

She put her empty shoulder bag in a free trolley and steered it purposefully down the busy aisle, trying not to notice a middle-aged man asking an attractive brunette to recommend the best tinned plum tomatoes.

'Want some help?' said a gruff male voice, as Lauren reached for some olive oil on the top shelf.

'I can manage, thanks.'

The man had puffy eyes and stank of nicotine.

'Do you shop here often?'

Lauren cringed. 'Hardly ever,' she said, as uninvitingly as possible.

The man grinned leeringly. 'My lucky night then.'

'I don't think so.'

'Can't tempt you to a bit of stir-fry?'

Lauren ignored him. She wouldn't be able to take a thing with him breathing lustfully down her neck.

'All right then,' the man tried again. 'How about you tell *me* what you fancy?'

'Solitude,' Lauren retorted, wheeling her trolley sharply away from him.

This had been a terrible mistake. The sooner she got home the better. She began to throw things randomly into her trolley, edging the more expensive items into her rapidly bulging shoulder bag. Checking that no one was looking, she pushed them in further out of sight, then with deliberate casualness, tossed her cardigan on top of the bag. As she reached for a packet of dried Porcini, she became aware of someone standing close to her. Lauren stiffened. Only moments before she had stashed a blank video cassette into her bag. Her heart beat irregularly. Had Mr Nicotine followed her? Had he seen her take it? But the man she turned to was tall with glossy shoulder-length hair and French racing-blue eyes. Wow!

'I bought some of those in Italy three weeks ago. I couldn't believe the difference in price.' The man smiled, revealing flawless white teeth. 'What are you cooking?'

Lauren gulped, her mind still on video cassettes. 'I hadn't thought. Mushroom risotto probably.'

'Your husband's in for a treat. That's one of my favourites!'

'Actually, I'm not married.' She couldn't believe she'd just said that.

'But you've developed a passion for Farley's Rusks?'

Lauren laughed, relaxing. 'They're for my son. He's addicted to them.'

The man extended his hand and shook hers with a reassuring firmness. 'I'm Charles.'

She was just about to respond when a young man with a goatee and cropped blond hair, approached them with a laden trolley.

'Can't leave you alone for a moment, can I?' he said to Charles.

Charles grinned. 'I've been making friends with a beautiful woman. Harry this is—I didn't get your name?'

'Lauren,' she smiled warmly at Charles who was the best-looking man she'd seen in months.

'We've been discussing risotto dishes,' he said, 'I'm hoping Lauren will give me some tips for our party on Saturday night.'

'Please do,' said Harry with a smile that didn't quite reach his eyes. 'He's *hopeless* with risottos. They always end up sticking to the pan.'

'Oh, and yours are so much better,' jibed Charles good-naturedly.

'Darling, *I'm* not the one who does the cooking. We both know where my talents lie.'

Charles blushed. 'The main thing is to keep stirring and add plenty of liquid,' he said, winking at her.

'I'm always telling him that,' rebuked Harry, who continued to refer to Charles in the third person even though he was only standing a foot away.

'Yes. Well, it was nice meeting you both,' said Lauren hot with embarrassment, 'and good luck with the party.'

She never returned to that supermarket.

Erratic Carter approaches his watershed
says Ed McNab, reporting from London on the Yank trying to rekindle his career at the greatest of the Grand Slam events. Max Carter, once ranked two in the world, is approaching an age when most of his contemporaries are thinking about retiring. Not so Carter who is here in London to launch his long-awaited autobiography and to try and regain the Wimbledon title he so memorably won six years ago. Carter, whose last great triumph was back in 1991 when he won the Australian Open, has been plagued by a series of injuries. Last year was an unequivocal disaster for the thirty-three-year old and there were rumours that he was thinking of retiring.

'I guess it had to happen,' he said, 'you can't go on playing the kind of tennis I've been producing indefinitely. I'd had three really great years. It was just unfortunate that my ankle started playing up. My mind was on other things. I wasn't focused. But I've been working real hard on my game. I feel pretty confident.'

He'd have to be. Even two years ago Carter was finding it increasingly difficult to finish matches that were there for the taking. Since then, the tell-tale signs of self-doubt; double faults, hitting wide, problems with the toss on serve have proliferated alarmingly. Carter, who can claim as much

*as $100,000 just to make an appearance on court, is up
against stiff competition. The upward rise of hard-hitting
baseliner Wolff Bohakari must surely be a threat, along
with former champion André Agassi. Another contender is
the big server Luke Falkner. The popular Canadian seems
unstoppable. In January, he beat Pete Sampras in the final
of the Australian Open in Melbourne and this week took
the Stella Artois title.*

Max lowered the newspaper and swore.

'What's up, sugar?'

'They're writing me off, that's what. Calling me a has-been.
God damn!'

Tiffany leaned over his shoulder. 'Does it say anything
about the book launch?'

'You're kidding,' he snorted. 'They're not interested in
my book; they just want to talk about my apparent loss of
confidence.'

'But you're playing just great.'

'Not everyone shares your point of view, Tiff. But I'm
going after that title. It's now or never.'

'You can do anything if you put your mind to it. What say
we stroll into town. We could have lunch at that restaurant
in Beauchamp Place (she pronounced it Bowshamp). Who
knows? We might get lucky and see Lady Di.'

But Max's mind was elsewhere. Consigning the newspaper to the bin, he strode angrily into the bedroom and
began throwing his kit into a bag.

'I'm going down to the courts to practise. I'll get one of
the courtesy cars to drive me in.'

'But what about lunch?'

'Guess Di'll just have to wait. Rain check, okay?'

'Fine,' she said as he closed the main door. But just what
the hell was she supposed to do for the next four hours?

*   *   *

Lauren sat in front of her dressing-table mirror dabbing
Shalimar on her wrists and trying to decide what to wear.
For a moment she considered her reflection then drew a
brown line around her lips. She filled in the gaps with
a plummy matt lipstick. To her eyes she added only
mascara. Her face couldn't take much make-up or she
ended up looking tarty. Upstairs she could hear Pippa
moving around with Tom. It was bathtime, his favourite
part of the day and he was shrieking and splashing with
all the joy and energy of a healthy child – he would be
two in a couple of months. Normally she liked to bath
him but Alan was due any moment and she hadn't finished
dressing.

Earlier, Lauren had received a call from her mother. Kay
had done her best to sound cheery as she explained why
they had decided to sell their small Tuscan villa, but Lauren
detected the strain in her mother's voice. The Lloyds business
was obviously getting to them both. If she could just find
a buyer for the land Josh had bought in Colorado, she'd
gladly give the proceeds to her parents.

Her eye fell on a letter she had received that morning
from Josh's father. In it he had written about the death of
his wife. Helen Kendall had undergone an operation to
remove a cancerous growth from her right kidney and at
first it was thought the operation had been a success. The
cancer had, in fact, spread to her lymph system. In spite of
massive chemotherapy treatment, within six weeks she was
dead. The letter moved Lauren deeply. Here was a man who
had lost the two people closest to him in the world and yet
he wrote with a curious optimism. She picked it up now and
reread the end;

It is not my intention to distress you with this news, Lauren.
Although a great physical distance separates us, I think of
you as my daughter. I would like to know more of the woman

my son loved. Josh suffered a great deal as a youth. He carried
emotional scars around with him, allowing them to affect his
life – until he met you. With your love, Lauren, he was able
to grow, finally to let go of the past and, I hope, forgive. I
will always be indebted to you for giving him that. Perhaps
you will think it strange my writing to you like this when
we know so little of one another – these have been difficult
times. But please believe me when I say you have been in
my thoughts. There will always be a home for you here in
Australia. Although my darling wife suffered from illness
throughout her life, I had almost forty years of happiness
with her. That's forty years more than most. What right
then have I to feel sorry for myself because she is no longer
with me.

Lauren lowered the letter to her lap and stared out of
the window. So Josh *had* suffered as a child. But how?
The letter didn't explain. Was that because Doug Kendall
assumed she already knew? Lauren pictured Mrs Kendall's
blue eyes bequeathed to her son, the sharp inquisitive nose,
her sad, grieving smile.

'Both my babies gone. Oh, Doug, what now? How am I
going to find the strength to carry on without them?'

The phone rang, interrupting her thoughts.

'I'll get it,' Lauren yelled up to Pippa, thinking it was
Alan.

'Lo. It's me.'

'Sukie. I thought you were going to call me back this
morning?'

'I know. Sorry. Something came up.'

'Have you spoken to Mum?'

'Just now. You know they're selling the villa?'

'I can't believe it's reached that stage. They've had it for
fifteen years.'

'Dad's under real pressure. I know how he feels.'

Lauren could hear her sister inhaling cigarette smoke. 'What's up with you?'

'Nothing. Everything. Luke and I have been fighting. I said some pretty rotten things.'

The doorbell sang through the house. Lauren glanced at her watch. Alan was early. Damn.

'You two are always fighting. I'm beginning to think you do it just to add spice to your sex life.'

'*What* sex life? Sometimes I wonder what's the bloody point.'

'He may not make bells ring but he's genuine in the way he feels about you. I really like him.' There were voices in the hall. 'Sukie, will you be in later?'

'You've got someone there? Oh, that's right, I forgot. You're seeing your hot date.'

'Only he's arrived early and I'm still in my underwear.'

'Glad you haven't lost your touch.' Sukie was sounding more like her usual self. 'What's he into?'

'From what I could gather, he's worked as an agent and a tournament director. More recently he's branched out and formed a sports clinic.'

'He's got money then.'

'Ye-es, Sukie, Alan's got money.'

'Not sure about the name, though. Where did you meet?'

'Alan's involved with Tuff's European division. He turned up at one of the shoots and we started chatting. His mother had just died so we had something in common. Ended up having this heated discussion about private homes for the elderly.'

'Cheerful.'

Lauren laughed. 'Sukie, I've got to go. You can give me the third degree later on. I shouldn't be late.'

'Make the most of it.'

She had just hung up when there was a knock on her bedroom door. For one horrible, irrational moment Lauren thought it was Alan. She grabbed a towel to cover herself. But a moment later, Pippa's head appeared.

'Mr Tarrent's arrived. I've put him in the drawing room and given him a drink.'

'Thanks. I'll be right down,' said Lauren, feeling foolish. 'Is Tom all right?'

'Fine. But, er, your copy of *Possession* is a bit of a mess. I caught him trying to flush it down the lavatory. I've put it in the airing cupboard to dry.'

'Oh, God. He's got this obsession with that loo. Will you be okay for tonight?'

'I'm going to catch up with studying – there's a lot to get through,' Pippa pulled a face. 'So don't come rushing back on my account.'

Lauren's hands were sweating as she threw on a pair of midnight-blue velvet trousers and a chiffon shirt. She had considered the silver dress she had pinched from Harvey Nichols but it was too sexy and she didn't want to give Alan the wrong idea. This was silly, she thought, slipping her feet into sling-back shoes. He seemed harmless enough. And it was only dinner. But the moment she opened the door to the drawing room and saw Alan standing there, she knew it had been a terrible mistake.

'Alan,' she smiled, extending her hand to him.

The restaurant was five star. They were sitting at a corner table with a white cloth and stiff pink napkins. In the centre, a candle flickered next to a small posy of freesias. Alan dipped another moule into hot, buttery liquid then used his teeth to scrape the shell contents into his mouth.

'The best in town,' he murmured, smacking his lips pleasurably. 'Sure you won't change your mind and try one?'

Lauren shook her head. 'I'm not much of a shellfish fan.'

She had been thinking about Tom, about the recent

nightmares he'd been having and how hard it had been to leave him tonight. At least, when she had risked going up to check on him there had been none of the usual tearful scenes. She had found her red-pyjamaed son on his back, arms flung above his head, his face smooth and calm with sleep. She was worried about his throwing things. It had started about six months before when he had taken to hurling anything he could physically pick up over the first-floor banister, into the bath, or like tonight, down the loo. Did this mean he was unhappy?

'Paté good?'

Lauren focused her gaze on Alan. 'It's delicious.'

'I thought you'd like it here.' He broke his roll in two, smothering it with butter and stuffed the larger half in his mouth. Then he picked up his glass and touched it to hers. 'To a profoundly beautiful woman.'

'To the chef,' she said in response.

Alan downed the last of the moules and relaxed back in his chair. A silver cuff link shaped in a pound sign on one side, a shark on the other, caught a ray from one of the sun-like spotlights. It winked expensively at her.

'I didn't think you'd come tonight,' he said as the next course arrived.

Lauren was surprised. 'Why ever not?'

'Just the way you were the day we met. You seemed a bit on edge.'

'I don't remember that.'

'I'd heard a few rumours about you and, well . . .' Irritatingly, he chose this moment to take another mouthful of wine, 'something Ripley said made me wonder if asking you out was the right approach.'

He made Tuff's art director sound like Dr Anthony Clare. Unconsciously Lauren folded her arms.

'Intriguing. Are you going to tell me what Ripley said?' She hated herself for asking.

'Now,' he said, wagging a finger at her, 'I don't want you
to take this the wrong way . . .' Lauren's smile tightened.
'He seemed to think you'd put a wall up as far as men were
concerned.'

Lauren speared an olive. 'I had no idea Ripley took such
an interest in my personal life.'

Alan held up a defending hand. 'I didn't say I agreed with
him. I'm glad he was wrong.'

'He had no right.'

'Perhaps not, but no harm was done. I hope I hav-
en't offended you.' Lauren shook her head. 'Have some
more wine?'

'Just a drop.'

Some of the Burgundy splashed onto the white tablecloth
leaving a pink stain.

'How's Tim?' Alan asked, changing the subject.

'Tom.'

'Sorry. I knew it started with a T.'

'He's fine. Growing so quickly,' she said, instantly wishing
she was at home with him now. 'Before I know it he'll be
starting school.'

'Must be a bit of a bind having to look after him by
yourself, I would have thought.'

'I have a nanny. She helps.'

'I was always working too hard for any of that,' said Alan,
his voice lacking even the slightest trace of regret. 'I get on
really well with kids but that's because I make sure they're
someone else's.'

Their plates were cleared away and a third bottle of
wine arrived, even though Lauren insisted she'd had
quite enough. Alan produced something that resembled
a Cumberland sausage from his breast pocket. He lit it
and smiled speculatively at her through a haze of smoke.
Something about his eyes made her feel uneasy. She picked
up her water glass and drank from it.

'How about some cheese or dessert?' Lauren shook her head. 'A flaming sambuca? It goes very well with the chocolate mousse.'

'No, really. I couldn't eat another thing.'

'What if we were to have them wrap some up and take it back to your place?'

She was offended by the intimate suggestion. 'You haven't been invited.'

Raking dark hair back from his forehead, he blew smoke from the side of his mouth. 'I like a woman that knows her mind. Okay, then. We'll go back to mine. It's closer anyway.'

A waiter appeared and swept crumbs from the tablecloth with a small silver brush.

'Alan,' she looked him in the eye, 'I think I should make it clear that my feelings for you are strictly platonic.'

The corners of his mouth curved into an impudent smile. 'To be honest, it's not your feelings I'm interested in right now.'

'I beg your pardon!' The waiter had become inordinately leisurely in his work. 'Just what are you insinuating?'

'I'm saying that I don't buy women dinner who don't fuck.'

Both Lauren's and the waiter's jaw dropped.

'Oh, come on. Spare me the scene, Lauren. You knew what tonight was about.'

'I *thought* I did. You obviously had other things planned.' She was pink with rage.

Alan glanced irritably at the waiter as if to say go away, then back at her. 'Why don't you calm down. Finish your wine.'

A mobile shrieked from inside his jacket. The waiter scurried off towards the kitchen door, frantic to pass on the goss from table three. With infuriating casualness, Alan removed the mobile and pressed the on button.

'Alan Tarrent. What's going on? No. Don't take it to him.
You wait for him to come to you,' he said down the phone,
keeping his eyes on Lauren.

'How much? Not a chance. I went through all this with
him last night. Fifty grand or there's no deal. Hang on,' he
put a hand over the mouthpiece and said to Lauren, 'I'm
taking this outside, but I haven't finished with you yet.'

Oh, yes you bloody well have, thought Lauren as he left.
Swallowing her anger, she signalled for the waiter.

'I'd like the bill for everything I've had tonight,' she said,
trembling, 'and could you also order me a taxi.'

By the time Alan returned, the waiter was peeling off
the top copy of her American Express receipt. He eyed
Alan warily.

'What's this?' Alan asked, as she slipped it into her purse.
'What's going on? I didn't ask for the bill.'

He glared accusingly at the waiter.

'But I did.' Lauren rose from her chair.

'So you've decided to run after all.'

She smiled thinly. 'You're better at observation than you
are on subtlety.'

'Well, if you're expecting me to take you home now,' he
said sulkily, 'you can forget it.'

'I'd like to forget this whole evening. In fact I'd like to
forget ever meeting you,' she leant forward so that her
mouth was against his ear. 'And let me tell you *Mr* Tarrent,
a geriatric Rastafarian covered in putrid warts and reeking
of body odour would make a more arousing bed partner
than you. Have I made myself clear?'

'Mrs Kendall?' She turned to the dithering pink-cheeked
waiter who hadn't been party to so much excitement since
the night Jack Nicholson and Warren Beatty had dined at
the restaurant. 'Your taxi's arrived.'

'Thank you,' she said, and without a backward glance,
followed the man out.

By the time she got home, she was silently gibbering with rage. I'll get him fired, I'll tell all his colleagues, so help me. I'll . . . She paused in the hall. Why were all the lights out? And what was that noise? She could hear her son upstairs shrieking his heart out. TOM. If anything had happened to him . . .

Lauren fled upstairs to his room and flung open the door. He was standing up on his bed howling.

'MUMMY!' he wailed, holding his arms out to her, 'MUMMY, MUMMY!'

'*Darling.* Oh, my little angel. You're soaking! Did you have another bad dream?'

'Yes,' he whimpered, 'croc'dil.'

He wailed against her breast as she rocked him back and forth, soothing him with kisses and comforting words.

'There, there, my angel. Mummy's back. Mummy's back. She'll make the bad crocodile go away.'

When he finally drifted off to sleep, she went in search of her nanny. Why the hell hadn't Pippa been looking after him? Her bedroom was empty, so Lauren went back downstairs.

'Pippa,' she called, opening the door to the drawing room where she could hear faint echoes of music, 'Pippa, are you . . .'

She halted in her tracks. For there bathed in moonlight on the floor was her nanny writhing around with a strange man. Neither of them had any clothes on. They were so intent on what they were doing that they hadn't heard Lauren come in. Furiously she snapped on the light.

'What the hell's going on!'

'OooohmyGod!' shrieked Pippa, leaping up and snatching a cushion to cover herself. 'Oh, Mrs Kendall! *Please* don't be cross.'

Lauren was appalled. 'What is this!'

They were both throwing on clothes in a mad frenzy.

'It's not what you think,' begged Pippa.

'Oh, really! I suppose you're going to tell me you were studying human biology?'

The young man's gaze was fixed on the floor.

'My son's upstairs crying his eyes out. He could have been *really* sick and you're down here with, with this . . .' Lauren was almost stuttering; would this nightmare of an evening ever end?

'This is my boyfriend, Rod,' stammered Pippa.

'Well, I'm very happy for you, but as far as I was concerned he could have been ANYONE!'

Pippa's face matched her shrimp-coloured T-shirt. 'We didn't mean anything by it, Mrs Kendall. I'm re-ally sorry. And I *was* studying. How was I to know Rod was going to stop by?' Frantically, she jabbed a sheepish Rod in the ribs, 'Go on. *Tell* her!'

'Um, yer,' he mumbled ineffectually, then began to jangle change in his pockets. 'It's like she says.'

But for Lauren it was the last straw. 'Pippa, I want you to go upstairs and pack your things. You're not fit to look after my child.'

'But Mrs Kendall . . .' the full implication of Lauren's words were beginning to sink in.

'Right now!'

'But you can't just chuck me out. Not now, in the middle of the night. I've nowhere to go.'

'You should have thought of that before you started screwing your boyfriend in my house. If you've got problems finding somewhere to stay why don't you go back to his home!'

Rod panicked. 'Oh, no! Me mam will *kill* me!'

'*Ro-od*!'

'I'll give you an hour to collect your things. Then I'm calling the police.'

The house was very still after they had gone. Lauren

lay on her bed with Tom sleeping as still and sweet as a saucer of milk in her arms. She listened to the faint, jaunty laughter of people passing. A tenuous strip of light ran across the ceiling. She gazed up at it, thinking back to a time when she had felt in control of her life, confident and strong. These days she wore herself out with interminable internal struggles, energy wasted on arguments with herself, attempts to justify her behaviour. Perhaps she had been too hard on Pippa. Should she at least have let her stay on until she had fixed up another job? And how was she going to do that without references? But Pippa wasn't a child. She was in her mid-twenties, for God's sake. She should have known better. Lauren pressed her lips to her son's temples and closed her eyes. She had probably blown it with Tuff. No doubt Alan's ego would be seeking revenge after having been rejected. He had the connections. Would he try to get her sacked? Oh, but how dare he, she thought with renewed outrage? How *dare* he assume she was there for the taking? He'd treated her no better than a whore. She took in a deep breath to calm herself. Actually, there probably wasn't much Alan *could* do. They would be foolish to get rid of her now when the campaign was such an unqualified success. But to be on the safe side, she'd call Jane about it in the morning.

A plane droned by overhead. She listened to its dull roar, the silence that followed. Her mind drifted. The sky was still, black like an ocean; a graveyard for reckless divers. She saw her husband there, floating, blond hair spread about his face like a fan of coral, drifting in and out of a crevice in the reef face. She listened to the claustrophobic sound of his distressed breathing, sucking what little air was left in his tank as he began to lose control. She felt the icy fingers of water embrace his skin, pull him down into the silent well from which there was no return. She smelt his panic, his fear, the half-mad prayer he muttered as he sank like a stone into the sea's black mouth. Fool, she thought, as angry tears slid down her cheek, soaked the pillow cradling her head. Stupid irresponsible fool. What were you trying to prove? Didn't you once stop to think of the consequences, of what it would be like for Tom and me to go on without you?

The line on the ceiling shifted to the left and shrank slightly. Refocusing her eyes on it Lauren realised how precarious her own life had become.

At any moment she might crash.

Sukie arrived back in London to find Luke in a jubilant mood. Having beaten Michael Stich in a riveting four-set final at Queen's, he was now being tipped to win the Wimbledon crown. He didn't notice her damp, flushed skin or the fact that her blouse was buttoned up all wrong (a quickie on the way home). She'd watched the final with some reluctance on the hotel TV – Wolff's idea not hers. She would much rather have spent the time having Wolff focus his attentions on her. Stretched out in front of him in her new Chantal Thomas lingerie, she had done everything to tempt him with lacy stockings, a push-up bra and French knickers. But he had shown remarkable resistance. When it came to work, Wolff was belligerent: tennis first, her second. No room for manoeuvre. In the end, she had realised, it wasn't in her interests to argue. Chasing balls was Wolff's life and if she wanted him she also had to accept his commitment to the game. She didn't like it. The seemingly endless stretches of boredom made her want to scream and holler in frustration. The hours and hours he spent away from her, playing, practising, training, left her feeling as jealous as a deceived wife. But although she didn't share his passion for the sport, Sukie could understand parallels between playing on the circuit and being on a film set. Isolation and long hours, you existed in a sealed world with its own peculiar routines.

The same people incestuously cropped up over and over again. Cities you passed through once, twice, three times remained unmoved by your absence.

Sukie had spent four days in Manchester. When Wolff had asked her, she had felt as though she had been given a slice of heaven; four days seemed a lifetime, beyond her greediest imaginings. But how quickly the days had evaporated. Having once revelled in her new-found fame with Luke, Sukie these days longed for anonymity, only because it meant she could be seen in public with Wolff. On the other hand, there was something deeply erotic about exchanging cool, never-seen-you-before glances, knowing that by the end of the day they would be between sheets devouring one another. Most of her time was spent cooped up in her hotel room with aching thighs after having spent another sleepless night. They would separate, damply, in the early hours of morning like two opposing rugby teams after a furious scrum. The intensity of her feelings had come as a surprise. She loved sex. The bed arena was where she was at her most confident, most in control. But with Wolff it was all passion and fury. She found herself doing and saying things that shook the very foundation of her emotions. In the morning he would leave her reeling from the intensity of their love-making and sluggishly she would pass the time watching the Movie Channel and daytime soaps, forbidden to answer the phone in case Inge called. Or she would doze, marvelling sleepily at Wolff's remarkable stamina. How was he able to produce such sensational tennis with so little rest? After the claustrophobic few days she had spent with Luke she quite enjoyed having the days to herself but come the evening she was always champing at the bit for Wolff's return. She could never get enough of him. Always he left her feeling hungry for more.

Wolff lost in the final and accepted his defeat with remarkable restraint. Even the press remarked on his sportsmanlike behaviour. Was this, the *Telegraph* suggested, the effect of fatherhood?

'I don't mind answering questions about my tennis but I don't like to talk about my personal life,' was Wolff's response in a press conference. Of all the higher-ranking players he was known for being the most intensely private. Very occasionally, a dry sense of humour would creep into his conversation, but only after a big win.

Back in their hotel room packing his stuff, Sukie begged Wolff to stay on for just one more night. But he had been adamant.

'I have to get back. Wimbledon starts on Monday. I *need* to practise.'

She was stroking his back. It was smooth and hard as wood, 'I know, but couldn't you . . .'

He placed a finger to her lips. 'Sukie, this title means everything to me. There is nothing in the world I want more.'

'Not even me?'

He gave her an odd look. 'If you understood me you wouldn't ask that question.'

'But why do you have to go now? Why not tomorrow?' she groped for a cigarette hating the pleading tones in her voice.

'Because I lost and because Inge will be expecting me. Do you have to smoke that thing in here?'

Angrily, she turned on him.

'Yes, I do! Damn Inge, damn you! I wish we'd never met,' and she pulled defiantly on the cigarette so that the end glowed orange.

But Wolff took it away. 'Don't say that,' he murmured fiercely against her ear. 'Don't *ever* say that.'

Luke was on such a high when Sukie got back the following lunchtime he failed to notice her sullen mood. He had gone out and spent four hundred quid on a computer game and now couldn't put it down. It seemed a ludicrous thing to buy. Sukie couldn't even work out how to turn it on. But then when it came to gadgets, particularly ones to do with music, Luke was like a child. Mutely, she mourned all the things she could have spent four hundred pounds on. Her imagination took over and she began contemplating what she would do if she won the National Lottery.

She tried to make an effort for him; he was so transparently pleased to see her, like an eager puppy. But she just felt guilty and on edge. At least he didn't constantly nag her about smoking. He was good like that. She had noticed with some alarm that since the start of her affair with Wolff she was smoking twice as much. Neurotic cow. If only she could stop thinking about him. Relentlessly she tortured herself with questions: What was he doing now? What was it like being back with Inge? Did he burn with jealousy thinking about her with Luke? Was he thinking about her at all? She pictured him padding, naked and proud, across his bedroom to join Inge. Did he fuck his wife the way he fucked her? Were Germans better in bed? Sukie's mind festered. Her skin crawled with curiosity. She feared his priorities. Who, if it ever came down to it, would he choose?

Practice courts at Wimbledon were like gold dust. Over the three-week tournament period (with one week for the qualies), time on the sixteen outside courts was restricted to thirty minutes unless two seeded players were practising together. Then they could play for an hour. Aorangi Park's adjacent practice courts weren't as tight, but still hard to come by. Luke had managed to get a practice court for every day and the morning after her return from Manchester, Sukie agreed to go with him on the offchance she might see Wolff. Someone had earlier spotted him dropping off the twins at the Aorangi Park Pavilion crèche while he practised. But unfortunately by the time she arrived he'd already gone.

'Got some party he's taking the twins to,' a player's

wife had explained. 'Have you met them yet? They look
just like Ingeborg, don't they; big blue eyes. And all that
white-blonde hair. Nothing like their dad. He's always
bringing them down. Likes to show them off when he
gets the chance. I did overhear him booking up for later
this afternoon.'

Sukie's hopes rose.

'Luke,' she said casually on their way back to the hotel,
'I'd completely forgotten this afternoon. Mum's birthday is
coming up and I'd promised to go shopping with Lauren.
Do you mind?'

'That's cool. Donald wants to meet up in an hour. One or
two things he wants to run by me – you'd only get bored.
Want me to have the car drop you off somewhere?'

'No. Don't worry. I'll take the tube.'

'Since when did you ever take the tube over a free lift!'

'When the traffic's bad,' she said quickly. 'It took us ages
to get back.'

'You're right.' He kissed her on the mouth and slipped
a wad of notes into her hand. One undeniable fact about
Luke was his unstinting generosity. 'Get her something nice
from both of us. Okay?'

'Thanks.' And because she was feeling happy, she reached
up and kissed his lips.

'Mmm,' he murmured approvingly, 'I should let you go
shopping more often.'

As the Rover courtesy car pulled away from the hotel
and into Buckingham Gate, Luke watched Sukie, handbag
swinging in one hand, skipping hurriedly across the road.
He cast a roguish eye over her, taking in the wonderful
curves, the large expanse of thigh where her short, tight
skirt had ridden up, the lacy blouse she was wearing with
tiny buttons running down the back. She had just reached
the other side when something fell from her purse. He called
out her name to attract her attention but she didn't hear him.

Daydreaming again, he thought fondly, and raced to catch her up.

'SUKIE!' he yelled. 'Hey, wait up!'

That was when he heard the horn. Luke turned just in time to see the Rover Sterling courtesy car plough into him.

18

Charlotte and her friend Francesca were watching the fourth day of Wimbledon. They had removed the cushions from the sofa to the floor and were lying on them. Tennis racquets lay abandoned nearby along with sweat tops and three battered tins of Slazenger balls. During a slow patch between Michael Chang and the Frenchman Cédric Pioline, Charlotte flicked through the channels.

'Wait a minute. Go back to ITV. It's Michelle Gayle. Oh, she's so *smooth*.' *Smooth* was Fran's new word of the month. 'I always thought she was really good as Hatty.'

'Why did she change her name?'

'She didn't, silly. Don't you remember her in *EastEnders*?'

'Yeah-us,' Charlotte lied, who never watched soaps.

Fran's eyes were fixed to the screen. 'Bet she gets her pick of men.'

'You're prettier,' Lottie said loyally.

'D'you really think so?' Extravagantly, Fran rolled over on to her back and tossed her thick blonde hair so that the locks dangled over the edge of the cushion. 'Ricky says he can't keep his hands off me.'

Charlotte gazed at her with envy. 'Your new boyfriend?'

'He's amazing.'

That was how Charlotte felt about Fran. Right from the time she'd first visited her friend's house and listened to some kind of hot, jungly music that gave her goose bumps; when Fran's elder sister Lisa, who was a professional make-up artist, had offered to work an elaborate magic over Charlotte's pale face with her brushes. But best of all was when she'd admitted to Fran she was diabetic and all Fran did was shrug.

'So's my cousin,' she'd said. 'She has to inject four times a day. I think it's cool to be different.'

It was then that Charlotte privately swore to be Fran's friend for ever.

'So,' she said now, 'what do you and Rick get up to?'

Forgetting her Hollywood pose, Fran flipped back onto her stomach and cradled her head in her hands, 'Well,' she said breathlessly, 'sometimes, in his car . . .'

'He's got a car?' Charlotte squeaked.

'A Toyota. Take my advice; don't go out with someone your own age. They've got nothing going for them.'

Charlotte whacked her friend with a cushion, 'Listen to *you*!' Then curiosity got the better of her. 'How old *is* he?'

Melanie appeared in the doorway, 'Either of you girls like some tea? I've just put the kettle on.'

'Oh, Mum, go *away*!' Charlotte snapped. 'We're having a private conversation.'

'Sorry I spoke. And mind your shoes on that sofa. I don't want any accidents.'

'All right. All right,' Charlotte waved an impatient hand. Why did her mother always do that? It wasn't as if she had friends round very often.

'Well?' she urged Fran, once Melanie had gone.

'He's over twenty and he's very sophisticated.'

'When do you get to see him?'

'As often as I like.'

Charlotte's face grew heavy with scepticism.

'Well,' Fran rushed on, realising her credibility had slipped a notch, 'after practice anyway. We have to be discreet.'

'It must be serious.'

'Oh, it is!' Fran leant closer, conspiratorially. 'We're talking about getting married.'

Charlotte rolled her eyes and giggled. 'You'll have to sleep with him then.'

'We might not wait,' Fran said nonchalantly, and gave another toss of her glorious locks.

Charlotte was shocked. 'Fran, your parents would kill you if they found out.'

'The only time my parents notice anything is when I lose matches.'

Charlotte sighed. 'I know what you mean. I get stick from Hugo *all* the time. And he isn't even my real dad.'

For a moment they lay in contemplative silence. Fran gazed into the distance, Charlotte gazed at Fran. She had never met anyone like her. Everything Fran did was somehow colourful and intriguing. She felt drawn to her warmth, her beauty, like a moth to a flame.

'Did you ever get to know your father?' Fran asked curiously.

'He was a very famous tennis player. He taught me *everything*.'

Now it was Fran's turn to look impressed. 'You never said.'

'You never asked. That bracelet you're always asking to borrow, the one I keep by my bed.' Fran nodded eagerly. 'He gave it to me.'

'Wow! You're so lucky. My dad never gives me things like that. What happened to him?'

'Oh,' Charlotte said mysteriously, 'he was murdered.'

'MURDERED!' Fran's eyes were like saucers.

'Shhh,' warned Charlotte. 'Mum'll hear us.'

'God! You *poor* thing. Murdered! Wow! I've never met anyone who knew a dead person. That's so smooth. Who was he?'

Charlotte cast a furtive glance towards the door. 'We don't talk about it,' she said in a hushed voice.

'Oh,' said Fran. 'Gosh!'

High on victory, Charlotte decided now was the moment to produce her trump card. 'And another thing; I've just gone on the pill.'

Fran's big, soft mouth went slack with wonder. 'When?'

'Started last week.'

'But you said you didn't have a boyfriend?'

'It's got nothing to do with boys.' She said 'boys' as if it was a dirty word.

'Then how come you're on the pill?'

'Because I am.'

'Prove it.'

'I would but Hugo keeps my packets.'

Fran sat bolt upright. '*Hugo* knows about it?'

'It was his idea.' Charlotte wondered if perhaps she had gone too far, said too much. It was supposed to be a secret after all.

'Why would Hugo want to put you on the pill?' Fran asked.

'Because my periods were affecting my game – I got really bad cramps and stuff. Look, Fran,' she urged, wishing now that she hadn't mentioned it, 'Mum doesn't know anything about it. I'm not allowed to tell her so you must promise not to say a word – to *anyone*! Especially not at school.'

'You can trust me. I'm really good with secrets.'

Melanie's head reappeared, 'You two *sure* you wouldn't like some tea? I've made a lovely cake.'

'It does smell nice,' admitted Fran, as baked cinnamon smells wafted into the room. She glanced hopefully at Charlotte.

'Oh, very well then, Mother,' Charlotte relented. She waved a regal hand above her head. 'We'll have it in here.'

Melanie hid a smile. 'Yes, your ladyship. Coming right up.'

The moment the door was closed, the girls collapsed into peals of laughter.

*   *   *

Luke opened his eyes and blinked against bright ceiling lights. He had no idea where he was or how long he had been there. He focused on a wall, a man wearing a mask, rows of beds. There was a sound, a faint rustling noise. Brow knitted with concentration, he closed his eyes and tried to identify it.

'Mr Falkner? Mr Falkner? Can you hear me?'

Someone was calling to him. He opened his eyes a second time and gazed into a sea of freckles. His mother had freckles but this woman was too young to be his mother. The face smiled at him.

'How are you feeling?'

The nurse picked up his wrist between her fingers and took his pulse. He wanted to say something to her, tell her what pretty hair she had, that she smelt of laundry powder and fresh rain, but the words slipped from his grasp long before they reached his mouth. Something was on his chest. Christ, it was heavy. Luke shifted slightly and was shocked by the sudden scalding pain. He groaned.

The freckled nurse looked concerned. 'Bad is it?'

'I'm wha—t happ—?'

'You've got quite a bit of bruising. Try to lie still now.'

'Buwhathmadder me?'

He felt a sting in his arm, reeled from the clinical smell of antiseptic. He thought he could see Lauren but the room was growing dark. Voices, low whispers coming from the bottom of a well. Someone calling from the bed next to him. Then a louder voice. A man's. The room spun. In his head he saw a tall structure, a skyscraper covered in scaffolding. Something toppled from it. A shadowy figure. His arm flinched as he tried to stop himself falling from a great height.

'Just try to rest. All right, Mr Falkner?'

'No,' he said. '*NO!*' and shut his eyes.

*   *   *

When he next woke he was somewhere else. Soft light this time, coming from a window. He opened his eyes gradually, letting in the room by degrees – tiny dots on the green wallpaper, a fat, rusty radiator. An armchair. And flowers. Lots and lots of flowers. The air was sweet with their scent.

'Luke?' said a voice. 'It's me.'

She was sitting next to the bed. He noticed that she was wearing sunglasses. And the dress. He hadn't seen it before. For her benefit he managed a weak smile.

Sukie smiled back, nervously he thought. 'Hello.'

'Water,' he croaked.

She manoeuvred the cup to his lips, tilting it slightly. 'Not too much,' she warned. 'They told me just to let you have a sip. You can have more later.'

She put the cup to one side next to several cards. On a table near the window was a basket of fresh fruit wrapped in cellophane and tied with a yellow ribbon. When Sukie removed her sunglasses she had dark rings under her eyes. 'How are you?'

He raised a feeble thumbs up.

'Do you remember what happened?'

'A car,' he said, wincing as the pain in his chest returned with force.

'I saw it happen, Luke. You just shot out in front of him. Thank God the driver had his wits about him. You could have been killed.'

'Take more than a car. When did you arrive?'

'Just now. About ten minutes ago,' she looked away. 'I—I can't stay long.'

'Can't say I blame you. Hospitals freak me out too. Let's locomote out of here together.' She gave him a look. 'Okay, so I get to stay. But while you're here do you have to sit so far away? I'm sick, baby, but I ain't contagious.'

Sukie moved over to the bed and sat on the edge. Somewhere in the distance a door banged. The radiator gurgled in response. A green-uniformed woman popped her head round the door.

'Got some more flowers for you, Mr Falkner. I'll just pop off and see if I can find a spare vase. You've used up almost our entire supply!'

Sukie looked remorseful. 'I didn't think. I should have brought some.'

'Forget it. It's you I want, not flowers. How long have I . . .?' He faltered, his chest heaving from the effort of so much talking.

'A while,' she told him, not quite meeting his eye. 'You've had some surgery but you're going to be fine. Absolutely fine. The doctors are very pleased.'

He didn't like the sudden brightness of her voice.

'How long, Sukie?'

She bit her lip. 'Three days.'

'Three days! I've been here THREE days!' Wincing, Luke turned his head away, his world crumbling.

'Listen to me,' she said with sudden firmness. 'It's *not* the end of the world. So what if you missed Wimbledon. There's always next year.'

'You don't understand.'

'Luke, it's *just* a tournament.'

But she no longer had his attention. He was crying. Leaning forward Sukie placed a hand over Luke's and held it tight. Nothing further was said. There seemed to be no point. Instead, she studied the peaches and strawberries and mangoes clustered round the centrepiece of pineapple in the basket, listening to Luke's tight, jerky sobs.

Not for the first time Sukie felt utterly useless.

Every August the National Junior Championships of Great Britain are held in Nottingham. For hundreds of young

hopefuls it is the most important tournament of the year
with months of training invested for the event. Success in
the National could bring sponsorship deals, national training,
tours abroad. But competition is fierce and the tournament
carries the additional pressure of being very public along
with high expectations for those participating. The lucky few
connected to members of staff at the Nottingham Tennis
Centre get to stay in their homes. The rest have to make
do with nearby bed-and-breakfasts or, if they can afford it,
a hotel.

Charlotte and Fran had both entered and found themselves
in competitive roles. But Fran, who had started playing when
she was seven, had the upper hand. Seeded number three
in the under-fourteen event, she automatically qualified for
the main sixty-four draw. The unseeded Charlotte had first to
qualify. Most players hated the 'qualies' because it meant you
had to win three matches (played over the preceding week)
just to reach the tournament. Once through, it was likely they
would draw a seeded player in the first round, and if unlucky,
they might find themselves out of the tournament after only
a few hours.

For Charlotte the tournament had very nearly been over
even before it had started. Stuck on the M1 in a tailback
fifteen miles long, Hugo had got her there with minutes
to spare before the sign-in. Had she missed the draw she
wouldn't have been allowed to compete. Charlotte routined
her first opponent, a pretty but ineffectual player, with an
encouraging score of six-one, six-two. Her second match,
however, delayed for two hours due to rain, was more
of a fight and went to three sets. Watching in the second
row, Hugo received several raised eyebrows for bellowing
at Charlotte after she dropped her serve. Nerves rattled and
clearly embarrassed, she lost the second set, and was down
love-three in the third before she was able to pull herself
together.

Chris, one of Sutton's fulltime coaches had driven down to support not just Charlotte but four other Sutton pupils playing in the tournament. Realising the pressure Charlotte was under he watched silently from his seat, nodding encouragingly when she glanced in his direction. Hugo frowned nearby. He disliked the man, critical of what he saw as a laboured approach in bringing Charlotte's game on. But he tolerated the LTA coach because without him (or rather without the backing of the LTA), Charlotte's chances of making it were negligible.

Hugo was waiting for Charlotte as she came off court.

'Bit touch and go out there,' he said, nodding briefly to a passing official. 'Why didn't you come into the net more?'

Charlotte gulped thirstily from a bottle of lemonade. 'Don't know,' she gasped, wiping her face against her sleeve, 'lost my concentration for a bit in the second set. She was serving really well.'

Hugo consulted his notepad. 'You only served two out of twenty second serves to the backhand.'

Chris joined them. 'Well done, sweetheart,' he said, putting an arm round her shoulder. 'You did what I told you. Stuck with the plan and I'm really pleased. You played a good match today.'

Charlotte flushed with pride, 'Thanks. Do you know who I'm up against next?'

Chris glanced at the form he was holding. 'Abigail Heally. Won her last round in straight sets. She's good, but you're better. So don't go getting yourself worked up about it. Plan on getting a good night's sleep, okay?'

He directed his gaze at Hugo as he said this. It would be just like Hugo to get Charlotte back on to the practice courts and have her work out for another hour.

'I'll just run up to the office and hand in my result,' Charlotte said to Hugo. 'Meet you back at the car in ten minutes.'

*   *   *

She was fifteen minutes late. Hugo was drumming his fingers on the car roof when she arrived.

'Sorry,' she mumbled, as he unlocked her door, 'got waylaid.'

'I've been speaking to your mother.'

Charlotte looked at him. 'Did you tell her about my win?'

'Of course. We didn't have long to talk. But she was pretty chuffed with the news.' He started the ignition. 'About this win today, I thought you showed courage out there,' Charlotte blushed at the rare compliment, 'but I don't want you getting complacent in spite of what Chris said. There's still a lot of work ahead. Next week's going to be a tough one.'

Yes. Yes. Yes . . . Charlotte's mind wandered. Relaxed and happy from her victory, she sank back in her seat and watched people wander in and out of the main exit. There was Chris talking to the Centre manager and one of David Lloyd's coaches. Behind them emerged her opponent from the last round. Carrying a Prince kitbag, the girl looked miserable. That could have been me, she thought sympathetically, then steeled her heart. She couldn't afford to become emotional. Not now. It would be the undoing of her game.

'. . . get up first thing tomorrow and work on your toss. No good blaming double faults on the wind.'

As Hugo pulled out, he was made to wait while another car reversed into a space ahead. Which was when Charlotte caught sight of Fran. She was with a man – an old man, and he had an arm draped intimately around her shoulder. Charlotte blinked. Was this the elusive Ricky? Surely not. But with a sinking feeling in her stomach, Charlotte could tell he was by the way Fran was lapping up his every word. Charlotte had imagined someone tall and slim with dark brown hair. Not a paunchy man old enough to be Fran's father.

'Charlotte,' Hugo's voice, 'you're not taking any of this in, are you?'

'Sorry. It's just that Fran's over there with her new boyfriend. She's been banging on about him for ages and I was curious to see what he looked like,' she pointed them out. 'Over there.'

Hugo's gaze followed the direction of Charlotte's finger and found them just before they disappeared into Ricky's car.

'That's not her boyfriend,' he said jocularly. 'That's Rick Lamb. Her new *coach*. I was talking to him about the new number one court underway at Wimbledon only yesterday. Used to play professionally. Now works for the LTA.'

Fran's coach! Charlotte couldn't wait to get to a phone.

Luke was in hospital for two weeks. While he lay in his comfortable green room having morphine dreams, the All England Club saw their biggest turnout ever despite the weather which was cool and cloudy, the occasional tantalising ray poking through the clouds.

Wolff, for the first time in his career, reached the final. Although he lost, his performance at Wimbledon was worth $47,588 and his ranking broke back into the top twenty. Germany regained the title, and the LTA got an injection of fourteen million pounds to put towards finding the longed-for British champion.

In a show of independence Sukie had managed to get rid of her tenant and reinstated herself back in her old Notting Hill Gate flat. With the exception of a patch of damp in the bathroom and a small black cigarette stain on the lino of her kitchen floor, the flat was transformed. A freelance interior decorator, Sukie's ex-tenant had used her skills to cheer the place up. Sukie was secretly thrilled with the improvements but because her permission hadn't first been sought before the work commenced, she held on to the deposit, claiming untruthfully that she wanted the flat restored to its former decorative state.

Luke had broken a foot, suffered concussion and bruising to the head and chest and fractured his right leg in two places.

Advised by his surgeon not to travel for at least one month, Luke checked out of hospital and moved in with Sukie. One of his first visitors was Lauren.

'Hey,' he grinned down at her from the front door. 'Sorry I took so long. I was up on the roof catching some rays.' He patted the plaster on his right leg. 'This thing kinda slows me down.'

'If this is a bad time I could always come back?'

'Lauren, it's never a bad time when you visit. Come on in,' and he grabbed her hand as though he were afraid she'd escape, before hobbling awkwardly back into the flat.

Following him down the hall Lauren clutched the flowers she'd brought him in her free hand. A stale smell of fried food hung in the air.

'Hear you've been working without me,' Luke said, over his shoulder.

'You didn't miss much. Just a reshoot then this dreary lunch party I had to attend on the Thames. No one decent to talk to. It would have driven you mad! Oh,' she said as they entered Sukie's tiny sitting room, 'I see you've made some changes. Quite a transformation. It's lovely.'

'You should see upstairs. Not that I can take any credit. Sukie's last tenant did it all. Think she works for one of those glossy house magazines.' He lowered his rangy frame onto a worn armchair and gestured at the sofa. 'Take a load off.'

Lauren removed a guitar and sat down. 'You look so well.'

'You look pretty good yourself.'

'I can't believe how quickly you've recovered.'

'Nothing like a dose of R&R,' he said lightly. 'Still, it's tough. First time in years that I've been sick.'

'It must be purgatory for you. I hope Sukie's proving to be a good nurse?'

'Pretty good. Yeah,' his eyes dropped to his wristwatch. 'Say, she should have gotten back by now. I said you might be coming over.'

'It doesn't matter. It was you I wanted to see.'

'She's got some project she's working on. Won't say what. Not to me anyway.'

Lauren picked up traces of bitterness in his voice. 'There's nothing wrong?'

'Between Sukie and me? We're fine. I admit it's hard for us both adjusting. This apartment can get kind of crampy.'

Lauren smiled. 'I think it was meant for someone a foot shorter than you.'

He laughed. 'Can I fix you some coffee or something? For once, we've got a stocked fridge.'

She shook her head. 'I can't stay. I left Tom with my next-door neighbour and promised I'd be back by one. She's been so much help. I wouldn't want her to feel taken advantage of.'

'Well, I appreciate the visit. In fact I wanted to thank you for coming over to the hospital all those times. They sure made a difference.' It wasn't said, but she knew he was thinking about Sukie; after her first visit she'd only been back to see him once.

'How's Tom?' he asked. 'I'd like to see the little fella sometime.'

'You'll have your opportunity next week. I've invited you and Sukie round for dinner.' Lauren read the surprise on his face, 'She hasn't told you yet?' Typical of her sister. 'Max and Tiffany are coming too. It's not often I can get you all in the same city at the same time.'

'Sometimes I wake up and forget just which city I'm in.'

'Will you be coming to Max's book launch on Friday?' she asked him.

'Decided against it. The press'll be looking to get shots of me – don't think I could face all that just yet. It's Max's night. I don't want to ruin it for him.'

'I don't think Max would see it like that but I can understand your reticence.'

Luke glanced down at his hands, his mood suddenly serious. 'Look, Lauren. While you're here – I don't suppose anything was mentioned at Tuff?'

'In what respect?'

'It's just that with me like this,' he scuffed the arm of the chair with the flat of his hand, nervously, she thought, 'I was kind of wondering if they were thinking of making changes?'

'How could they? Both our contracts are good for two more years.'

'Yeah, but with clauses. Mine expires if I don't play a minimum of ten events a year.'

'Then you've got nothing to worry about. You'll be back on court in no time.'

He grimaced. 'That's what I'd thought. Give it a couple of months for this to heal.' Again he tapped his leg.

'I sense a but.'

'There are complications. The tendon in my right knee has partially snapped. If it doesn't mend naturally I may need another operation. That would keep me out of the game for the rest of the year.'

Lauren's face fell, 'Oh, Luke. Just when everything was going so well for you.'

He jutted out his bottom lip. 'I got unlucky. Most of my life's come real easy. I always took what I had for granted. *Christ*, I used to laugh at guys watching what they ate, working out at the gym all hours of the day, the time they

spent practising down at the courts. I never had to do any
of that shit. Just played because I loved it.'

'And now?'

He looked at her, his expression almost one of bewilder-
ment, like a child whose parent had shouted at him for the
first time. 'Now is different. I can't take things for granted
any more.'

Lauren gave a sad little smile. 'None of us can, Luke,' she
said, reaching out for his hand, 'none of us can.'

'Hello, Wolff.'

His hands dampened, he felt his stomach falter, stumble
as he turned to face Sukie. She was wearing a crushed
velvet dress in Titian red which was so tight it left
little of what was underneath to the imagination. Her
hair had been recently cut much shorter than he had
remembered. But she had the kind of round, even-featured
face that could take the severity. Her large blue eyes
looked huge.

Kittenishly she smiled at him. 'I thought you'd be here.
You look dreamy in that tux.'

'I feel uncomfortable.'

'You shouldn't. I didn't come here with Luke.'

'How is he?'

'On the mend. Determined to run before he can walk.
You players are all the same. But I don't want to talk to you
about Luke,' she lowered her voice. 'When can I see you?'

Wolff surveyed the room. 'I don't think it's a good idea.'

Her eyes grew serious. 'Wolff, don't make me beg. It's
been almost three weeks. I'm going out of my mind. I *must*
see you – alone.'

He was compelled by the urgency in her voice to look at
her. God, she was lovely. He ached to have her. Instinctively
he wiped clammy palms against the sides of his trousers.

'Still at St James's?'

'No. The tenancy lease on my flat expired. We've moved back there – temporarily,' she added suggestively.

'Same number?'

'Yes.'

'I'll call you.'

'When?'

He had no time to answer. Inge joined them. Wolff dragged his gaze away from Sukie and smiled at his wife. If Inge was surprised to see them together she hid it well. Proudly she held up a copy of Max's book.

'Isn't it good? And finally I managed to get him to sign this for me. You should see. Such a queue of fans. Women mostly, of course. Hello, Sukie,' she said warmly. 'I wish I could wear a dress like that. You look wonderful! Doesn't she, Wolff?'

Sukie's eyes darted briefly to Wolff's. 'Thanks. So do you.'

'Mmm. Maybe not. But why should I care. I have my two beautiful little girls.'

'Yes,' said Sukie feebly.

'Are you going to read Max's book?'

Sukie waved her cigarette in the air. 'I expect so. I've always wanted to find out the nitty gritty of Max's past.'

'How is Luke?' Inge asked

'Up and about – driving me crazy.' Sukie laughed lamely.

'Poor Luke. It is such bad luck for this to happen to him now. But anyway he has you to take his mind off it.'

There was a hellish pause.

Wolff's hands were damp again. The musky smell of Sukie's perfume was driving him insane. It prevented him from thinking straight. He had to get some air.

'They're serving up the food. Let me get something for you both.'

Inge smiled. 'Thank you, darling. I'm ravenous.'

But Sukie shook her head. 'Not for me. I came here with someone. I'd better go and find him.'

Wolff marched off in the opposite direction, Sukie's eyes big with secret messages burning in his brain. He did not wait to find out if the two women had continued talking nor did he look round.

Lauren, sitting opposite Max, was deep in conversation with an Italian Olympic committee member. They were discussing Alan Tarrent and she listened with interest to his comments. Although loquacious and charming, it was Alan's truculent side that was more well known – certainly to her. He had made many enemies, not least among the press. One unfortunate journalist, new to the job, had quoted a few of Alan's comments and promptly found himself dragged into a storage room and his head banged against a concrete wall until he promised to retract what he had written.

The committee member stopped in mid-sentence. 'He's not a friend of yours is he? I'd hate to have put my foot in it.' The noise level in the room had climbed to such a level he had to shout to make himself heard.

Lauren smiled sourly. 'Alan Tarrent is no friend of mine.'

A waiter was pouring Max more wine when suddenly he put down the bottle and plucked a programme from the table.

'Señor Carter, I *big* fan of yours. It would be an honour if you would to sign this for me.'

'Look, I . . .'

With a nose for trouble the maître d' was instantly at Max's side.

'What are you *doing*!' he snapped at the waiter, his Roman profile twitching. 'You're *not* to bother Mr Carter. Is that understood? Go back to the kitchen and finish your work this instant. I'll speak to you later.'

Mortified, the waiter fled from the room.

'Terribly sorry, sir. The man's new.'

'Hey, no problem,' Max winked at Lauren.

Sukie leaned across him, gazing at Lauren's dress with envy. 'Been on another shopping spree, Lo? Whenever I see you these days, you seem to be wearing something new. You want to watch you're not becoming a compulsive shopper.'

Lauren cocked her head to one side and looked down, not wanting the conversation to continue.

'I think you look stunning in it,' whispered the Olympic committee member, taking her silence for embarrassment.

Lauren smiled at him gratefully.

Someone banged on a table. A representative of the publishers was introduced and said a few words. Then Max got up and waited for the surge of applause to subside. He made a brief speech, cameras exploding excitedly in his face. Lauren joined in the applause. Many players looked incongruous and ill at ease in formal attire. While appearing relaxed on court in front of an audience of fifteen thousand spectators, when faced with a television camera they quickly dried up. Max was a rare exception. Confident, suave, articulate, he was the media's dream interviewee.

At this very moment he was being beset with questions. One of the journalists asked him.

'What do you plan to do when you retire?'

'Probably become a journalist,' he said, deadpan. Everyone laughed.

Wolff watched without listening. He felt—it wasn't a feeling he could define, only that he must have her. In all his life he had never physically desired a woman so much. He couldn't explain why. Just being close to her but not being able to touch her had been intolerable. He reached the buffet table and automatically took the white plate handed to him by one of the waiters. As he indiscriminately piled his wife's plate with food, he thought of the twins and what this would do to them if Inge ever

found out. The affair was wrong. He knew it. He *knew* it,
but it was as if some madness had gripped his soul. Like an
alcoholic in a bar, he couldn't resist another drink. Or could
he? Had he really put his feelings to the test? He loved Inge,
desired her. In her he had all the qualities a man could wish
for in a wife. She deserved better than this. He resolved not
to call Sukie. To put her from his mind. Then he pictured
her full pale body, naked on the floor, arms open to him,
thighs apart, and the image of Inge, mother earth, smiling
and lovely, holding the twins, faded into the background.
The two impressions interwove, each stimulating confusing
feelings: guilt, desire; remorse, love.

A noise caught Wolff's attention. Turning, he saw Sukie
with a tall man with white-blond hair. Wolff recognised
him as Luke's part-time doubles partner. Undeniably good-
looking, the man was a well-known rake. His arm circled
Sukie's waist and he bent down to whisper something in
her ear. Whatever it was he'd said Sukie found hysterically
funny and collapsed against him with laughter. A liquid chill
ran through Wolff's blood. Why couldn't he do that? Why
didn't he have the ability to make a woman laugh? All his
life he had been accused of being too serious, too intense.
It had never bothered him much. But at that moment he
was consumed with jealousy, filled with desire to smash the
man's smug face to pulp. Then he saw his wife approaching
him. He forced himself to calm down.

'*There* you are. Did you forget me?'

'*Desolé, chérie. Aqui tiene.*' He handed her the plate.

Inge laughed. 'French and Spanish together? That is new
for us. Oh, but why not?'

She picked up a salt cellar and sprinkled a little onto
her food. When she looked up her expression was one of
concern. 'You look pale tonight. I hope you're not catching
a cold.' She put her free hand to his brow.

Wolff pulled away as if stung. 'I'm fine,' he snapped,

watching Lauren Kendall leave the room. 'Don't fuss me.'

He was immediately contrite, but Inge's eyes merely filled with familiar affectionate laughter.

'No, of course not. I shouldn't do that. What a terrible crime it is if I show everyone how much I love my husband.'

Lauren went in search of the Ladies. On her way out, she passed a couple standing in the doorway. She overheard the man say,

'Kiss me.'

'Why?'

'Just do it.'

Lauren had to cross the lobby to get to the loo. As she approached, she saw two men deep in conversation. One of them was Max. The other was the Spanish waiter who had earlier pestered Max for an autograph. Moving closer she was able to pick up their conversation.

'. . . still have that programme?' Max was speaking.

The waiter fumbled in his pocket and handed it to him.

'You got a family?' Max asked, scribbling an inscription across the top.

The waiter nodded. 'Three very beautiful boys. Like me, señor, they're all tennis fanatics.'

'That so? Tell you what—'

'Henriques, Meester Carter, Pepe Henriques.'

'Okay, Pepe. I'm playing in an exhibition match two weeks from now. How about you turn up and I'll have tickets for you and your boys at the main gate.'

The waiter's face lit up. 'You would do this for me? Oh, Meester Carter, is incredible! How I can say *thank* you. You do very good thing for me.'

Max handed back the man's programme and smiled. 'I've put the date and venue on the back. But take a tip from me; don't go telling your boss.'

Lauren slipped undetected into the Ladies.

The bathroom appeared empty. Sitting on a velvet-covered stool, Lauren gazed into the mirror and dabbed at the corners of her eyes with her little finger and smoothed her eyebrows into neater lines. 'Kiss me.' The man's words echoed in her mind and she had a sudden vision of herself standing at the entrance of a restaurant with Josh's arm wrapped possessively around her shoulders. 'Kiss me.' How many times had she heard him request, no *demand*, the same thing whenever they went out. It occurred to her now why he used to do it. It was his way of telling all the men in the room that she belonged to him. His property. She tried to picture him in her mind. But his features blurred in and out of focus. Something wet had materialised on her hand. Lauren smudged it with her index finger. Appalled, she realized it was a tear. She felt more rise to the surface of her eyes. You can't, she told herself astonished by the sudden tug of emotion within her. Not now. Not here.

She forced her train of thought to change direction and unwittingly remembered Sukie's surprise tonight at her designer dress. *You want to watch you're not becoming a compulsive shopper.* Did that mean she knew what Lauren was up to? Lauren's hands ran across the pale blue satin of her dress. She had to be more careful before things got out of hand. There had already been too many slip-ups. She couldn't afford another. Earlier that day Sukie had asked to borrow an outfit for Max's book launch. Specifically she had requested the Calvin Klein dress Lauren had pinched from a department store. But having slipped it into her bag without trying it on, it had later proved too big for her. Lauren had thrown it out.

'What do you mean, you got rid of it?'

'It didn't hang right,' Lauren had lied; 'the hem puckered. I washed it to see if it would make a difference. But that just made it worse. I took it down to Help The Aged.'

'A *Calvin Klein*!'

'It was ruined. Don't keep going on.' From her wardrobe Lauren had grabbed a red dress in desperation. 'This would look stunning. Why don't you try it on?'

'What size?'

'It'll give.'

Lauren had got away with it this time. But for how much longer?

A loo flushed and a heavily made-up woman emerged. She looked at Lauren as she rinsed her hands.

'Have we met?' she inquired politely.

Lauren shook her head and manipulated her features into a professional smile.

The woman dried her hands then helped herself to some hand cream provided for guests. She then reached for a matching bottle of *eau de toilette* and sprayed a generous amount onto her chest.

'Are you sure?' she asked again, throwing Lauren another curious glance. 'I'm usually good with faces and yours seems very familiar.'

Lauren was fixing her lips. 'I must have one of those faces.'

'Perhaps. But . . .'

She wasn't going to get away with it. 'I'm part of the Tuff sports campaign.'

The woman nodded. 'Of course. My husband was saying only yesterday what a success it's been.'

'Really?' Lauren tried to sound pleased without encouraging further conversation.

'I . . .' The woman paused, clearly embarrassed, and with a sinking feeling Lauren guessed what she was about to say. 'It was an absolute tragedy what happened to your husband. We were all devastated. Do you know I can still remember it as though it were yesterday.'

Me too, thought Lauren, me too.

A young woman entered the room. 'Mother, *there* you

are. I've been looking for you everywhere. Dad's getting restless. I think you should come.'

The woman raised her arms in exasperation. 'He's not still going on about missing Giles, is he? I've lost count how many times I've told him Giles will wait. Oh, all right, I'm coming.' The woman checked her teeth, then once more locked eyes with Lauren in the mirror.

'Well,' she said apologetically, 'it was nice meeting you.'

When she had gone, Lauren slipped into the end cubicle and removed her shoes. Generally she avoided high heels. She hated the discomfort, the restriction they imposed and she didn't need the extra height. But tonight, on show for Tuff, she had felt obliged. Now she removed them – it felt as if a pack of particularly vicious rodents had been gnawing at her toes. Wriggling blood gratefully back into her feet, she turned sideways to withdraw some loo paper and noticed a twenties-style silver sequinned bag on the floor. That woman must have left it behind. Lauren picked it up and opened it curiously. Inside, she found a phial of pills – they looked like Prozac – a lipstick, two used Kleenex, silver compact, grubby twenty-pound note and a diamond ring. Held up to the light, she saw that it was genuine. Too big for her wedding finger, she slipped it onto the next one. Though still a little loose, she gently moved her hand so that the diamond sparkled enticingly under the lights. In a flash Lauren decided she must have it. But what to do with the bag? She couldn't take just the ring. Too incriminating. *Don't. Walk away.* Heart pounding, Lauren shoved the diamond inside her bra. It felt cold, its small, sharp edges bit into her flesh. She flushed the loo and straightened her dress. She tried forcing the silver bag into her own but it wouldn't fit. Too big. She unlocked the door and searched around the room for somewhere to hide it. Her eyes found the paper towel container. *You don't have to do this. You can just walk away or hand it in to reception.* Frantically, Lauren ripped free several towels and wrapped the bag inside them. Hurry. Before someone sees you. Entering a different loo this time, she jammed it into the sanitary bin. Then she fled.

She slowed her pace as she crossed the lobby floor – no Max this time. The concierge smiled at her inquiringly as she approached his desk.

'Could you get me a taxi?'

'We have several waiting outside, madame. If you'd like to follow me.'

Outside it was raining. The doorman followed her out, shielding her with an umbrella. In the safe anonymous gloom of the taxi, Lauren let her head fall against the back seat and closed her eyes. Fool. *Why did you do it? What if that woman goes back. If you didn't mean to be found out, then why did you leave the bag? She will guess it was you. What if she had already returned?* Shut up, I don't want to hear this. *But you must. It's got to stop.* She felt wrung out by the argument within herself. I should have stayed, Lauren realised. It would have looked better. She could go back. Return the bag to where she had found it. Or hand it in. No. Too late for that now. But she must hide the ring, get rid of it somehow. Throw it away? Oh, she thought, raising a trembling hand to her forehead, what in God's name is happening to me?

19

The following Wednesday, the day of Lauren's twenty-seventh birthday, temperatures soared into the eighties. Determined to make more of an effort socially, Lauren celebrated the event by throwing a small dinner party. Luke and Wolff's long-term, on-off court battle made it difficult for her to invite them both, but the problem resolved itself when Inge's parents decided at the last minute to fly over for the weekend to see the twins. After a disastrous first-round defeat at Wimbledon, Max was determined to make a come-back at the US Open but had delayed his and Tiffany's return to the States by twenty-four hours. Also invited was Anna Harrison, a friend from Lauren's modelling days who was spending the night, and as a gesture of thanks Lauren had included her next-door neighbours, the Masons, who had often looked after Tom.

They all arrived laden with gifts and cards which Lauren left stacked in the hall to be unwrapped later. Windows had been thrown open to the warm night, long-stemmed roses from the Masons' garden adorned the beautifully laid table, conversation mingled with Simon and Garfunkel on the stereo. The hot and sour pickled prawns had been swiftly demolished. The main course was met with equal enthusiasm.

'This is exquisite!' drooled Jill Mason, plunging her fork into her salmon steak. 'What have you cooked it in?'

'Avocado and crème fraiche sauce,' said Lauren, handing round a bowl of baby summer vegetables. The tan she'd caught from sitting in the garden highlighted her beauty. 'I can't take the credit unfortunately. The recipe comes from my mother.'

'Burnt toast and Pot Noodle was as far as my mum's culinary skills stretched,' said Anna Harrison ruefully. 'Dad did all the cooking at home.'

'One of those New Age men, was he?' teased Henry Mason, a financial adviser who was going bald.

'Not a chance. It's just that he refused to eat anything Mum made. He worked as a chef for a top hotel,' she explained, flicking stray black curls from her forehead. 'Brilliant mind and a perfectionist – a hard act for anyone to follow. My three sisters and I all left home feeling totally inadequate which is probably why I became a model.'

'Oh,' said Henry ineffectually, 'yes, of course.'

Tiffany helped herself to some couscous. 'Guess that's how you know Lauren? From working together?'

A brief mischievous look passed between Lauren and Anna who smiled. 'We've had some pretty racy times.'

Luke shifted eagerly in his chair. 'Right on. Now the conversation's getting interesting.'

Sukie rolled her eyes. 'Do you *have* to be so predictable?'

'What about you, Jill?' said Anna, wanting to include Henry's shy wife in the conversation. 'I know you've got two little ones but do you get time for anything else?'

A stone overweight in all the wrong places and with a capricious thatch of light brown hair, Jill Mason was almost apologetic with her smile. 'Charity work mostly. I was a nurse before I met Henry. Gave it up when we got married.'

'That's hard slog, isn't it?'

'What – being married to Henry?' Max winked at Jill.

Good-temperedly she joined in with the amusement. 'It was hard, you're right. Overworked and underpaid but hugely rewarding. I must admit I do miss my job but the children are so small and – well, it would be impossible to go back now.' She glanced at her husband; but Henry wasn't listening. Dazzled by Tiffany's gleaming smile and dancing eyes, he was finding the flattery of such a knock-out woman irresistible and had immediately launched into one of two areas he felt comfortable with; cricket and finance. He'd spent the last five minutes trying to persuade her into taking out a pension plan.

'Same thing on the circuit,' said Luke, generously spreading butter on another bread roll. 'It's like you get used to travelling constantly then suddenly you've got a family and the routine's gotta change. Man, I'd *love* to have kids but you've gotta be making big bucks to do it *and* be able to keep on playing.'

Jill smiled at him. 'How many children do you plan on having?'

'Four. Maybe five. I'd like a few.'

'Well, don't look at me,' said Sukie, stabbing at her half-finished meal with a fork. 'I'm not a breeding machine.'

'Oh, silly,' said Lauren, giving Luke a reassuring smile.

'I'm now working as "a friend" of St Mary's. In fact,' Jill admitted, turning to Max, 'I've been a little calculating. We're holding a charity auction next weekend and as Lauren said you'd be here tonight I brought along a copy of your book. I was hoping you'd sign it. You don't mind, do you? The money we raise will go to a good cause.' She gave him a pleading look that said; this would mean a great deal.

'Sure. Want to do it now?'

Triumphant, Jill rushed off to find her bag.

'You *are* good,' said Lauren warmly. 'This means so much to her.' She took a sip of her wine. 'Tell me, how are the book sales going? I meant to ask earlier.'

'Real well. Trouble is half my time's taken up with signings,' he waved his hand indicating that the subject didn't interest him much. 'Got to get my mind back on the game – the US Open's approaching fast.'

'Will you visit your parents while you're out there?'

'I should. I owe them one,' he shook his head ruefully. 'Fact is I don't get over to Oakland anywhere near enough nowadays. You think you've got all this time to spare, then one day you wake up to find your folks have grown old.'

'What about Ruth?' Lauren asked, thinking about the mentally and physically handicapped sister he rarely mentioned. 'Are your parents still taking care of her full time?'

'Not any more. They're no longer up to it. Ruth's now in a home. She's well looked after and it's close by, so my folks get to visit each week. What about *your* plans?' he said, clearly uncomfortable talking about the sister he loved but whose severe disability caused him incalculable guilt.

'Tuff's organised a press week on the QE2. It'll be the usual mixture of press, buyers, players. I'm going along to do my bit. It'll be a five-day crossing to New York – they'll fly us back. Rather exciting as I've never done a cruise before and I can even take Tom. Shame Luke won't be going. I've got used to having him around. He's been so much fun to work with – cheers me up.'

'Is that what you need – cheering up?'

'No, not really,' Lauren glanced around at her animated guests and smiled. 'In fact, I'm really enjoying myself tonight. I'd forgotten what fun it is to have people round. We used to do so much entertaining. It's stupid of me to cut myself off just because Josh isn't here any more.' She put a hand over Max's and squeezed it gratefully. 'I'm so glad you were able to be here.'

'Me too,' his eyes grew nostalgic. 'Something just occurred to me.'

'What?'

'We've known each other for almost five years.'

Lauren was amazed. 'Has it really been that long?'

'Feels like nothing to me.'

Jill returned in a breathless rush as though she was afraid Max might have changed his mind in the time she was gone.

'Here we are.' She placed the book and a fountain pen in front of him.

Henry, who had been waiting for a good moment to mention the sixty-eight he'd scored before lunch during last weekend's club match against the Old Etonians, realised to his horror that he'd lost Tiffany's attention. Perhaps he'd overwhelmed her by introducing too many policy schemes into the conversation. In his experience, women often were a little daunted by money. He glanced at his wife for help, then saw Max signing her book.

'Aha! There you go. Now what did I tell you, angel? Said it would be all right, didn't I?' Smugly, Henry sat back in his chair and gave a satisfactory sniff as though the success of the autograph had been entirely his doing.

Lauren began clearing plates. Sukie gave her a hand out to the kitchen, desperate for a break from the dreadful Henry, who had next targeted her with a pension plan.

'Thanks for putting me next to bore of the year,' she muttered, easing her hands into a pair of yellow washing-up gloves. 'He's done nothing but quote pension statistics all evening.'

Lauren giggled. 'He's probably terrified. He doesn't get to meet girls like you very often.'

'It's the Texan he seems to have the hots for, not me.'

'Who's this?' Max had followed them through and put down several stacked plates next to the sink.

'We're talking about Henry.'

'Right. Thought I could hear him giving you the lowdown on health insurance.'

'Don't!' said Sukie.

'Relax. He's on to cricket now.'

Sukie groaned. 'That's even worse.'

Max picked up a spare dishtowel and helped Lauren with the drying up.

'Sukie,' he said carefully, 'don't you think you were being a bit hard on Luke earlier? None of this can be easy for him.'

'What do you mean?'

'Just that he's had a rough ride. He needs support not antagonism.'

Sukie's mouth curved into a vinegary smile. 'I'm not going to mother him, Max, if that's what you mean. He can take care of himself. Luke just needs a break from the game. He'll bounce back.'

'Maybe not. When guys like Luke get injured, they can lose confidence once they return to the game. You don't go all out for points in the same way because in the back of your mind you're worried about something going.'

Sukie laughed. 'Worry isn't part of Luke's vocabulary. He plays by instinct – *you* told me that. I'll lay a bet you'll be the first one moaning when he whips you off court in the Australian Open.'

Lauren frowned. 'But that's less than four months away.'

'So?'

Max placed a dry glass on the table. 'Sukie, I don't think you understand. Luke could be out of the game for a lot longer than that – hasn't he explained this to you?'

Sukie paled. 'What do you mean? He said his injuries weren't serious.'

A look passed between Lauren and Max.

'Perhaps because he didn't want to worry you. But you should know that Luke may never again reach the level he's at now.'

This horrible prospect hadn't even crossed Sukie's mind. 'You don't honestly believe that?'

'It happens to players all the time. You put your whole

life into the game and with one shot it can all go. Luke's going to need plenty of support. That means you've got to be patient with him.'

Swallowing the concoction of guilt, dread and anger battling within her, Sukie plunged a caked pan into the soapy water and attacked it with a scouring pad.

'What you're saying is all very well but it's hardly fair to make this *my* problem. Sooner or later, Luke's going to have to face reality and learn to fend for himself.'

'Hey,' said Max swivelling round, his voice a fraction too bright, 'it's the man.'

Standing at the door was Luke, looking cheerful in a red gingham shirt. He hadn't heard, thought Lauren. Thank God.

'Henry's suggested playing something,' he said, hobbling closer.

'That's a surprise,' muttered Sukie. 'Let me guess. Monopoly!'

'I said I'd come and find out if you've got any games.'

Lauren laughed. 'There are plenty for two-year-olds.'

'Perfect,' said Max.

'Have a look in the cupboard under the stairs,' Lauren suggested. 'There are stacks of them I put away – board games mostly. You're welcome to root around.'

'I'll do that. You going to be long in here?'

'The plates don't wash themselves, Luke,' Sukie snapped, peeling off her gloves.

'Chill, Sukie,' he said, grinning.

'And since you're in such a hurry, *I'll* find the games and *you* can finish off this lot! It's too hot in here and I need a cigarette.'

Tossing a baffled Luke the gloves, she marched out of the room.

'What'd I say?'

'Ignore her,' said Lauren, 'she's just being bloody-minded.'

Max winked at him. 'Glad to see you've got your woman firmly under control.'

Back in the dining room, Henry was setting up a game of Articulate with all the enthusiasm of a four-year-old. Tiffany topped up her glass with Chardonnay then passed the bottle across the table to Luke.

'Guess you won't make it to the US Open?' she said.

'Not this year.'

'Shame,' said Anna. 'My boyfriend watched you play at Queen's – he's a real fan. We both are.'

'Reckon Luky here's got a few tennis years in him yet,' said Tiffany with a smile.

'Unlike you, hey Max?' Luke winked at his friend who along with Lauren had surfaced from the kitchen. 'He was winning grand slams when I was still a boy.'

Max cuffed him gently round the head, 'You make me sound antique.'

'What was it like, winning Wimbledon?' asked Jill who had followed the championship for years and secretly fancied Max.

Emotion flooded into his face. 'Nothing, and I really mean nothing, compares with winning Wimbledon.' Then Max smiled, charming them all, 'Except perhaps winning it a second time.'

Anna was watching Henry spin the arrow in the centre of the Articulate board. 'Is it still a buzz? Do you still love playing?'

'I love *winning*,' Max said frankly, 'and I love the money and attention that goes with it. But there's a price for all that.'

Luke nodded. 'Too right.'

'The fame, you mean?' Anna suggested. 'The invasion into your private life?'

'From the time you pick up that racquet, you feel the expectations of others telling you your one responsibility is to win matches. Luke here won the Canadian Open when he was nineteen. I got my first grand slam title when I was twenty-one. You can't arse around to do that. You've got to put a hundred and fifty per cent into your game. When you play a grand slam you almost have to put yourself in a cage for two weeks. You can't let anything distract you. What makes me pissed is that the press seem unable to understand that. You come to do Wimbledon and all they want to know is what you do in your spare time.'

'Yeah. Like what shows you've seen, which exhibitions you've visited,' added Luke. 'I ain't got time for Van Gogh. One day I have a four-hour match, next day I'm resting, day after I'm working out and then you're back playing for real again.'

'Poor Luke,' said Sukie, embarking on her fourth glass of wine, 'you've obviously had a rough time of it.'

Max smiled dryly into his glass. 'There speaks the expert.'

Lauren sent her sister a warning look.

'What I want to know is why lesbianism is so rife in tennis,' said Anna.

'Have you seen any of them lately?' said Sukie. 'It'd be much the same as fucking a man.'

Henry spat out his wine.

'Gigi Fernandez is pretty cute,' Luke said easily, 'and Steffi's got one of the hottest bodies I've ever seen.'

Sukie smiled witheringly. 'But *she's* not a lesbian, is she?'

'Fact is,' said Max, ignoring her, 'there are only the four grand slams and Liptons in Miami where the sexes mix. The circuit's a lonely place for these girls. It's not like they can just go out to bars and pick guys up. Their only other option is to sleep with their coach – unprofessional – or sleep with each other. Happens all the time.'

Lauren rose. 'Who wants coffee?'

Anna, who had caught a flight from Zürich at seven that morning and was struggling with fatigue, smiled gratefully. 'I'd kill for a cup.'

Henry emitted a froggy laugh. 'No need to go that far.'

Max held out a hand and stopped Lauren. 'Before you go, I'd like to say that that was a hell of a meal.'

'Here, here,' agreed Henry. 'You'll have to show Jill how to make that spicy prawn thing,' he smacked his lips greedily. 'We can use it to bribe the boys at the club – raise the level of their game.'

Sukie rolled her eyes heavenward.

'A toast to Lauren,' said Max, raising his glass, 'for her kindness, her friendship and generosity.'

Lauren dropped her head.

'Here, here,' Henry said again, also raising his glass. 'To the birthday girl.'

'To the birthday girl!' they all chorused.

Then they began to sing 'Happy Birthday' and Lauren fled from the room.

Jill pulled a sympathetic face. 'I'll give her a hand with the coffee.'

'Oh, but—' Henry looked disappointed, 'I thought we were going to play a game? I've set it all up.'

'Perhaps later, darling,' said Jill gently.

Everyone wandered through to the drawing room. Henry was soon rambling on about cricket again, this time to Sukie. Anna was telling Max that she had never had to worry about her weight – in fact she had trouble keeping it on. She later proved the point by eating an unmodel-like number of chocolate truffles. Sukie, bored to the point of insanity, walked restlessly across the room away from Henry. Her period was due. She felt bloated and overweight and was regretting having eaten so much. Luke's eyes trailed her. She was wearing a black dress which ended in a sheaf of wispy chiffon. Running an admiring hand up the back of her thigh just before leaving the Notting Hill flat, Luke had discovered she wasn't wearing any knickers. With a gleam in his eye now, he pulled her down next to him on the sofa.

'Don't,' she tried to wriggle away.

Luke grinned, 'Why not? You love the attention.'

'Not tonight. I'm not in the mood.' She glared at Tiffany's slim feet in expensive shoes.

'Of course, the Test Match against the West Indies was a masterpiece of classic batsmanship,' Henry, the sound club cricketer was saying.

'You're always in the mood.' Playfully, Luke bit the back of her neck.

'We got thrashed by the Aussies, but Darren Gough was something else. Six wickets for . . .'

'Luke. *Stop.*'

'What the hell's eating you tonight,' he muttered angrily.

'Nothing!' she snapped. 'I just don't want to be mauled.'

He released his hold as though burned. 'Go then. Don't let me stop you.'

Jill returned with a tray of coffee. She offered a cup to Sukie.

'Not for me,' she muttered, slinking to the furthest corner of the sofa.

'How about you, Luke?'

He nodded resignedly. 'Looks like it's going to be a long night.'

Jill put down the tray.

'Tell me if this is the wrong moment,' she ventured, having been encouraged by Max, 'but this auction next week. I was wondering if you might have a small tennis relic you'd be willing to donate? It wouldn't have to be anything expensive and it would be for a good cause.'

'It always is,' said Sukie rudely, lighting another cigarette.

Jill's smile slipped an inch. 'I'd quite understand if

you said no. You must get asked this kind of thing all the time.'

Luke threw Sukie a dirty look. 'I'm sure I can drum up something.'

'Why not give her your racquets and your kit while you're about it,' Sukie muttered. 'It'll be *months* before you'll be needing them again,' she glared at him accusingly.

Her remark had been meant exclusively for Luke but unfortunately Tiffany overheard.

'Dear me,' she tutted, a sly expression settling on her features, 'have we a lovers' tiff?'

Sukie turned on her. 'What's it to you if we are. Try keeping your beaky nose out of other people's business!'

'SUKIE!'

This from Lauren was followed by a paralysed silence while everyone waited to see how Tiffany would react. To their amazement and relief, she broke into a genial laugh.

But this merely incensed Sukie further. 'What's so bloody amusing?'

'Relax, honey. Just trying to lighten the atmosphere is all. I thought we were having a party.'

'Anyone else for coffee?' Jill stammered.

'Love some, darling,' said Henry. 'Make it two sugars, if you will. Man's got to splash out once in a while.' Contentedly, he sank further back into his comfortable armchair. 'We had a similar situation take place last week. Do you remember Jill, darling?' Henry chuckled expansively to himself, while Sukie puffed mutinously on her cigarette. 'Anthony and Rosie, old friends of ours,' he explained to the rest of the room, 'had a *blazing* row. Turned out Anthony had been bonking the au pair. There was the most godawful scene.'

'Henry, dear, I don't think this is quite the time.'

But Henry, simple soul, failed to catch the warning note in his wife's voice and carried on, deaf and blind to the mounting tension in the room.

'The au pair was sacked on the spot and Anthony got his marching orders. He ended up in a scruffy bedsit in Clapham. Imagine! You should have seen the size of the house he had to leave behind.'

Anna giggled.

Sukie was still glaring at Tiffany. 'What is it you find so funny?'

'Sorry?' said Henry, assuming she was addressing him.

'Sukie,' Lauren warned.

'Well, I'm *sick* of her condescending ways. Dressed up like some stupid Barbie doll,' she said cuttingly, her lips thinning unattractively. 'She thinks because she's got money she can behave exactly as she likes.'

Henry looked at his wife as if seeking an explanation.

'Cut it *out*, Sukie.' This time the warning came from Luke.

For Henry, the penny finally dropped. He tried to defuse the situation.

'I really do think we should all remember that we are guests in Lauren's house . . .'

'"I really do think—"' Sukie mimicked. 'Why don't you just piss off back to suburbia, you dreary little . . .'

Luke banged his fist on the coffee table. 'That's enough! I'm taking you home.'

Sukie laughed demonically. 'You're not taking me any-where, you idiot. God, you're so *thick*. Hasn't the penny dropped yet?'

'Sukie, PLEASE,' begged Lauren. She glanced imploringly at Max. Do something, she seemed to say.

Max got up and clapped his hands, '*O-kay*, guys. How about we cut the cake?'

But Luke held up a hand. 'No, Max, I wanna hear this. Let her say what's on her mind.'

For a moment Sukie continued smoking, then she leaned forward in her seat towards Luke. 'If you really

want to know I can't *stand* being in the same room
as you.'

'I say, steady on,' stammered Henry.

'It's over, Luke. It has been for a long time.' A nervous tick
began to throb in Luke's throat. 'I don't want you touching
me any more. I don't want you in my life. It's finished, finito,
kaput. Is that clear enough for you?'

Luke's face was drained of colour.

'Darling,' said Henry, standing up, 'I really do think it's
time we got going. The babysitter . . .' he finished lamely.

But with one look, his wife silenced him.

'You *suffocate* me,' hurled Sukie, her eyes blazing and
hateful, 'to the point where I feel I can't breathe. You're
selfish, egotistical, you think people find what you say
funny when really they're laughing at you.' Relentlessly she
continued her assassination. 'You're about as sophisticated
as Pee Wee bloody Hermann, and if anything needs working
on it's your performance in bed.'

'Jesus,' muttered Max.

'*Bitch*!' Luke glared at her murderously. Then rose
abruptly from the sofa.

'Luke, she doesn't mean . . . Please don't . . .'

'I'm sorry, Lauren, I really am. You don't deserve this
shit.'

He cast one last look of disgust at Sukie. Then, hobbling
with as much dignity as was possible with a leg in plaster,
he exited the room, slamming the front door behind him.

No one spoke. An unrepentant Sukie sat wreathed in
cigarette smoke, exhaling through her nose like a dragon.

'Well,' said a miffed Henry to no one in particular, 'I think
that's put an end to our little game of Articulate.'

'Good one, Sukie,' said Max.

Lauren grabbed the coffee tray, swallowing rage. 'You
really have perfected the art of making a man feel small.'

Tiffany got up in disgust and looked at Max. 'Honey,

I'm going upstairs to freshen up. I need a change of scene.'

Sukie glared at them all, furious with herself for having got herself in a state which she could no longer control.

After that the party quickly deteriorated. Everyone made feeble excuses about getting home. Anna escaped to the kitchen on the pretext of finishing the washing up, but Lauren guessed she didn't want to face Sukie before going to bed.

In the hall Lauren waited with Max while Tiffany was in the loo.

'Any idea what brought that on?' said Max in a lowered voice.

'I knew they had their arguments.'

'That wasn't an argument. That was World War Three.'

'I felt so helpless. There didn't seem to be any way of stopping it.'

'I think that's how we all felt. Look, it's done now.'

'Yes,' Lauren said bitterly. 'Poor Luke.'

'What can I do?'

She raised her shoulders helplessly. 'Speak to him. Tell him she didn't mean it. God, I don't know. Perhaps she did. It was probably just the alcohol talking. She'll feel terrible about it in the morning.'

'I get the feeling she's pushed it too far this time. Luke has his pride.'

'Of *course* he has. I'll go round and see him tomorrow. He might talk to me.' She put a hand to her face. 'It's an awful thing to admit, but there are times when I'm truly ashamed of Sukie.'

'It's not your problem, Lauren. It's something she's got to work out herself.'

'I realise that. But why did she have to be so cruel – to *Luke* of all people.'

Max pulled her close, wrapping her in his arms. 'I'm sorry,

baby,' he murmured, his mouth against her ear. 'It shouldn't have happened – not on your birthday.'

Something in his voice made her pull back. Her eyes searched his face. 'Max?'

'Ready to go?' said a sharp voice. Tiffany was watching them from the bottom of the stairs, her evening bag glittery in one hand.

'Sure, honey.' Max released his hold on Lauren.

'Tiffany, about tonight,' Lauren had regained her composure. 'I don't know why Sukie behaved the way she did – she was unspeakably rude to you.'

Tiffany linked a proprietorial arm through Max's. 'She had a bit too much to drink is all.'

'Well, I think you're being very understanding. Don't let it put you off coming back another time.'

Tiffany smiled in response but Lauren detected hostility. Her sister had placed her in a very invidious position and she wasn't enjoying the experience. Upstairs she found a grim-looking Sukie lying prostrate on her bed.

'I think I'm going to be sick,' she announced dramatically.

Lauren was unmoved. 'I'll get you a bucket.'

'Lo?' croaked Sukie, when she returned.

'What?'

'I *had* to tell him. I couldn't go on like this. Not with Wol— well, with things the way they have been.'

'No.'

'You understand, don't you?'

'It's not me you should be saying this to,' said Lauren, thinking of Luke. Sukie was doing what she had done all her life. Running away when things got serious – a heartbreaker, a professional saboteur. From the door, Lauren switched off the light. She didn't want her sister to read the coldness in her eyes.

'Go to sleep, Sukie. We'll talk about it in the morning.'

*   *   *

Max switched on the light and chucked the room key onto the bed.

'Eight okays since we left Lauren's. Want to tell me what's eating you?'

'Nothing's wrong with me. Just that I could have done with some support tonight.'

'Hey,' Max held his hands up in defence. 'That wasn't my script back there. Whatever's going down with Luke and Sukie is their affair.'

'She behaved like a bitch and you did nothing to back me up.'

'You handled it fine. And anyhow I didn't want to make the situation worse for Lauren.'

'Heck no. Can't go getting our little princess upset, now can we?'

Her remark confused him. 'What are you trying to say?'

She gave a humourless laugh. 'For the record, Max, I know what's going on.'

'Glad someone round here does.'

Tiffany sniffed haughtily and took off her shoes. 'I'm going to take a shower.'

'Again? You had two already.'

She turned on him, pink with indignation. 'But I'll just bet you wouldn't be complaining if Lauren Kendall had suggested that. Any opportunity to get *her* panties off.'

Max reddened. 'Just what the hell is that supposed to mean?'

'Come *on*, Maxy, baby. You think I'm blind? You think after being with you all this time I don't know how you work? You've got the hots for her, major league. At least have the guts to admit it.'

He gave an indignant laugh. 'You crazy woman. I'm not admitting anything, 'cause there's nothing going on. I've known Lauren for years. She was married to one of my oldest buddies.'

'Convenient that he's dead then, isn't it?'

'*THAT* was way out of line.'

'And you can go to hell!'

'I think I preferred okay better,' he muttered as Tiffany slammed the bathroom door.

She sat on the loo and stared glumly at the floor. I'll lose him if I carry on like this. Me and my big mouth. She hadn't meant to say any of it. It was obviously the wrong way to play it. She had no proof, no real ground to stand on. But what was she supposed to think when he hadn't come anywhere near her in weeks? He claimed it was down to his punishing training. It left him depleted of energy. But she knew him better than that. When it came to sex Max could keep going for hours.

Half an hour later she re-emerged from the bathroom in the hotel's towelling robe and climbed into bed next to him. The light was already off.

'You okay?' he asked gently.

'Mmm,' she mumbled, softening, hopeful suddenly, ready to forgive. Then he went and spoiled it all by rolling onto his side and saying,

'Boy, I'm beat.'

She lay there for a moment wrestling with questions. Then she spoke into the darkness. 'Did you ever fantasise you were with someone else while we were making out?'

'Rosanne Barr once crossed my mind.'

'Be serious.'

'Baby, I am.'

She persisted. 'Have you?'

A pause. 'Is this still about Lauren?'

She lay rigid.

'Because you're wrong if it is.'

'Am I?'

Max sighed. 'Give me a break, will you, Tiffany! I've got to be up in five hours.'

After a few moments his breathing deepened. Tiffany lay in silent indignation with her back to his, carefully sticking to her side of the bed. By morning she had made up her mind not to accompany him to the Open. Maybe a bit of space would help mend the frays of their relationship.

The turnout for this year's Junior National in Nottingham had been disappointing. Fans and family members had found their enthusiasm dampened by the relentless, grumbling skies. They sat around in gloomy groups, huddled under umbrellas, armed with rainproof jackets and flasks of hot coffee. It went on record as having been the worst August in twenty years. For the players this had meant a great deal of hanging around. Lounging in their sweats, they filled the boredom with snacks, card games, daytime television. Then the last day of the tournament brought a sudden reprieve. The sky cleared and the sun, keen to make up for lost time, beamed down on the courts. The car park filled, nets were measured, plastic chairs put back outside. The Midland Bank flags fluttered lazily in the light breeze.

Having made it through the qualies, Charlotte had defied all odds and gone on to demolish spectacularly five more opponents in the main event. Now she had reached the final. But she was up against her old rival Serena Rutherford who held the title for the twelve-and-under and was tipped to win again in the under-fourteen.

Serena had been one of eleven boys and girls lucky enough to be offered a place at the Rover-sponsored Bisham Abbey. Combining academic work at a local school, they returned to Bisham for all their tennis coaching and training. Every minute of their day was filled with a comprehensive schedule of fitness, individual coaching, medical supervision, tournament schedule organisation, match play at home and abroad. There were some who questioned the benefits to youngsters from the age of twelve residing full time at the Buckingham-based school. Away from the emotional support of their families, they had no social life and little time for recreation.

None of this, however, concerned Serena. Now Bisham's number one ranked player, she had cruised through her rounds dropping only one set to Fran in the semifinals.

'I've been watching her play,' Hugo said to Charlotte as they watched Serena's frighteningly strong forearm swing freely during her warm-up with the resident Bisham fitness trainer. 'She's a classic Chris Evert clone who likes to stay in the back court and blast. Her weakness is that she doesn't move her feet. She gets her opponents to do all the running.'

Charlotte nodded, chewing pensively on the side of a nail. 'I've played her before.'

'Then you know what you've got to do.'

'Force her to the net.'

'Exactly. She'll play with strength but don't let yourself get worked up about it. Concentrate on what we discussed,' Hugo advised. 'We've been through it all. Don't stiffen up. Keep loose. And remember, fight like bloody hell.'

'This is the Midland Bank girls single final fourteen-and-under,' the umpire announced from his chair, 'between, on the left of the chair Serena Rutherford from Sussex, and on the right of the chair, Charlotte Roach from Wimbledon.'

There was a sprinkling of applause. Head dipped, Charlotte fiddled with her racquet strings but allowed her eye briefly to stray. The Serena contingent took up most of the front row, Mrs Rutherford deep in conversation with Bisham Abbey's psychologist on one side, on her other side, Serena's boyfriend who, according to Fran, was training to be an Olympic swimmer. Next to him was Mr Rutherford and his two older daughters – slimmer, less pretty versions of their sister. Two rows behind, Fran was laughing with some of the other players. Further along was Melanie wedged next to Hugo. He had rung the day before with news that Charlotte was in the final. Melanie had dropped everything and come up by train. She tried not to show her feelings, but Melanie found it nerve-racking to watch her daughter play. She knew how badly she wanted to win. Charlotte was jogging up and down on the spot trying to warm her muscles – over the course of the week the court surface had taken its toll on her body. Melanie smiled encouragingly, but Charlotte hadn't seen her. Oh, well, she thought stoically. Probably doesn't need inspiration from me. Always was a self-contained girl.

There was a sudden high-pitched shrill. Hurriedly, Hugo removed his pocket-sized cellular mobile from his jacket and pressed the on button. His eyes were fixed on Charlotte as he snapped into the mouthpiece. Moments later he slipped the phone back into his pocket, the main button now firmly switched off. He was determined to get no further interruptions.

There wasn't much Charlotte could do for the first set-and-a-half. Serena, with her gym knickers and ginger ponytail swinging behind her, controlled all the big points, using her strength to run Charlotte around the court. Opportunities to come back were few and far between, but when Charlotte had her first of two break points in the fifth game, she failed to convert them. In under an hour the score was six-three, three-one to Serena. The fateful day of her eleventh birthday at the Rutherfords when Charlotte had so convincingly lost to Serena now came flooding back. Was history about to repeat itself?

Beetroot-red, she shook herself out of her mood and tried to work out a game plan. She wasn't playing badly. It was just that Serena's powerful slogging prevented her from getting in to the net. She had her *racing* round the court. Charlotte glanced up at her family. Melanie was biting a nail, Hugo looked grim. But Charlotte was nothing if not tenacious. She *refused* to give up. When another Rutherford winner screamed past her, Charlotte clamped her teeth. Sooner or later Serena would get complacent. If she could just hang on to the match.

Then serving at forty-fifteen to take a lead of four-two, Serena missed an easy backhand. Lapse of concentration or was she getting tired? It was the first hesitant shot she had hit and Charlotte sensed an opening. Ignoring a nasty blister on her right heel, she attacked the next two points by scampering to the net, then went up to advantage with a lovely drop shot. Serena's confidence was rattled and she produced an uncharacteristic double fault. Suddenly it was four-three and the match had come alive. Spectators leaned forward in their seats.

'Come on, Charlotte!' Fran yelled excitedly.

Charlotte was suddenly another player. She produced some dazzling shots as she dashed about the court with extraordinary determination, growling as she attacked each shot. No longer the underdog, the score levelled to five-all then went to a tiebreak. It looked as though the set was Charlotte's. Then the scales tipped and once again it was Serena putting on the pressure. She breached Charlotte's defences with a flood of gloriously hammered winners, taking a quick six-two lead. It gave her four match points.

'Oh dear,' sighed Melanie.

Hugo held a hand to his head in disgust, the strain he was under showing in his deeply lined face. 'Bloody hell! She's let it go. She's as good as handed it to her.'

'It's not over yet,' Melanie said grimly.

'No?' snapped Hugo, seeing his dreams of success going down the drain. 'She needs a *miracle* to pull this one off.'

Furious with herself for slipping behind again so quickly,

Charlotte projected her rage into her shots and produced five straight winners bringing her not only set point but cheers from her supporters. Serena shook her head in disbelief. The match wasn't going according to script and she looked mightily put out about it. As for the Rutherford camp, their expressions matched the menacing black clouds that had just drifted overhead. With straining necks, spectators wondered if the match would have to be postponed. But this wasn't a concern for Charlotte. Her mind was on winning. She would *not* give Serena an inch!

Her first serve went wide. She played it safe with the second. Anticipating this, Serena blasted a return to the back corner. Charlotte scampered after it and had to lob it blind. Serena wasn't as quick as Charlotte. Stumbling, she made a cross-court pass which fell short. Charlotte was ready and went in for the kill. With Serena out of position and helpless she made an easy forehand winner. She yelped victoriously.

The rest was straightforward. Her confidence in shreds, the favourite flailed her way through the last set, finally losing three-six to Charlotte. With a temper that had been rising for some time, Serena furiously hurled her racquet to the ground. It brought a gasp from the crowd.

'Game, set and match to Miss Roach.'

The umpire's voice was half-drowned by the shrieks of excitement from Charlotte's camp. Fran jumped up and down whooping with joy. Hugo's expression was one of astonishment and delight. Melanie held her hands to her mouth as if in prayer, smiling proudly. By contrast, the Rutherford family gathered their belongings in silence, gazing alternately at the ground and the heavens. Anywhere, it seemed, but at each other. Mrs Rutherford looked thunderous. Her mouth was set in a tight, downward line.

'There'll be hell to pay, mark my words,' said a mother,

nodding in her direction. 'I wouldn't like to be in Serena's shoes.'

For Charlotte the thrill of winning after having been so far behind, and then saving four match points, was almost indescribable. The following morning a picture of her flushed, beaming face appeared in the local paper. Some of her words had been quoted.

'You play tennis for matches like this one. It's what it's all about. Not for money, not for anything else. Just knowing you won because you didn't give up.'

A journalist overheard Hugo describing Charlotte's performance.

'Once she's got hold of that ball,' he said proudly, 'she won't let go of it for anything. She's like a little terrier.'

'Little terrier'. It was a name that would stick.

Beside her in bed, Wolff watched her put a cigarette between her lips, inhale deeply, then blow bluish smoke up towards the ceiling, her throat stretched and pale.

'Wolff?'

'Mmmm?'

'Do I look nice in my sleep?'

'Yes.'

'But what do I look like exactly?'

'Same as you do now except that your eyes are closed.'

'Be serious.'

'I am.'

'Then tell me.'

He traced her lips with a finger, 'Why do you think I'm running late when I leave your bed? Because I'm always tempted back into it.'

This obviously pleased her. She propped herself up on one elbow.

'Hungry?'

'Ish.'

He had seen her earlier preparations in the kitchen. Rolling onto his back, he peeled the used condom from his penis and dropped it into the bin next to the bed.

Sukie coiled her arms round his neck and nibbled one ear. 'Then why don't I feed you.'

He glanced up to smile but there was such a soft moisture in her eyes he found he could hardly bear to look at her. He meant to say something then, but the phone rang. Kissing him on the forehead, she picked up her dress and crossed the room.

'It's Mum,' she whispered. 'I'll take it next door. Why don't you have a bath. Supper'll take about half an hour so you don't have to rush.'

He had arrived late at her flat by almost an hour. Perhaps he had expected her to be cross with him. And why shouldn't she be? Their time together had such restrictions. But when she opened the door he had read only pleasure on her face. She threw her arms around his neck and pulled him eagerly into the warmth.

'A whole night,' she had murmured, 'I can't believe I have you for one whole night!'

He could hear her moving around now in her tiny kitchen, softly humming to herself. He gazed morosely at a vase of fresh flowers wondering what the hell he was going to do. This wasn't what he had planned. He had come to tell her that it was over between them, that he couldn't see her any more. He had convinced himself that what he was doing was right – for all of them. But Sukie had looked so vibrant, so provocative, his resolve had faltered. Once again he found himself falling under her spell. Sitting in front of her fire he had started to say something, but then she had taken his hand and slipped it inside her silky dress, pressing it against her small plump breasts and he'd thought: I want this. What can be the harm?

Oh, but he could see the inescapable hole he was digging

for himself. Lying here on her bed, the task of explaining began to seem even more inconceivable. The continual deception, the lies he was feeding both women had to stop. But how could he tell her? How? Night after night he would wake up troubled and restless. The strain was becoming so bad that it was even beginning to affect him physically. His game was coming apart. How much longer could he keep up the pretence: how long would it be before Inge found out? His wife was no fool. He sighed, feeling the weight of the world deep within his soul.

When the affair had first started he had justified it by blaming Inge for trapping him into a marriage he wasn't ready for. All the months of Inge's pregnancy, the thickening gracelessness of her – was it any wonder he had strayed. He was still only twenty-four. Too young to be burdened by such responsibilities. But that was unfair and untrue. What he'd done was to let his feelings of hatred towards Luke blind his judgment. He had looked at the Canadian and thought; I want what you have; I deserve your freedom. And now that he had it?

Sukie popped her head round the door holding a dishcloth in one hand.

'No bath?'

'Maybe later,' he said summoning a smile.

'Well, you're in for a treat tonight. I'm preparing a feast!'

'What are we celebrating?'

'Us,' she said it triumphantly, moving across the room. Then she bent down to kiss his lips. The gesture was light, almost imperceptible. 'I love you,' she whispered.

Sukie, he thought, once she had returned to the kitchen. He felt impossibly sorry for her; for her misguided choices, never more so than of him; her blinding vulnerability that she tried so hard to conceal and yet so utterly failed to do. He thought about her body that had given him so much pleasure, had so instinctively known what he liked. He could feel his hands around her waist even now, the silvery trail of her appendix scar which only an hour ago he had run his tongue along, and down further to her surprisingly thick thatch of pubic hair.

When, heavy-footed, he eventually surfaced from the bedroom, Wolff found Sukie in her small sitting room lighting candles. The room was full of the hot fragrance of lamb and rosemary.

'What do you think?' she asked proudly.

He gazed at the table laid for two: flowers, linen napkins, ivory-handled cutlery. And there – the Venetian glass bowl he had bought for her birthday filled with floating orange flowerheads, and mauve candles. He had come here to use anger as a defence. Instead he felt only a terrible helplessness.

He suddenly realised he couldn't go through with it. He couldn't face her with what he must say.

'Wine,' he said, slapping his forehead, 'I forgot the wine.'

'Oh, don't worry. I've got a perfectly okay bottle of Sainsbury's plonk in the fridge.'

'No, I mean the wine I bought earlier. A special vintage. It's in the car. I'll just get it now.'

She looked pleased. 'Okay. But hurry back.'

He closed the door of her flat and took the stairs down to the ground floor. At the entrance his hand held the front door slightly ajar. He took several gulps of the autumnal air as though he had just thrown open the window of an overheated and stuffy room, trying to still the sickening churning within him. Then, resolutely, he slammed the door shut. Wolff walked to his car parked two streets away, turned the ignition and drove off. Sukie, upstairs in the warmth of her snug one-bed flat, pulled the lamb wrapped in puff pastry out of the oven and placed it triumphantly on a serving dish.

She was still humming as she carried it out to the table.

*   *   *

Wolff drove home with a blinding headache. It got so bad that he'd had to stop at a late-night chemist and get some aspirin. Twenty minutes on and the pills still weren't working.

Inge saw instantly what was wrong with him. Making him some camomile tea, she gave him his migraine tablets and put him straight to bed.

'My poor baby,' she said, gently undressing him, 'is it very bad?'

'Just let me rest for a while, will you?'

Almost three hours had lapsed by the time she came to bed. But Wolff wasn't asleep. He couldn't. The pain in his head throbbed punishingly and he had lain there in the dark listening to the sound of heavy rain. Eyes by now accustomed to the dark he watched his wife unfasten her watch and place it on the chest of drawers. Noiselessly she undressed. Each discarded item revealed more and more of her big bony body. She eased back the duvet sliding her naked form in beside him. As she did so a wave of the gardenia she always wore filled his nostrils. He was overcome by nostalgia, of love for her. He wanted to confess, to tell her about Sukie but the smell of his wife's body was too heavy. No words would come. Instead he reached out, sinking against her softness, her attentive, watchful silence, her warm forgiving flesh.

And when his tears surfaced, she began to rock him gently as if he were a baby, humming a German tune he didn't recognise.

20

It was hard to measure the extent of Sukie's anger and sense of betrayal. Her affair with Wolff had lasted for almost sixteen months. Not once had she dreamt it might end this way. When it had finally dawned on her that there was no bottle of wine in his car, that Wolff had had no intention of returning to her flat, she'd spent the rest of that night drinking tea. Cigarette followed cigarette as she gazed mindlessly out of the window and the sky turned from black to petrol-blue, to a flat, soulless grey. Numb with shock, her mind refused to digest what had happened. She just waited. For a few hours time stood still, until, like a dentist's anaesthetic, the numbness had eventually worn off and she began to feel the pain.

Weeks went by and rage continued to eat at her. At first she tried to justify what he had done. Wolff had panicked. He had felt unable to go through with it even though he loved her deeply. Perhaps his wife had followed him to the flat, threatened him with the children and dragged him back home. Sukie could have forgiven him that. She could have forgiven him almost anything. But not this silence. Not this awful place in the dark she now found herself in. '*Friday*,' he had said, the last time they had spoken. '*We'll be together again Friday*,' he had murmured the words into the phone and she had swallowed his promise whole. Wolff, she realised blackly, picturing his compellingly unhandsome face, was a complete and utter shit. That morning, shattered and dazed, desperate for a comforting shoulder, she had actually tried calling Luke. She wasn't sure why. Reassurance, forgiveness maybe? Then she realised she didn't have a number for him. She thought about leaving a message with his agent. But what could she have said had he called back: I need you? Forgive me. I'm sorry? Absolutely not. And thank Christ she hadn't. When she was finally able to see more clearly, she realised it was much too late for a reconciliation. Luke would *never* have her back. She was certain of it. She had been the cause of too much pain. And now she was getting paid back. Only now it was Wolff who was doing the hurting – to her.

The days passed, grey and empty. With no job, no tenant paying her mortgage and no Luke to bail her out, she had once again fallen behind with her payments. The rates were due, the gas board wanted two hundred and thirty quid, yet she did nothing about it. There wasn't anything to motivate her. Sometimes she panicked and thought about phoning her father. He would help. She never for a moment doubted his generosity, not when it came to his precious daughters. One plea and the chequebook would miraculously emerge from his desk. But she couldn't face asking him. Couldn't bear to read the kind, pitying look in his eyes.

She hadn't loved Luke. She had been in love with the idea of him – his success and all the trimmings that came with it – the glamorous lifestyle, the first-class treatment, recognition. Being with him had elevated her position, made her feel powerful. People knew who she was. When her face was caught by cameras at tournaments, they asked questions. They looked at what she had and they envied her. That was what she missed, not the tennis. She couldn't have cared less if she never saw another match. And yet without it her life was empty. A large, gaping hole. She had nothing to fill it.

She thought about Wolff with an intensity she would never have thought herself capable of. Even in rage and indignation she continued to burn for him. Night after night she hovered by the phone willing him to call. He *had* to. Until then she felt unable to turn her attention to anything else. She had no plan. Couldn't think about this rut she had dug herself into. Instead she slept until noon then sat around watching afternoon black-and-white films on TV. Surely he must soon realise that she meant more to him than his wife. But the days turned into weeks, hope turned into despair and Sukie turned to her only consolation. Alcohol.

An old boyfriend with powerful connections in the publishing world had managed to wangle her a membership to Groucho's. Having finally given up all hope of Wolff calling, Sukie began dropping in on the trendy Soho club most evenings. On her own tonight, she had found the club unusually quiet. Stephen Fry had made a brief appearance with two chums but left soon after, no doubt in search of a larger audience. About to follow suit, Sukie was putting on her coat when a glass of champagne was presented at her table.

'The gentleman over there bought it for you,' the waitress pointed to one of the heavy leather sofas.

Expecting a pot-bellied, boring old fart, Sukie did a double-take at the sensational-looking man watching her from across the room. Late thirties, she guessed, and beautifully dressed, he had thick chestnut-brown hair and cheekbones to rival Paul Newman's. His were the sort of looks that would have demanded her attention anywhere. But what really stopped her in her tracks was the way he was watching her. It was with the same insolence that had so struck her in Wolff.

Sukie's heart somersaulted.

She reached for her pack of cigarettes next to the bed, flicked her lighter and swallowed smoke deep into her lungs. Lying on her back she could feel the swell of his buttocks, the firm promise of his hairy thighs. With her free hand she stroked his chest, enjoying the heat from his body.

'I admire your stamina,' said the man lazily. 'Are you always this eager or have you something to prove?'

Sukie rolled onto her stomach and gave him a silky smile. 'Don't tell me I've worn you out?'

'No. I'm just not feeling particularly horny tonight. It's probably the weed.'

'Funny, it seems to have the opposite effect on me. It's good stuff. D'you have any more?'

'You're welcome to what's left.'

She stretched, content for the first time in weeks. Then turned back and studied him.

'I don't usually give men compliments, but you have an incredible body. Are you a sportsman?'

'Nope. I just like to keep in shape.'

'What do you do?'

'Bit of this, bit of that.'

'You don't have to be quite so evasive. Or don't you like talking about your work?'

'I do that all day.'

'Perhaps you're a spy?' Sukie took another drag then handed him the roach. 'Tell me, do you usually pick up women so casually?'

The man smiled, shaking his head. 'Let's just say I have a weakness for redheads.' He looked at his watch. 'I've got to be making a move.'

'Not now?'

Her good mood quickly faded. He was already getting dressed.

'I'm catching a flight back to New York in three hours.'

'But it's four a.m.!' Shit. She didn't want to sleep alone. Not tonight. 'Can't you at least stay for a cup of tea?'

He laughed. 'What is it with you English broads and your tea?'

'What is it with you Americans and your coffee and cinnamon rolls?' she retorted.

'Touché. Tell you what. I'm back in three weeks. We'll make an evening of it then.'

Sukie pouted. 'You're fobbing me off.'

'Says who?' he was hunting for something in his jacket.

'Men always say that when they don't want to see you again.'

'If I hadn't wanted to see you I wouldn't be suggesting it. Now what's your number?'

Speculatively, Sukie watched him zip up his trousers. 'I don't even know your name. How can I have dinner with a man whose name I don't know?'

He walked over to the bed and placed two joints in her lap.

'That particular dilemma is easily solved. I'm Roe Lewis,' he said, and grinned.

'Pass me that towel, will you, darling? I don't want to drip.'

Melanie held her wet hands over the sink while her husband chucked her the dishcloth she'd left hanging on a chair. Work, which he was bringing home from the office with increasing frequency, littered the kitchen table.

'Can't you finish that later?' she suggested, wondering if the rock music coming from upstairs was still too loud. He'd already yelled once at the girls.

'Not a chance. I've got a meeting first thing in the morning. This report *has* to be ready.' He scratched his head in frustration.

'Any joy with Brian – about sponsoring Charlotte?' Brian was one of Hopkins' company directors.

'No go, I'm afraid. He liked the idea but— ' Hugo turned his chair round to face her. 'I was hoping I wouldn't have to say this, Melly, but there's a chance that Hopkins might go under.'

She sat down in an adjacent chair, clutching the teatowel, 'Do you think they will?'

'Hard to say at this stage. We're all pulling together but things have got pretty serious.'

Melanie contemplated the alarming prospect of Hugo's being without a job. 'What will happen if they do?'

'Well, for one thing, it'll mean there'll be no spare cash flow to support Charlotte's tennis. I've got a bit put by to keep us going, but not for long.' He leafed through the papers in front of him then held up a handful of faxes. 'Do you realise this week alone I've had four sponsorship offers; free racquets, shoes, kit, but none of it cash.' He threw the faxes down in disgust. 'I just wish we were in a position to refuse the vultures. All those calls, the ignored letters I wrote asking for their help.'

'But surely now,' tried Melanie, 'with the National behind her? It was such a big win, after all.'

'It's helped. The LTA have offered to contribute towards her expenses but it's simply not enough.'

Melanie grappled hard for a solution. Then one came to her. 'I have an idea,' she said looking at him thoughtfully. 'But you mustn't get cross if I tell you.'

'I'm all ears.'

'I was thinking,' she said gently, knowing how important the address was to him, 'that we could sell the Eaton Square flat.'

'Out of the question.'

'But it's the size of a postage stamp.'

'I need it,' Hugo said desperately.

'You never use it.'

'It's good for business.'

These were just excuses. They both knew it. But for some reason, Hugo had it in his head that having a smart address meant you'd made it in life. Melanie knew better than to push him.

'All I'm saying,' she said, kneading tension from his shoulders, 'is that you should think about it.'

A terrific thud vibrated above their heads followed by muted squeals and laughter.

Hugo glanced up at the ceiling and frowned. 'Just what the hell are those girls up to now?'

'*Missed!*' giggled Fran, lifting the pillow and aiming it squarely at Charlotte's head.

Charlotte retaliated with a cuff to Fran's legs. 'Because you keep on duck-diving.'

'Your tough luck, isn't it?' And Fran leapt onto the bed, using her pillow as a shield.

Whack! Thump! Whack! Thump! Pillows flew backwards and forwards with gathering force as the girls' excitement escalated. Escaped feathers floated haphazardly above the war zone. Wicklow pawed at them, his green eyes huge and frenzied. One particularly strong blow knocked Charlotte off balance and sent her crashing into the wall.

'Ouch!' She raised both hands in defence, 'No, Fran. Stop. My head. I think it's bleeding.'

Fran let the pillow fall from her hand and jumped off the bed.

'Where? Let me see.'

Charlotte winced. 'Careful.'

Gently Fran parted the hair and inspected a small angry graze.

'There's a bit of a mark but I don't think it's serious. TCP should do the trick. That's what Mum always uses.'

'There should be some in the bathroom cabinet.'

'I'll get it,' offered Fran.

'Not like that!' Charlotte squealed in a panic. 'Hugo might see you.'

Fran glanced down at her exposed bra and tittered. 'Might

make old bossy boots's day.' All the same she buttoned up
her shirt before leaving the room.

Minutes later she was back with antiseptic and a wad of
cotton wool. 'Hold still,' she ordered, suddenly matron-like,
'it might sting a little.' Charlotte bit her lip as the powerful
disinfectant made contact with her skin. Wicklow jumped
on to her lap, treading claws into her skin. Gently, she eased
them off.

'There you go,' said Fran. Aiming carefully, she threw the
cotton wad into the bin.

Charlotte dropped the pillow she had been fighting with
to the floor and sat on it. Lifting her legs from the ground
she practised her stomach exercises. 'Are you excited about
the Orange Bowl?'

Fran yawned in response and popped a Refresher into
her mouth.

'I've never been to America before,' Charlotte panted.
'What's Miami like?'

'Lots of palm trees and flash cars.'

Charlotte held her stretched-out legs about a foot from
the floor and counted to ten. 'You don't sound very
enthusiastic.'

'Why should I be?'

'Playing abroad. It's the next step up. I think that's exciting.
Whew!' She relaxed her legs.

Fran yawned. 'Yes, well, I'm not going.'

Charlotte stopped what she was doing, 'Not going?'

'Changed my mind.'

'You can't have.'

Fran sniffed. 'Well I have.'

'And what does Ricky think about it?'

Fran's expression grew dark. 'I don't give a flying toss
what Ricky thinks. I wish he were dead.'

Charlotte blinked. 'What happened?'

'I don't want to talk about it.'

Whenever Fran said she didn't want to talk about something, Charlotte knew the truth would surface soon after. She didn't have to wait long.

'Ricky and me split up.'

Charlotte was dumbstruck. Fran had said they were in love. They were going to get married.

Fran flicked her perfectly formed blonde curls. 'He dumped me,' she said flatly. 'He was worried someone would find out, so he finished it.'

Charlotte climbed onto the bed next to her friend, 'Oh, Fran, I'm really sorry.'

Fran dropped her voice to a conspiratorial whisper as though afraid she might be heard downstairs. 'I told Mum and Dad that I didn't want him as my coach any more and they hit the roof. They wanted to know why but I wouldn't let on – not that I owed Ricky anything, the rotten slimebag. I just didn't want all the hassle. To tell you the truth I'm sick of it all.'

Of Ricky? Her parents? Not tennis, surely?

Fran lay back on the bed and gazed up at the ceiling, the same ceiling Charlotte had for years studied in the hope of finding inspiration, answers, hope. 'I don't want to spend my life on a tennis court. I don't want legs like a bulldog or skin that feels like cracked leather because I'm in the sun all day long. I want to be feminine. I want to wear pretty clothes and look like Michele Gayle.' She twiddled a small gold stud in her right earlobe. 'I want to do normal things like go out with my friends and not have to get up at the crack of dawn just so I can fit in practice before school.'

'You *can't* just throw it all away.' Charlotte was appalled. Everyone at Sutton said that Fran was destined for a great tennis future.

'Well, why not? I don't enjoy it any more – haven't done for months. I've decided I want to become an actress.'

Charlotte was trying to keep up. 'Have you told your parents?'

'Dad went ape. Shouting and banging his fists, saying how I was selfish and irresponsible, that I didn't appreciate the amount of money he'd invested in my career.' Fran's lovely eyes filled with tears. 'All my life I've done what others have wanted me to do. Just for once I want to do something for myself.'

'Don't cry, Fran. Don't cry.'

Tears spilled down her friend's face. Charlotte was confused. She caught her reflection in the dressing-table mirror and wondered; am I feminine?

'What will you do?' she asked as Fran mopped her eyes.

'Don't know. Talk to Mum. Try and win her over. Make her understand. At least she'll listen,' Fran sniffed. 'They can't force me to go on playing.'

Charlotte looked at her friend helplessly. What could she say? Tennis was her life. It meant everything to her. She had thought it was the same for Fran, but now the very foundations on which Charlotte had built her dreams felt split, ruptured.

Fran's confession threatened everything Charlotte believed in.

It had taken Inge almost an hour to get the twins to bed. Even when they were asleep, Inge had stood, stock-still, listening to their breathing, as she had always done, right from the day they were born. Gretal, with her weak lungs, had suffered another asthma attack and Miriam had taken full advantage of the situation, working herself into a hyperactive state. Not for the first time Inge had resorted to putting a few drops of whisky in Miriam's milk to calm her down. Finally peace was restored to the house. Satisfied that Gretal was comfortably settled for the night, Inge returned to the kitchen to finish supper. With some luck she might have half an hour to

work on her Italian. These days it was so hard to find
time for anything and she was very much behind. Tying
an apron round her waist, she switched on the intercom
that was connected to the twins' room upstairs. Not that
she anticipated further disruption. But some habits were
hard to break.

Inge was adding more paprika to the goulash when the
phone rang. It stopped before she could get to it. Never
mind. If it was important they would call back. She ran the
hot tap and began the washing up. The ringing resumed. She
hastily wiped her hands on a dishtowel, but again it stopped
before she reached it. Inge frowned, a tiny worrying thought
niggling in the back of her mind. When the phone rang a
third time she was ready. She picked up the extension by
the door.

'Hello?' she said, her voice uncharacteristically aggressive.
No answer. 'Who's there?'

'Is Wolff around?' a voice finally asked. Female, distant.

'He is in the bath. May I give a message to him?'

A long pause. 'No. Look ... forget it,' and the line
went dead.

Inge slowly replaced the receiver. If this was one of those
pranksters again. About two months ago they had started
getting anonymous phone calls. The caller never spoke,
but Inge could sometimes hear breathing down the line.
Horrible. So horrible. The calls often came in the middle
of the night, dragging them from a deep sleep. Worried
about the twins, Inge had begged Wolff to do something,
at least go to the police. But Wolff had shown a strange
reluctance. He said that if they ignored it, the calls would
soon stop. He had been right about that. Shortly after, the
calls *did* stop and Inge had let the subject drop. But now
her fears returned.

She could hear Wolff banging around in the bathroom
upstairs. He'd be wanting his supper. She was worried

about him. The migraines were getting worse. And he
hadn't been sleeping well, dozing off and on, waking
often with a sudden start as though he had something
weighing on his mind. Once, recently, Inge woke as he
jerked awake but when she'd asked what was wrong he
had become cagey, distant. Nothing further had been said.
She knew better than to press him.

She had just finished the washing up and had forgotten
all about the calls when the ringing suddenly resumed.

'I'll get it,' Wolff yelled from the landing.

The overhead floorboards creaked as he made his way
back to the bedroom. She waited for Wolff's angry voice,
but after a few moments she heard the ping of the phone.
She scolded herself for being so foolish.

The stew looked thick and creamy. She dipped her little
finger in then put it to her mouth, sampling the sweet meaty
taste. It needed more salt. Inge debated on what vegetable
to have with it. She took a broccoli head from the fridge
and sliced it into four quarters with a sharp knife. The
twins' intercom crackled. She could hear Gretal's gentle
wheezing. Poor darling. Perhaps she should go up and
check the steamer. Then she heard another noise. A voice.
Her husband's. Surprised, she stopped to listen. At first she
thought he was talking to one of the girls, then she realised
he was on the phone. He must have taken the mobile into
their bedroom. Why, for heavens sake?

'. . . not to call me here. I know I wasn't fair . . . true I
handled things badly, but you must understand . . .'

He was talking in whispers. Inge strained her ears but
she could only hear snatches of the dialogue.

'No. Impossible . . . be the point?' There was a long delay,
followed by a sigh. Who *was* he talking to? 'Look. Okay. I
will . . . No. Not there. I prefer . . . more . . .' Gretal had
started coughing which meant that Inge missed what was
said next.

'. . . can't do this. You understand? . . . for me. All right then. Monday . . . one o'clock.'

She heard the ping of the mobile then the snap of the aerial being clicked back in. There was a faint rustling. Gretal whining in her sleep. Wolff was talking to her, trying to get her on to her back to aid her breathing. Then silence.

'Darling,' Inge ventured, when her husband appeared towelling his wet hair, 'who was that on the phone?'

'When?'

Comprehension filled Wolff's face. 'Ostoja. He wants to go over some new techniques on my game.' He plunged the wooden spoon into the goulash and tasted it. 'Tastes really great.'

Inge lavishly added cream and some chopped parsley. 'So, when are you seeing him again?'

'Who?'

'Ostoja.'

'Monday lunchtime. We don't have any plans, do we? I'm not forgetting anything?'

'No. But I was thinking Ostoja was in Florida.'

'He came back early,' Wolff held her gaze. 'You believe me, don't you?'

'Of course,' said Inge, turning her attention to the broccoli.

But for the first time in her marriage, she didn't.

That morning, Sukie dressed with careful deliberation. She had it all planned. Nothing could go wrong. Tonight Wolff would be hers again, she felt sure. If only she could get rid of the bags under her eyes. She hadn't been sleeping well lately. Stress did that to you and lately she had plenty to feel stressed about. Her face looked drawn and peaky. Ruthlessly she slapped on more blusher.

In retrospect she thought perhaps it had been stupid to call him. But what else could she have done? Twice she'd

lost her nerve, hanging up after only a few rings. Then *she*
had answered the phone, which had thrown Sukie. She had
been convinced it was going to be Wolff. Had the German
suspected anything? These days Sukie referred to her rival
as 'the German'. Less personal that way, less complicated.

She waited until 12.45 before leaving. She still had some
pride. Although she could ill afford the luxury, she took a
taxi. Bugger the bus. It was too cold to stand around outside.
She felt weak with dread. Now that the moment had come,
her nerve had gone. What the hell was she going to say
to him?

The Chiswick wine bar was busy. Packed tables, crowds
jostling for drinks around the bar allowed her to slip through
anonymously to the back. She cast a few furtive glances
around for Wolff but there was no sign of him. The shit
hadn't arrived yet. Stalling for time she went to the loo,
flicked her hair into a more orderly state and reapplied some
perfume. Then she got herself a drink at the bar and smiled at
the attractive barman. To pass the time she would normally
have flirted with him but today she lacked both energy and
inclination. She glanced at her watch. 1.15 p.m. Should she
stay at the bar or try to find a table? When Wolff arrived she
didn't want him to think she'd been waiting long. Maybe she
should chat up the barman. Make Wolff jealous. On second
thoughts, tactics like that had never worked with Wolff.

People were leaving. Grabbing her drink she went and
sat at an empty table. Her heart thumped uncomfortably.
This was ridiculous. When had she ever been nervous about
meeting a man? Since her encounter with Wolff, echoed a
voice in her head. She picked up the menu and read it
without taking in a single word. She couldn't have eaten
anything anyway. Her stomach felt as though someone had
squeezed it dry like a sponge. Three men at a neighbouring
table were having a heated argument.

'She should have *told* me,' one of them said feelingly.

'Mate, I know just how you feel. I went through it all with Carol.'

'But she should have bloody TOLD me. Not kept me dangling like a bloody puppet.'

'Yer, all right, Steve, mate, keep it down.'

Was that what Wolff was doing to her? Dangling her like some poor miserable puppet? How many times had she sat around waiting for him, becoming more impatient and frustrated as the minutes ticked by. And when he did appear, no sheepish apology, no attempt to explain what had delayed him. Around her someone's horsy laughter, the whir of an overhead fan, the clinking of glasses. It was suffocatingly hot. Sukie's mind wandered.

'Didn't we meet earlier?' his firm, capable hands on her waist. She could still feel them burning her skin.

'No, but that is what you wished.'

'You're very sure of yourself.'

'Why not?'

Why not? Why not? She glanced at her watch. 1.35p.m. The bastard was thirty-five minutes late. How could he do this to her. *He* was the guilty party. *He* should be the one suffering, not her. She rubbed her moist palms on her skirt. She felt sick. A waitress appeared.

'Are you ready to order yet?' she asked pleasantly.

'Actually, I'm waiting for someone. He's a bit late. But I could do with another of these in the meantime.' She held up her empty wine glass.

'No problem. I'll be right back.'

'How long have you been seeing him?' Their first date together. Wolff dwarfing her already tiny sitting room as he wandered around with a restless energy, picking up photos, ornaments and inspecting them. The same careless way his eyes appraised her.

'Luke and I?' she had stammered. 'It's not very serious.'
'You mean you're available?'
'Only if I want to be.' Hard to believe how confident she had sounded back then, playing the game.
'And do you' he asked, 'want to be available?' The pull of his eyes. She found them irresistible.
'Yes.'

The waitress returned with her drink. It was a different wine. Oaky, like an Australian Chardonnay. Smoother than the first. She gulped it greedily. A glass smashed. Startled, Sukie turned towards the noise. It was the irate man his friend had called Steve at the next table. He had slumped forward onto his arms in despair. One of his friends was helping the waitress clear up the glass, the other ruffled the man's hair, a mixture of compassion and embarrassment on his face.

'S'all right, Steve. You two'll work it out.'

The third man scraped back his chair, 'Come on, mate. Reckon we'd best get him out of here.'

Her wine glass was empty. She looked at it numbly. When had she finished it? She couldn't remember. A dark-haired man was approaching her. Sukie froze. But he wasn't Wolff. He walked straight past her table and into the Gents. A couple, pawing one another sat down at the table the three men had just vacated. They sat close together, hands and legs entwined. They began kissing with shameless abandon. Sukie tried not to stare. She lit her fourth cigarette. Almost two o'clock. The bastard wasn't going to come. And she'd been so sure he would. If not to see her then at the very least to stop the German from finding out about their affair. She had warned him. Hadn't he believed her? Or was he really stupid enough to think that she wouldn't carry out her threat?

She rose purposefully, anger singing in her ears, and made

her way on unsteady legs to the bar. Her head was spinning. Should have eaten something.

'Watch it, love. You almost took a tumble then.' A face loomed up beside her. 'Come on. Cheer up. May never happen.'

Sukie released a tight, brittle smile. 'I hate people saying that.'

'Oh,' he said expansively. 'Sorry I spoke.' He shifted his gaze back to his paper. An obese man pushed in between them and bellowed his order to the barman.

Sukie edged away as he squeezed out again, two brimming glasses of wine balanced precariously in both hands.

'He must be mad.'

'What?' Sukie turned to the man on her left again. 'Who?'

'The bloke who stood you up.'

'Yes. Well,' said Sukie, some of her anger defusing.

He fixed his small birdlike eyes on hers. 'A great-looking woman like you. Needs his head examined.'

'Try telling him that.'

He signalled to the barman who promptly arrived. 'Jimbo, get this girl a drink, will you? And make mine a double.'

'What'll it be, luv?'

She gave the man a smile, mellowing. 'A glass of white wine, thanks.'

He'd pushed his newspaper to one side. The first thing she read was, 'Babs does it with a horse.' She raised an eyebrow.

The man chuckled. 'Lives of the rich and famous – usual day-to-day stuff. If you're interested there's a piece here that I—well, read it and tell me what you think.'

But Sukie's eyes were fastened on a picture at the bottom of the social page. Luke and Lauren together, holding hands. Faces tilted towards the sky, they looked unspeakably happy. Sukie felt the skin on her face tighten in dismay. She read the caption underneath.

Rumour has it that Tuff's glamorous couple have turned
their relationship into more than a professional one. Our
reporter couldn't get hold of the widow of Wimbledon
champion Josh Kendall to comment, but was able to catch
Luke Falkner coming out of Piccadilly's Planet Hollywood.
The Australian Open champion had this to say: 'She's the
woman of my dreams. I've never known happiness like it.'
Falkner was seeing twenty-five-year-old Sukie Miller, but
the pretty strawberry-blonde has been unable to compete
with the love volleys served by her older sister Lauren.

Bitch. Bitch. Bitch. Luke had been hers. He'd loved her and
now Lauren had him. How dare she? How *dare* she. Rage
singed through Sukie's veins. The unfairness of it all. But
then that's how it had always been. No matter what, Lauren
always landed on her feet. Everything came easily to her. It
was as though she had a guardian angel watching over her.
Sukie wondered if she was going to throw up.

'You all right?' said the man. 'You're as white as a
sheet.'

She attempted to pull herself together. 'I should go.'

'At least finish your drink. You've hardly touched it.'

She thought she had. Must have been another one. Why
not? She had nothing better to do. She sank back on the stool.
Someone walked through the door but it wasn't Wolff. The
last flicker of hope in her died. Sukie raised her glass. 'What
shall we drink to?' she said bitterly.

'How about to fame and money?'

'I'll certainly drink to that, and to two-timing little shits!'
she added with venom.

'I'll drink to that too.'

For a moment they sipped in companionable silence.
Sukie closed her eyes. The alcohol wasn't having its
usual desired effect. She could feel a clawing headache
coming on.

'Got the time, mate?' someone yelled in the background.

'Just gone two thirty.'

Two thirty. An hour and a half late. She had a sudden image of Wolff's body, the muscles compact and tight like the strings of a newly strung racquet. How she ached to feel it again.

'Haven't you got to get back to the office or something?' she asked the stranger, wishing now to be alone. To wallow.

'One of the advantages of being freelance is you get to choose your own hours,' he said with a slight bitterness to his voice. 'I tried working for others but it didn't work out. How about you?'

'Unemployed.'

'I take it you've had a bad day?'

'Oh, I'm having a *wonderful* day,' her eyes slid back to the paper. 'I just found out my sister's been sleeping with my ex.'

The man raised an eyebrow. 'Nice.'

'Isn't it? I suppose I should have expected it from him,' she said suddenly ludicrously self-righteous. 'I knew about his reputation with women long before we'd started going out. But Lauren!' She gave an incredulous snort.

The man was gazing at the paper. He looked up at Sukie then back down at the paper, his eyes growing wide with astonishment. Sukie missed this. Her mind had wandered.

'Do you watch sport?' she slurred.

'I like a game.'

'Tennis?'

He shrugged carefully. 'I watch Wimbledon when it's on.'

Sukie fixed him with her gaze. 'Have you ever been to the Australian Open?'

'A number of times.'

'Me too. As a matter of fact I was there for the semifinals

in January,' she said, thinking of the game between Luke and Wolff. 'And d'you know what I was thinking as I watched the match? I thought: How many of you millions of people watching today can say you've slept with both the players on court. I mean that would be like you going to a world cup final and saying that half the players on the pitch were your best mates.'

The man had gone very still. 'You could say that.'

'*God*! When I think of all the things he put me through,' she continued, leaning towards her neighbour and drunkenly stabbing his chest with a finger as though he was the one at fault. 'I could tell you stories that would knock Princess Diana right off the front page. That would show him, wouldn't it? That would show the snake!'

People were staring at her. She must have been shouting. Sukie picked up her glass and drained the contents.

'Show who, Sukie?' the man probed.

'I'd show . . .' He'd called her Sukie. How did he know her name? She couldn't remember having told him. Her thoughts jumped about sporadically. What had they been talking about? Tiredly, she rubbed at her headache.

'Who did you want to show?' repeated her neighbour.

Show? Show? She began to feel swimmy. Sukie giggled. 'Ah. And wouldn't you like to know!'

'Yes. Very much.'

The man's voice had dropped to a conspiratorial whisper. 'Sukie, it is Sukie, isn't it?' She gave a heavy nod. 'How would you like to make some money?'

She looked at him uncomprehendingly.

'How would you like to sell me your story?'

'Hey. D'you work for a paper?'

'I told you. I'm freelance.'

Sukie blinked. 'How much money?'

'That would depend on what you've got. But I'd make it worth your while.'

'I, er,' Sukie tried unscrambling her mind. 'Look, I'm not feeling very good. Have you got an aspirin?'

'Jimbo'll have something. He's got an Aladdin's cave behind this bar. Never know what he's going to pull out next.'

'You talking about me again, Col?' said the barman, catching the tail end of their conversation. 'Don't you go listening to him, miss.'

Col grinned, flashing a row of saffron-stained teeth. Then he tilted his head towards her empty glass and said,

'Now then, what about a top-up?'

Max peered down at the brightly lit street six floors below. 'Hang on, Frank,' he said putting a hand to the mouthpiece. 'Honey, your cab's here.'

'Already?' called a voice.

'The man did say ten minutes. Can you get the door? It's buzzed three times. Sorry, Frank,' he said, resuming his phone conversation, 'go on. The USTA want . . .'

Tiffany emerged from the bedroom, her arms half-hooked into a coat. She crossed the room and opened the front door. 'Luke!' she exclaimed. 'We thought you were in London.'

The towering Canadian grinned. 'I was until this morning. Caught the overnight flight. Tuff wanted me to take part in a fashion show they've organised at the Beverly Center. It's not like I have any other commitments. It's the menswear so you might want to come along.' He peered at her more closely. 'You've done something to your hair. It's different – I'm mean it looks great.'

She smiled, enjoying his confusion. 'It needed cutting. But what about you? You look like a new man.'

'I feel it.'

'That's obvious. Did you want to see Max?'

'If he's around?' The door obscured Max from his vision. She opened it more fully.

'Come on in.'

Max, still on the phone, waved an acknowledging hand.

'What's with the bags?' Luke asked, almost tripping on three suitcases stacked near the door. 'You guys planning a long vacation?'

Tiffany buttoned up her coat. 'I've gotten tired of L.A. I'm moving back to Wichita. For a while, that is, until I can sort a few things out.' He noticed some of the sparkle dim from her wide brown eyes.

'Oh,' he said, quickly appraising the situation. 'Look, if this is a bad time . . .?'

'Oh, Luke, if you only . . .'

Max had hung up. 'Luke, my man,' they shook hands. 'It's good to see you looking so well. How're you shaping up?'

'Better every day,' he tapped his plastered leg, 'and I get to ditch this mother next week.'

A car honked in the street below. Tiffany picked up her handbag and an overnight case. 'I've got to get going. Wish I could stay and catch up with your news, but maybe next time, hey?' She smiled bravely at Luke.

'You want me to give you a hand with those?' he offered.

'I got it,' said Max, throwing a bag over his shoulder, the other supported in his free hand. 'Look, buddy, I won't be long. Help yourself to a drink. There's a stack of beers in the cooler.'

Tiffany reached up and kissed Luke on the cheek. He caught a whiff of her perfume. 'Bye, you,' she murmured. 'Take good care of yourself.'

'Yeah. You too.'

Max was back minutes later.

'Look, buddy,' Luke began uncomfortably, 'if I've interrupted something here . . .'

'Forget it. You did me a favour.' Max withdrew two beers from the fridge and tossed one towards Luke. 'I'm not big on goodbyes.'

'Things didn't work out then?'

Max collapsed into a chair and clicked open his can. 'Her decision, not mine. Bottom line was Tiffany wanted more than I could give her. She's hurting now but I think we'll remain pals. I hope we will.'

'That takes some doing, man. I envy you.' Luke was thinking about Sukie. 'Sure as hell never worked for me.'

'I'm not saying it's easy. These things never are. I'm going to miss her like crazy, but I've done the right thing – for us both.' Max ran a hand through his hair. 'Anyway, what brings you round?'

Luke shuffled his feet.

'Oh,' Max gave a perceptive nod, 'a woman.'

'I didn't plan it. Man, it was the last thing on my mind. After Sukie, I swore that it would be the last time I'd get involved.'

Max laughed. 'I've made the mistake of doing that too.'

Luke took a slug of beer, 'I don't know how to explain it. It's not like we didn't know each other. Fact is we'd become rather close. Then last week—Jesus, things happened and I know it sounds corny but she just blew me away.'

'She sounds special.'

'She is. I never thought someone of her class would be interested in me. She knows all this stuff and—' Luke gave a dry, shaky laugh. 'Look at me. I'm a nervous wreck just thinking about her.'

An uneasy thought suddenly flashed through Max's mind.

'Max, it's Lauren.'

The thought turned sour. Max blinked. Blood spots rose before his eyes. He felt breathless as though someone had kicked him viciously in the ribs. 'Lauren,' he repeated stupidly.

'Can you figure it? Me and Lauren.'

Max spoke carefully. 'You slept with her?'

Luke chuckled. 'Man, that's what I've been trying to tell you.'

Luke had slept with Lauren. The hairs stood up on Max's arms. 'When did this all happen?'

'After Lauren's party. I was feeling pretty choked about Sukie. When Lauren called up, asked me to come round,' he shook his head, as though he couldn't believe it himself. 'I don't know, it just happened. Guess we both wanted it. I've been walking on air ever since. Only— '

Max wasn't sure he could take any more.

'There's been some stuff about us in the papers. I was dumb enough to talk to a reporter. Next thing I know it's in print. They made a whole big deal out of it. Made it sound like more was going on than really was. Thing is, I don't think Lauren's going to be too pleased about it. I thought you'd know how to handle it.'

Max was trying to keep up. 'Why me?'

'Because you're her friend. Because you know her.'

'Know her?' Max's voice sounded far away.

'Yeah. Listen, will you stop repeating every goddamn thing I say.'

The sun came out suddenly from behind a rain cloud, flooding the room with warm light. Lauren's lovely face flashed with extraordinary clarity in Max's mind. Not just her face but also her voice, her gestures – he could even smell her. In that instant, it dawned on him that he loved her. He'd protested so vehemently, but Tiffany had guessed right all along. It was just that he hadn't seen it. He felt a fierce desire to punch Luke in the face, smash his vile confession into oblivion. Then the cloud slotted itself back in front of the sun and the room returned to grey.

'Max?'

Luke was talking to him. 'What?'

'You think it will affect things? My having been with Sukie?'

'That's something you'll have to ask Lauren.'

'You're right. I should talk to her. Can I use your phone? I wanna see if she'll fly out for a few days.'

Luke left shortly after. Alone, Max gazed at the floor, his can of beer in one hand flat, forgotten. At that moment, everything about the room imprinted itself on his mind for ever; the pale blue carpet, the folded pine shutters, the illuminated hall doorway. The phone rang twice but he ignored it. There was no one he felt like talking to. All he could think about was Lauren and Luke, Luke and Lauren. Their names continued to ring on and on in his head like a nursery rhyme until he could stand it no longer.

The beer can crinkled in his hand as he squeezed it. Some of the liquid spilled out onto the carpet. He rose abruptly and walked to the door. But when he reached it, he paused.

In a sudden explosive outburst, Max clenched his left fist and slammed it into the wall.

21

On Friday Sukie woke to a raging hangover. The room was dark. Tomb-like. For a moment she panicked. She couldn't remember a single detail of last night. Her mind was empty as though someone had scooped out the inside of her skull like a melon leaving nothing but a useless piece of rind. She lay still for a moment assessing the damage before moving.

Birds were singing outside her window. Sukie winced. Did they have to make so much noise? Groping for the bedside lamp she switched it on. The room swam murkily into focus; carelessly drawn curtains; open wardrobe doors exposing bursting, chaotic contents. There were shoes and clothes strewn across the floor covered in mud. *Mud*! How the hell had she got *mud* on her clothes? Gallivanting through country fields wearing a thin dress and strappy heels in the cold? Hardly her idea of having a good time – and it *was* cold. The room was like a bloody fridge. Why hadn't the heating come on?

The phone shrieked in Dolby stereo. Sukie recoiled, threw the bedclothes back over her head and waited for the ringing to stop. It continued with infuriating persistence.

'All right!' she snapped and picked up the receiver.

'Where the hell have you been?' barked a voice.

Sukie held a groggy hand to her temple. 'Do you mind not shouting. I've got a splitting headache.'

'You'll have a lot worse to deal with by the time I'm finished, you little bitch.' Max. In a foul mood. 'You've really gone and done it this time.'

Sukie groaned. 'Not that sanctimonious tone, Max. Not today. Can't you call back tomorrow when I'm feeling more up to this?'

'It's a bit late for rain checks, Sukie. *Christ*, no wonder you're so goddamn miserable. You sit around on your butt expecting life to be one great big Hallmark card, and when it doesn't go your way you fuck it up for everyone else.'

Sukie was fumbling for some paracetamol in her bag which she had found under the bed. Apart from the pills, her house keys, a mottled lipstick and a battered comb, blonde hair trapped in the grooves like dental floss, it was empty. What had happened to her make-up – and purse for that matter? She had cashed her last fifty quid yesterday.

'Great,' she muttered, 'bloody great.'

'Sukie,' hissed Max, 'you'd better be taking this in.'

'I don't respond well to shouting. What's the time?'

He sighed audibly. 'Three o'clock – in the afternoon. Tell me you haven't just woken up?'

'What's it to you if I have. I'm sick.'

She was searching for something to swallow her pills with, but the only thing to hand was a coffee cup with a few dregs in the bottom. A layer of unsightly mould coated the top. She chucked it in the bin.

'Oh, God,' she moaned, 'I think I'm dying.'

If she was hoping for sympathy, Max was the wrong person to appeal to.

'Take it from me there's not a single soul out there who gives a shit how you're feeling.'

His indignant mood was obviously on Luke's behalf. With difficulty she swallowed the paracetamol.

'Max,' she soothed, 'I know you and Luke are good friends, but I don't see why I should get all the flak. He's hardly been a saint . . .'

Max cut her off. 'You just don't get it, do you? A lot of people are hurting right now, two of whom may end up separating because of you.'

What on earth was he rabbiting on about now? Sukie held the receiver away from her ear. 'Will you stop *bloody yelling*!' she yelled. 'If you just rang to give me a lecture then I'm going to hang up.'

Silence down the phone. 'I guess you haven't heard?'

'Heard what?' The paracetamol had got stuck halfway. She swallowed several times, forcing the pill further down her throat.

'When was the last time you bought a newspaper?'

'Max, I'm about to be sick.'

'It's what you deserve.'

'That's *it*! I'm hanging up now.'

'Go right ahead. But buy yourself a copy of the *Informer*. I think you'll find it an education.'

Little shit. She disconnected the phone and took another paracetamol – she couldn't remember whether she'd taken one or two. Intending to have a shower she staggered into the bathroom and instead threw up. One of the pills flew into the toilet bowl undigested. The rest was watery, insubstantial, the colour of tea. Groaning, Sukie splashed her face with cold water then limped back to bed. When she woke a second time she felt marginally better and ventured downstairs to make herself some coffee. The answer machine was jammed with messages. She ignored it – she couldn't think of a single person she wanted to talk to. There was a letter caught in the letter box. She tugged it free and wandered with it into the sitting room. The *Informer* was stamped across the top of the thin envelope. The *Informer*? Hang on. Wasn't that the paper Max had been banging on about? Intrigued, she ripped it open and read the *Informer* compliment slip dated Wednesday.

Have left countless messages but no joy. Couldn't have done it without you. You're a star! How about a drink on Friday? Col.

Who the hell was Col? The name didn't register. Clipped to the back was a cheque. Sukie's blood ran cold. Made out in her name it was for £50,000.

'*Mum!*'

'In the kitchen.'

The front door slammed shut and there were sounds of excited footsteps. Charlotte burst into the room followed by Fran and Hugo.

'You're back early,' Melanie said smiling. 'I wasn't expecting you until seven. Hello, Fran.'

'Mrs Butler.'

Charlotte threw her bag down and collapsed into a chair, glancing automatically at the press cutting of herself at the Junior National taped to the fridge door.

'The court lights went out on the practice courts,' she said, annoyed. 'We had to wait in the viewing room for ages. Then after all that we got sent home.'

Melanie looked at Hugo. 'Isolated power failure,' he explained. 'They managed to track down the janitor but he couldn't work out the fuse box, so no play tonight, I'm afraid.'

'Never mind. I'll make tea for everyone. Will you stay for supper, Fran?'

'Yes, she will,' said Charlotte. 'I've already asked her.'

From the fridge she removed her insulin then got out the plastic ice-cream container in which she kept her monitoring equipment. These she set down on the table. 'How long will it be before we eat?'

'About half an hour so you can take your shot now,' said Melanie, scooping one of two piles of washing separated into colours and whites from the floor. She shoved clothes into the washing machine.

'Anything I can do to help?' Fran volunteered.

Melanie smiled. 'It's all done. Just heating up in the oven.'

Hugo took a copy of the *Informer* from his briefcase and opened it to the centre page. 'Have a look at this,' he said to his wife.

'What is it?'

'I wouldn't bother, Mum,' said Charlotte, using the Monojecter to prick the end of her thumb. 'It's just some stuff about Lauren's sister.'

'Caused a *sensation* at school,' said Fran theatrically. Wicklow rolled himself against her legs, purring sonorously.

'Who's Wolff Bohakari?' asked Melanie, skimming through the article.

'Mum, you remember – the French Algerian who lost to Josh in the second round at Wimbledon.' Charlotte squeezed the side of her thumb until a tiny bead of blood formed. This she carefully smeared onto a testing strip then pressed the button on the biosensor. 'He's been bonking Sukie Miller.'

'That'll do, Charlotte,' warned Hugo.

'And he's married!' added Fran. 'I think she did it for the money.'

'Lauren's the one I feel sorry for,' Charlotte said passionately. 'I never did like her sister.' The biosensor beeped and she jotted down the result in the diary she kept.

Fran was looking at her friend curiously. 'Have you met her then?'

'Oh, I know Lauren really well. I stay in her house all the time.'

'How come?'

Charlotte's eyes slid towards her mother. 'I'll tell you later.'

But Melanie wasn't listening. Memories of Josh's infidel-
ities had all come flooding back. She studied the photograph
of Inge with her twins and she thought: I know exactly what
you must be feeling. I've been there too.

Pushing the paper away, she pulled her dark hair back
into a knot.

'I think I've got better things to do with my time than
read rubbish like this,' she said. 'They should be allowed
to sort their lives out in private.'

'That's exactly what I said,' said Charlotte, wondering if
she could sneak round to see Lauren before she left for
California.

'Off!' Hugo snapped at Wicklow who had leapt heavily
onto his lap. 'Get down, you wretched cat!'

Wicklow jumped as if scalded and left the room in a
sulk.

Melanie's mind was hurtling back through time. It was
mid-morning, she was driving her father's old Ford, clouds
of poisonous fumes coming from the old engine, with
three-year-old Lottie strapped into her seat in the back.
Somehow she had managed to undo her seatbelt and was
crawling about on the floor. With one eye on the road,
her free arm clutching her daughter, Melanie rear-ended a
green Toyota at an intersection. A young man got out of the
car. Through her dirty windscreen she watched him bound
over. He was wearing scuffed Reebok shoes and shorts that
showed off his long muscular legs; his blond hair reached
his collar, his skin was smooth and golden as if he'd just
been on holiday.

The Toyota turned out to belong to a friend – who, she
never found out. He took her for lunch – take-away coffee
in polystyrene cups and sandwiches which they ate on their
laps on Wimbledon Common. She had thought it so romantic
at the time. She liked the way he took time to play with her
daughter – the attraction with Lottie had been instant and

mutual. Bouncing her on one knee, he told Melanie that he was a tennis player. Recently arrived from Sydney, he was looking for somewhere to stay – his friend's sofa in Earl's Court wasn't a suitable long-term arrangement. Did she know of anywhere? No, she didn't. But she thought he was the most beautiful man she'd ever seen. He looked, she thought, like a film star. By the time they left the park it was dark and he followed her back to Gladstone Road for supper. Worried about his age, she had half-heartedly resisted his advances. But from the moment he'd entered her home, she was already out of her depth and within a fortnight he had moved in.

'Does it hurt?' Fran was asking as Charlotte stuck a syringe into her abdomen.

'I've got used to it now.'

Melanie dropped four tea bags into the teapot, her mind on her daughter. A noise had disturbed her last night and Melanie had left her bed to investigate. Charlotte's room was empty, the pillows on the bed dented, the duvet pushed back to reveal the creased white bottom sheet. Melanie had crept downstairs, avoiding the bits that squeaked – Hugo's ears, even in sleep, were sensitive. The sitting-room door was slightly ajar which was odd because she always closed it before turning in for the night. She put a hand on the knob and edged it open. The room was in darkness except for the coruscating light from the television. Charlotte was watching a video of Josh playing at the Australian Open. It was years old, taken during the early part of Josh's career but Melanie recognised it immediately. He'd played sensational tennis that day, only to be massacred by South Africa's Wayne Ferreira in the second round. Charlotte was kneeling inches from the screen, freezing a close-up frame of Josh's face. She just sat there, bathed in the white-blue light of the machine, obsessively running the film backwards, then forwards, hoping to find – what?

Steam belched into the air as the kettle boiled. Melanie opened a cupboard and took down four mugs.

'Why don't you girls go next door and watch some TV while I fix supper? I'll bring your tea through in a minute,' she said, shooing the girls out of the room.

'What are we having?' Hugo asked, once they were alone. The paper had been folded away in a drawer.

'Lasagne.' There was something indefinable in Melanie's eyes.

Hugo approached his wife, circled his arms around her waist and kissed the back of her neck.

'Actually, while we've got a moment alone there's something I wanted to show you.'

'Can't it wait?' said Melanie, feeling suddenly very tired.

'No, it can't.'

He took an envelope from his briefcase and handed it to her. 'A solution,' he said mysteriously. 'I decided to take your advice.'

She unfolded the sheet of paper inside. It was a copy of an estate agent's particulars drawn up for Eaton Place.

Hugo had put his flat on the market.

Lauren heard the car pull up in her drive. From the bedroom window she watched him step out and lock the door. Max. She rushed downstairs to greet him.

'It's been *ages*. I was so worried you weren't going to come,' she threw her arms round his neck. Max accepted the embrace then disentangled himself after a polite pause.

'Something came up. I won't be able to stay long.'

'Oh, all right.' She was thrown by his rather cool, offhand manner. 'Come in. You've got time for a drink at least?'

He asked for coffee. Strong and black. When she brought

it through into the drawing room she found him reading the *Informer*.

'Didn't think much of the quality of writing.' She tried to make a joke of it.

Max dropped the paper onto the coffee table in front of him. 'When did you find out?'

'Wednesday.' She handed him his coffee. 'I had journalists bugging me for three days.'

'They're relentless.'

'I won't have to put up with it for long. Tuff have asked me to fly to the States for some more promotional work. I leave in two weeks.'

There was a pause. 'What about *your* immediate plans, Max?'

He shrugged. 'I've got the Paris indoor event, then it's back home to California,' he looked uncomfortable. 'Have you spoken to Sukie yet?'

'Last night. She called to say she was driving down to my parents.'

'That fits. Running away again.'

'I don't suppose she feels she has much choice. In her position I'd probably have done the same.'

Lauren fiddled with her drink, waiting for Max to say something. When he didn't, she said,

'I think I'd realised she was up to something as far back as my party. The signs were all there.'

He looked horrified. 'You telling me you knew about the affair with Wolff?'

Lauren shook her head. 'I'd worked out that Sukie was seeing someone; I just didn't know who.'

Max frowned. 'You seem to be taking all this in your stride.'

'How else should I react? Getting angry won't solve anything.'

'She screwed your best friend's husband!' he snapped, feeling a prick of self-righteous indignation.

Lauren reddened. 'Since when did it ever bother you whether a woman you slept with was single or married?'

Max shifted his gaze.

'I'm sorry,' she added quickly, 'I shouldn't have said that but Sukie's my sister. If I don't defend her, who will?'

Max felt his frustration bubble to the surface. He banged the flat of his hand against the arm of the chair. 'Jesus, Lauren, Sukie's a big girl. She can handle it. Why won't you just face up to the fact that this mess she's in is of her own making.'

'I know.' She sat down next to him on the sofa. 'It's just that I've always been there for her. She doesn't have many friends to turn to.'

'That's no goddamn surprise,' muttered Max. 'Look, whatever guilt trip you've been carrying for her over the years has gone way beyond the call of sisterly love. It's time Sukie learnt to sort out her own battles.'

'Will you calm down. I don't like what's happened any more than you – my heart goes out to Inge, but we shouldn't be arguing about it.' She ran a hand rhythmically up and down her arm as she spoke. It was an extraordinarily sensuous action but she seemed unaware that she was doing it. 'Can we call a truce?'

For a moment his resolve weakened. Like a thirsty man his eyes drank in her face, searching for some sign of encouragement. He sensed her vulnerability. He could do it – now. He could crush her to him, lose himself in that wonderful body. The one he had been dreaming of for so long.

'Lauren, I—'

'I heard about you and Tiffany,' she said, throwing him off tack.

'News gets around. Who told you?'

'Luke.'

'Oh, right.' Max's voice was cold again. 'Just what *is*

going on with you two? I mean, where does he fit
in?'

'Luke's been very good to me.'

Max felt a fresh swell of anger. I'll bet he has. 'And just
how am I supposed to take that?'

Lauren looked flustered. 'I don't know what else to say.
If you're asking me if I'm in love with him then the answer's
no.' Max frowned. 'We spent one night together, Max, at a
time when we needed each other.'

'But I thought . . .?'

She shook her head. 'It was never going to be anything
more, but that's not to say I regret what we did. I've done
nothing to reproach myself with,' she sighed. 'Oh, Max,
don't you think I don't continue to yearn for Josh? I'd give
anything for him to be back alive, but the truth is he's gone
and I have to get on with living my life the best way I can.
I'm not made of stone, nor can I go on being the grieving
widow for ever.'

He looked away.

She tried again. 'Don't you want me to be happy?'

'That's a dumb question to ask.'

'It's just that you seem so angry. What have I done?'

Suddenly unable to help himself, he raised his eyes to
hers and exposed the vulnerability in them. 'What do
you think?'

Lauren read the truth and gasped.

'No!'

He grinned ruefully. 'Sucks, doesn't it?'

'Oh, Max.' She put her hand out and covered his but he
snatched it away, trembling. 'I'm sorry,' she said gently, 'I
had no idea.'

'No, I guess you didn't,' his voice was bitter. 'But I wouldn't
get too down about it. I've no shortage of offers.'

Lauren bit her bottom lip. 'The last thing I wanted to do was
hurt you. I really value you as a friend. *Please* believe that.'

Max got up from his chair. 'You know all the right things to say, don't you, Lauren?'

'Max, please . . .'

'Gotta go.'

'Can't we at least talk about it?'

'We just did.'

She stepped towards him but he pulled back as though he couldn't bear her to touch him. He turned from her and walked away, out of the house, out of her life. She watched his back receding down the drive until he was no longer in sight.

Oh, Max, she thought glumly as fat tears spilled from her eyes, ran freely down the bridge of her nose. What have I done to you?

The room is flooded with light as she returns to the bed. Her progress is hindered by the extra weight she carries and the hot, sleepless night she has spent, but her movement are soundless. She eases herself back under the sheets, lets her head sink against the pillows. She feels the strong kick of life, impatient, deep within her. Her husband stirs at her side. Lying on his back with one hand thrown above his head, the scar is exposed; pink-white and raised, marring the otherwise smooth skin. Gently her fingers explore its edges, lingering across the distorted line. His eyes open. With an air of puzzlement he looks round the room. Then his gaze finds her.

'I overslept again, didn't I?'

She watches him yawn and stretch like a well-fed tiger and she says, 'I'm afraid.'

'Afraid, angel?'

'I'm afraid of losing you.'

He puts a hand to her mouth to block her words, her fear. Presses his face into her neck with such urgency that she can feel his stubble burn her skin, bending her to his will until she forgets, relents, gives in.

Wolff had been gone eight days. Each evening at six o'clock he had phoned to speak to the twins, to reassure them of his love and commitment. But Inge had been very firm. She absolutely would not see him. Nor would she have him in the house. Not until she had decided what to do. And in that she wouldn't be rushed. It was the final anonymous phone call that had done it. Things came to a head after supper when Wolff had suddenly broken down and confessed to his affair with Sukie. Wretchedly, with his hands thrust through his hair, he talked about how it had started, the madness that had seized him so that he had risked losing all that mattered most to him. He couldn't look at her as he described the inevitable breakdown of the affair. Inge contributed little to the conversation. She just sat there numbly listening to him talk, her face expressionless. When he had finished, after he had told her how much he loved and needed her, after sobbing into her lap over and over again, repeating that life without her and the girls was meaningless while she remained upright and angry, she had asked him to pack his things. No tears, no angry recriminations. Her request for him to leave within the hour was made quietly and calmly but in an emphatic tone. Wolff had had the sense not to argue.

Inge's attention drifted from her Italian textbook in which she was making no progress. The twins were scribbling on a mini blackboard – or at least Gretal was. Miriam was banging a chalk end on the arm of her chair. Thank goodness for the girls. Being so involved with them helped fill the gap. Inge gazed at them with fierce love. She had been thinking a great deal about what she was going to do. Returning to teaching was a possibility – it seemed silly not to make use of her language skills. But it was still too soon to be making long-term decisions. She had to explore her pain before she could begin to heal. It wasn't something she relished, but she was strong. She would get through this. For her own sake and more importantly for the twins'. Above all else their needs must come first.

Last Saturday, without warning, Miriam had switched on the television – something she was forbidden to do – and there he was, vivid in colour. They were showing highlights of a tournament in Stockholm. The sight of her husband struck her as though she had been pierced by a long sharp needle. She remembered then how often he had slid into bed beside her smelling strongly of soap and secrets. How comfortably he appeared to move from one woman to another, drifting into sleep, his breathing even, his warmth and smell just as they had always been during their marriage. She felt anger and anxiety rise to boiling point. How *could* he have? How was he coping without them? What was he thinking? She no longer knew. The gulf between them had grown so wide.

She realised she was crying. He doesn't deserve my tears, she thought miserably; he has himself to blame for what has happened. She wondered how she could bear the pain she was feeling which left her feeling weak and helpless. Weary with grief she lowered her head onto her arms and watched her tears form a pool on the kitchen table.

Miriam was still banging. She glanced round at her mother mischievously, but her mother wasn't looking. She was hiding in her arms. Was this a new game? Clambering down off her chair, she approached the table. Her mother's shoulders shook.

'Not worry, Mummy,' Miriam said in an anxious voice. 'Don't cry.' She stroked her back.

'No!' Gretal said in a panic, her tiny mouth trembling dangerously.

Inge raised her head and smiled at the twins through her tears.

'How silly Mummy is. She's been cutting onions again and it has made her eyes sting.'

'Uh-oh,' the girls chirped in unison, '*Si-lly bi-lly.*'

Their smiles were full of relief.

Sukie walked into the drawing room and scraped her shin on a rough edge of the wicker log basket. 'Bloody, fucking hell!' she cursed, rubbing her hand across the offended area.

'I see you're in one of your more cheerful moods,' said Robert Miller turning his head. He was on his knees in front of the inglenook fireplace, scrunching up bits of newspaper. The Labradors, tired out after their daily exercise, were snoring gently at his feet.

'What happened to the walk?' he said, hauling himself up stiffly to collect the basket.

Sukie blew her nose. 'Too cold.'

'Oh, I don't know. Wind's up a bit but it might put some colour back into those cheeks of yours. You can't go on skulking around the house for ever.'

'I'm not skulking.' Sukie dropped heavily onto the sofa, kicked off her shoes and drew her feet up under her. She was coming down with flu but she wouldn't mention it. Her father wasn't known for acknowledging frailties of the body. For as long as she could remember he had worked ceaselessly through colds, bouts of influenza, even a severe attack of food poisoning that had left him weak and shaken but still standing, still working.

'Where's Mum?'

'Upstairs trying to put young Tom down for his nap. Been a bit grizzly today. Missing his mother, no doubt.' The log basket squeaked as Robert pulled its heavy weight towards him. 'I expect Lauren's plane will have arrived by now. Weather'll be better in California.'

Sukie glanced out of the window. It was a raw afternoon, with the midwinter fields bare and colourless. This time last year she had been basking in the Johannesburg heat. Luke was playing in the ATP world doubles championships and if she remembered correctly, had reached the final round. It occurred to her that she had been happy then – all that sun and the sea, laughter and fun. Would she ever again recapture it with someone new? She wondered if Luke was out there now. It was more probable he'd be in Florida, but as she hadn't seen or spoken to him since Lauren's birthday party, and since none of his friends would talk to her, his whereabouts remained a mystery.

It was almost four in the afternoon by the time Sukie had arrived back at the Elgin Crescent flat. Facing her sister's wrath that morning for ruining her birthday party had seemed a preferable option to Luke's wounded gaze. Slipping the key into the lock she had braced herself for a showdown but the flat was empty. It smelt slightly stale as though no one had been there for days. Upstairs in their bedroom she was shocked to find his things gone. Everything. Luke had taken her at her word and moved out, left as she had intended him to. It was just that she hadn't expected it to be so soon, nor so final.

'Pass me the matches, will you?' Robert had his head bent under the hood of the fireplace.

Reluctantly Sukie got up from the sofa and handed him a box from the coffee table. She felt like playing a game, something to take her mind off the recent events but she didn't expect much sympathy from her father. Not after the recent rows. She'd escaped to her parents' house because she thought they'd understand. What she hadn't bargained for was her father's furious reaction. She'd never seen him so beside himself with rage.

'You're very quiet today,' he said now.

'I was just thinking. About what I'm going to do for a job.'

She hadn't mentioned the *Informer*'s cheque – she was loath to make the situation any worse for herself than it already was. The cheque had been stashed away upstairs in the small side pocket of her handbag. She hadn't cashed it although the prospect of escaping from the UK for a few weeks had been very tempting; Sri Lanka, Hong Kong, the Seychelles all glimmering like jewels in her mind. She might still go. Only there was her future to think about. And that was a big concern.

Robert Miller threw some more kindling on the fire. 'In my opinion,' he said, striking a match, 'you've come out of this whole ugly affair pretty damn lightly.'

'Daddy, I don't want to talk about it,' she said, blowing her nose.

'No, I don't suppose you do.'

'Well, we've been through it all. I've said I'm sorry. What else do you want me to say?'

Robert lit his pipe. 'Isn't there a small matter of fifty thousand pounds to be considered?'

Sukie looked sharply at her father. 'How did you find out?'

Robert stamped on an escaped spark that had landed on the carpet. 'You can't keep things like that quiet. Frankly, I think you should give the whole damn lot to charity.'

Sukie's hackles rose in defence. 'I'm not the only guilty party. You forget that someone else was involved.'

'I'm not forgetting anything. The man's been a bloody fool but I suspect he's suffering enough now that his wife's thrown him out.' The tabloids had been full of Wolff and Inge's separation.

'It's what the rat deserves.' Like a recalcitrant nursery-school child, Sukie glared at the logs already alight.

Robert folded his arms and contemplated his younger daughter. His look struggled between disgust and pity. 'I wonder if you'll ever grow up.'

Sukie chewed the inside of her cheek. Flames licked the logs hungrily and hundreds of tiny orange sparks flew up the chimney. 'You might have some understanding for the way I'm feeling.' Sukie's voice was peevish in an attempt to forestall tears.

'No, Sukie. This time you've gone too far.'

She looked into his brown eyes behind wire-rimmed glasses and began to cry.

'You've all turned against me.'

Robert turned on her furiously. 'Don't you dare try that one on, young lady. Don't you *dare*!'

'I can't help it,' she sobbed, screwing a tissue up into a tight little ball.

'God, child, why does *everything* have to be such a drama with you? When will you learn that you can't burst into tears every time you're confronted with a problem?'

Sukie sobbed more wildly. 'But you don't understand. You've *never* understood me.'

'Sukie, I can read you like a book. You'll never change.'

'Darling?' Kay was standing in the doorway. 'Whatever is the matter?'

'Sukie and I are having a row.'

'Oh,' Kay nodded sagely. 'Then I'll leave you two alone.'

'Wait Mum,' said Sukie, panicking, hoping for some support. '*Please* don't go.'

But Kay ignored her daughter's pleas. Very softly the door closed behind her.

LIGHT

*When I was a child, I spake as a child
I understood as a child, I thought as a
child: but when I became a man,
I put away childish things . . .*

Corinthians 13:1

22

Lauren stepped out of the drugstore into the warmth of the day. She limped urgently towards her rented car, fishing keys from her shoulder bag. In her haste to leave, she had knocked her shin against a metal railing. The injured leg throbbed, demanded attention, but she ignored the pain. No time for that now. She shouldn't have done it today. It hadn't felt right. Cameras were everywhere and her timing was off. *You're taking too many risks.* She knew that but she'd pinched the stuff anyway.

Her key was in the lock when she felt a hand on her shoulder. Lauren swung round. A black man of immense size towered above her. She thought, as he removed something from the inner pocket of his jacket, he was going to rob her. Lauren's blood ran cold. Did he have a gun? Was he going to shoot her?

Discreetly he held up the badge for her inspection.

'L. Johnston, security. I'd like to talk to you for a few moments.'

Her heart started again, hammering sickeningly against her ribcage. 'Yes?' she said faintly, groping for the sunglasses on her head and slipping them onto her nose.

'Could you show me the inside of your bag, mam?'

'My bag?' she repeated. She couldn't think. Her brain felt scrambled.

'You have merchandise belonging to the store.'

'You're mistaken. All my things have been paid for. Here,'

lamely she held out the brown paper shopping bag, 'see for yourself. The receipt's inside.'

A clammy trickle of sweat had begun to work its way down her breast bone. The man's black eyes bored into her.

'Oh, this is *ridiculous!*' she said indignantly, putting on her best Home Counties voice. 'Do I look like someone who would steal?'

'If you'll just cooperate.'

'But I object,' Lauren looked around desperately, lowering her voice. 'You can't prove anything.'

'Mam, we have you on tape.'

Her palms felt damp. A woman with two small children had stopped to watch. What must they think? She held her hands up in mock surrender.

'All right. You've found me out. I've been a naughty girl.'

The detective took the bag and led her back inside the store, away from the sun, away from freedom. His massive hand held her arm, gently but firmly. Despite Lauren's brave demeanour, he was practically supporting her.

'I feel so embarrassed,' she stammered, conscious of the sick, thudding of her heart. 'I've never done anything like this before.'

No response from her captor.

People were staring at them. Whispering, pointing. They knew why she was being brought back in. Her stomach felt tight and gassy. Air conditioning blew above their heads. She was sweating. What were they going to do to her? The things in her shoulder bag would be obvious, she realised that, but would they find the necklace she'd stuffed into her knickers? A young child was sucking a Hershey bar, its chin covered in chocolate; an obscenely overweight man was having an argument with his wife, belly wobbling like set jelly as he waved his arms in anger. Lauren contemplated making a run for it, only the security man's grip on her arm was too tight.

Still holding on to her, he stopped to speak to one of the cashiers. The girl was wearing a brown uniform and munching gum with furious speed. Lauren recognised her. Less than five minutes ago the girl had rung up her items. A long queue had formed. Customers waiting to pay looked at Lauren with mild interest. The black man leant down and whispered something in the cashier's ear. It seemed to go on for ever. The chewing ceased then began again, faster than before. Blue-mascaraed eyes glanced at Lauren and frowned.

She was led away to the back of the store. The cashier followed. It was like walking through a film set. Nothing seemed real; garish strip lighting, clinical white walls, staff members crowding round the coffee machine, snatching a five-minute break. She felt exhausted. All the excitement of getting away with not paying had evaporated the second she'd felt the security man's touch. By the time she was seated in a small claustrophobic office, her hands were shaking so badly she had to sit on them. One brief signal from the guard and the deputy manager rose abruptly from his desk and left the room. Lauren clenched her hands, like a rider on the Big Dipper, bracing herself for the next heart-stopping dip.

'What'd you do to your leg?' Johnston asked her, lowering his huge frame into a metal chair.

Lauren kicked out her right leg and inspected the shin. A deep gash about three inches in length ran vertically along the bone. Blood had congealed into a thick crust, her tights had ripped exposing a darkening bruise the size of a small child's hand. She looked at the wound uncomprehendingly. When had she done it?

'You want to clean that up?'

'No,' she said, 'I'm fine.' She wanted to get the ordeal over with.

In silence the black man removed the contents of her shoulder bag and laid the stolen items out on the table; pot of Elizabeth Arden face cream, eyeshadow compact, hand mirror, jar of vitamin D. In a daze Lauren wondered why she'd taken them. She realised she had no use for any of them.

He began totting up the money she had in her purse. 'About seventy-five dollars here in cash,' he looked at her obliquely, 'plus chequebook and plastic.'

Lauren hung her head.

'I've seen you in here before,' said the cashier. A moment passed before Lauren realised she was speaking to her.

'That's impossible,' she said rather too quickly. Had the girl recognised her from the Tuff campaign?

The cashier directed her next sentence at the detective. 'She seems real familiar to me.'

'No. I'm er . . . I'm just a tourist. I've never been here before.'

The security man silenced the cashier with a look and took a form from a drawer. 'I need to get from you some information.'

'Information?'

'Yes, mam. I need your name, *a*-ddress, social security number.'

Lauren's panic flared again. 'Couldn't you just let me go? I'll gladly pay for the things I took. I don't know what came over me. It's never . . .'

The security guard tapped his fountain pen impatiently against the desktop.

'If you'll cooperate, this won't take long.'

He asked her what she did for a living. She lied, said she worked as a secretary. Where did she live? Randomly she gave him the name of a hotel. Had she taken anything from the store before? No, she'd already told them that. Did she have a police record? Of course not. Was she aware she could go to jail? She was beginning to feel faint. It got worse. When they made her stand against a white wall to take a polaroid Lauren broke down.

'I don't know what made me do it,' she sobbed. 'I could lose my job. PLEASE,' she begged him, 'I have a child. My family. Bills to pay . . .' She realised she sounded hysterical but she couldn't stop herself.

'Mrs Kendall . . .'

But Lauren continued to wail.

'If you don't stop crying right now, I'm going to have to call the police.'

His words had the effect of a slap in the face.

'I'm sorry,' she sniffed, pulling herself together. The store detective looked relieved.

'You want me to get someone?' offered the cashier. 'I could go get John. He's on the floor.'

'No, please don't. I'm fine now. Really,' said Lauren quickly. She couldn't cope with anyone else grilling her.

'What's going to happen to me?' she said, wiping her eyes.

'It's the store's policy to prosecute,' the security guard looked almost apologetic.

Lauren's heart stopped. She mustn't let that happen. 'Am I allowed to make a phone call?' she asked.

'Local?'

'Yes.'

Johnston glanced at the cashier whose mouth was temporarily hidden by a large pink bubble. She cracked it with her lips then resumed chomping.

'Okay. But make it quick.'

'Can I go somewhere a little more private?'

'Right here's all you've got.' Resolutely he folded his arms as if to say, don't push your luck or I might just change my mind. He gestured to a phone on the desk. 'Press zero. It'll get you an outside line.'

Lauren took a deep breath then lifted the receiver. I shouldn't be doing this, she realised in a moment of sanity. It will only make matters worse. But there was Tom to consider, and *his* welfare *had* to come first. What other choice did she have? Only one person could help her now. The one person she could trust.

She pressed zero and called Max.

Within the hour a car pulled up at the rear door, enabling Lauren's exit from the store to be far less dramatic than her arrival. She wasn't sure what Max had done to get her out and she didn't ask. Drained, she sank exhaustedly into the passenger seat, her blue eyes hidden by dark glasses. She was vaguely aware of travelling towards West Hollywood, a four-storey Marlboro Man looming preposterously in the foreground; the monstrous Château Marmont. Before long she had fallen into a helpless half-dream.

From the highest point of the Post Office Tower she flees down a spiral staircase. She has ink on her hand. It worries her but there isn't time to wash it off. Behind her she hears running footsteps; urgent, angry-sounding. She is afraid! On she runs half-tripping, half-stumbling, her heart frantic. She is like a fox outnumbered by a drooling, bloodthirsty pack of hounds. Far below she can see the ground. They're gaining on her. Closing in. She urges her legs on. Hurry. If she can just reach the bottom. But like air it eludes her.

Nearby someone is sobbing. 'My babies,' the voice wails, 'both gone. Both gone.'

Her hands fly to her ears. The pain in the voice sears through her like cut glass but she cannot, must not listen. She grows dizzy. Her mind shrinks so that she is unable even to remember her own name. Below her the earth seems nothing more than a pinprick. Her eyes blur. She is falling.

A heavy hand lands smartly on her shoulder and yanks her to a halt.

'DON'T!' she screams.

Max held her door open. 'C'mon,' he said gently, 'let's get you inside.'

Nothing was said until later that night. It had been a quiet supper as neither of them had much of an appetite for food or conversation. With the meal out of the way Lauren went out on the veranda and watched the sun dissolve into the horizon. By the time Max joined her the sky had turned charcoal-grey and was streaked with pink.

'Looks like it's going to be another scorcher tomorrow. Here. I thought you could do with this.' He held out a glass of wine.

'Thanks,' she said, taking it. 'Whose is this place?'

'Mine. I've only had it a month, so you should feel honoured. You're my first proper guest. Oh, don't worry,' he said, registering her surprise, 'you're quite safe.'

'I was thinking about Tom.'

'I already called your parents.'

'You didn't mention anything about . . .'

He looked at her as if to say what do you take me for. 'Relax. All I said was that you'd postponed your flight for a day as you didn't feel up to the journey. They were cool about it.'

'And Tom?' She seemed anxious still.

'He went swimming today. Had a ball apparently.'

'In the outdoor pool! But it's *freezing* at this time of year. What's Mum thinking of? He'll catch his death.'

'From all the hollering I could hear in the background he sounded fine to me. C'mon, Lauren. Your folks know what they're doing.'

She smiled, relenting. 'Stupid, I know, but I just can't help worrying about him when I'm away.'

He caught her little shudder. 'You're cold?'

'A bit. But let's not waste the view,' she said, turning back towards the panoramic scene before them. 'I can see why you bought this place.'

Max sighed, lost in thought for a moment. 'I feel sane here, away from it all. I'd like to think this is where I'll end up.'

'I'm thinking of getting away myself.'

'Oh?' He glanced at her. 'Where to?'

'Australia.'

Max shook his head, not understanding.

'Josh's father died last Monday.' She dropped her head, incapable for a moment of speech. 'A massive heart attack.'

Max was immediately contrite. 'Lauren, I'm really sorry.'

'You know he wrote to me – twice in fact. He hoped I'd visit him, said he wanted to get to know me better.' She rubbed a hand across her brow as if there was dirt there. 'I never went. I never even made the effort.'

'You can't blame yourself for that.'

'Oh, but I do, Max. Because you see he was my last link with Josh, and now he's gone there's no one left.'

'How did you find out?'

'I got a call from the family solicitor. He wanted to discuss the contents of the will.'

'Why you?'

'Because it seems Doug Kendall's left everything to me – well, to Tom, actually. A large chunk of the inheritance is to pay for his education.'

'I see.'

'I have to go, Max. I owe it to Josh. Maybe then I can finally lay his ghost to rest.'

'If you need some company . . .'

She looked at him gratefully. 'I think I have to do this one on my own.'

They both fell silent. Max surveyed the night, drank in the heady scent of jasmine. He watched a bird silhouetted against the moon as it flew past then disappeared into the black sky. Far below, the city lights winked at him. 'Look,' he said eventually, with effort, 'can we talk?'

Lauren turned to him. 'Of course.'

He gazed pensively into his glass trying to formulate his thoughts. 'It's happened before, hasn't it?'

'What?' Lauren was being deliberately obtuse.

'The stealing.' He saw her mouth tighten. 'It's just that I'd like to know why.'

Lauren sighed. 'Max, I've already explained about today. It was a stupid mistake.'

Max fixed her with his gaze. 'How long's it been going on?'

'Don't,' she tried to sound hurt. 'Don't do this.'

'So I'm overstepping the mark a little. But that's okay because we're friends, aren't we?'

'This isn't the way I'd treat a friend.'

'Tell me what's making you so mad?'

'Nothing. I'm not,' but her voice had grown sharp and aggressive.

'Oh, yes, you *are*,' Max pushed. 'Fact is I've never seen you so mad. You're practically killing me with that look.'

She quickly averted her eyes. 'Be careful you don't say something you might regret.'

'Oh, come on, Lauren. Don't you think we're beyond playing games?'

She rose to her feet. 'I'm going to bed.'

He blocked her path. 'No you're not.'

'Let me pass.'

'I want to have this out.'

'And I said that I was tired.'

'Lauren, *talk* to me. Let me in on what's been going on?'

She glared at him furiously. 'You wouldn't have a bloody clue!'

'Try me.'

Angrily she pushed him aside only Max grabbed her arm.

'Let go!' she screamed, panicking. But he pushed her back down into the chair and held her there with his strong hands.

'Let go of me,' she pleaded, her voice breaking. A searing knot swelled in her throat and she couldn't swallow.

'Not until we've talked this thing through. Something's happened to you, Lauren. I don't know. It's like you're a different person.' He brought his face closer to hers. 'You've got *so* much going for you and yet you . . . God, you seemed prepared to risk it all for some lousy cosmetics.' He shook his head in frustration.

'What about Tom, for Chrissakes? Kay and Robert? Your friends? Your contract with Tuff? Didn't you ever stop to think you might lose all that?'

She couldn't speak. She glared at him with loathing.

'Okay, you got away with it today, but what if I hadn't been there to bail you out? What if they'd sued and the papers had gotten hold of it? Hasn't there been enough shit from them already? You put it *all* in jeopardy. *Jesus*, Lauren. It's like you're asking for that stuff to happen. I don't understand you any more.'

'STOP!'

She put her hands up to her face as though she could shield herself from his penetrating gaze. Warm, silent tears ran like rain down over the bridge of her nose. Her shoulders hunched and shook. She felt sick, frightened out of her mind. She wanted to retreat to a dark, silent place and sleep, shut herself down from having to think. If he would just leave her alone. But his questioning was relentless. How could she explain to him what she couldn't even explain to herself? What could she say? I'm sorry, Max. I was feeling low. I wanted comfort? I needed a new lipstick to cheer myself up?'

Ashamed she buried her face further into her hands and said in a flat voice. 'Why don't you leave me alone?'

'Because this isn't finished. *Listen* to me,' he said, shaking her angrily. '*Nothing's* changed. Do you understand? What you did today and all those other times – I don't know how long it's been going on – it was irresponsible, yes, but it doesn't change the way I feel about you.'

Tears were running down her cheeks. She looked up and examined his face. He had screwed up his eyes as though confronted by a bright light. When he opened them again his expression was one of despair.

'Why do you deliberately hurt yourself?'

'I don't.'

He took her chin in his hand, forcing her to meet his gaze. 'Stealing is self-destructive, Lauren. You carry on like this and you'll end up in jail. Is that what you really want?'

She found she could hardly breathe. Perhaps she'd faint.

'Nothing's changed. I'm still the same Max,' he insisted. 'It's still me. I'm *not* rejecting you, I'm just rejecting what you've done.' Tenderly he wiped the tears from her face.

'I love you, Lauren. I've always loved you. But it's got to stop. You know that, don't you?'

'Yes,' she whispered, 'yes.'

They sat up through half the night talking about it. Lauren held nothing back. What would have been the point? He knew so much already. But with each confession she felt as though someone was hitting her head against a stone wall, rendering her weaker and weaker. She cried in waves. Exhausted, she would collapse against his chest soothed by his deep voice, his hands, until she felt strong enough to continue. By the time he put her to bed she had a crippling migraine.

When she opened her eyes, she focused on the bedside clock and saw that it was five thirty in the afternoon. She had slept uninterrupted for almost fifteen hours. She tried to recall the events of last night with Max but she had trouble distinguishing what was real from the bad dreams that had followed. Feeling dreadful, she hauled herself out of bed, ran herself a bath then lay in it crying.

Elsewhere the house was still. She wondered where Max had gone. An hour later she tried his room but it was empty. The clothes he'd worn last night were thrown carelessly on the floor as though he had undressed in a hurry. Downstairs, she found a note on the hall table, pinned under some change. It read, 'Gone out for a couple of hours. Have taken the mobile if you need me.' Two hours. She had no idea what time he had left.

She wandered into the conservatory and sat down. Last night flooded back in grim sharpness. Max knew everything. Weak with shame Lauren hid her face in her hands. It was a redundant gesture as she was alone in the house. But the shelter of her hands provided some small comfort. The confession to Max had left her drained. He had opened her up like a surgeon and taken a good look at her exposed entrails. She had braced herself, ready to read shock, disappointment, disgust flicker across his face, because that was how she felt about herself. Once again Max had surprised her.

She had a sudden image of Luke Falkner asleep, his arms flung wide across her bed like a child who had nothing to fear from unconsciousness and the night. It was his transparent need, his complete lack of guile that had attracted her to him. The brief affair hadn't lasted. It was never meant to. Luke had resisted the split but she had no regrets. They had reached out to each other at a time when they both needed comfort.

There was a mark on her sleeve. Gently Lauren teased it off with a nail, careful not to tear the delicate fabric. The expensive shirt had designer label written all over it, yet she couldn't remember which shop it had come from or if she had paid for it. The same vagueness applied to most of her wardrobe; her hoard, her addiction. What had the stealing really been about? How had things got so out of hand? The stolen items had no emotional value. They added nothing to the quality of her life. Nor was it about money. Her earnings from Tuff meant Tom's and her own futures were secure. And finally, with the sale of the Colorado land Josh had bought, she'd even been in a position to help her parents with their Lloyds payments.

Why then the compulsion? Why take the risk?

She turned and gazed out of the window, crying again. It seemed that having started she couldn't stop. The shimmering sunshine was incongruous with her mood. Foliage and flowers in abundance, petalled heads highlighted to an almost surreal intensity of colour. When she tried to think of what she was supposed to do to repair her life her mind went blank. Yet repair it she must.

I'm tired, she realised, releasing a deep shuddering sigh. Weary of trying so hard, appearing to be on top of things, pretending to take everything in my stride because that was what I wanted everyone to think. While the me, the real me was flailing, struggling to keep above the water's surface. She slipped back to the events of yesterday, her journey from the supermarket to her car, the humiliation of being caught, the interrogation that followed. Was that what she had been waiting for? The authoritative hand on the shoulder? Had the stealing been her way of saying: look properly? See beyond my surface – help me?

Something Max had said to her last night sprang to mind. *'Nothing's changed.'* He was wrong about that. Already a great deal had changed.

Only somehow the realisation no longer terrified her.

23

Christmas came and went in dismal wind and rain. There had been talk of snow but it didn't arrive until February by which time spring buds had already appeared – tricked by unusually mild weather. Then a dramatic change. The shortest month of the year brought blankets of snow. Chaos reigned as the entire country froze under the icy grip, causing motorway traffic jams for up to thirty miles; snow ploughs worked through the nights but many roads were rendered too precarious for travel. Overturned juggernauts lay abandoned by the wayside like dead animals. Schools in more remote areas closed.

Wolff was untouched by the chill of winter. He had spent the last six weeks in the Southern Hemisphere. Not only had he enjoyed a second summer but he had also reached the semifinals of the Australian Open. Suffering from a shoulder strain, he hadn't expected to get past the second round, so his win had gone some way towards lifting his demoralised spirits. His mood today, however, was wary. In fact, sitting now on this brand new sage-green Conran sofa breathing in wonderful cooking smells wafting through from the kitchen, he was feeling distinctly tense. He hadn't been back to the Vicarage since Christmas. Absurdly he had been worried the twins might have already forgotten him.

The strain of his marriage breaking up had been enormous. He wore the emotional scars like a soldier returning from war. Every day was like an endurance test. It wasn't simply the pain of Inge's absence but also the additional

day-to-day burden she had left him with. The endlessly
tedious demands of cooking meals, laundry, ironing, shopping, packing. It all wore him down. How the hell had Inge
managed? She was good about letting him see the twins when
he was in town, but the short visits and subsequent returns
to his rented two-bed flat in Fulham proved so painful, he
preferred not to go at all. His worst fear was that Inge
would leave one day and take the twins back to her native
Germany.

He had coped with the separation by throwing himself
into tennis. For as long as he was out on court, his mind
was focused on the game. It was the single productive area
in his life. With Australia over, he had returned to Europe
ready to dive right into the snow and wind and the indoor
circuit. Physically he had never been fitter – his body was
lean and hard as granite. But although his eyelashes seemed
thicker than ever, his hair was falling out. At twenty-five
Wolff, resembled more a man in his thirties.

His unease came from his wife's own lack of it. Since he
had seen her last, Inge had altered greatly. Gone was the
stoical gaze, the belligerently folded arms, the dark circles
under her eyes that bespoke endless sleepless nights. At the
front door she had greeted him with a wide confident smile.
There was no surprise, no regret in her face, nothing in her
gestures that could be construed as encouragement. Not that
he had expected her to take him back with open arms. It
was clear she'd need time to think things through and Wolff
accepted this. Punishment might erode some of the abject
guilt he had carried round like a slab of stone chained to his
neck. But while he had been out in Melbourne's Flinders Park
winning matches there had been hope of a reconciliation. It
was what had kept him going. Now he wasn't so sure. He
felt like an intruder in his own house.

The twins at least had been pleased to see him. They
fell upon him, jumping up and down in their matching

flower-printed little dresses and wool tights that bagged around their knees, showering him with thrilled smiles and kisses.

'Dada, Dada, Dada, Dada,' Gretal had whispered in a fierce monotone, small arms anchored to his neck as though afraid he'd disappear if she let go.

He noticed instantly that along with the Conran sofa, other changes had been made to the house during his absence. Why did that make him feel so angry? In the sitting room his poster had been taken down from the wall above the fireplace. The gesture had an ominously final note to it.

'Oh, I've missed you both,' he said, nuzzling the twins with the beard he had recently grown until they shrieked with joy. 'Have you been good girls?' Two pale round faces nodded earnestly. 'Because I brought you something back from Australia.'

'*Presents! Presents!*' they both squealed, bouncing up and down on him.

'Okay,' he said, surrendering. 'In the hall, in the green bag.'

Miriam scampered out of the room. 'Me, me, me!' she cried. 'I'm going to be first.'

Gretal, who had developed a nasty cough, left more reluctantly, hovering next to her mother until the distant sound of rustling of paper became too tempting.

'I can bring you some coffee if you like?' Inge suggested. She was standing by the door wearing chinos and the pink and green flannel shirt he liked so much. Coincidence?

'Aren't you going to join us?'

She shook her head. 'My next student will be here in a moment.'

Disappointment crushed him. Not having seen her for so long, he had hoped she'd spend some time with him.

'So, you're teaching again.' He said it to try and keep her in the room – with him. 'Which subject?'

'French mostly. But some German too. I enjoy it.'

'That's good.' He tried out a smile. 'And you're working from home?'

She inclined her head, 'It's more practical this way.'

'Are you okay for money? You only have to ask me if you need more.' She nodded curtly as though she found discussing finances with him unpleasant. Her hand hovered on the doorknob.

'Inge, please,' he hesitated, rejecting the sudden urge to beg, 'at least stay with me until your student comes?'

'Yes,' bossed Miriam, back in the room. She was clutching a large koala bear. 'Mummy stay.'

Inge sat down – on the chair furthest away from him he noticed – and pulled Gretal onto her lap. The beautiful old engagement ring he had given her, a half-hoop band of diamonds, gleamed on her wedding finger.

'What's this, my little angel? Have you got a koala too?' she asked her asthmatic daughter.

Solemnly Gretal nodded, 'Yes' she said, wide-eyed, 'but he's hurt-ed his ear. He's resting.'

'I see.'

Inge looked at Wolff. He shrugged apologetically. 'Got crushed a bit on the way home. I can fix it,' he smiled again. 'You look incredible,' he said, meaning it.

'I feel well. It is good to be teaching again. I've missed it so.' Wolff winced at the implication.

There was a pile of books on the floor, leaning to one side like the tower of Pisa. And two dusty boxes she must have brought up from the cellar. Inge had obviously been having a sort-out just before he'd arrived.

'I notice you've taken down my picture. Any reason?'

She wasn't as embarrassed as he'd expected her to be. 'We had a bit of an accident.' We? he thought. Who the hell was we? 'The glass had to be replaced. Actually it is good you mentioned it. You've reminded me to collect it. It has been ready for days now, I think.'

Obviously not one of her priorities, he thought bitterly. Gretal began to twiddle a piece of hair above her ear.

'Did you want to have it?' Inge asked.

'No,' he said quickly, 'that wasn't what I meant.'

The doorbell rang. Inge lowered Gretal to the floor. 'That will be Mary,' she said. 'I must go.'

Wolff panicked. 'Inge,' he said in a rush, 'I've been doing a lot of thinking . . .'

She looked at her watch and smiled pleasantly. 'If you want some coffee you are welcome to use the kitchen while you are here.'

Did she have to make his presence sound so temporary. 'Can we not talk – maybe after your lesson?' Unconsciously, he had switched to French.

She answered him in English. 'Not today. Mary's here for two hours. After that I have a meeting with some other mothers. It's impossible.'

'Dinner then?'

'Mummy's going out to dinner,' said Miriam smugly. 'She's got a pretty new dress like mine.'

There was a pause. 'I see.' Wolff swallowed his anger.

'It's in Mummy's cupboard. Shall I show it to you, Daddy?'

'Not now, Mirry.' Inge lifted her pale hair in both hands and dropped it neatly down her back. 'So,' she said, 'I leave the girls to look after you.'

Wolff recognised a brushoff when he heard one.

'I'll make Daddy's coffee,' volunteered Miriam. 'I'm good at it.'

'There,' said Inge, as though the matter was settled, and she left the room. He could hear her going quickly along the hall to the front door.

'Shit,' he muttered to no one in particular.

Miriam climbed onto his knees. 'Are you coming home, Daddy?'

In despair he looked at the space that his wife had only moments ago filled. A sudden homesickness for Inge swelled in his throat. 'I don't know, chérie,' he said. 'I really don't know.'

Charlotte could tell Esme was having an off-day the moment her grandmother opened the door. She had on that dire pale-blue housecoat she wore to do the cleaning, her hair was still in curlers and she'd forgotten to put her teeth in.

'You're early,' the old woman grumbled, wandering back into the living room waving a yellow duster. Hermann was in his basket, lined with a stiff and hair-strewn rug, looking sheepish. Lately he'd developed an antisocial habit of hurtling after strangers, his toothless gums bared threateningly in a snarl. Afraid he might hurt someone and have to be put down, Esme had started adding tranquillisers to his food.

Charlotte hugged her grandmother affectionately. 'How are you, Nana?' The room exuded a strong smell of oxtail.

'Mustn't grumble,' Esme cast a beady eye over Charlotte's appearance: ponytail, leggings, bulky sweater and boots. 'You mind my clean floor with them boots,' she warned. 'I've been having a tidy-up.'

Charlotte followed her through. Articles of food had been removed from cupboards and put on the floor. A pair of washing-up gloves draped the side of a bucket of soapy water.

'I'd have had it all cleared away in another half-hour,' Esme continued, patting one of her curlers that had loosened and threatened to come out. 'Why d'you wear them things anyroad? They look as though they were made for a man.' Charlotte glanced down at her boots which were heavy and black with thick soles and eyelets rimmed in brass.

'They're trendy, Nana. Loads of girls wear them.'

'Aye. I dare say they do.'

Esme disappeared up to her room to change and Charlotte reestablished order in the kitchen. Despite being handicapped by a sprained wrist she managed it quite well. While she waited for the kettle to boil, she studied the postcards and pictures pinned to the wall. There were lots of the Virgin Mary shrouded in blue and golden robes, baby Jesus on her lap looking middle-aged and worldly. Another picture was of Jesus on the cross. She tried to imagine what it would feel like to have a nail hammered through your hands and feet then decided she'd rather not. Her eyes dropped resentfully to her right wrist. She had sprained it a month ago. Sutton's physiotherapist had advised her to rest it for six weeks. Heedless of the warning, she had tried to play in a friendly match but the pain had flared up the moment the first ball had been struck and Charlotte had been forced to pull out.

The tiny Bushy Meade house was quiet but if she kept very still she could hear Hermann's sighs and snuffles, the gentle movements of her grandmother upstairs. She walked over to the sink and gazed out at the small garden taking a battering from the sleet and wind. A small tree shivered, its fragile branches frozen stiff. Hermann's faint pawprints in the thin layer of snow were still visible from his last walk. Charlotte sighed. I'm lonely, she realised unhappily. The last four weeks had been interminably slow. Bad weather had kept her indoors and irritable with inactivity. But it wasn't just the frustration of not being able to play that was getting her down. There seemed to be nothing to do except read, watch telly or go to the gym and work on her exercises. She had always been a solitary person, happy with her own company, but with Fran gone and Lauren away so much these days, her life seemed utterly dull. She missed her friends dreadfully.

Three days before the monotony was broken when a

parcel had arrived from America. It had been sent by
Lauren and inside, carefully packed in tissue paper, was
a tiny CD Walkman. Lauren had even added half a dozen
of the latest CDs. Charlotte was thrilled, having hankered
after one for months. Her mother, purse-lipped, had said
she should send it back as it had obviously cost a great deal
of money. But Hugo, surprising both women, had argued on
Charlotte's behalf. In the end it was agreed that she should
keep it.

Esme finally reappeared still wearing the housecoat, but
she had combed her hair neatly and fixed a pair of favourite
M&S diamanté earrings to her ears. The false teeth, deposited
at night in a red plastic mug, now filled her mouth.

'Now then, what's up with you?' she said to Charlotte, once
they'd carried the cups and saucers into the living room and
settled themselves on the sofa. 'You've got a face as long
as a pole, and you've got skinny again. Come on, have a
teacake. It'll do you good.'

'I'm not very hungry, Nana,' Charlotte said, trying to
remember what time she'd taken her last insulin shot.

'Not like you to turn down my cooking.' Esme switched the
fire on and the small logs flickered with electricity. Charlotte
gazed at them. There was something magical and hypnotic
about the colours; a clear blue with flickers of moody green
and purple.

'Tell me what they had to say about this wrist o' yours?'
Esme meant the physiotherapist.

'He wants me to keep the bandage on for another
week.'

Esme clucked sympathetically. 'Well, duck, a week's not
long. Then you can get on with winning again.' Charlotte
dropped her head.

'Eay now. What's all this?'

'Nana, I don't think I'm good enough.'

'Don't be daft. This doesn't sound like my Lottie.'

'I told you about Fran giving up tennis – and she was loads better than me.'

'You beat her in National, didn't you?'

Charlotte considered this. 'But she had the tougher draw. It keeps on going round in my head. Fran was brilliant. She could have made it to the top – everyone said so.' A sigh, deep and full of frustration. 'Why did she go and chuck it all in?'

Esme sniffed. 'She didn't have staying power, I expect. Anyroad, I seem to remember something about her wanting to go on stage?' She tapped Charlotte's knee. 'Now you listen here, lass; her decision's got nowt to do with you.'

Charlotte raised her head and looked at her grandmother. 'I'm just so afraid of not making it.'

Esme's voice was firm. 'Oh, you'll make it. You just have to put mind to it.'

'The competition sometimes gets to me,' Charlotte mumbled. 'I know I shouldn't let it. Just that it used to be easier, it used to be fun. When I walk on court these days, I think: this player can beat me.'

'Expect they think same thing about you.'

Charlotte began fiddling with a crocheted cushion cover.

Esme put down her teacup. 'Your granddad may have been a simple man, but he knew a thing or two. He used to say anything on earth worth having, first has to be earned.'

'But what if hard work isn't enough? I worry about losing all the time. Sometimes the night before a big match I get so nervous I can't sleep.'

Esme looked pensive. 'Do Melanie and Hugo know owt about this?' She waved a bony hand, 'About way you feel?'

Charlotte pulled a face. 'Sort of. But I know they're worried about money and stuff and we've all been getting on so much better lately that I didn't want to . . .' to hide her confusion she swallowed some tea. 'I thought . . .' Charlotte's voice faltered because there seemed to be no adequate words to express how she really felt. She rubbed her nose with the back of her hand.

Esme frowned. 'D'you want to carry on playing? Because if you're not enjoying it any more . . .'

Charlotte gave a little gasp. 'Nana, tennis is my life.'

'All I'm saying, pet, is you're plenty young enough to start again with summat else.'

This startled Charlotte. She had never stopped to consider alternatives. Fran's defection from the game had made her question her playing ability but there had never been any question of giving the sport up. A fleeting dread seized her, but a second later it vanished from her mind. She shook her head, resolute once more. 'No,' she said solemnly, 'I'd rather fail than give it up.'

'Then you've just got to remember one thing: if you're going to carry on, do it for yourself – not because Hugo wants you to, or for that matter owt else. Listen to your heart and listen to it well. It won't steer you wrong.'

She leaned forward and gave Charlotte's wrinkled brow a quick little kiss. 'Now go on,' she said kindly. 'Drink your tea up. Your problem, my little luv, is you're too much like your mother.' Esme's small sharp eyes danced. 'You like to worry.'

'Mr Butler, I've got that Kennedy chap on line two. Shall I say you're in?'

'Not again! The man's becoming a bloody nuisance.' Hugo peered at the wall clock. 'Tell him to call back during business hours. It's late and I'm going home.'

From under his desk Hugo withdrew his briefcase, checked he had all he needed, keys, wallet, then walked along the narrow hall where his coat hung. It was almost seven o'clock and he felt unspeakably tired. At his desk by eight every morning, he was still catching up with a backlog of work by the time he was due to leave. Too many interruptions, that was half of it, and not enough delegating. But at least the threat of liquidation had been lifted. All that hard work with the team pulling together had finally paid off. And for that he was thankful.

Sometimes when he thought about his flat in Eaton Square he felt pangs of regret. But Melanie had been right when she'd said he never used it and he couldn't go on living the dream indefinitely. He had never been cut out for that kind of life. He liked to think of himself as part of the aristocracy but his working-class roots were the real truth and always would be. He felt he'd reached a stage in his life when he could finally accept and like who he was. Becoming a family man had done that. A sheik had bought the flat. Hugo hadn't entirely approved of his Arab purchaser but the full asking price had been offered and Charlotte's tennis career could continue. He felt good about what he'd done.

Outside, it was bitterly cold. The blue Fiat was on the opposite side of the road sandwiched between two other cars. Wrapping his coat round him more securely, Hugo darted across the pavement, careful to avoid dangerous patches of ice. Inside the car his breath fogged thickly.

He kissed his wife. 'Been waiting long?'

'A few minutes. I was afraid I might be late. The traffic from Kensington was hell.' She slipped the car into gear and reversed until she had enough room in front of her to manoeuvre. 'How was your day?'

Hugo grimaced. 'I'm being hounded by a client who claims we tricked him into paying over the odds – a very tedious matter. Anyway, what were you doing in Kensington? I thought you were coming straight from Esme's?'

'I had some shopping to do.' She turned right into Pelham Street. There was a frivolous note in her voice, as though something exciting had happened to her. 'Tell me about this client.'

Hugo clicked in his seatbelt. 'Two people had offered the full asking price on one of our properties so we suggested they put in a sealed bid. This chap Kennedy offered an extra five grand which got him the house. He's pissed off because he found out the first buyer had pulled out without making a bid. Thinks we conned him, to use his disgusting term.'

It had started to rain. Melanie flipped on the windscreen wipers.

'What time is the table booked for?' she said, changing the subject.

'Eight o'clock. Turn right here. No, not that way,' he said, remembering the roadworks, 'Putney Bridge is down to one lane.'

The rain was coming down harder now. The car windows had fogged up. For a while they drove in silence, Melanie squinting to see through the rain, Hugo going over events of the day in his head.

'Before I forget,' he said suddenly, turning the air vent on full to clear the windscreen, 'we've got a clients do on Friday.'

Melanie threw him a sideways glance. 'Which Friday? Not the 24th?' She could see from his expression that it was. Her face fell, 'Oh, Hugo, *not* the 24th. I asked you to keep that free *weeks* ago.'

He raised his hands in mock surrender. 'I'm not exactly thrilled about the office planning my evenings for me but I'm not in a position to argue. Anyway, what's so important about the 24th?'

'I had something planned.' She looked sulky. 'A surprise.'

'Can't you change it for another night?'

'*No*, Hugo, I can't.' They had stopped at some lights and Melanie turned to him in dismay. 'This is really important to me. I was counting on you being there.'

'I can't very well be in two places at the same time.'

'Then tell the office no – put my needs first for a change.'

He was offended. 'That's a bit unfair. You know very well that you and Charlotte are my first priority.'

'Then say you'll come.'

He threw back his head in exasperation. 'I'm not cancelling anything at work unless I know what it's for.'

Her mouth took on the same stubborn set so often noticeable in Charlotte.

'Oh, now come on, Melanie.' He massaged his temples anticipating an argument. 'Be reasonable.'

The lights changed. Angrily she put her foot down and the car jerked forward along the Brompton Road.

Morosely he gazed through the windscreen. This was most unlike her. She never usually made a fuss about office parties. This surprise she was getting so worked up about – what the hell was it? Hugo racked his brains. His birthday wasn't until August. Melanie was a Capricorn. It couldn't be anything to do with their anniversary because they'd only recently celebrated it. He scratched his head, baffled. Maybe Charlotte could shed some light on the matter. He'd have a word with her when they got home.

The car turned off the Talgarth Road towards Hammersmith Broadway. Hugo glanced at his wife. She was crying.

'Melly?' It seemed that by speaking her name he'd made the situation worse. Tears now streamed down her cheeks. Her face was scrunched as though she was suffering a great deal of pain. He put a hand to her head but she pulled away.

'Darling, whatever is the matter?'

'I've tried,' she sobbed, as rain lashed against the windscreen, 'tried—make you understand— '

'Of course, you have.' Hugo kept a concerned eye on the road, 'Darling, get in the left lane.'

'But you won't— ' her voice was jerky as she shifted

the Fiat into the middle of the road. 'You refuse—what's important to me— ' The car roared along the broken line between the lanes of traffic and she manoeuvred it into a space seconds ahead of a Rover.

Hugo caught his breath. 'You're not making any sense.'

'I feel so *useless*,' she wailed, screwing up her eyes. 'I want to be more than just a wife to you.'

'You're a wonderful wife and someone I love very much – darling, *please* watch the road.'

They were crossing Hammersmith Bridge. A double-decker bus approached them from the opposite lane, its wheels spraying the small Fiat with fans of rain. Instinctively, Melanie swerved the car to the left then back again, narrowly avoiding a crash into the bridge wall.

Hugo bit his lip to stop himself from snapping. Castelnau Road stretched out before them. 'Pull over,' he said to the still sobbing Melanie. 'Come on now, *pull over*. You're hysterical.'

'I don't *CARE*!' she wailed. 'I'm a woman – it's my prerogative to be upset!'

'Melanie, if you carry on like this we'll both wind up in hospital!'

This seemed to sober her. She drew up in front of Trinity church, just past the small village of shops. Hugo leaned across and pressed on the hazard lights.

'Right,' he said, handing her his handkerchief, 'what's all this about?'

Accepting the clean square of cotton, she blew her nose and mopped her eyes. Woodenly she gazed out at the rain, her voice drained of emotion.

'When you asked me to marry you I thought at the time, this is it. This is what I've waited for all my life. I'll be happy now. No need to go on searching because you – and Charlotte – were all I wanted, all I'd ever needed. For a while I really believed it,' she sniffed, looked down at her hands. 'I worked hard at being a good wife and mother. I thought that if I could make you both happy my role would be a fulfilling one. But I was wrong. I realise that now.' She sighed and shook her head slowly. 'Oh, I'm so bad at explaining, but I want you to understand. You see, I felt that if I didn't do something for myself I would break up into little pieces – literally.'

Hugo swallowed nervously. They never had conversations like this. He began manufacturing calamities; she was having an affair; she wanted a divorce. My God. Had he been so neglectful, so monumentally blind that he hadn't even seen it coming? He regarded his wife in doleful silence.

'You're kind, considerate, generous, Hugo,' she turned to face him, 'and I know you love me. You've always been very good at showing it. It's just that you don't respect me.'

His jaw dropped. 'That's simply not true.'

She held up a hand to silence him. 'Let me finish. Something happened to me a while ago. It's been going on for about three months now.'

Hugo's hands gripped the seat. So it *was* an affair. Oh, God, let it not be true.

'Maybe I should have spoken to you about it earlier but I was afraid of how you might react— '

Perhaps it was punishment for not having valued her enough, not having loved her enough. Only the truth was he did – madly. The best thing he'd ever done was to get married. Only he hadn't realised it until now – at the very moment he was losing her. Anguished, Hugo closed his eyes.

'I had hoped you'd trust me to do the right thing in the end. But now you've forced me to tell you.'

He held up a hand. 'Enough. I don't want to hear this. I refuse to just sit here quietly while my wife tells me she's seeing another man.' He fumbled angrily for the door handle and stepped onto the pavement. 'Quite frankly if you are seeing someone,' he shouted above the noise of the traffic, ducking his head so that he could see her, 'I'd rather you kept the sordid details to yourself.'

He began to pace, muttering to himself. He hadn't bothered to close his door.

'Hugo,' she called. '*Hugo!*' No response.

Melanie got out of the car, slamming her door so quickly that it almost caught her heel. She stormed round to the other side, catching him up.

'What are you talking about!' she yelled, grabbing his arm. '*What* affair?'

He was already soaked. '*Yours*. The one you've just been banging on about, the one that's been going on for three months. I won't take it, Melly, you hear?' He was waving his arms about furiously. 'You're my WIFE and I'm not going to let you just walk away from our marriage! I *LOVE* you.'

The fog cleared. 'You thought I was seeing someone?' Melanie shook her head in disbelief. 'Oh, Hugo. You clot you, you daft bloody fool.' Not once in their marriage had he ever heard her swear. 'If you really want to know what I've been up to then shut up for once in your life and I'll show you.' Grabbing his hand she pulled him to the back of the car and opened the boot. Various oblong and square-shaped brown packages had been carefully packed against one another.

'Do you know what those are?' she shouted, proudly pointing inside. 'They're my paintings and they've just come back from the framer. I've got my first exhibition, Hugo. A gallery in Thackery Street liked them enough to finance and organise the whole thing.'

Hugo gazed at his wife in astonishment. Light from passing cars transformed her – her face pale green, her dark hair suddenly haloed in gold.

'Yes,' she said, her eyes shining. 'Me. Stupid little Melanie who nobody thought was capable of managing more than the ironing, the occasional part-time job. *This* was going to be my surprise. I did it because it needed doing, because I wanted to. But mostly I did it for us. I don't want to be just your housekeeper, Hugo. I want to be someone you can be proud of. Can't you understand that?'

She had rendered him speechless. A moment ago his world had come to an end. Now the lights had been switched back on again. He gazed at his wife as if for the first time: mascara bleeding black rivulets down her cheeks, rain dripping from her hair, sodden clothes. How beautiful she looked to him. In an instant he envisioned her success: great reviews, followed by bigger exhibitions, fat cheques, media demands. It all threatened him, but he pushed the fear aside. Instead he opened his arms.

'I've been selfish,' he said, against her hair, 'a selfish bloody fool. But I'll make it up to you, Melly, I swear it.'

She pulled away from him, blinking back rain, her eyes searching his face. 'What about the 24th? Will you be there?'

For a split second she could see echoes of the boy he had once been flash across his face. Hugo's mouth widened into a smile.

'Just you try and stop me.'

24

My dear Dougie,
It's possum time again. The bold little critter careered around
the roof of our bedroom all night and when I stomped out
at dawn it just peeped over the edge. You'd think he'd have
run away but not a bit of it. I thought of you and chuckled.
The pest controller has been called and peaches, for bait, are
ready . . .

I'm on the veranda snatching a few minutes of peace for
myself before the house rouses itself into madness. It's a
beaut of a day, clear enough to see for miles across the
tabletop mountains. Sometimes, like now, the trees on the
mountains look so blue I can almost see smoke rising –
how I love this place. Moving out of the city was the best
thing we ever did. The cicadas are making the most awful
racket. Don't know what they have to complain about; they
say it's been about the driest and mildest winter on record
(how mild can you get?). When I can snatch some free time I
really must resume work on the garden before it turns into a
jungle. It's rank with neglect. Maybe one day, eh, Dougie?

I meant to write days ago. I know how worried you've
been, but there's so much to do with the kids home from
school and Helen being the way she is. The doctor comes to
see her about once a week. He says it's clinical depression,
whatever that means, but that the drugs he's given her will
help. Some days she's like her old self: cooking meals, talking

*to the kids like she hadn't a care in the world. We've even got
her to play Mum's old piano – d'you remember 'Wollalonga
Lula?' It was always one of my favourites. Then she just
wanders off to bed and doesn't get up for three, sometimes
four days. I've got to admit it's hard seeing her like that, it's
hard adjusting. Wish I could do more.*

*How's young Josh taking it all? When I spoke to him on
the phone he seemed not to know what had happened. He
even asked me when Brett was coming home – the mind can
play awful tricks. I didn't know how to answer the poor boy.
Maybe you can bring him on your next visit. He loves the
farm and things might be better with Helen by then. She
still hasn't mentioned his name but she will – in time. We
must all be patient. I know it's hard with Helen not being
home but don't blame Josh. He's still so small, Dougie. He
doesn't understand.*

*Oh dear, I can hear a kookaburra which means getting
up time – after church we're taking the kids to the Jenolan
caves. See you on the 8th. Until then take good care of
yourself. Our love and thoughts are with you both.*

Lauren lowered the letter, her brow knotted in confusion.
The contents disturbed her. She had always imagined Josh's
childhood a happy one. But this letter suggested otherwise.
Had his mother had a breakdown? Who was Brett? And the
correspondent – the scrawled signature at the bottom of the
letter was illegible. A relative perhaps?

She was on her knees surrounded by dusty suitcases,
rolled-up rugs, two, three, four boxes which she had found
shoved under the double bed. An electric fan that looked
like a boat propeller whirled rhythmically above her head;
muslin sheets hanging from curtain rails bellied against vast
windows. Sunlight poured through them across the bleached
parquet floor and fractured around furniture, a bucket and
mop, piles of yellowing newspapers. She had meant to have

this room cleared hours ago – there was so much to do still before the weekend and the onslaught of prospective buyers coming round. Discipline was needed but the letters she'd found were utterly compelling. Greedy to discover more, Lauren pulled out another box and ripped it open. Inside was a stack of furry-edged photographs thrown together with no attempt having been made to catalogue the events. One followed another as Lauren foraged amongst the contents. Most of the subjects meant nothing to her although she did recognise early shots of the Vaucluse house. What a surprise that had been – her first real view of it. Somehow she hadn't expected it to be so huge. When Doug Kendall's solicitor had picked her up from Sydney airport, he had painted a very different impression, glibly suggesting it wouldn't take her more than a few days to sort everything out. That had been almost three weeks ago.

Lauren was about to abandon the photographs for one of the other larger boxes when something caught her eye. Later, she would remember the moment when she picked it up and held it towards the light: the rawness in her knees from kneeling on the hard floor, the bark of a dog in the street outside, the heat of the sweltering afternoon sun. The shot was a three-by-five black-and-white, brittle with age. In it was a young child of approximately four, standing against a backdrop of gum trees. The child's slim body was naked; it looked as though he'd been running and had stopped short a few feet from the camera. White-blond hair fell in soft curls to his shoulders and in his right hand he was dragging a wooden tennis racquet. His grinning gaze was directed at the camera as though he knew the photographer well. On the back of the shot someone had scribbled *J. Fourth birthday, Perth, '74.* Lauren's heart skipped a beat. Josh. She'd never seen a shot of him as a child. He bore an uncanny resemblance to Tom.

A shrill peal rang through the house. Someone was at

the door. She glanced at her watch. Four o'clock already. Where had the time gone? Reluctantly pulling herself up, she shook the stiffness from her limbs and went downstairs, the photograph and letter still in her hand.

A plump woman with a thatch of orange hair was standing on the porch. She seemed anxious.

'Mrs Willis?'

The woman picked up a bag at her feet. 'I had a sudden panic that I'd come on the wrong day. We did say Tuesday, didn't we?'

Lauren smiled reassuringly. 'Come on in,' she opened the door to its maximum width. 'You look as though you could do with a cup of tea.'

Lauren led her into the kitchen which was, in her opinion, by far the prettiest room in the house. Large colonial-type doors opened on to a bordered garden and overlooked the sea. A young boy wearing navy shorts was racing after imaginary adversaries with a toy gun.

'Sit down, won't you?' Lauren beckoned to a chair onto which Mrs Willis settled her weight. Her perm was a little too tight. It was at odds with her sweet round face and jolly smile. 'Did you have an exhausting journey?'

'Not too bad. The train took me most of the way. I got a taxi from the station.' Curiously Mrs Willis glanced around the graceful room, already stripped of half its contents, bulging bin bags, their plastic necks secured with rope, boxes labelled and sealed with masking tape stacked in a corner.

'Funny thing,' said Mrs Willis, shaking her head. 'I only left this place a few days ago but it already feels different – like I'm in another house.'

Lauren filled the kettle and plugged it in. 'Does it make you sad coming back? I mean you were here quite a while.'

'Right up until Doug died. My hubby passed away three years ago, bless his heart. What with the kids all grown up and off leading their own lives – well, it seemed the right thing to do. Besides, there wasn't anyone else.'

Lauren looked at her lap. 'About the will . . .'

Mrs Willis waved her hand, wrinkled and stained with sunspots. 'Oh, I know all about that. And it's a good thing too.'

'Then you don't mind?'

'Mind!' her splendid breasts jiggled up and down. 'Did you think that was why I came today?'

Lauren was embarrassed. 'Well, no. But if I'd been in your position . . .'

'My Jim left me well provided for. I don't need the money. Dougie did what was right when he left it to your little boy.' She gestured towards the stacked boxes. 'Looks like you've been working hard.'

Lauren grimaced. 'Slow work in this heat and there's still so much to do. I hadn't realised how long it would take to clear a house of this size. We were meant to be leaving on Monday but I might have to delay the flight another week.'

'That wouldn't be so bad, would it? February's a gorgeous month to be in Oz – it's not so hot and you don't get the rain either.'

'In some ways I don't want to leave at all. Vaucluse is so beautiful. It would be easy to stay here, let time take its course. But I have a life back in England, commitments. And Tom has his school.' The kettle boiled. 'How do you take your tea, Mrs Willis?'

'As it comes, love. And indulge my vanity and call me Rachel. Makes me feel younger.' Freckles disappeared into the creases of her smile.

Lauren put some biscuits on a plate. 'TOM!' she yelled into the garden. 'Do you want some tea?'

The young boy raced into the kitchen. He had a pale pointed face with two bright red patches on his cheeks. The intensity of the sun had bleached his fair hair almost white.

'Bumble bees!' he said, slightly out of breath, throwing his tanned arms around his mother's waist.

Lauren smiled over his head at Rachel. 'A new word,' she mouthed, and shrugged.

'Can I have some more mango juice?' he begged.

'All right, but first you should say hello to Mrs Willis. She's your great-aunt and she's come a long way to see you.'

'Hello, Mrs Willis,' he said politely, staring wide-eyed at her tangerine halo.

'Goodness. Don't you look like your father,' Rachel's voice was wistful.

He shrugged his small shoulders and looked down at the floor. His long lashes made fans on his cheeks.

Lauren ruffled his hair and handed him a glass with a straw stuck in it. 'There's your mango juice. Why don't you take it outside. You can come and talk to Mrs Willis a bit later.'

'Okay,' he said, then leant up to whisper in his mother's ear.

She patted his bottom. 'I'll explain later. Now go on. Scoot.' He scampered off happily, juice spilling from the glass he held in both hands. 'He'll be out there for hours,' said Lauren, proudly watching him go. 'I should really live in the country. Look at him. He's in his element.'

'Josh was the same at his age,' said Rachel. 'I can't get over the similarity. Seeing Tom just then was like stepping back in time.'

Lauren brought the tea to the table. 'I'm sorry. I didn't think.'

'Don't be. I'm very glad I came. Dougie talked about you a great deal.' Lauren dropped her eyes. 'You know, after Josh left for Europe we heard so little from him. Always travelling, that boy. He seemed to lead such an exciting life. But between you and me he wasn't the best of writers. Oh, you know, we'd get the occasional postcard but it was hard reading between the lines.'

'Which reminds me.' Lauren retrieved the letter she'd found earlier. She handed it to Rachel. 'Can you make any sense of this?'

The older woman read it very carefully. When she finally put it down, her face was as white as flour.

'Where did you find this?' she said in a whisper.

'Upstairs. In a box under one of the beds.'

'Lauren . . .' she seemed to be struggling for words. She ran a worried hand across her wide, pleasant face. 'Look, love, I don't know you well enough to know how much you've been told.'

'The letter means nothing to me. I was curious but if this is painful for you— '

'Oh, *no*. You've got that all wrong. It's how this might affect *you*.'

'Me!' Lauren flinched.

'All this,' Rachel glanced at the letter, 'it happened such a long time ago. Why go resurrecting it now? Keep the memories you have of Josh intact.'

'Rachel, if there's something I should know, then please don't keep it from me. I came here to bury the ghost of my husband but I can't do that unless I fully understand the man I was married to.'

She looked uncertain.

'Please, Rachel.'

'If you're really sure?'

Lauren held the woman's solemn gaze. 'I'd like to know.'

'Then all right, I'll tell you.' Rachel drained her teacup, almost as if the hot liquid held restorative powers. Hands folded in her lap, she began to talk.

Doug Kendall was the first man Helen Thorowgood slept with and she married him soon after. Their partnership was a happy one. Doug worked as a sports instructor at the local boys' school. Helen worked behind a Revlon counter in Rose

Bay but gave up her job when she fell pregnant. Throughout
her pregnancy she blossomed, embracing her new role with
both arms. Friends and family members who saw her with
other babies referred to her as a natural mother, born to
raise children. That label stuck until the birth of Josh. Then
everything changed. Suffering from post-natal depression
Helen rejected her infant. She wouldn't breast-feed him.
She refused even to pick her son up. For almost a year
it was down to Doug to carry full responsibility for his
family, undertaking the role of both parents while his
wife lay in a morose state in bed. By the time Josh was
old enough to walk, Helen's condition, with the help of
prescribed drugs, had stabilised. She started venturing out
of the house again. Finally she moved back from the spare
room into her husband's bed. There was even talk of her
returning to work.

Then she got pregnant again and the situation at home
quickly deteriorated. The Kendall's second son born six
weeks prematurely, was delivered by Caesarean. He was
a sickly, fretful baby who cried frequently. Helen made
little effort to bond with the infant, paying him only
the slightest and most necessary attention. Most of her
time, as before, was spent in bed. Months passed with
no sign of improvement and as they couldn't afford a
live-in minder, Doug was forced to give up his job and
seek part-time work.

One afternoon, shortly after Josh's fifth birthday, Doug left
the children alone with their mother. This wasn't unusual.
Josh was often left to look after his younger brother. The
six-month-old Brett was in his cot supposed to be sleeping
but he'd been crying for over an hour. His mother, lying
feeble and wan next door, ignored the cries, but Josh
abandoned his toys and went into his brother's room.
Standing on a stool he was able to lift the fractious Brett
out of his cot. Josh's hands felt dampness. He tried to calm

the baby repeating the same words he'd often heard his father use. He put his brother's face against his and kissed it. But Brett was now hysterical. He kicked, struggled and squirmed in his brother's arms, his cries becoming wilder and shriller until the inside of Josh's head began to hurt. When the baby wouldn't stop its crying, Josh began to shake it, but Brett was so heavy Josh lost his grip and the infant slipped through his hands and fell to the floor, banging the side of his head against the wall. With difficulty Josh picked his brother up and put him back into the cot, making sure that he was warm enough by tucking the blankets in. At least Brett had stopped crying. Satisfied, Josh gently closed the door, went back downstairs and resumed playing with his toys.

Rachel shook her head. 'When Dougie later returned Brett wasn't breathing. He rushed the baby to hospital but by then it was too late. Brett was already dead. He died of a fractured skull.'

Lauren's hands flew to her mouth. 'Oh, my God!'

'The whole thing was a horror story,' Rachel continued. 'I can remember it as though it were yesterday. My husband and I were in bed when Dougie called us. He was in such a state. Apparently little Josh had taken a kitchen knife and stabbed himself several times in the hand.'

The scar, thought Lauren. He hadn't been in a fight at all.

'Of course, Jim and I came down right away, did what little we could. The police had to interview Josh,' she sighed, lost for a moment in memory. 'Poor little ticker. D'you know what he told them? He said that he'd been bothered by the crying and didn't want his mother to be disturbed.' She shook her head. 'Fancy a child of five saying that.

'Right after it happened, Helen came to stay with me and my family – well, Dougie was in no fit state to look after her himself. I think what everyone was most afraid of was that they'd take Josh away but as there was no evidence that Josh had been previously aggressive, Brett's death was declared an accident. Poor Helen was later charged with negligence and committed to a residential treatment centre for psychotherapy.'

Lauren hugged her body as if chilled. 'I can't quite take this in.'

The older woman placed a chubby hand on Lauren's arm and patted it maternally. 'Of course you can't. It's a big shock for you, you poor love.'

'But your brother. It must have been awful for him.'

'Yes, it was.'

'I'd always thought the Kendalls had had such a happy marriage.'

'And they did. You mustn't go thinking otherwise, Lauren. Helen loved Dougie very much and in her own way she loved Josh too. It's just that she had this condition that crippled her. She's not to blame for what happened any more than Josh was.'

Lauren's gaze moved out to the garden. Her son was lying on his stomach with his legs up in the air and crossed at the ankles, his glass of mango now empty. He seemed to be having an intense conversation with the grass. Lauren realised that Josh would have been about the same age as Tom when the accident had happened. It seemed inconceivable.

Rachel's gentle gaze settled on her. 'Lauren,' she said gently, 'don't let what I've told you spoil your memories of him. Perhaps I shouldn't have told you but you've got to understand that it was an accident. Josh never meant anyone any harm. He was always such a lovable little boy. He just wanted to do the right thing.'

Later when Rachel had gone, Lauren drove down to Neilson Park, taking Tom with her. Since arriving in Australia she had taken to swimming there every day. It was a magical evening as she drove the rented car along Hopetown Avenue with the top down, Tom waving his arms in the back. Her hair whipped in the wind like clean laundry, sunlight danced on the ocean ahead like glitter. The orange explosion of evening looked oddly triumphant. It reminded Lauren of Rachel Willis.

Finding a flat rock she sat on it, breathing in the sharp smell of the sea. She watched her son skip through the waves, stopping from time to time to retrieve a sea treasure that caught his eye. Four young men were playing a riotous game of volleyball, their tanned torsos gleaming proudly against the creamy sand. In Lauren's hand was the photograph of Josh. Compulsively, she kept looking at it, searching for some tell-tale sign of an event so devastating it had ripped his family apart. A sentence she hadn't thought of in years sprang to mind: *Judge each passing face by the colour of its smile.* You never could tell, really, what went on behind a smile. She thought she knew Josh, but she had only known bits of him. She remembered the photograph with the lock of hair she'd found in an old boot soon after his death. Now she could put a name to the baby. It was Brett, Josh's brother. Despite the horrible circumstances of Brett's death, Josh had kept it with him all those years.

She could see Josh, a vibrant animal, out to enjoy life to the full. He was striding up and down their garden in his bare feet, wearing jeans, a bottle of beer in his hand, humming to himself. Lauren closed her eyes, trying to see him better in her mind. Would it have made any difference to the way she'd felt about him had she been told the truth? Would knowing have stopped her from marrying him? In her heart she knew it would not. The capacity to love far outweighed the rational boundaries of the mind. Had she been given the opportunity to do things all over again she would still have chosen Josh, scars and all.

A tall dark man stepped out of the sea and dripped over to his towel: a family collected up their belongings ready to go home, abandoning sand castles and rubbish: a crouching Tom was drawing pictures in the sand with a twig. What had it been like for Josh? Lauren wondered, shouldering a secret of such monumental weight, a secret that had lasted his lifetime? Secrets got into your blood, consumed you like parasites until they took you over completely. How well she understood that. To feel trapped, miserable and alone. The pattern of stealing had controlled her as long as it had remained hidden. It might have continued to do so had she not finally been caught and forced to talk about it with Max. She hadn't taken a thing since it had happened. Not that she'd had much opportunity lately, but when she did go shopping now, even for food, she was careful to take only a bag large enough to hold her purse and keys. The urge remained, but each day it grew weaker. Already she felt less menaced by it, more in control.

Tom was calling to her, his high-pitched voice carrying above the sound of the sea. Responding with a wave, she walked towards him: her brightness, her son. She owed it to him to shed the dust of her past. The stealing was the first step, but it was just one of many. She still had a long way to go. As much as she had loved Josh, she loved life too. If she was to find new happiness she had first to let him go.

She had reached the water's edge. Waves lapped around her bare ankles, sand shrank beneath her weight, left wet footprints. Time stood still as she gazed one last time at the photograph that had already become so precious to her. She held it up to her lips. *Goodbye, my darling*, she whispered. Tom was running towards her. She could hear him shouting but his face was a blur. She couldn't see him properly. The sun was too bright. Tears stabbed her eyes. Savagely, she wiped them away. He mustn't see her like this.

'Mummy!' he cried, leaping into her arms and sending them both tumbling, half in, half out of the water. Tom's blue eyes grinned at her with all the recklessness of youth,

'Got you!'

'Yes,' she said, surrendering to the game, 'you have,' and began, very weakly, to giggle.

Neither of them noticed the black-and-white photograph being carried out to sea.

25

– SEVENTEEN MONTHS LATER –

Melanie bent forward towards the dressing-table mirror. It reflected a face she was still getting used to. The new shiny sleek bob fell like a bell around her face. It added a slant to her eyes, made her look more feline. She was both startled and enchanted by the effect. Last night Hugo had said he was falling in love with her all over again. She smiled at herself, thrilled at how her new life was turning out.

'Darling!'

Melanie cast one final look at herself in the mirror, smoothed down her Monsoon silk dress and grabbed her bag from the bed. 'Coming,' she called.

Hugo was waiting at the bottom of the stairs. He felt stirred by the appearance of his wife. 'I'm a lucky dog,' he said admiringly, 'bloody lucky.'

Melanie blushed. 'Did I hear someone at the door?'

'A courier. He brought these.' He handed her half a dozen navy caps with a sporting logo on the front. 'I had other offers but this particular company's agreed to pay £1,500 if we wear them for the TV cameras.'

She slipped the cap on to his head. 'Suits you,' she said, kissing his nose. 'Now, is the video set?'

'Yes.'

'Keys?' Hugo nodded.

'What about the camera?'

'Damn,' he clicked his fingers, 'it's in the office. We'll

have to take yours.' For the umpteenth time that morning
he cast a fretful look at his watch. 'Have you called your
mother to say what time we're picking her up?'

'Twice.'

'You're *sure* she'll be ready?'

'Hugo,' she ran a hand through his thick greying hair
and said very gently, 'you mustn't worry. We've masses of
time. Just try to calm down or you won't make it through
the day.'

He took a deep breath and attempted a smile. 'Yes,' he
said, 'I'm just feeling a bit edgy. I so want it to go well.'

Melanie's mouth softened. 'I know that. But you've done
all you can, darling. Just try to enjoy it. We may never be
part of anything like this again.'

Minutes later, a slightly calmer Hugo guided the Jaguar
towards Bushy Meade. It was a scorchingly hot day.
Windows were rolled down letting in petrol fumes and
summery smells. Beyond them was a playing field with white
dots of cricketers. The air was full of Sunday sounds; the
shriek of children, a church bell ringing, the merry click
of bat upon ball. Melanie, looking cool and lightly tanned,
relaxed against the leather upholstery. Through the open
sun roof she dreamily watched the duck-blue sky swim by.
Oh, what a perfect, perfect day, she thought happily.

Next to her, Hugo shifted uncomfortably in the heat. He'd
gained a few pounds, a result of spending less time in the
gym. But he still looked good for his age and he wore his
deep tan with pride. Slipping a pair of Carrera sunglasses
onto his nose, he reached for his wife's hand.

Melanie went in to fetch Esme. Hugo elected to wait in
the car in the hope it would speed things up. After an
interminable wait, the front door opened and Melanie disappeared inside. Hugo drummed impatient fingers against
the steering wheel feeling increasingly anxious. He watched
an elderly man with medals on his chest throw breadcrumbs

at pigeons. Two minutes, he decided he'd give them two minutes. But moments later both women reappeared. Hugo's sense of relief rapidly turned into one of incredulity. Esme, a terrifying vision in purple, with green shoes and a green hat that didn't quite match, hobbled towards the car.

'Christ!' he muttered.

'Wanted to do my bit,' she climbed stiffly into the front passenger seat, reeking of lavender. Hugo dutifully helped her with the seatbelt.

'I'm *so* excited,' she fluttered, fishing out an antique-looking camera from her bag.

'You should be, Mum,' said Melanie from the back. 'This is quite a day for us all.'

Hugo gunned the car into gear and pulled out into the road.

'Can we stop along the way?' said Esme, 'I need to get film for this.'

Hugo gave a sigh of exasperation. 'Why did you leave it until now to tell us, Esme. We could have sorted this out yesterday when we had more time!' Melanie frowned warningly at him in the rear mirror.

'Damn,' he muttered under his breath.

'Won't take a minute,' said Esme, hearing him.

They had to try four newsagents before they found one open. A wooden-looking Hugo waited in a bus lane while Melanie ran into the shop. Taxis swept in and out of Wimbledon station. A bus pulled up in front of him disgorging passengers. Melanie returned, waving a film. Just as Hugo pulled out, another bus lurched in front of him.

Unthinkingly, he drove all the way up Wimbledon Hill only to find many routes blocked off by traffic wardens. He'd forgotten that roads became one-way systems during the championship. AA signs were everywhere. Village lampposts were adorned with purple and green ribbons. From pub walls flower baskets hung in celebration.

By the time Hugo drew up outside Gate 5 in Church Road he was in a thoroughly bad mood. Gone were the vast crowds that had queued over the last fortnight in hope of a Centre Court ticket. All that remained were barrier railings, plastic tarpaulins and rubbish littering the ground like leaves.

'You two go on ahead while I park the car,' Hugo suggested, wanting a few minutes alone to calm down. He handed Melanie two tickets. 'I'll meet you inside.'

They got as far as the Fred Perry statue when Esme decided she wanted a cup of tea. With twenty minutes to spare, Melanie took her to the tearoom, a place where agents and tournament directors frequently met to negotiate guarantee deals for the players. While Melanie joined the queue, Esme fumbled around in her bag for a mint and in the process dropped her gloves. A small boy, emerging from the loo with his mother, stopped to pick them up. He was dressed in a shiny red-and-white Power Ranger suit.

'What a good boy,' said Esme gratefully as he handed her the gloves.

'The promise of an ice cream always does wonders for his manners,' said his pretty mother, ruffling his hair affectionately. 'Come on, Tom,' she took his hand, 'we're running late.'

Lauren Kendall left the tearoom with her son, blonde hair swinging freely down her back. She pictured the little old woman wearing the colours of the All England Club in her mind and giggled. Tom wasn't alone in his bizarre choice of outfit.

Outside, on the last day of the championship, it was mostly staff and connoisseurs – tennis buffs who had bought tickets months ago – who remained. Nevertheless the club was seething with life and everyone, even the officious club officials were smiling. It was as though there was something intoxicating in the air. One of those miraculous English summers that made winter seem utterly improbable.

Lauren's pace was unhurried as she walked past beds of roses and neon-blue hydrangeas, the splits on either side of her skirt showing off her brown legs. She passed stands selling glossy lilac programmes thick as bibles; green-and-white seat cushions for hire; the competitors' lounge where the hottest topics of debate were how to get a Wimbledon driver who had spare complimentary tickets and meal vouchers, and where to find London's trendiest hang-outs. She stopped to watch the Chelsea Pensioners having their photo taken. Against a backdrop of glossy Virginia creeper they looked resplendent in their crimson coats. Tom attacked his ice cream which had already begun to melt.

A gleaming Bentley pulled up outside the royal enclosure. A crowd gathered as the driver got out and held open the rear door. A blonde head emerged from the building. Several excited shrieks of '*Diana! Diana!*' pierced the sky but the chaperoned princess disappeared instantly into the back of the car. Moments later it pulled smoothly out of the gates.

'She had William with her,' someone said. 'Did you see? Did you see?'

The Last Eight Club had been designed for all quarter-finalists of the championship. Lauren stood at the entrance, her eyes adjusting to the light and searched the room. With a sudden yelp of excitement Tom let go her hand and ran towards the bar. He leapt into the arms of a man standing alone.

'Hey!' cried Max, 'what have we got here?'

'An obsessed Power Ranger fan,' said Lauren joining them. 'Can you imagine wearing nylon on a day like this?' She kissed his cheek. 'I hope you haven't been waiting long.'

He handed her a brimming glass. 'You timed it perfectly.'

'Champagne? What a treat!'

'Can I have some?' Tom asked, skinny arms linked around Max's neck. 'I've had it before. It's got bubbles.'

'Sure,' said Max, ignoring the warning look on Lauren's face. 'Unless you'd rather have the Pepsi I ordered for you?'

Lauren giggled. 'And that's got bubbles too.'

Max put the confused Tom down. 'Tell you what, go talk to Warren behind the bar. He'll fix you up with something.'

They took their glasses over to a free table. Max spoke first. 'Did you catch the men's final?'

'Missed it. We got a bit behind – Tom insisted on making pancakes. Who won?'

'Wolff. Made mincemeat of the Swede. Never seen him play so well.'

Lauren beamed. 'That's a fiver you owe me, Max. Oh, *good* for Wolff. Nothing like a reconciliation to spur a man on. Inge must be thrilled.'

'Yeah. I'm glad they worked it out.'

A harassed-looking man approached their table. 'Mr Carter,' he said breathlessly, 'they need you back in fifteen minutes for more interviews.'

Max nodded briefly, his eyes on Lauren. 'Tell them I'll be there.'

For years NBC had made it clear that when the time came for Max to put down his racquet, the network had a place for him as a TV commentator. Until recently Max had scoffed at the idea, determined to make the comeback he yearned for. But each year that dream slipped further from his grasp. He worked hard, played in all the tournaments he entered, but things finally came to head after he had dinner with his old doubles partner.

'Max,' said his friend, 'you're missing shots you made look easy when you were sixteen.'

The advice was simple: put 150 per cent back into the

game or get out. Perfectionist as he was, Max realised that his moment of glory had been and gone. It was time to move on. That same week he signed with NBC.

Lauren was watching him. 'Having doubts? About quitting, I mean?'

He looked almost wistful. 'Sure, I have them. Leaving the circuit was a tough decision to make. Probably *the* toughest. But the fat lady sings for us all and I never liked the idea of being a has-been.'

He drained his glass and looked at his surroundings as if for the first time.

'You know how much I love this place, Lauren,' he said. 'No other grand slam affects me in quite the same way. I mightn't play any but I'll always be a Wimbledon champion; my name'll always be up on that board. That's a good feeling.'

'Of course it is,' Lauren squeezed his hand, smiled the Mona Lisa smiled that had first bewitched him. 'You were one of the best.'

Tom returned clutching a bottle of Pepsi with a straw inside.

'Mummy, it's started,' he said eagerly.

Lauren's eyes flew to the TV monitor on the wall. 'Hell, it has too. We must go or she'll never forgive us.'

'Can you come, Max?' Tom begged, as both adults rose from their chairs.

'Not this time, champ. I've got work to do. But the new Power Ranger movie's out now. How about I take you next week?'

'Oh *yes*!' Tom said, thrilled.

'You'll get no peace now,' murmured Lauren, reaching round the back of Max's collar to tuck the label in.

'I like it that way,' he said, gazing at her. Their lips touched briefly. 'Call me later?'

'Aren't you coming round?' she looked disappointed.

'Didn't know I was invited.'

'You're always invited,' and then she was gone, like a wisp of rose-scented smoke, a gentle wave swallowed up by the sea-swirling crowd, the maze of outside courts.

He followed her out, his mind focused once again on work. Meandering towards him was Sir Cliff Richard, self-conscious in a mint-green jacket. A severely burnt umpire, who looked like a pickled lobster, stopped to buy an ice cream. Nick Bollettieri, in his wraparound sunglasses, was leaning against a wall talking animatedly to Mary Pearce. As Max neared Centre Court, his eyes latched onto a familiar frame, inches taller than everyone else. Luke Falkner looked quite different. Gone were the shoulder-length loopy red-gold curls. Now he wore his hair tightly cropped and he'd grown a beard. The overall effect was less pretty, more aggressive, but Max thought it suited him better. Luke wasn't alone. For a moment Max thought the beautiful woman on his arm was Lauren, the resemblance was so striking. But on closer inspection her eyes were too close together and the blonde hair had come from a bottle.

'Say, Max!' the Canadian leapt towards him. 'Man, it's great to see you.' He introduced the woman, 'Mary Ann, this is my old buddy Max, Max Carter.'

'Hi,' she giggled, giving him a wide, toothy smile.

'Saw you made it to the second round.' Max kept his voice light.

'Yeah. I'd liked to have gone further but it felt great being out there. I'm starting to feel really positive about my game again.'

'When do you go home?'

'Tomorrow. As I made it to the mixed doubles semis I thought I'd stay on until the end.'

'I'm glad things are working out,' said Max carefully.

Mary Ann was glancing at people walking by. She looked restless.

'So,' said Luke, 'what's the scoop?'

'Not much.'

'You ever see Lauren?'

'Actually, you just missed her. She was here about five minutes ago.'

'No,' he looked disappointed, 'how's she doing?'

Max looked him straight in the eye. 'I'll be honest with you, Luke. I've never seen her happier.' Max's smile shone with an exaggerated bonhomie. 'She's really got her life together.'

'That's good. That's good.'

'Honey,' said Mary Ann petulantly.

'Yeah, okay, baby, we're going.' He shrugged apologetically at Max. 'Guess you've got interviews and stuff, hey?' Max nodded. 'Hang on until next year and it'll be me you'll be talking to.'

'You said it,' said Max.

He watched Luke go and cast his mind back to the last time he'd seen him play. Physically, Luke had never looked better, but he was half the player he'd been before the accident. The star quality wasn't there any more. Gone also were the days when he could go straight into any tournament he wanted to compete in. His ranking had slipped staggeringly from eleven to a hundred and seventy on the computer – he'd had to qualify for Wimbledon. Two years ago it would have seemed inconceivable, only Max had watched it happen to countless talented players. One minute launched towards stardom, the next crawling their way back up from the bottom. But with Luke? Well, with Luke there had been such promise, such dazzling talent; a young, supremely confident player equipped with all the shots in the book. Now the magic in his racquet was gone. He would never get it back. Max shook his head sadly. Sooner or later someone

was going to have to tell him the truth – either that or he'd
figure it out for himself. But then what? The game was his
life. What the hell else was Luke supposed to do?

It had been the hottest championship in almost twenty
years, all the more unusual without the interruption of
rain. Record amounts of suntan cream had been sold at the
on-site chemist, twenty-eight tons of strawberries had been
devoured, scores of people who had become so engrossed in
the tennis that they had forgotten to eat or drink, were treated
for heat exhaustion by the St Johns Ambulance People as
temperatures soared into the high nineties.

While the bookmakers were rubbing their hands with glee
after Wolff's defeat of the Swede – a former champion who
had attracted the highest bets – another player was defying
all odds on a neighbouring court. The girls' singles junior
championship was underway on court number one, one of
the best places in the world to watch tennis as the seats
were almost on top of the court.

Charlotte Roach was up against the Italian number six
seed, Marisa Di Nunzio. Her Latin opponent had shoulders
that would have made most linebackers drool with envy.
She was a six-foot Amazon and weighed 160 pounds. To
the five thousand seated in the stands it was like watching a
rerun of David's meeting with Goliath. So it was no surprise
when the first set was a six-three romp. Like David, it was
Charlotte who had taken it *not* the Italian.

At the start of the match only four thousand of the eight
thousand seats had been filled. Word that the British girl
was one set up and serving at four-three in the second,
however, had spread like wildfire. The stands were now
packed. As Lauren and Tom slipped into their seats, Hugo,
Esme and Melanie tried to relax in the players' enclosure.
Hugo had made up his mind that just making it to the final
had been his stepdaughter's triumph. Now that Charlotte

had surprised them all by taking the first set, however, Hugo's attention was completely focused. His eyes never left the court. Even during the changeovers, he was deaf to everything else going on around him.

One nasty moment arose when Marisa thunderbolted the ball straight at Charlotte, striking her in the midriff. Charlotte doubled over, balancing herself with one hand on the ground. The anxious crowd inched to the edge of their seats, but sighed with relief as Charlotte pulled herself up and returned to the back of the court. Stoically, she raised a hand to indicate she was all right.

'And they say the Empire's dead,' said an old man in a panama hat proudly thrusting out his chin. Forgetting that she'd always told Charlotte off for biting her nails, Melanie began to chew her own.

The incident seemed to shake Charlotte's concentration. She dropped the next three consecutive points, allowing the Italian back into the match. Throughout, Charlotte had nimbly danced around the onslaught of shots from her opponent. But she couldn't maintain this level of tennis indefinitely. They had been playing for an hour and twenty minutes. The temperature was a hundred degrees and both girls looked exhausted. Also suffering were the lineswomen wearing tights and heels – one of them had earlier fainted and had been carried off for medical attention. In their green and purple uniforms, the ball girls and boys squatted, ran, stood to attention, rolled the yellow balls.

It now looked as though the match might go to a third set. Would that be the undoing of Charlotte? She was the one that had been doing most of the running. When Marisa cracked a backhand return that flew past Charlotte right down the line, Charlotte's shoulders sagged visibly. Four games all and serving thirty-love up, the Italian loomed. As a weary Charlotte walked to the baseline, the crowd started clapping. At first it was slow, sporadic, but by the time Charlotte had turned to face her opponent, almost everyone had risen to their feet, clapping and shouting, trying to will her back into the game.

Galvanised by the support, Charlotte came up with two brilliant returns, levelling the score to thirty-all. Marisa hit an easy forehand pass wide in the next. When the Italian missed her first serve, Charlotte was ready to pounce. She hit an awkward return to the Italian's backhand and rushed to the net. The volley was a winner. Five-four to Charlotte and her turn to serve.

Twice in the next game the Italian took the lead. Twice Charlotte fought back. Tom Kendall, chin supported in his hands, watched enthralled. At his side, Lauren was reliving the memory of Josh and the last time he'd played on Centre Court, just a few feet away. Strange, she thought as Charlotte dived after the ball, how history repeated itself.

The rallies were getting longer. Back and forth, back and forth, whack, whack went the ball, until the spectators could hardly bear to watch. At thirty-all the Italian lashed wildly at the ball. It soared high into the air. Up and up until it seemed to meet the giant crane with its camera's panoramic eye, until it became difficult to see properly against the deep, cloudless blue of the sky. With it went the hopes and fears of the British spectators desperate for a home win. As it reached its peak the ball seemed to hang motionless, poised like a bird over its prey. Then it rapidly began to descend. Eyes peeled, a puce-red Charlotte positioned herself, racquet poised, then whipped the smash to the back of the court. The crowd went crazy.

'Forty-thirty,' said the umpire.

'I can't look,' squeaked a voice. 'Tell me what happens.' Nervous titters rippled through the crowd. Standing behind the last row of seats an army security guard furtively popped a nut cluster into her mouth.

Charlotte took her time as she walked back to the serve

line, bending on to her haunches to flex tired muscles. She closed her eyes and breathed air deep into her lungs. Sunlight struck the gold bracelet she wore on her left wrist, tiny racquets dancing in time to the exhausted beat of her heart. There was a paralysed silence. It was so quiet a bird could be heard chirping in a nearby tree. For many, Charlotte's victory would mean hope, hope that they too might one day achieve a similar dream. Because if this gutsy slip of a girl plucked from obscurity could do it, then anything was possible. Others recalled the Rudyard Kipling quote above the door in the members' hall leading to Centre Court:

> If you can meet with triumph and disaster
> And treat those two impostors just the same.

Charlotte Roach opened her eyes and stepped back to the line. Deliberately she bounced the ball five times. As she fixed her gaze on her opponent, she took a deep breath. It seemed to those watching that all her nerves fell from her with the sweat from her brow. She threw the ball high into the air and served for the championship.